Pride Publishing books by Nicole Dennis

Southern Charm
Rules of the Chef
By the Numbers
On the Green
When in Bloom
Following the Law
According to Design
Saving the Wedding

Southern Charm

SAVING THE WEDDING

NICOLE DENNIS

Saving the Wedding
ISBN # 978-1-83943-796-0
©Copyright Nicole Dennis 2022
Cover Art by Kelly Martin ©Copyright Month year
Interior text design by Claire Siemaszkiewicz
Pride Publishing

SAVING THE WEDDING

Dedication

To all the Charm fans who waited a long time for
this one.
To Tammy Cook Green, thanks for naming
Charmed Occasions.

Chapter One

Stepping outside on a Saturday morning, Gavin Hartfield, the creator of Charmed Occasions, the wedding and event-planning company within the Southern Charm Bed & Breakfast, touched the Bluetooth wireless earpiece that wrapped around his ear to reset it. Then he adjusted the microphone.

A trio of calls with immediate hang-ups buzzed his phone.

He pulled it out and checked the screen. The area code was from Atlanta, his previous hometown.

There was one person who kept harassing him, no matter how many times he changed his number.

A flicker of a panic attack increased his heartbeat. *Again. All of this. All over again.*

He wanted the bastard to leave him alone.

"No. No. Concentrate on the wedding. They deserve your full attention—not an asshole who can't let go."

"Help! Gavin! You there?"

Wincing at his assistant's voice, Gavin wanted to rip the entire headset away. "Yes. I'm here. Use the volume control. Please."

"Sorry, sorry," Victor MacArtney said. "Better?"

"Yes. What did you call for, Victor?"

"The family member acting as the cameraman for the virtual part is here. His name is Ryan. He wondered if he could follow you for all the pre-wedding stuff to show the family and guests waiting in their online group."

"I'll meet him inside. Have him wait by the entrance."

"Gotta keep some of our secrets and tricks. Right?"

"Right."

"Will do, boss."

Shrugging off the earlier panicky sensation, he checked his tablet to update the list and timings for the wedding of Michael and Charles. Since the pandemic had changed everything, they'd pushed back their wedding multiple times until it was considered safer, when everyone would have been vaccinated. Once they'd chosen this Saturday, they were determined to exchange their vows and rings. They'd selected Occasions' smaller package with a gazebo wedding and a brunch reception. The rest of the extended family, friends and co-workers had been invited to a virtual party in a Discord group that would be livestreamed by Ryan. The grooms kept the ceremony and reception areas subdued, simple, with a few splashes of flowers and a single pale-blue accent color against the natural background. It suited the older couple, who were both in their early forties. Now he needed to make their dream wedding come true on this July morning.

"Gavin, we have a problem!" Victor said while racing over.

Gavin wondered what disaster Victor had created this time. "Where is Ryan?"

"Left him inside like you said."

"What is that?" Gavin focused on what Victor held in his hand.

Victor held up the battered birdcage. "One of the birdcages fell while the lighting team tried to hang it in the gazebo. A few pieces of metal snapped. Luckily, Jude hadn't added the flowers or that would be another disaster. Ryan didn't film anything. Would make it even—"

"Don't even go there."

"Yeah. True. What should we do?"

"First, calm down. There is always a solution. You must learn that part of the job."

"Okay." Victor spun the damaged item between his hands.

Gavin inspected the cage and realized they couldn't repair it. They would have to discard the item. *Okay, minor disaster, but there's always a solution. Focus on that.* "There's no fixing this cage."

"What's the solution?"

Gavin tapped open the inventory program and scrolled to figure out his options. "Okay. Aisle 3, Bin C. There's a matching cage that's a little smaller, but it'll work. Toss that one, remove it from the inventory list and get the replacement."

"Will do."

"Please tell them to be extra careful. Those are our only white cages. We'll have to be on the lookout next time we go shopping. And don't go through the main entrance. Avoid the camera."

"Promise. Keep out of sight until it is all fixed and perfect. Understood." Victor raced off.

"What next?" Gavin waved to the violinists. While he talked to Victor, the pair of music students had arrived and begun practicing. They'd worked an Occasions wedding before and knew the drill. Then he returned inside to weave his way to the kitchen.

"Morning, Malcolm, how are we progressing?"

The sous chef, Malcolm Bissete, chopped and diced with a massive chef's knife. If Gavin used one of those, he would be afraid of losing a finger. "I'm not going to be filmed. Right?"

"The camera guy is waiting by the front entrance. I'll keep him contained. This was agreed upon between Occasions and the grooms."

"Okay. Too busy to deal with that nonsense. Stupid pandemic."

"I know. I know. At least we get to go back to some normalcy."

"True. Anyway…progress check. Right." Mal didn't look up throughout the entire conversation but kept his attention on his work. "Cocktail hour is done and ready." He scooped the ingredients to a bowl. "The cocktails will be made fresh to order. Zak is on his way and will mix everything. Unlike me, he knows what he's doing."

Mal went to the warming oven, plucked out a couple of pieces, plated them and passed it to Gavin. "These are the egg-white tartlets with bacon, Gruyère and sun-dried tomatoes. The other is the mini-French toast. I added dark maple syrup, so it bakes into the bread. Nothing should bother your lactose issue. Both grooms requested alternative milks."

"I missed one of my favorite parts of every event — the tasting element."

"Still not going to share with Victor?"

"Nope. Not guilty, either." Gavin savored the hors d'oeuvres Malcolm had created to satisfy an early morning hunger before the actual brunch — something to offset the morning dip into alcohol. The cocktail hour would be celebrated with an option of mint juleps and Bellinis, along with coffee and tea. While the grooms and wedding party finished the pictures, the guests could enjoy some delicacies. "Wow. These are delicious!"

Malcolm slid over a cup of fresh coffee, doctored to Gavin's taste. "Appreciate it."

"What else is ready?"

"Katie's delivery guy dropped off the cake. It's waiting in the walk-in fridge. Simple but elegant, like one of the grooms, Charles, wanted. Katie loved how it came out and will add it to her social media pages." Mal pointed to another workspace. "I'm finishing the salad wraps and grilled vegetable tartlets. The frittatas are baking. The scones are done."

"Perfect. You rock." Gavin polished off the rest of the French toast, loving the flavor combination of cinnamon, nutmeg and maple syrup.

"It's a small event, so there isn't much to make. It'll be the same with Sunday's reception. I enjoy these little ones. I'm not running around like crazy to get everything done."

"There are going to be more of these smaller events until everything settles down."

"And people become comfortable in larger ones."

"Life came to a stop and changed. Now we need to figure out a way back," Gavin said between sips of coffee. "Just wondering. What are you going to do when Dorian finishes school and returns home? Will you keep helping with the event side?"

"I'll return to restaurant cooking with the occasional event-planning stuff for the larger groups. The restaurant side is my passion."

"What?" Gavin frowned in a playful, teasing manner, complete with the sad puppy-dog look that collaborated with his baby-blue eyes. "Don't you like working with Victor and me?"

"Not the puppy-dog eyes! No! No. Stop that." Mal snapped his towel at Gavin. "You're evil, man, just plain evil. Not going to sway me. Nope."

Gavin grinned while he dropped the look when he knew he'd gotten to Mal.

"Hey, I adore you, honest. I don't mind helping with the events if I'm needed, but I'm a restaurant kitchen guy. It's in my blood. I love the craziness of a busy evening."

"Understandable." Gavin finished the coffee and pushed the dishes back across. "I'll let you get back to things. Let me know if anything changes." He tapped his earpiece. "Unless you run into Vincent, then tap me on this."

"Always." After a flourish of the towel, Malcolm tucked it back around one of his apron's ties.

Gavin left the kitchen with a fresh burst of energy. Heading through the main restaurant, he studied a couple of people from the local businesses dressing the closed-off area for the reception. Pale-blue tablecloths with sand-colored napkins and chair covers united the area. A bounty of fresh flowers in shades of cream and pale blue added a beautiful fragrance. He loved everything the florist, Jude Sebastian, designed.

Taking a moment to adjust a couple of items and locate a missing placement, he returned outside. There he found Jude and his team setting up the last of the exterior floral arrangements around the gazebo and aisle. The lighting team finished adding pin-style lights around the gazebo that went with the strings of fairy lights. The natural morning sunlight would brighten the rest of the setting.

Though he discovered the second birdcage hanging, he couldn't locate his assistant.

Gavin tapped his headset. "Victor, where are you?"

"Helping Charles with his outfit. We have a loose button and a wobbly belly," Victor replied. "Don't worry. Ryan is still in the front entrance area."

"Okay. Keep me updated. I'll pick up our cameraman and check on the grooms next."

"Will do."

Gavin stepped closer to the dark-haired florist where he was tucking pale-blue and cream flowers into the birdcages. "Hey, Jude." Memories of the Valentine's Day surprise he'd created for Jude at Dr. Elliott Sheffield's request to reveal their new home flashed through him. It had been one of his most memorable moments.

"Morning, Gavin. Wonderful day for a wedding." Jude shifted his attention from the cage and flowers toward Gavin. He let out a low appreciative whistle. "Looking pretty dapper this morning. I like the paisley suspenders."

Every single time they met, the florist commented on Gavin's combination of bow ties and suspenders. They were his look, his trend and something he'd started with his first wedding. In a way, they remained his good-luck charms. If he needed to go a bit more formal, he had a collection of vests and a few coats more reminiscent of earlier centuries. There was a touch of steampunk style to some of his wardrobe. Today, he'd chosen gray-checked pants with a long-sleeved white button-down shirt. Due to the steamy early-July morning, he'd rolled the sleeves up his forearms then set off the look with gray paisley suspenders and matching bow tie.

"How many pairs of suspenders do you have?"

"Lost count a while ago," Gavin admitted. "Same with the bow ties. At least a couple hundred, if not more, of each type."

"Damn. How are we to know what set to get you for your birthday?" Jude let out a low whistle. "Sheesh. You probably have every single style and pattern."

"No, not everything. Still missing a few sets, and more are always being revealed and designed. My collection is always growing. I'm not stopping anytime soon. There's some higher-end ones I didn't pick up."

"Do you have a wish list?"

"Multiple ones."

Jude laughed.

"Still can't get Doc Elliott to try them?"

"Nope. Claims they get in his way in the ER."

"Riiiiight."

"Silly doctor of mine," Jude said. "He prefers his boring scrubs."

"He's still a keeper. Does he have a twin?"

Jude laughed and shook his head.

"Damn. Too bad he broke the mold."

"Oh, I'm not giving him up for anything."

"Don't blame you." Gavin cupped his fingers under one bloom that was tucked into a stylized vase set on a pedestal. "These are gorgeous."

Jude caressed one petal with a fingertip. "The one you're touching is a morning glory. I adore that sky-blue color. The others are a combination of white mini cala lilies and ruffly double tulips. It took a bit of luck for me to find these white hybrid nerine lilies. They're the perfect addition to intersperse among the foliage. After sending the grooms a picture, they became excited and gave me a bit of extra budget to find them."

"I remember their excitement about it."

"Crazy how that happens. Anyway, I chose Italian ruscus, eucalyptus and fern combinations to finish off the centerpieces and accents. Smaller versions are on the tables," Jude said. "The grooms chose a boutonnière of a single morning glory flower and two strands of Italian ruscus. I delivered those earlier."

"Other than tulips, I have no clue about what you just said. Tell me more."

With a chuckle, Jude pointed to the different white flowers while he named each one. Then he did the same with the foliage—a touch of green to add to the plain palette. After the explanation, he let out a sigh and stretched from side to side. "Man, am I beat."

"It's barely seven."

"Been up since four to finish these. Plus, Elliott got called in for an emergency. I'd hoped these crazy nights were gone after the pandemic, but nope. That's life with a doctor. Whenever Elliott gets up, Dawson barks and asks for a trip outside. Though not part of his training, I relaxed on things since I don't need the canine support as much. To top off the craziness, Sigi meows for someone to fill his food bowl right that very second or he will tell everyone of the injustice," Jude grumbled. "Crazy feline."

Gavin chuckled at the latest rant over Doc Elliott's gray cat, Sigmund, a former stray who had adopted the doctor. Dawson, Jude's Medical Alert companion, was a sweetheart of a Golden Labrador. "Yikes, sounds like you need a nap."

"After we're done with the set-up, I'll grab a catnap at home…probably with the cat," Jude said.

"What about Dawson?"

"At home I keep things relaxed. He can pass out on his doggy bed like the good boy he is. The cat could care less about boundaries." Jude shoved a hand through his dark hair. "Even with a nap, my day remains full. I need to finish the final touches on tomorrow's flowers, and I have a few other orders to fulfill."

"Better to be busy than have nothing to do."

"Tell me about it. I'll take a busy day any time. While the Charm went through renovations, I wasn't sure the shop could remain in business. Things got dicey. Then the pandemic hit and… Seriously, I thought I would lose the entire store, but—"

"You kept things alive."

"It was strange. One commenter of my Facebook page asked if he could purchase a basic arrangement online and pick it up curbside. There were a hundred comments wanting to do the same. I wasn't anything like those massive online stores, just a small local business, but Elliott nudged me to do it. Took a week to create a few arrangements, take pictures and post them to the website. Got a dozen orders the first week. Then it increased every week. It was"—Jude shook his head, tears in his sky-blue eyes—"amazing."

"Something special that happened throughout downtown."

"Our town knows how to come together in a crisis."

"With business returning to Occasions, I get to keep you hopping."

"Don't get me wrong... I love it, and I'm never going to complain. It's just a hectic schedule. Customers don't want me to remove the online site. I get requests and orders every week. When you mix what's happening at my store with Elliott's schedule, yeah, not much time in between everything."

"Hope you guys can figure out something."

"Luckily, the shop is earning enough to hire a couple of more people, so I hope it will lighten things. I want to hire another flower artist."

"Other than being rundown, how have you been feeling?"

"A helluva lot better." Jude wasn't bothered at all by the question he must hear multiple times every day. Most folks in Breeze knew about Jude's seizure and diabetic conditions. "This glucose monitoring device is a wonder machine. I have lots of energy and not a single seizure in six months."

"Good to hear things are settling down health-wise." Gavin glanced around. "Where's Dawson?"

"Curled up on the higher porch." Jude pointed in a different direction, then let out a whistle of three altering tones.

A soft bark replied. A golden furry head appeared by the railing. A bright-blue vest shaded his upper body.

"Napping on the job, huh?" Jude teased his furry pal.

Dawson whined.

Gavin chuckled at the pathetic sound. "Looks like he found a sunny spot."

"Of course... It's his newest pastime adventure. He hasn't had much to do since Elliott and my diabetes coach stabilized me."

"Not that you mind."

"Nope. I don't mind him having some lazy times. He's always a working dog."

"Jude, we need you," one of his assistants called out.

"You're being hailed. Talk to you tomorrow," Gavin said.

"We'll be here with a different palette. Vibrant roses and massive flamingo-pink peonies. I enjoyed collaborating with those ladies."

Gavin could say the same about the female couple exchanging vows during a sunset wedding the next day. They were a true delight to help create their dream day. The ladies worked together with Gavin, even with their different opinions. For this event, however, he communicated with Charles far more often than Michael.

With everything nearly completed, Gavin headed inside. Bracing himself, he adjusted his bow tie and fixed one of his sleeves. Putting a smile on his face, he walked toward the front reception area where Victor had left the cameraman, Ryan.

"Hey, everyone," a young man called out while he turned with an iPhone held out on a selfie stick. "Here is Gavin, the fabulous event planner for Charmed Occasions. He designed everything with Charles and Michael. Hello, Gavin, I'm Ryan, the narrator of our livestream. Could you say hello to our virtual guests and explain a bit about the Southern Charm B&B and Charmed Occasions?"

"Hello, Ryan. Welcome to the Southern Charm Bed & Breakfast." Gavin waved to the camera. "Hello to all the guests of the wedding of Charles and Michael. I wish all of you could be here in person, but I understand the concerns. It's a bright, warm Saturday morning here in Shore Breeze, Florida. Southern Charm is based in a southern antebellum-style home." He continued with an explanation about the building, the location and both businesses. "Now that the boring stuff is over, we'll get to the fun part. Ryan, could you swing the camera around our grand front reception area."

"Sure. Here we go, folks," Ryan said while he moved the selfie stick.

"This is the front reception area of the Southern Charm. The guests can gather here before the celebrations. Our local floral designer, Flowers in the Breeze, added arrangements along with touches from Blissful Cloths. Here is our sign with the grooms' names and wedding date. There is another sign offering directions for locations, plus a guest sign-in book," Gavin explained. "Occasions adds these extra touches to all our events."

The front doors opened.

"Hello, Whitney," Gavin greeted the local wedding officiant, Whitney Becker, when she stepped inside. "This is Ryan. He's filming the livestream for our virtual guests. Everyone, this is our officiant, Her Honor Whitney Becker."

"Hello, Gavin, Ryan and everyone online. I hope you're all having a wonderful day." Whitney waved to the camera.

Gavin motioned out of view to hold off the filming. From his understanding, the grooms had specified things to Ryan, after Charles' cousin had requested to be the cameraman.

Recognizing the symbol, Ryan took over the narration and headed off.

"Something new to get used to," Whitney said.

"Yet another part of our new reality." Gavin moved them farther away. "How are you this morning, Whitney?"

"Doing wonderful. You're looking sharp as ever. How are you holding up?"

"Hanging in there, like always. A couple of hiccups, but everything is progressing," he said. "Would you like some coffee and scones? It'll be another half-hour."

"That would be awesome. I need another hit of caffeine—especially since I'm going to be on camera."

"Malcolm will hook you up with the good stuff. Don't worry. You'll do great…like always."

"Thanks. I'll find my own way." She waved a hand. "Such a flatterer."

"An honest one."

Then his earpiece buzzed.

He received word that Jude and Blissful Cloths had finished. Everything was ready outside with a few things left for the reception.

With that over, he waved Ryan back to continue filming.

Together, they greeted some guests. Still cautious, he kept his distance and waved, though he handed over business cards when a few requested his information. They were welcome to head outside and enjoy the morning. At the same time, he reminded them about Ryan, the camera and the sign-in book.

When they left, he connected with one of Charles' groomsmen to alert them to the early arrivals. They would oversee seating the guests and making them comfortable.

"Time to check in on our grooms," Gavin said to Ryan and the camera.

* * * *

Hours later, with the newlyweds ensconced in the honeymoon suite, Gavin watched the guests scatter, either to spend time in Shore Breeze or make their way home.

"Victor, get with the trades." Gavin checked everything on his end-of-event list in his cramped office. "All linens can return with them. We have different colors tomorrow. Help them reorganize everything back to the restaurant order so Dakota can open. Cecile wants to begin filling tables with customers."

"Got it. Disassemble and spread out the flowers throughout the tables?"

"Yes. Return all the other inventory to the storage area. Please keep it all organized."

"Will do. I'll get the cart now," Victor said.

"If you finish up early, join me outside for the breakdown."

"Okay."

Gavin left his tablet but kept his earpiece in place. Then he returned outside to find the trades appearing for the breakdown.

"Keep the chairs here. Stack them on the lowest deck where we can bring them to the beach. Same with all the pillars. I checked the weather, and no storms are expected. The rest of the items go to storage," he said. "All the lights come down."

With those directions, everyone got to work. Gavin never considered the option of stepping back and not working. It wasn't how he wanted to run his company. It didn't take long to get the small number of duties finished.

Victor arrived with the pushcart to retrieve the storage items.

"I'll print a list of what we need for tomorrow. Put it all on the cart, but leave it in storage," Gavin said. "I'll close the books for this event." He waved to all the trades. "Thank you, everyone. See you for tomorrow's wedding." Then he returned to his office. Once he sat down, he removed the earpiece, connected it to recharge and rubbed his ear.

Then his office phone rang. Stopped. Rang. Stopped. Rang. Stopped.

The caller ID flashed with an unknown number. The area code…Atlanta.

"Go away. Go away. Go away, you bastard. Stop hunting me."

Closing the book on the wedding, Gavin submitted all the final invoices, payments and checks through the system the Charm's accountant, Chandler Braddock, had created to operate the Occasions' event-planning and catering services. He adored the simple interface and integration. Then he checked off all the lists in the binder version. He printed what reports he needed to add to the client's binder. As the final touch, he stuck a bright red 'Finished' sticker and scribbled the date. Chandler and the computer system would alert him if anything hadn't been paid, but he maintained the back-up for any troubles.

After replacing the binder, he selected the one for tomorrow to prep what he could. He printed the inventory list and left it on the desk's corner for Victor. Then he contacted the vendors with a reminder. After catching a glimpse of the ladies enjoying a joint bachelorette party at one of the clubs on bar row, Gavin knew nothing would deter this wedding.

At the same time, Gavin noticed two bars next to each other were shut down with 'For Sale' signs. A bright orange sticker from the county tax collector office warned of the closing due to unpaid taxes. Rumors had spread about the town council wanting to change and revitalize bar row to make it more upscale. It was something the mayor had campaigned about during his re-election.

Unfortunately, there were more than a few stores that had closed during or after the pandemic. It was a sad sight to see the empty stores, but hopefully new entrepreneurs would fill those shops.

Opening his inbox, Gavin noticed a recent email from another client. There was a little more personal history. While he was looking for anything else he might have missed, a knock pulled his attention away.

Samuel Ashford leaned against the doorframe and slid one hand into a pocket. "Hey there. Simple event this morning. The couple looked happy."

"It was small but special. They didn't want a lot of pomp and circumstance. Charles' nephew used his iPhone to livestream everything. That was a little crazy, but we kept it contained. Hopefully, we'll get more business from their guests, who asked for my card. It's taking time, but people are learning it's safe to celebrate weddings and life again."

"Awesome. We can always add more to the calendar — and even more when we get that event space finished."

"Any updates on it?"

"Not yet. Sully and his crew are working away. I gave them the go-ahead to use their power tools after the group moved inside."

"Thanks. Power saws and drills aren't the thing you want to hear at a wedding ceremony, especially when it's being streamed."

"Sully understands."

"Do you think Sully will talk Chandler into marriage?"

"He's whittling him down, but Chandler remains stubborn." Samuel ventured deeper into the cramped office and dropped into a chair. "You need more room than this broom closet. I'm sorry we didn't have anywhere else for you, but we reorganized to make as much space as possible during the renovation."

"I'll have more room in the new event building. I can wait. The inventory is more important to store properly than an office for me."

"Thanks for being accommodating."

"You know I'm happy to be here and creating these wonderful celebrations."

"Feeling more like home?"

"Every single day. Charmed Occasions is my dream company."

"Good," Samuel said. "Everything is going good then."

"Yes, Victor is an immense help. Speaking of my trusty young assistant..." Gavin smiled when Victor poked his head around the door-frame. "Everything put away?"

"In its correct place and checked back into the system," Victor said.

"Perfect. Here's the list for tomorrow." Gavin stretched to lift the paper from the corner.

Samuel ended up taking it and passed it back to Victor.

Victor scanned the items.

"Don't forget the pedestals are outside on the lower deck, along with the chairs," Gavin said.

"I'll get it all ready."

"When you finish, you can head out. Excellent work as always, Victor."

"Great. Good to be able to do my job again. Thanks, Gavin. Bye, Samuel," Victor said.

"There's something we need to discuss," Gavin said after Victor had left. He swiveled and plucked a green binder. He slid out a folder from a pocket and opened it. Then he turned around a to-do list and pushed it closer to Samuel.

"What's this?"

"The list for your wedding." Gavin tapped a pen on the desk. "Which starts with the date. I can't move forward on anything without a date. That influences everything from invitations to trades. Why bother figuring out a theme or colors if we don't know when it'll happen?"

Samuel let out a frustrated breath.

"You have been ignoring me since my arrival. I know you've been engaged a little longer than I've been around. What's the delay?"

"Even though he proposed, Dakota doesn't want to commit to anything. I try to bring it up, but—" Samuel shoved fingers through his hair. "Oh, I don't know what happens. If I push, we argue. That sucks…big-time. I don't want to—"

"Rock the boat."

"Yes. Stupid, I know, but—"

"Stop. Stop," Gavin interrupted. He hated seeing Samuel in pain about something that should be wonderful. "Planning a wedding shouldn't be stressful. That's my part, to deal with the stress. It's something wonderful to look forward to celebrating the start of a whole new part of your life together." He walked around the desk to crouch next to Samuel's chair.

"How do I even bring up the subject if he's going to run away?"

"It means he isn't ready."

Samuel held up his hand to reveal the glinting band. "Then why give me the ring?"

"He loves you with everything inside him. There's something holding him back from a commitment."

"Something influencing him from his past."

"Possible." Gavin shrugged. "Do you know much about it?"

"Some, but not all of it. He's close-mouthed."

"Same with Malcolm and Reece."

"Why do they do that?" Samuel leaned back with a frustrated sound.

"Who knows." Gavin placed a hand on Samuel's knee. "I'm sorry to make you upset. It wasn't my intention."

"There's more to the situation—obviously more than even I know."

"Hey, what's going on in here?"

They turned their heads when Chandler called out.

"Wedding shit," Samuel said.

Chandler rolled his eyes. "Is that idiot still dancing?"

"With his mouth sewn shut," Samuel added.

"Let's go dig into a tub of Cherry Garcia with extra chocolate syrup," Chandler said. "We'll figure out a way to get him to talk."

"Good idea," Gavin said while pushing up to his feet. He leaned back against his desk.

"Do you want to join us?" Chandler asked.

"Lactose-intolerant, otherwise I would dive right in," Gavin said.

"Damn. Right. Forgot. Missing out on the precious Cherry Garcia. Oooh, and Phish Food." Chandler *tsk*ed while he commiserated.

"It sucks, but I can't miss what I never had." Gavin shrugged. "Anyway, I have emails to go through, including one from my ex."

"Ex?" Chandler and Samuel asked together.

Gavin winced at the slight slip. "It came down to personal issues for me, and I didn't want it to hurt Arthur. I screwed up even worse when I delved into a different relationship with a co-worker, so my relationship went to hell." *The co-worker now calling, hanging up and harassing me, not that I'll say it aloud.*

"One of the reasons that led you to submitting an application," Samuel said.

"Yes, that was the main reason," Gavin said. "Arthur found his true love a year later. Now they're engaged. After they got vaccinated and cleared, he emailed me to create a beach wedding. He didn't trust any other coordinator but hoped we could get beyond our past. I told him we could. So—"

"Ouch," Samuel said.

"I can get through it. Honest," Gavin said. "He's not the one I want to avoid. I consider Arthur a good friend. I miss seeing him."

"We'll be here for you. If anything gets odd or difficult, you call on us," Samuel told him.

"I will. Promise." Gavin waved them out. "Go get high on ice cream and chocolate."

They chuckled while they left.

Gavin focused in on the upcoming wedding of Arthur Carlton and Neil Bardon. Arthur had found love with an older man who loved and doted on him. He would maintain the same high level of attention to detail. While he wouldn't let anything ruin Charmed Occasions' growing reputation, he remained nervous. After the disastrous turn in his relationship with Maury, Gavin had taken a long hard look at himself.

Since his college boyfriend had cheated, Gavin thought it had been something about him that had screwed with things. He'd withdrawn behind powerful internal walls to protect himself from that devastating feeling and protect his low self-esteem. For some reason, he always expected the worst would happen after the simplest argument.

The same insecure feelings rose when he had been with Arthur. That had led to arguments until their split. Gavin couldn't figure out how to fill the damaged parts of a tear-stained heart locked within the cage of insecurity. While he desired to find the right partner, he needed to learn to cope, trust and act from a secure place. From his exterior image all the way down to deep within, he never quite felt comfortable. This issue echoed when he was with anyone—even when he had been younger. He'd never gone club-hopping *or* bed-hopping.

When he'd first gotten together with Maury, he'd thought he'd found his true relationship—a partnership where he felt secure and loved—but

Maury had pushed him too fast into physical stuff. Gavin hadn't readily responded. Over the months, Gavin had known that things would become worse, but he couldn't bring himself to call an end to it until Maury had snapped one night and hit him. Gavin had called things off and closed all contact.

Except they had continued to work at the same company.

After things soured with Maury, he'd stayed in Atlanta for another year until he'd seen the Southern Charm ad. Unwilling to face his past, he'd accepted the Charm offer, left all he knew behind and begun again. During some research, he'd learned that his sexuality difficulties could stem from being demisexual. He couldn't respond sexually to a partner without a close-knit emotional bond.

All those issues had sharpened when the gorgeous EMT, Xavier 'Gray' Grayson, had pretty much dismissed him during the Halloween festival. Samuel had dressed Gavin in bright white leggings, a thin white tank, big ears and a freaking fluffy cottontail stuck to his ass to transform him into the White Rabbit. His only clothes were a plaid vest and an oversized pocket-watch and chain. Everything showed in that costume, and still the man had turned away. Something had to be wrong. He'd known Gray was gay, since he'd laughed and flirted with other men.

Would he ever get the chance to plan an event for himself? Would he be able to stand at the end of an aisle, in front of friends and families, holding hands with a man he loved?

Whenever things went bonkers, he made sure none of his personal issues interfered with his work ethic.

That meant enacting that promise right now.

Gavin stared at the email from Arthur, who planned on arriving within the week to approve all final versions. No matter how he felt, Gavin would have to face his past…and Arthur.

Shit, he wasn't sure how this one would end.

Then there were the damn calls. Maury was behind them. There was no one else who was that vindictive or evil.

Again, no matter what, Gavin knew he would figure out everything.

Chapter Two

Grayson heard the radio call come through.

"Base, this is SB-P2 on scene."

"SB-P2, report."

"Two-car accident at South Zephyr Road by the corner of A-3 and the cinema. Possible injuries. Require EMT. Request back-up assistance to restrict access to the crime scene and onlookers."

"Set the perimeter. Control the crowd. Additional responders are on their way."

"On top of it. SB-P2 out."

Immediately alert, Xavier 'Gray' Grayson listened. All the while, adrenaline raced through his blood to prepare him for the upcoming scene. Even as the chief paramedic, he went through a two-days-on and one-day-off shift. While it seemed a little chaotic to most folks with a regular day job, Xavier was used to the hours. This week he was on day shifts but would soon shift back to nights with the next rotation. On top of this schedule, he also went to college to pursue his nursing degree.

"Let's go. That's our call," Xavier called out to his EMT partner and good friend, Norman Perry.

"Crazy amount of calls for a summer afternoon," Norman muttered.

"Complain. Complain. We could be back in a pandemic."

"No thank you! Never again!"

They climbed into the rig and within minutes were on scene. Norman reported their status.

Stepping out, Xavier snapped his blue gloves in place and checked out the entire situation.

In the first car, the driver extracted himself from his broken vehicle. He kept one hand pressed against his bleeding temple to staunch the blood. He cursed while he circled his car, inspected the damage and tugged out his phone. With only one hand, he tapped something on the screen but appeared to just be taking pictures.

The male driver of the second car remained behind the wheel. The front and driver's side windows were smashed. Bits of shattered glass scattered across the road. The shards sparkled like diamonds in the morning sun. He moaned, belched in a loud disgusting fashion and whined.

"Shit, we have a damn drunk," Norman muttered.

More screaming and high-pitched crying.

"The cars aren't the only accident. Something else happened. Something worse," Xavier said.

As if proving his words true, someone screamed out, "Here! We need help over here!"

Xavier turned his head at the cries.

"SB-P2 to Base, secondary scene active. Additional injuries. On my way to secondary scene," the deputy said. He rushed around the front of the smashed vehicles to the smaller group. "Gray! Norm! Over here!" He waved to alert the EMTs.

"Go ahead. I'll get the gurney," Norman said.

Xavier raced across the chaos, his bag in hand, and followed the deputy.

Together, they discovered the second scene. This one involved a small bicycle mangled underneath the wheels of the first car. The thin frame of a preteen boy was sprawled across the pavement and sidewalk, his limbs bent in odd ways. There was a slight glistening of blood.

Two more boys with their bicycles stood by their friend. Tears streamed down their faces. The taller blond boy waved to get their attention.

"The car. The car swerved. It hit... It hit Adam. We didn't see it coming. We had the light to use the crosswalk," the boy called out in between hiccups and sobs. "He's hurt. He's hurt bad. Ya gotta help him."

"*Base, SB-P2 on second scene. Adolescent victim. Male.* How old is Adam?" the cop asked.

"Twelve. We're twelve." The boy snuffled and swiped the back of his hand against his snotty nose. "We were heading home after a movie."

"*Age twelve,*" the cop relayed the information on his radio. "*Was on a bicycle. Crossed with light at crosswalk. Side-swiped by car. Located under front bumper of first car with bicycle. EMT Grayson with me.*"

"Update. We'll give immediate EMT attention and evac to the boy. Alert clinic to send second bus for the drivers," Xavier said after a quick assessment.

The cop repeated Gray's attention to the dispatcher.

"*Copy, SB-P2. Responders alerted to changes. Clinic on notice.*"

Additional sirens wailed. More patrol cars arrived on scene, surrounding it. Deputies stepped out, and each went to work on a specific task. Multiple deputies corralled the onlookers. Three others rolled out and secured the yellow crime scene tape at different points to block everyone. They used it to contain the scene and possible evidence. The Crime Scene SUV arrived, and the familiar face of Keegan Donaghue slid out to survey the area. Other deputies moved through the crowd, probably to locate witnesses, while the remaining deputies assisted the accident victims.

Xavier concentrated on the wounded boy. Then he lowered his gear and crouched next to the victim. Norman followed him with the rest.

Keegan joined them but quietly took his pictures from multiple angles without interrupting anything. He set a marker next to the bicycle and another one close to the boy's position. Then he pulled back to another section of the massive scene to begin the rest of his work.

"Hey there, my name is Gray," Xavier said to the groggy boy. "Can you tell me your name?"

"Adam. His name is Adam," his teary friend said.

"Thanks. And what about you?"

"Jaime. This is Morgan."

The third boy wiggled his fingers at his name.

"Hi, Jaime, Morgan. I'm Gray, and this is Norman. We're going to take care of Adam. Okay?"

Jaime sniffed up tears and snot, then he rubbed his lower arm under his nose. "'Kay."

"Good. Jaime, Morgan, I need you to listen to the officer here while I help Adam. Okay? He's going to ask you some questions about what happened, and I need both of you to tell him the truth. Don't be afraid to tell him everything, because anything could help Adam. Okay?"

"'Kay." Jamie stepped closer to the officer.

Morgan moved to the officer's other side. "He gonna be okay?"

"That's what I'm going to figure out."

"Step back over here with me, boys. Jamie, how about you tell me how the day started?" the officer said while pulling out his pad and pen. He led them back a few steps.

Xavier went through his primary assessment. He checked Adam's airway, breathing and circulation. He felt concerned at the boy's quiet, slow responses to his questions.

Passing the drivers to another pair of paramedics, Norman comforted the almost-hysterical children and double-checked their health. Leaving the deputy in charge of them once it was clear they weren't hurt, the EMT returned to assist Xavier. "What do we have?"

"Suspect a head injury, possible spine damage. Need a child-size neck brace," Xavier ordered. "Adam, we need to wrap a special brace around your neck to protect it. It's a little uncomfortable, but we need to do this."

"'Kay," Adam mumbled.

"Responses are slow, simple, repetitive. He's not fully answering anything," Xavier said and went through his secondary assessment while Norman secured the brace. This detailed head-to-toe assessment took in everything during the physical examination. He noted any changes in the skin, flicked a small light to check the pupil response, listened to the chest sounds, palpated the abdomen and moved his hands to check for any pain, tenderness and deformities. Together, they untangled the boy from the bicycle. Xavier placed pads against the wounds on both lower legs and secured them in braces, noting possible broken bones.

After the second assessment, Norman nodded. "I concur with the head injury."

"Right. Recheck his vitals every ten minutes." Xavier adjusted the backboard. "Get ready to move him."

Norman checked and rattled off the vitals.

"Load and go. We need to get him to the clinic."

Together, they rolled Adam carefully to his least-wounded side and strapped him to the backboard. Adam cried out in pain. With a pair of deputies, they lifted and secured the board to the gurney.

A woman appeared within the crowd. "Adam! Adam!" Frantic, agonized fear cracked her voice.

The boy opened his eyes, bleary, darkened with pain. "Mommy!"

"Adam!" The screaming mother shoved past everyone in her desperate attempt to reach him.

Two deputies moved to intercept and keep her away from the scene.

"No, that's my son! Adam!" she screamed.

"The EMTs are working on him, ma'am. Let them help Adam," the deputy said.

"Adam! Baby, Mommy's here. Okay, baby, Mommy's here."

"Mommy..." Adam said.

Xavier softened his expression. Grateful to get a response out of the boy, he stopped the gurney next to the opened doors. Then he checked over Adam once more. He went through all the vitals. "Hey, Adam, remember me?"

"Gray. Like the color."

"That's right. I need to ask a few more questions."

"'Kay."

"How old are you, Adam?"

"Twelve…and a half."

"Twelve and a half. Wow. Were you at the movies with your friends?"

"Yeah. Saw *My Little Pony* movie. Summer special. Dollar." Adam's voice was thick with slurred words.

The symptom warned Xavier that something was happening within Adam's brain.

"Did you like it?"

"Yeah."

"Who is your favorite pony?"

"Rainbow Dash."

"Nice choice. I'm more like Fluttershy, because I enjoy caring for others."

"You like ponies?"

"Love them."

"But you're big."

"Doesn't matter. Still like the ponies. I'm a proud 'brony'." Xavier checked the boy's pressure, not liking how it had dropped. "How are you feeling, Adam?"

"Hurt. Want Mommy."

"I know, and we'll get her over here." Xavier flicked his penlight in Adam's eyes and noted the change in the pupils. "Where is your helmet, Adam?"

"Forgot. Home. Mommy gonna be mad."

"It happens. You didn't want to be late for the movie. Can you tell me where you don't feel good? Or can you point to where it hurts?"

Adam blinked, tried to move, but tears filled his eyes. "Uh-huh."

"Okay. What's happening?"

"Can't move. Hurts."

"Okay. Everything will be okay, Adam. I know you're scared."

"Mommy?"

"We'll get her." Xavier placed a hand on the boy's hair to offer comfort. "A lot is going to happen, but I'm not leaving your side. Your mom will be there, too," he said. "The same thing will happen at the clinic. A lot of lights, people asking questions, and activity, but all of it will help you get better. Okay?"

"'Kay." The boy paused, blinked and looked away. After a long moment, he returned his vacant gaze to Xavier. "Scared. Mommy..."

"I know." Xavier looked at his partner. "We need to go. Definitely a head injury, no helmet. Don't like the look of his legs. Get the mom here and explain what's happening. You drive. I'll stay with him."

"Got it!" Norman raced away to find the mother.

"We're moving out," Xavier said to the cops. "Clear a path."

"On it," a deputy said. A bunch of them moved ahead to push the crowds farther away from their path to the clinic.

"We got a short ride, Adam, so we'll be there in a quick minute," Xavier said.

Xavier moved the gurney into place until it hit the back to collapse the legs and he pushed it inside. After Norman returned with the mom, he helped her step up and pointed out the extra jump-seat. "Buckle in, please."

"Thank you. Adam, baby, I'm here. I'm here," she said while she moved. She dipped down to kiss his forehead.

"Mommy!"

"I know, baby. Hang on."

Xavier climbed up but paused to glance across the crowd. His gaze stopped on a pair of baby-blue eyes. He lowered his study for a second to catch sight of the bow tie and suspenders. Then he held the baby-blue stare for another moment.

Gavin. That's his name. The wedding guy. What is he doing here?

With a shake of his head, Xavier closed the doors and concentrated again on young Adam while Norman drove them away.

Chapter Three

Returning to the Charm after that insane visit to town, Gavin got the call that he had a waiting groom. He double-checked his appearance and straightened his bow tie. This time he chose a set of a dashing blue jacquard, a navy and black checkerboard pattern that had the smallest hint of crimson accents, along with a leather crosspatch on the suspenders. He paired the set with a deep red shirt, navy pants and suede ankle boots. He headed down the hallway, turned the corner and stopped short. He braced himself with a hand against the wall.

Arthur Carlton stood near the front desk. A yellow spinner suitcase rested near him while a backpack hung from his shoulder. He wore his prematurely silver hair in a longer style but maintained his preppy appearance in his dress.

"Hello, Arthur! Welcome to the Southern Charm Bed & Breakfast." Gavin stepped around the final corner. "I hope you had a wonderful trip."

Arthur looked up from signing the electronic pad. He tucked his credit card back into the wallet then he smiled. The simple action lightened his deep blue eyes. "Gavin." He enfolded him in a warm embrace.

A little surprised, Gavin hesitated a second but returned the affection. Arthur always had the warmest heart and nature—one of the sweetest men, a hugger.

"So wonderful to see you again. You're looking happier than when I last saw you back in Atlanta," Arthur said. He placed a hand against Gavin's cheek and studied him. "There's warmth in your eyes and cheeks. You don't look stressed."

"I'm away from it."

"Away from *him*."

Gavin nibbled on his lip and glanced at Elise. He gave Arthur a quick nod. He didn't regret telling Arthur what had happened with Maury. Arthur had pushed him into sending his application and getting the hell out of Atlanta.

"Has he contacted you?"

"I get some calls. Don't know what it means. I'm ignoring them. That's about all I can do."

"Damn, that's not good. You don't need any more trouble. This seaside town agrees with you."

"It's not just the town. This B&B is a wonderful place and so are the people here."

"You feel at home," Arthur said. "You feel safe."

After a rough childhood with an alcoholic father, a mother struggling to keep it all together and multiple moves from one dump to another, Gavin had never truly felt home anywhere—at least until he'd moved to Shore Breeze, found his new house and a position at the Charm. He realized his past had altered and affected his self-esteem issues.

"I do. This is a wonderful place, a caring family. Charmed Occasions is everything I wanted in an event company."

"I can't wait for you to show it off to me."

"I think you'll enjoy it." Gavin slid a hand into his pocket. "How is Neil?"

"Busy with work, which is why he's not with me. He sends his regards and thanks for your helping us. Let me finish with the check-in and we can catch up. Can't wait to hear how you're doing and how we'll make this wedding spectacular. It'll be one of your favorite events. I'm sure of it," Arthur said and returned his attention to Elise. "Sorry… I didn't mean to ignore you."

Elise waved away his concern. "It's wonderful to see friends get together."

"I couldn't wait to see him again." Arthur winked at Gavin. "Is there anything else you need from me?"

"Nope. I have everything, but I do need to give you something." Elise handed Arthur the key with a scallop shell charm and B&B tag. "This is your key to the Calico Scallop Room."

"A key?"

"It's a metallic strip key instead of the old-fashioned tumblers and locks," Elise explained. "The owners wanted to keep the quaint nature of a B&B, but with added security. When you check out, the keychain with the charms are yours to keep, as a reminder of your stay."

"What a wonderful memento. So unique and different. Thank you," Arthur said.

"Would you like to show Mr. Carlton to the room, Gavin?"

"Sure," Gavin said. "You've got a choice, Arthur. Stairs or elevator?"

"I can climb stairs. Hey, I work out three times a week, sometimes more. I'm getting buff." Arthur fake-curled his arm to show off his biceps.

"Come on, Mr. Bodybuilder."

Laughing, Arthur tucked his wallet back inside the backpack and slung it over his shoulder. Then he snagged the suitcase's handle and followed Gavin. "Show me the way."

Leading him up to the second floor, Gavin took him to a water-view room. "Here's a tip. It's the easiest way to remember the rooms." He pointed to the light-box with a scallop shell glass design. "The charm on your chain matches the door light. The backside of the charm has the floor number."

"Oh, that's gorgeous," Arthur said and caressed the edge of the box. "How unique to mark the doors. So much cooler than boring numbers."

"All the shells can be found in Florida waters. The boxes were added with the renovations. A local artist created all the charms and lights. If you're interested in checking out his work, he has a studio and gallery downtown."

"I would like to see his work, perhaps to find something for Neil."

"How about I let you settle in for a few hours? You can unpack, clean up, check out the Charm and the beach. We can meet at the doors to Southern Delights for dinner. My treat."

"Sounds good." Arthur slid the key into the lock and opened the door. "Where can I find the Delights?"

"Downstairs across from the front desk. It's a top-notch restaurant that features local seafood and ingredients."

"Oh, I do remember seeing the sign about the restaurant. I can't wait to try it."

"It's where most receptions happen. We're building a new event space, but it's not going to be ready until October."

"Definitely want to check it all out."

"I'll see you soon, then." Gavin walked away.

"Hey, Gavin."

Gavin stopped by the staircase and looked back down the hallway.

"It's good to see you again. I made the right decision to ask for your help." Arthur placed a hand on the doorframe and leaned on it. "I don't want to cause you any pain. Please tell me if anything bothers you."

"It's wonderful to see you. There's no pain. I promise. Some regret about how things ended, but I'm happy you found love with Neil."

"Okay. Wanted to make sure before we finalize things. If you're hurt, I don't want to add to it."

"You're not. I promise. I want to be the one to help make your dream day come true."

"See you at dinner."

With a nod, Gavin went downstairs.

* * * *

Hours later, Gavin met Arthur by the front desk with his messenger bag hanging from one shoulder. "Good evening. Hope you had some time to rest. Like the room?"

"It's great. So peaceful to listen to the ocean. How about you?"

"Doing okay. Hope you don't mind if I relax a bit." Gavin rolled his neck back and forth. Then he tugged loose the bow tie and pulled it free. After folding the strip carefully to prevent wrinkles, he tucked it into one of the outer pockets in the messenger bag. To further relax, he unbuttoned and folded back his shirtsleeves.

"End of a day?"

"Another long one, but I enjoy them. Ready to eat?"

"I am."

"Excellent. Follow me." Gavin led him to where diners gathered by the double wood and engraved-glass doors leading to the restaurant, Southern Delights. The area was filled with people waiting for a table. Many stood outside waiting for a notification to buzz their phones. He wound them through until they reached the hostess station.

The elegant hostess, Cecile, turned to them with a smile and a raised finger. She touched the headset and spoke something about clearing three exterior tables and resetting them. Then she tapped something on a tablet with a stylus. "Evening, Gavin, sorry. Things are a bit busy. I fear my busboys are a little slack." She glanced at Arthur and gave him a nod. "Hello there. Who are you?"

"Hi, Cecile. This is a Charm guest and one of my upcoming grooms, Arthur Carlton. He'll be marrying his fiancé, Neil, in a couple of weeks. He's here to finalize some details," Gavin introduced. "Arthur, this is the Delights' fabulous hostess, Cecile LeClair. She keeps things running smooth throughout the restaurant."

"Other than the kitchen. That's Dakota's territory," Cecile said.

They chuckled.

Arthur cast odd, confused glances at them.

"Everyone steers clear of the kitchen when Dakota rules over the ovens and fire. He has a typical hot chef's temper and tongue," Gavin said, "accompanied by very sharp knives."

Arthur snorted when he caught the inside joke.

"Welcome to the Southern Charm and the Delights, Arthur," Cecile said.

"Thank you, I'm happy to make it here."

"Is one of the Charm reserved tables open?" Gavin asked about the quad of tables kept aside for Charm guests or employees.

"I have two. One outside on the patio and another inside," Cecile said.

"Your choice, Arthur," Gavin said.

"Inside, please. The humidity is a little stifling. I need to acclimate a bit longer," Arthur said.

"Understand. It happens a lot to our guests. Follow me." Cecile scooped up a pair of fresh printed menus and led them past the doors. The place was packed with diners, scents of delicious food and patio doors opened to enjoy the music of a pair of guitarists playing outside. Cecile moved with ease. She stopped at a table that was by the windows but closer to the kitchen.

Stepping up to be a gentleman, Gavin held the chair for Arthur. "Please."

"Thank you," Arthur said.

"Gavin!"

At his name, Gavin looked around to find Chandler and his partner, Sully Tarleton, at a nearby table. Chandler waved and Gavin returned it. The taller blond, Sully, also waved hello.

"Thought you would have left by now," Chandler said.

"Oh, no, I have a special guest with a better offer than an empty home." Gavin motioned to Arthur, who smiled at the couple.

Chandler and Sully laughed.

"Without fail," Sully said.

"Hey. You know I try." With another wave, Gavin dropped his messenger bag in a free chair. Then he settled in the chair across from Arthur, who continued to sit during the teasing exchange. The amused look remained in place on Arthur's face. "What?"

Arthur tilted his head toward the couple. "Who is that?"

"The one in the glasses is the Charm's accountant, Chandler Braddock. The tall fellow is his partner, a local carpenter and contractor, Sullivan Tarleton, but we call him Sully," Gavin said. "They're good friends."

"Partners?"

"A wonderful couple. Chandler got pulled into this place by Samuel Ashford to review the previous owner's books. Samuel's family acquired half of the Charm's ownership and Samuel was sent to the Charm to figure out what to do. Instead of destroying everything, Samuel chose to save it. Sully did the renovations. They met during that time. I didn't hear the entire story, but it's one of those special love stories. There's something special about this B&B that influences love stories."

"I hope to get some of this influence for Neil and me during our day," Arthur said.

"It's my job to make sure that happens."

"Good to have you in my corner." Arthur waved the menu. "What's with these paper menus?"

"There's a reason—and not because of the pandemic. This was a thing before that happened. They're printed upon request according to whatever dishes the chef, Dakota Mitchell, decides to offer. Those decisions are based on the fresh ingredients he procures from the local dock, butchery and farmer's market. Sometimes he'll have similar-style meals for the same menu or each night will have specific specials. Either way, you almost never have the same thing twice when you visit Delights, unless you fall in love with one of their main dishes."

"Sounds wonderful."

"Good evening, gentlemen. My name is Amelia — Oh, it's you, Gavin." Amelia chuckled while she placed unique Delights' coasters in front of them.

"Sheesh. All I get. 'Oh, it's you.' Jeez, thanks, Amelia. I feel so special and welcomed," Gavin said, teasing her.

"Well, you didn't have your bow tie."

"What? Is that all that's bugging you?"

"You look different." Amelia waved a hand around her neck. "What happened?"

"I'm done with work and wanted to let loose to enjoy dinner with my friend," Gavin said and introduced them.

"Hello and welcome to the Delights, Arthur," Amelia said.

Arthur listened to their chatter with an off-sided smile. "Hello."

Amelia glanced between them. "What can I get you two to drink?"

"The house sweet tea. Light ice. No lemon," Gavin said.

"So...the usual."

Gavin sent an air kiss at the sass.

Arthur flicked a fingertip along the menu's edge. "Is there a bar available?"

"Yes, we have one outside during the summer. What would you like? We have some excellent house wines or local craft beers?"

"Icewine Martini. Shaken. Double. No olives."

"Icewine. Don't hear that one too often. Lemme check to see if they can make that for you," she said.

"If not, a regular martini. Made the same."

Amelia jotted down the extra note. "Lemme go check with our bartenders. I'm sure Zak will know it. I'll return and take your orders." She headed for the nearest open patio door.

"I've heard Icewines are potent. How are they?" Gavin asked.

"I could use a bit of potency tonight. It has a sweet upfront attack followed by the typical back-end dryness from the vodka. It's a combination of grace and potency. Not many places have Icewine, though, so it's hard to get," Arthur explained.

"What is it?"

"It's a type of dessert wine made from grapes that have been frozen while still on the vine. The sugars don't freeze but the water does. This ends up creating a more concentrated grape juice. By the end of the process, it creates a smaller amount of more concentrated, extremely sweet wine. Canada has one of the best ones on the market, but there's an American brand growing in popularity."

"How do you know all this?"

"Neil first introduced me to the drink. We learned more about it when we worked on the graphics and campaign for an advertising project. We tried a bottle, mixed it different ways and got hooked on the martini blend." He flicked the edge of the menu. "It's funny what you can learn when designing graphics or ad campaigns. They sometimes bring you products you have no idea what they are but need to learn to design for the job."

"How is it working with Neil all day and living with him? You're never apart."

"Our departments don't always work together, only on certain projects. I do prefer working for his company than the previous one."

"Now you have me intrigued to try it," Gavin said.

"If they make it, but not from my glass. It'll be a little too much for your first try. I would try a small glass straight from the bottle with some ice."

"Should we serve it for the reception toasts?"

"I would enjoy that if it's possible," Arthur said.

"I'll look into it."

"You're in luck," Amelia said after returning to their table. "Zak recognized the name. He ended up ordering a case when someone asked about it for a dinner party—not one of yours, Gavin."

"Oh, thanks so much for pointing that out."

"Can't get all of them."

Arthur snorted at their byplay.

"Zak's making your drink right now."

"Excellent. Thank you. Could I have a water as well? Light ice. Lemon," Arthur said.

"Of course." Amelia jotted the note. "Have you decided what you want, or do you need more time? Perhaps you would like to start with an appetizer? I recommend the mini crab-cakes or hush puppies."

"Arthur?" Gavin asked.

Arthur selected one of the spring lettuce salads with Israeli couscous, grilled gulf shrimp and vegetables and a light herb vinaigrette.

"Good choice. What about you, Gavin?"

Gavin chose one of the new specials with the freshwater blue crabs, orzo, fresh herbs and vegetables. "Toss in an appetizer of the mini crab-cakes with both sauces."

Amelia double-checked their choices, scooped up the menus and left them alone. She returned a few moments later with their drinks, a pair of small plates, a basket of fresh-baked bread and a plate of herbs. She poured olive oil onto the herbs to create a dip. Then she left again to retrieve Arthur's drink.

"Both sauces?"

"There's a house remoulade and an aioli. Both are wonderful. And try the bread. It's made fresh." Gavin used a piece of bread to combine the oil and herbs. He ripped apart pieces of bread to dunk into the mixture.

Amelia returned with the crystal-clear drink in the martini glass. The bartender had chilled the glass to create a light frost appearance to accompany the name of the drink. She placed it front of Arthur on a separate coaster. "There you go."

Arthur took a tentative sip. He closed his eyes for a moment and nodded. "Perfect. Thank you."

"You're welcome. I'll be right back with the crab-cakes," she said and left them again.

Arthur took a longer sip and hummed in appreciation. "Good thing I'm not driving anywhere."

"Is everything okay?"

"Hmm." Arthur shrugged while he gave the martini glass a bit of a spin. "Bad news on the medical side for Neil. He spoke with his doctor earlier. I wanted to be there, but—"

"Came here instead."

"He insisted."

"What would you like to do?"

Taking another sip, Arthur sat up. "I want to finalize our wedding plans. No matter what happens, we've decided to move forward in our life. That means enjoying our wedding."

"Okay then. Want to start now?"

"Please."

Gavin lifted a folder from his messenger bag and flipped it open between them. He went over the details of the package Arthur had chosen, with available options or changes. They paused when Amelia dropped off first the appetizer and later their dinners. While eating, he explained everything Arthur should expect when they reviewed the different packages and added information about the layout and rehearsal timing.

"More than I expected," Arthur said when they finished the explanations and their meal.

"And a little overwhelming, but that's why you have me."

"Do you do this for every event?"

"More or less."

"Amazing. How do you keep it all straight?"

"An excellent electronic system, a whole lotta paperwork and a binder for each event. I simplified things where I could, but given the nature of this business and people—" Gavin shrugged. "I do what I can."

"Can we continue tomorrow? I need to speak with Neil about some of this stuff."

"Take the folder with you. This is your working copy." Gavin slid it closer to Arthur. "I'll make a note about the Icewine." He chose a pen and scribbled it down, then signed the check Amelia had dropped off. He jotted a note on the copy and stuck it in his bag. "Have a good evening. The ocean is very soothing if you leave the window open, kind of worth dealing with the humidity."

"Are you staying?"

"Not sure, there are a couple of things I need to finish. Nah, time for a break. I'm gonna head for a walk on the beach to unwind. Then I'll head home."

They left the table. Arthur headed to the stairs while Gavin stopped by the front desk.

"Good night, Gavin," Arthur said.

"See you tomorrow."

Chapter Four

After an extended shift in between long hours of studying for his two summer college courses, Intro to Philosophy and Applied Microbiology, Xavier wanted to collapse. Instead, he dove into remnants of energy to keep moving forward. There were eight more days. The last few classes were lengthy reviews to prepare for the exams. He would have to figure out the microbiology lab exam before the lecture class. It was a crazy schedule, but he needed the additional work hours to cover his bills. Soon he could revert to normal EMT shifts until the fall semester.

Xavier smacked the closest wall with his palm. He cursed the world and the air blue. "Sonofa... Why? Fuck me, why?"

As the paramedic supervisor, Xavier witnessed the absolute worst moments in life a human could potentially face — illness, accident, self-inflicted, homicide, brutal assault, overdoses, anything a human can do to another human when all morals, emotions and compassion were cast aside and forgotten.

For the most part, he could push past through the various atrocities and go to the next one.

Sometimes, there were cases he couldn't forget.

One of those specific cases had happened earlier.

One idiot had climbed behind the wheel of his car after enjoying a 'good summertime' getting completely smashed with his equally reckless drinking buddies and side-swiped a child riding home on his bicycle

"Gray, come on, man. There's no point beating yourself over what happened. There's nothing you can do to change fucked-up human nature," Norman said while he leaned his shoulder against the wall next to Xavier.

"The drunk bastard got his head jiggled, ten stitches above his eye and a fractured wrist. The other guy got a touch of whiplash and strained muscles. That kid...? That kid might never ride his bike again. What the fuck kind of fate is that? Going to movies with your friends on a bright summer day, and you end up in a hospital bed," Xavier said.

"Gray..."

"It sucks when kids are involved."

"Kids and idiots."

"They're the true innocents. What the fuck was that bastard thinking?"

"He wasn't—an alcoholic who needed his next fix. It's all they consider in their life and don't give a shit who gets in their way."

Xavier thumped his head back against the wall.

"We did what we could."

"Something more should be done."

"At least this isn't some wacky big city. Shore Breeze is a safe place—safer than most and especially for kids.

We would be up to our knees and elbows in blood and guts in some big city."

"Yeah. Yeah. I know." Another thump against the wall. Another grimace. "Still fucking sucks." Xavier shook his head. He pushed the heels of his hands against his eyes. His mind raced with all kinds of images from different scenes he witnessed as a paramedic. Even with his recent medication adjustment, his ADHD continued to antagonize and aggravate him.

"Hey, Gray," a nurse offered while she moved toward them.

"Hey, Kelli." Xavier lowered his hands after scrubbing his face. "Whatcha got for me?"

"An update on the boy you brought in earlier," she said.

"Really? Appreciate it. How is he doing?"

"The latest word from the pediatric ICU is Adam is out of surgery and recovery. He's in ICU under critical condition. The neurosurgeon is wary of potential brain swelling, bleeds and other possibilities."

"Right. No helmet."

"It puts him at a higher risk for complications. His youth, overall health and a child's brain plasticity to heal are favors in his odds, but nothing is for sure at this point."

"The same deal with any serious brain injury."

"Exactly."

"Which means…"

"There's nothing more you can do here," Kelli said.

"It's the end of our shift," Norman added. "We need to return to the station, clean the rig and go home."

"Listen to Norman," Kelli said. "Go home, Gray. You did all you could for Adam, and gave him the best shot at survival on scene."

"What about the drunk?" Xavier asked.

"Sober and in the custody of the sheriff's deputies. The doctor placed his wrist in a soft brace so he couldn't use it to cause pain or damage."

"Whining about the pain."

"Yes, and a headache. One of the nurses gave him two ibuprofen and told him to suck it up."

Xavier snorted.

"He's going straight to booking and a cozy night in a prison cell."

"Where he belongs. He could have killed that boy and not even realized what he'd done," Xavier said.

"No need to go down that road right now," Norman said.

"Go home, fellas. At least enjoy the rest of the night for some of us," Kelli said and walked away.

Xavier tilted his head back against the wall. A long-troubled breath rattled out of him. "Damn, this whole situation sucks ass."

"Come on, man. Let's get out of here. Been a long damn shift."

"Yeah. Yeah. Here—" Xavier tossed the keys to Norman. "You drive the rig back."

Norman caught the keys with a quick twist of his hand. He twirled the ring around one finger. "You got it."

Xavier finished the last of their paperwork while Norman drove back to the fire station.

"Damn, we need gas. Should I stop?"

"Yeah. Don't want to screw that up."

Norman grinned. "Riiight—"

"Don't go there." The rig had run out of gas during Xavier's first shift as a full-time paramedic. He'd never been so embarrassed.

Chuckling, Norman detoured to the nearest gas station. He got out to pump the tank full. Within minutes, he got them back on the route back to the fire station up the road from the clinic. Then he pulled the rig into their place in front of the opened door to their slot and they climbed out.

Like at the beginning of their shift, they ran through the checklists at the end.

"Clean up, wipe everything down and toss the trash. I'll hit the checklists and restock," Xavier said.

"No problem."

Xavier climbed into the back, grabbed the handwritten checklist he'd started twenty-four hours earlier and went through each step. The checklist made sure that all medical equipment worked, enough supplies were on hand for the entire shift and the vehicle itself was ready to drive.

At times, a previous crew could forget to replace the supplies they used. It happened. Xavier kept on top of each crew and made sure they took responsibility. The crews were small and the shifts long. Things got forgotten. Either way, Xavier tried to maintain consistency.

The final rig check took another hour. The morning ones could take up to two hours.

When he checked one of the portable oxygen tanks, Xavier cursed under his breath. It was empty. The previous crew had neglected to top it off, but marked it off as 'full'. Xavier noted the name with a mental jog to ream the idiot.

"Norm?"

"Yeah, boss?" Norman stuck his head around the edge.

"Take this inside and refill it." Xavier rolled the tank to the opening and helped Norman lower it to the ground. "Luke and Wendy screwed up on their list and didn't top it. We're damn lucky we didn't need this extra one."

"Yeah, we would have been screwed."

"Our patient could have ended up dead."

"Want me to find them and kick their ass?"

"Please. I'm too damn tired to do it myself."

"I'll take care of it," Norman said. "Anything else?"

"Bring back another box of medium gloves, a bottle of disinfectant and wipes."

"Got it. Be right back."

Xavier finished a half-hour later when Norman returned with the tank and requested items. Together they sprayed, soaped, power-washed and dried the entire rig from until it sparkled. Then Xavier signed off on the paperwork, had his partner jot his name to verify and let him drop it off.

"Drive the rig inside," Xavier said. "Close the door and drop off the keys on their ring for the next crew. I'm going to clock out and head home."

"Got it covered. Trust me. Go home. Get some sleep."

"Can't. Got some studying to do, if I can keep my eyes open."

"Don't push yourself too far." Norman clapped a hand on Xavier's shoulder. "See you next shift."

"It'll be double after my exam in the morning." Yawning hard, Xavier shook his head when his jaw popped. He made the mistake of looking at his desk. Cursing because he couldn't ignore it, he double-checked a pile of paperwork, signed off then dropped everything in the outbox. Finally, he clocked out.

Then he grabbed his backpack from his locker, located his keys and headed to the parking lot. He tossed his bag into the cab of his ancient Ford truck. Climbing in behind the wheel, Xavier rubbed his eyes.

"Five minutes and you're home. Five more minutes. Get with the program."

With the pep-talk, he cranked the key to turn over the engine. A couple of groans, clanks and the engine fired.

Xavier dragged the gearshift into Reverse, pulled out, shoved it into first gear and drove away. The roads were deserted. Since he didn't need to concentrate on traffic, the break sent his ADHD mind racing with anything that could face him back at the apartment.

It wasn't going to be a smooth drop into bed.

* * * *

His ADHD brain pounded at the idea of an empty fridge, freezer and pantry. There was no food for him to make a quick meal. He couldn't afford the expense of takeout. While he had another week of classes, he continued to look forward to the upcoming semester. The next nursing course was expensive as hell. The books alone would rip apart his budget.

"Really? Now? Come on."

His mind pointed out the empty shelves. *No food*. His belly grumbled.

"Dammit. Fine. Fine."

Xavier drove back across town and beyond to the grocery store. Within moments, he pushed a cart through the near-empty store.

While his mind jumped between all different items, Xavier circled the first two aisles. Then he stopped short and pulled out his phone.

"Stop. Stop. Stop," he muttered.

Xavier located one of his previous stored lists in the app. He double-checked the items and noted he would re-use everything.

With the list to calm his ADHD and give him focus, Xavier went through the entire store, checked out with ease and returned to the truck. He placed the filled totes on the cab's floor. Climbing back inside, he fired up the engine again.

"Come on, Old Blue, I need to you to keep moving. Cooperate with me, buddy, please," he coaxed the old Ford.

Driving back to the apartment, Xavier carried everything inside in one trip. He rested his elbows on the counter to catch his breath. He unloaded the groceries across the counter space to figure out what he had purchased. Exhaustion dragged at him, but his slight OCD drove him to organize everything into groups. He couldn't dump everything into the pantry and fridge.

If he kept his OCD somewhat fed and under control, he didn't have many ADHD moments because he kept his life structured and scheduled.

Norman and the other EMTs knew to never mess with his organization systems.

With all the groceries put away, he ruthlessly cleaned everything in the kitchen, packed the used totes together and set them in place. He repeated the procedures with his everyday bag. Grumbling, he snatched up the keys and hung them from the hook by the door. Then he kicked off his work-boots and placed them in their cubby space.

Satisfied that he'd prepared everything possible, he went to his bedroom and changed into a pair of sweatpants and faded T-shirt. Sorting out the laundry into precise color piles, he set up a small run of uniforms in the washer.

His belly grumbled with hunger.

"Okay. Okay."

Xavier returned to the kitchen. While his mind suggested multiple options for dinner, he settled on the easiest and fastest. He piled deli meats high on Chicago Italian bread with a few slices of provolone, slathered a combination of mustard, honey and dill and finished it with a couple of baby spinach leaves for some fresh crunch. He poured potato chips onto the plate and refilled his water glass. Since there wasn't a kitchen table, he settled on the sofa with dinner laid out on the coffee table. He clicked through Hulu and watched the latest episodes of *Arrow*.

After a few bites, Xavier heard his phone beep from a low battery. He cleaned off his hands and plugged it in. Then he double-checked his upcoming schedule, something he'd helped build with the firehouse captain.

Along with the electronic calendar, he opened his notebook planner and a pack of colored pens. He coordinated the paper planner with the electronic one to have everything laid out in front of him.

To keep his OCD and ADHD level, he maintained a constant oversight of his schedules. He would check and double-check everything before agreeing to the request—or sometimes suggest a different day. This issue drove his few boyfriends bonkers because he couldn't relax in the rigidity required to maintain his self-discipline.

He flipped one schedule to check out what was coming up for the fall semester. Thanks to his next class, a nursing one, he would be gone two full days and two lab days every week. It meant his work schedule would be tighter and longer over the weekends.

"Eight. Freaking. Hours. Kill me now."

The class was eight credits and meant he would be in one classroom for eight hours twice a week. Then he had two lab days consisting of another two-and-a-half hours each. He couldn't take an online version. This class had to be done in person and on campus.

"Why did I do this to myself?"

It would take every one of his coping strategies to deal with his ADHD over those long days. There were certain little things he required to control it — his rituals, triggers and strict schedules built on top of his daily maintenance medication. Then he carried an emergency supply if things flared out of control. Still, his disability varied day-to-day with some moments being harder to cope with than others.

After finishing dinner and cleaning his plate, he pulled out the applied microbiology books and worked through his last preparations for the lab exam in the morning.

When he couldn't shove anything more into his brain, he returned only the binder to the backpack and double-checked his pen and pencil supply. Once he'd confirmed he had everything ready for the exam, he dropped the backpack by the door. Then he tried to relax with a cup of herbal tea and another *Arrow* episode before bed.

When he couldn't relax, his energy level ratcheted up and he smacked his head against the sofa.

"Okay. Fine. I'll go for a damn run. Stupid brain. Stupid energy."

Xavier wrote the run in on the schedule to satisfy the OCD urge. Then he returned the cup to the kitchen but wrapped foil over the top to keep for his return.

After a quick change into his running shorts and sneakers, he shoved his phone into the armband and connected the wireless headset. He dropped his ID and house-key into another pocket on the band. Then he did a few stretches to loosen his muscles.

With easy, measured steps and one of his running mixes playing, he wound a loop around downtown, then past the apartment buildings and decided to go a bit farther. He followed the trail along the shoreline toward the Charm. Thanks to this extended circuit, hopefully, he could finish his tea and let his mind shut down. All he wanted was a few blissful hours of sleep.

* * * *

When he got closer to the Southern Charm, Xavier slowed down for a few paces. He popped out one bud to listen to the music playing on the patio. Though he didn't recognize the singer, he enjoyed the dual-played guitars. He popped the bud back in and hastened his pace.

Lost in the music, the twists of his mind and the pounding of his sneakers on the wave-soaked sand, he continued his path across the beach. Thanks to the limited lighting, there wouldn't be anyone this close to the water. If anyone were around, they would notice his movement and step away.

His path stopped short when he slammed hard into someone. His chest burned when a hard shoulder jammed against him. It cut into his breathing, made it harsh.

"What the hell?"

Their feet tangled, and it knocked them both off balance. With a flail of arms, limbs and cursing, they both dropped hard.

Xavier spit out sand, still cursing while his mind raced. *What the hell happened?* A male body half underneath him shifted. He noticed it was more slender than his broader frame.

"Damn it all. Didn't you even notice I was running? What the hell where you—?" Xavier stopped snapping and moving when the man yelped. His EMT instincts kicked in and adrenaline pumped while he hyper-focused on the situation and his demeanor altered. "What happened? Are you injured?"

"Ouch. You weigh a freaking ton," his 'victim' said in a droll tone. "Could you get off me? Please. Sorry... I don't roll around with strangers. Sand gets into some nasty places."

"Crap." Xavier carefully adjusted his weight until he lifted himself away from the man. He curled up to a sitting position, turned off the music and pulled out the earbuds. He tucked them into the armband.

Adjusting his position until what little light could shine upon his 'victim', he recognized who he'd run over.

The new guy at the Charm. The wedding guy.

"You're the wedding guy." The rather cute guy who wore suspenders and bow ties with every outfit—the one who reminded him a lot of Nate Berkus.

"Really? That's it? The wedding guy?" the man asked in the same droll tone while he met Xavier's stare. "We've met a bunch of times."

"Have we?"

"Am I that forgettable?"

"Depends on the situation where we met."

"Unbelievable."

"Name?"

"Gavin Hartfield. I'm the event planner and coordinator for Charmed Occasions at the Southern Charm."

"That's a mouthful."

"Official title, since you insisted," Gavin snapped back in full sass mode. "No, I didn't notice you running along the beach in the night. I was sitting here minding my own damn business when someone ran right over me."

"Hmm…sass. Nice."

"Ooh, snarky and annoying."

Xavier tried not to smile at all the sass and snark. "Do you know—"

"Xavier Grayson, but you prefer to go by Gray. Yeah, I know who you are."

"Guess we did meet or exchange names somewhere along the way."

"We did. Multiple times. Again, *you* forgot. *I* didn't," Gavin said.

"Sorry. I meet a lot of people in short spurts during my work."

"I'm constantly dealing with people myself, but I don't forget." Gavin pursed his lips for a second, then added to make his point, "Gray."

"Okay. Okay. I apologize. You can call me Xavier."

"Why? Is 'Gray' reserved for friends only?"

"No. I'm called both. I would like for you to call me Xavier." Xavier wanted to hear his real name from Gavin. For some damn reason, his mind insisted on the difference.

"Fine. Fine. Whatever." Gavin paused a few beats. "Xavier."

"When did we meet?"

"Do you not remember me?"

"I have ADHD, so my mind can go a mile a minute. Plus, I suck at remembering names unless you're one of my repeat EMT calls."

"Oh. Umm. Most recent was last Halloween when Doc Elliott introduced us during the Halloween festival—"

"Wait. Right!" Xavier snapped his fingers when the image clicked in his mind. "You were dressed as a bunny—"

"A rabbit. The White Rabbit from *Alice in Wonderland*," Gavin corrected. "Damn freaking costume."

"Rabbit. Sorry. Any other times?"

"Yes, there were others, but I can't remember right now when I'm. In. Freaking. Pain!"

"Oh, shit, sorry. Right."

"Yeah, yeah, forget about it. Look... You should get back to your run. I'll deal with whatever is wrong with me." Gavin pushed himself to a sitting position. He winced and yelped when he moved his feet. "Crap."

"That doesn't sound good. Let me look at it." Xavier moved until he crouched near Gavin's legs.

"Umm. No, I can manage."

"Who is the trained paramedic?"

Gavin grumbled. "You."

"Thank you." Xavier assessed the situation and cursed the darkness since he couldn't get a decent look at the injury, though he noticed he touched bare skin and toes. "Where are your shoes?"

"Duh. I took them off."

"Where are they?"

"Left them by the boardwalk. I wasn't going to ruin them by walking across the beach. Sand feels better on the toes."

Trying to ignore how slim Gavin's lower leg and foot felt within his hands, Xavier concentrated on his work. He palpated and manipulated Gavin's left ankle.

"Ouch. Ouch." Gavin whimpered and yelped. "Would you stop fiddling with it? Dang it. That hurts."

"Sorry. I don't mean to cause more pain."

"Duh. It hurts. What's wrong with my ankle?"

"Definitely not good, but I can't make a definitive diagnosis out here. It's too damn dark." Xavier looked back toward the light. "We need to get back to the Charm."

"Fine. Could you help me up?"

"And risk you injuring yourself further? No. That's not going to happen." Xavier crouched, slid his arms under and around Gavin. He scooped him close while he rose to his feet.

"Whoa! What are you doing? I can freaking walk—" Gavin flailed until he wrapped his arms around Xavier's neck. "*Eep!*"

"Just hang on." Xavier noticed Gavin's frame was small and light in his hold. "You don't weigh much. What? A hundred pounds soaking wet?"

"I don't know if I should smack you or thank you. Either way, my weight isn't your concern."

"It is if you're doing something bad to cause it."

"I am not! Put me down!" Gavin wiggled a little in Xavier's hold.

"Stop wiggling your ass or I'm going to drop you on it," Xavier snapped and juggled him. His adrenaline levels flagged while his exhaustion returned, along with frustration for the unexpected chaotic change. He needed those fleeting calm moments to get some decent sleep before facing a grueling lab exam. *Not the best situation.*

"Oh, sure, injure me even more. I—"

Xavier shushed him while he moved up the steps to the quiet porch. The guitar players had left. He went through the opened patio doors and headed for the kitchen and back hallway.

"Samuel? Chandler? Anyone here?" He didn't bother calling for Dakota or Malcolm, who would be busy closing the kitchen.

"Gray? What are you doing here so late?" Samuel moved down the hallway. "Gavin! Oh my God! What happened?"

"Gray— What—?" Chandler said. "Gavin?"

"Why are you holding Gavin, Gray?" Samuel asked. "Hold on." He rushed into the kitchen and dragged out a chair. "Here. Set him on this. There must be some reason you don't want Gavin on his feet. What happened?"

"We bumped into each other on the beach." Xavier placed Gavin on the chair. "The hard way."

"You ran over me...literally," Gavin corrected.

"You didn't move out of the way."

"Hello! Nighttime. There are no lights on the beach. No moon in the sky. All which means that it's freaking dark outside. I could barely see a foot ahead of me— and that was water," Gavin said.

Chandler snort-laughed and tried to smother it with a hand.

"Not helping, Chandler," Samuel said.

Needing to move forward with this chaotic evening before it set his ADHD ablaze, Xavier dropped to a knee and took hold of Gavin's foot. His bare feet stuck out from rolled-up pants.

"Where did you leave your shoes and socks?" Samuel asked.

"Outside by the last dock steps," Gavin said. "Don't let me forget about them."

"I'll go find them," Chandler said.

"Appreciate it, Chandler." Gavin offered him better directions to locate the shoes.

"I'll find them and leave them in your office." Chandler left to locate a flashlight and head outside.

"It seems you really like those shoes." Xavier double-checked Gavin's left ankle, since he could now investigate more clearly what he'd palpitated earlier.

Gavin yelped and squirmed in the chair. "Ouch! Yes. One of my favorites…suede."

"Suede?"

"What? I love suede oxfords or ankle boots. Like I said earlier, I wasn't going to ruin them."

"About as much as you love your bow ties and suspenders?" Xavier flicked the back of his finger against the suspenders. "Missing the tie."

"No, nothing outshines them," Gavin said. "The tie is in my messenger bag. End of the day I enjoyed a nice dinner with an old friend and upcoming groom. Then I wanted a quiet moment on the beach before I headed home."

"What's the verdict?" Samuel asked.

Xavier studied the swollen and tender ankle. He glanced between Samuel and Gavin. "It could be a sprain. I suggest a trip to the ER."

Gavin groaned. "Is that necessary?"

"Can you put any weight on it?" Samuel asked.

Gavin pushed up, using his right foot for strength and support. Then he shifted his weight a little. He almost collapsed and would have if it weren't for Xavier's hold. He shook his head. "Ouch. No. It hurts. A little weak. It won't support me."

"That's enough. Sit back down," Xavier said and helped Gavin sit again. "Do you have an ice-pack and towel? We need to get some ice on it to help the swelling. Perhaps another chair to elevate the joint."

"Right away." Samuel rushed off to get what Xavier asked for.

"What about the ER?" Gavin asked.

"We'll do this first to help with the pain and swelling," Xavier said. "Then we'll get you to the ER. Worried about the cost?"

"Always. You don't have to stick around. Samuel and Dakota can help me."

"I helped cause the accident, so I feel obligated. Plus, I know what is happening and can assist. My presence might help you skip the waiting line since we're not going by ambulance, my usual way."

"Here we go," Samuel said while he set up everything.

Dakota followed him into the hallway. "What's all the commotion? Oh..." He stopped to take in the situation.

"Had a bit of a run in," Xavier said. "Evening, Dakota."

"Gray. Out for a run?"

"Yup. Met up with a..."

"Speed bump," Gavin finished. "Me."

Dakota snorted.

Xavier placed Gavin's ankle on the other chair with a folded bunch of towels. Then he laid a towel with an ice-pack across Gavin's ankle.

"Yikes, that's cold," Gavin said with a grimace and a wince.

"Big baby," Dakota said.

Samuel smacked Dakota's arm with the back of his fingers. "Behave. I'll grab my things and Gavin's wallet. We'll get him to the ER." He disappeared down the hall.

"Wallet is in my bag in my car," Gavin called out.

Samuel returned and held out his hand. "Keys?"

"Umm. Oh. Here." Gavin wiggled to the side and pulled the small keychain from his pocket. "Slid off what I needed for my walk. Click this button once. Wallet is in the front pocket of my bag."

Samuel took the keys and left again.

Dakota leaned back against the wall. "What really happened?"

"Smacked into each other out on the beach," Xavier said. "We went down hard. I think Gavin's ankle rolled under him."

"Ouch," Dakota said.

"That's what I said. Multiple times," Gavin said.

"Not going to be fun to work with a bum ankle. Got a busy weekend?"

"Always. I'll put Victor to work. Let him do all the running around."

"Right. That won't stop you."

"I'll try," Gavin said with a game smile.

"You don't know the meaning."

"I'll learn."

Dakota snorted.

"Guess that never works?" Xavier asked, somewhat able to follow the conversation.

"He doesn't know the meaning of sitting down and being patient," Dakota said.

Gavin grumbled.

"What was that?" Dakota lifted an eyebrow.

Gavin kept quiet.

Dakota grinned.

Xavier knew he'd missed a few things.

Within minutes, Chandler returned with Samuel. "Found your shoes and socks. I left them in your car since I met Samuel there."

"Appreciate it, Chandler," Gavin said.

"I'm heading home to Sully," Chandler said. "Hope you feel better. Listen to the doc's orders."

Dakota snorted. "Told him the same thing. He's not going to listen."

Gavin grumbled.

"Oh, leave off. We'll take care of him, like we do all our Charm family." Samuel juggled his things and tossed Gavin his wallet. He kissed Dakota's cheek. "I'm going to sit with Gavin at the ER. Be home when I can."

"No problem. Keep our wedding planner safe." Dakota kissed Samuel's mouth before he could slip away.

"Up you go," Xavier said after he set aside the ice-pack. He scooped Gavin up in his arms.

"Holy crap," Dakota said. "Lifting weights, Gray?"

"He doesn't weigh anything. Don't you feed him? Thought you were a hotshot chef, Dakota," Xavier tossed back.

"Oh, he's so going to kick your ass when he gets a chance," Gavin said.

"Big-time kick your ass or chop your favorite bits into itty bitty pieces with his favorite knife," Samuel added. "Put him in my car." He unlocked the doors and opened the back door of the rich blue Lexus GX SUV.

"When did you get this?"

"Last year for my birthday present. It's so shiny." Samuel skimmed his fingers over the blue paint. "Still trying to get Dakota to trade in his rusty-crap Jeep, but he doesn't budge, so I got the shiny for me."

Xavier guffawed at the idea. "You'll never get him free of the Jeep until its engine blows up, busted and dead with no hope for recovery."

"I'm beginning to believe that. Sounds like you speak from experience."

"I'm not getting rid of my Old Blue."

"Old Blue?"

"My Ford F-150 truck. It gets me where I need to go, but he's not a pretty one." Xavier settled Gavin on the back seat and held his ankle still while he scooted across. He closed the door and climbed into the front passenger seat.

"Joining us?" Samuel hit the button to start the engine.

"Might as well. I can help you two get right in, let the doctor know what's happening and it's a quick walk home." Xavier tugged his phone free from the armband and dialed the clinic. He relayed the information about their new incoming patient with one of the nurses on duty. "Good news. Doc Elliott is on shift."

"Yay. One bit of good news," Gavin said.

Xavier glanced over his shoulder at Gavin. Not the outcome he'd wanted when he had started his nighttime run, but he would manage...like always. And this interesting latest introduction to the Charm's wedding planner? At least this time he wouldn't forget Gavin's name.

Chapter Five

When Samuel pulled up to the clinic's curb, Xavier helped Gavin out. He carried him to a wheelchair and settled him into it. Then he raised one foot-brace to secure the swollen ankle.

"Go on inside. I'll find you after I park," Samuel said.

Xavier pushed Gavin into the ER and straight to the check-in area. He snagged a clipboard, filled in the information about the injury and held it out to Gavin with a pen. "Here. You need to add the personal stuff."

"I hate this step. As if someone will see if you're worthy and allowed past the entrance gates." Gavin winced. "Any chance to get something for the pain? More discomfort, but—"

"I'll find another ice-pack in triage. You can't have anything until a doctor sees you. I'm not in my official paramedic role. Until I get back, fill in everything you can."

"Thank you, Xavier," Gavin said while he studied the paperwork.

Xavier tightened his grip on Gavin's shoulder before he left.

Gavin scrawled in his personal information. Then he plucked out his health card to add it. He was better off than most folks when it came to this little card that meant so much on such a flimsy piece of paper. "Thank you, Samuel, and Southern Charm for this wonderful insurance."

"Nope. Not the Charm. The insurance is part of Ashford Hotels, my family's corporation. We fall under their umbrella of benefits," Samuel said while he dropped into a chair.

"Oh, hey," Gavin said. It took him an extra minute to track Samuel's words. "You found a spot."

"Hmm. Not too far away. ER not too busy tonight. Guess that's a good thing for Doc Elliott and the rest."

"What do you mean about the corporation?"

"After explaining things, Dad insisted on covering everyone under their plan. In another three months, you're eligible to sign up for the 401(k) plan. A packet will be sent to you from the corporation's HR office."

"Good to know." Gavin finished scribbling down the insurance information and had Samuel double-check everything.

"Hey, Samuel. Here you go, Gavin," Xavier said when he returned. He twisted and cracked the ice-pack to activate it. Then he wrapped it around Gavin's swollen ankle. "Give it a few moments and it should get cold. Did you finish the paperwork?"

Gavin signed off on the last page. "Finished." He held out the clipboard.

"Let me see if we can get things moving. I don't care to spend all night here since I have an exam in the morning," Xavier said.

"What class?" Samuel asked.

"Applied microbiology lab," Xavier said.

"Yikes."

"Yup. Lemme see what else I can do." Xavier returned to the check-in area.

"What are you doing here? Thought you were off tonight... And that's not your paramedic uniform, Mr. Grayson," the late-night ER nurse said with a whistle. "I appreciate this look, though. Definitely a good one."

Xavier flushed and shook his head. He should have pulled on a tank top. "Didn't know I would be coming in here. Was out for a late run."

"You don't look hurt."

"Kind of ran into someone."

The nurse held up a hand to stop him. "Wait. You did *what*?"

"I ran over someone sitting on the Charm's beach. We slammed into each other. Then we twisted around, fell, and he rolled his ankle underneath our combined body weight and the sand."

"What are we going to do with you? What about the head lamp?"

"I'll make sure to wear it next time," Xavier said. It felt like the nurse scolded him as if he were a little boy. "I called ahead to notify Doc Elliott if he's not with an acute case. Could we jump the line a bit? I don't want to leave my ermm...the patient alone until I know someone is checking him out."

"School?"

"Final exam."

"Understand. Usually, I would say no since that's against our policy." The nurse tapped things into the computer system. "Okay. I can slip him in because it's you and things are quiet. The doc sent his acute patient upstairs. Can you bring him back to bay five?"

"Will do. Thank you." He tapped his fingers in a certain pattern that helped soothed his rattled chaotic brain.

"Head to bay five with your victim."

"Ha-ha. Thank you," Xavier said.

He returned to Gavin and Samuel, who now had a cup of coffee. Samuel texted someone on his phone while Gavin half-dozed.

"Hey, Xavier, any luck getting Gavin into the back?" Samuel asked.

Gavin bounced his head and blinked. He looked up at Xavier. "Need a nap."

"Not time for a nap. I got you in ahead of others." Xavier flipped up the brakes and pushed Gavin's chair. "You'll need to stay here for a little longer, Samuel."

"No problem." Samuel wiggled his phone. "Fully charged phone and an e-book. Got a re-read of a Jordan L. Hawk book. Love Whyborne. He's totally adorkable."

"Enjoy the story and your book boyfriend." Xavier pushed Gavin's chair away, hit the plate for one door to open and rolled Gavin's chair through it. Since he normally didn't head to the curtained bays but straight to the acute exam and trauma ones, it took him a minute to figure out the layout.

"Umm. Driver, are we lost?" Gavin asked.

"Shush. This isn't my normal side. Here we are." Xavier pushed the wheelchair into the curtained bay.

He scooped up the ice-pack and assisted Gavin onto the gurney.

"How long do we wait now?" Gavin twisted to lie back. He motioned for Xavier to raise the upper portion of it and he leaned back with a sigh.

"Don't know." Xavier tucked a pillow under Gavin's ankle and replaced the pack. Then he dropped into the side chair. He tugged out his phone to make a few notations to calm down his ADHD and OCD issues.

"Not too long if I have anything to do with it," Dr. Elliott Sheffield said when he stepped inside the curtain bay. His eyes widened. "Umm. Gray, you're out of uniform—like big-time out and missing a few pieces."

"Really? You? Come on. It's running gear." Xavier let out a long sigh. "Fine. I need a pair of scrubs. Please?"

Doc Elliott chuckled. "I'll get you a set." He backed up to the curtain. "Annie, could you get a pair of scrubs for Gray? Thanks." He returned to them with a grin. "Any particular reason for the attire?"

"Late-night run to work off the energy burst. My usual coping mechanisms before bedtime weren't working," Xavier admitted. "Plus, I have a final exam tomorr—" He checked his phone and shook his head. "Wait, no, this morning, so anticipation and worry heightened things."

"Do you need a consult to rework your medications?"

"Things are amped up during final exams. After them, I'll have a few weeks to settle down, just EMT shifts, and it'll steady me before the next semester. The run helped until I got to the Charm's beach and…" Xavier paused and glanced at Gavin.

"He ran over me," Gavin finished.

"We smacked into each other and took a tumble. His ankle ended up being the only victim. I hope," Xavier said.

"What were you doing on the beach, Gavin? I didn't think you would have a new position as a speed bump," Doc Elliott asked.

"Sitting above the tide line and chilling after a long day. My ex arrived earlier to finalize details for his wedding. We had dinner. Things were upsetting inside me and the ocean..." Gavin shrugged. "It has a peaceful effect. I needed to sit there — yes, in the dark — and listen to the waves."

"Then...bang?" Doc Elliott said.

"Yep. Became the speed bump."

"Doc Elliott? The scrubs you requested," the nurse, Annie, said, and held out a folded set of pale-blue scrubs.

Doc Elliott pointed to Xavier.

"Appreciate it, Annie," Xavier said after he stood to take them from her.

"A shame to cover all that gorgeous ink work," she teased. "Can I get a selfie to share? We'll break Instagram. How about a quick dance for TikTok?"

"No."

Laughing, Annie left them alone.

Xavier pulled the scrubs over his skimpy running outfit. "There. I feel better."

"Eeh. I like the other look," Gavin said. His tone sounded a little woozy.

"He's not on any pain medication," Xavier said.

"I'm tired." Gavin punctuated the statement with a jaw-cracking yawn. "I need to be asleep, not sitting on an uncomfortable gurney with a swollen ankle that's going to alter all my plans."

"Guess that means I'd better get to work before you fall apart." Doc Elliott manipulated Gavin's foot, asked a few questions, offered a pain scale while he evaluated the limb and joint. He asked Xavier a few questions about how he'd taken care of Gavin's ankle.

Gavin let out a few yelps, grimaced with a couple of movements, but answered Doc Elliott's questions.

"Can you put weight on it?"

"Yes, but it doesn't feel stable," Gavin said.

"I agree with your earlier assessment, Gray. The injury appears to be a light sprain," Doc Elliott said.

"Which means?" Gavin asked.

"The ankle bone isn't broken or involved. It's the ligaments and tendons surrounding the joint that became injured. I believe they stretched a little too far to make them uncomfortable, but I don't think they tore. This is an inversion ankle sprain, which meant your ankle turned inward and stretched the outer ligaments," Doc Elliott said and used his fingers to demonstrate what he was talking about along Gavin's ankle. "All your pain is located along the outside of the ankle."

"How bad is it?"

"According to your symptoms, I can label the injury a first-degree sprain, which is a good thing. The ligaments are stretched but not torn, because the sand protected you," Doc Elliott said.

"That's a good thing. Less recovery time. Less pain," Xavier said.

"Good to know. Got too much to do to be hampered by a bum ankle," Gavin said after another jaw-breaking yawn. "What's the next step?"

"I could order a radiograph and consult with a podiatrist," Doc Elliott said. "A tendon strain will not appear. And a podiatrist..."

"Could repeat everything you said hours later," Gavin said.

"Yes."

"Nah. I trust your diagnosis, Doc. Next step?"

"Wish all my patients were this easy going," Doc Elliott said. "You need to wear an air-brace during the day, along with using crutches, switch it for an ACE bandage wrap for the evening and additional supportive treatment. RICE."

"Rice? You want me to eat rice?"

Doc Elliott laughed and shook his head. "No. R-I-C-E treatment. R is for rest. For the first twenty-four to forty-eight hours. Limited movement and walking. Stay home."

"But..."

"Keep your butt home and in bed. Doctor's orders."

"Okay. Okay." Gavin held up his hands to give up the argument. "I'll figure it out. Next?"

"I is for ice. Use an ice-pack during the first forty-eight hours—every hour for twenty minutes at a time. I'll send you home with a couple of reusable ice-packs to alternate them."

"Got it."

"Compression is the next step. For the first forty-eight hours, I want you to wear the ACE bandage. Keep the wrap snug but not cutting off circulation. Your ankle will swell and release, so the bandage will need adjustments."

"Okay. I can do that. No shower?"

"Not for the first forty-eight. Afterward, you can take a shower, but replace the wrap when you get out.

Then you'll use the stirrup air-brace for another week, at least, for additional support during the day."

"Got it."

"E is for elevation. Try to keep your ankle elevated above your heart while doing the other three for as long as possible. Use a bunch of pillows. It'll be a little uncomfortable, especially at night, but it will help reduce the swelling."

Another yawn cracked Gavin's jaw. "Uh-huh, got it."

"You haven't remembered a thing I said."

"Probably not."

"I'll have it all written down. For the pain, you can take one 400mg ibuprofen pill twice a day. A third only if you're truly uncomfortable. I don't think you need anything harder."

"'Kay," Gavin said.

"He's falling asleep, Doc," Xavier said.

"So I see. Let him rest. I'll get with Annie, and we'll get everything ready for him. Are you driving him home?" Doc Elliott said.

"Samuel is in the waiting room. We left Gavin's SUV at the Charm. I'm jogging home when we're done."

"We'll get moving and get all of you out of here. I'll give all the instructions to Samuel for your care. Take a nap, Gavin, and I'll be back." Doc Elliott motioned to Gray. "Follow me, Xavier."

Gavin wiggled his fingers and snuggled back.

Xavier followed Doc Elliott out of the curtained area. He wanted to ask again about the child, Adam, from the accident. Instead, he held back and kept his mouth shut.

"Anything else, Gray?" Doc Elliott tapped notes into the tablet to update Gavin's chart. "Didn't expect to find you here with someone."

"My actions did cause the accident. It felt right to remain with him."

"Interesting to hear that from you." Doc Elliott glanced over at him. "Usually, you keep away from eligible bachelors."

"What? No. It's not…"

They moved farther away.

A young nurse went past them with a smile. "Good evening, Doc Elliott."

"Hello. Stacey? Right?"

"Yes."

"Enjoying your first month with us?"

"I am. This is a wonderful hospital."

"Excellent. Carry on, then," Doc Elliott said.

With a nod, she walked toward the curtained bays. "Good evening, Mr. Hatfield, I have your Demerol shot."

The name caught Xavier's attention because it was close to Gavin's name—Hartfield. "Hatfield?"

"Kenny Hatfield. Twisted knee. Possible broken fibula. Skateboard mishap."

"Ouch—"

"Not Hatfield," Gavin said, his voice rose. "No, I'm Hart—"

"Oh, shit!"

They rushed back toward the curtained area.

Doc Elliott whipped back the curtain in time to see the young nurse finish administering the shot of Demerol into Gavin's hip, since he didn't have an IV. "What are you doing?"

"Administering the shot to Mr. Hatfield," she said.

"Mr. Hatfield is a teenager in bay two. This is Gavin Hartfield in bay five."

"What? That's impossible." The nurse looked at Gavin and back to the doctor.

"Didn't you check the numbers and the charts? That shot is supposed to be administered through an IV port, not into skin and muscle. This man doesn't have an IV. What if he's allergic? You could have caused significant harm or death! Either way, your actions can be ruled medical malpractice," Doc Elliott snapped. "Kelli!"

The nurse burst into tears. "Sir, I didn't... I mean..."

"What is happening?" the head nurse for the night shift, Kelli Stratford, called out.

"Call security and administration. I want this nurse taken into custody. She administered a pain medication to the wrong patient without verifying identification and written orders. Why was she placed in charge of a powerful narcotic? She's been here less than a month," Doc Elliott ordered. "We may have to contact the sheriff, report this incident and see what they or the clinic's board recommend."

"I do not know. I didn't give her any orders for pain medication."

"Damn it all. Call security. *Now.*"

Kelli rushed to grab the nearest phone to contact security. She kept her gaze on Stacey, who didn't move.

Doc Elliott turned to Xavier. "Please stay a few moments longer. Keep an eye on him for any possible side effects. Call me immediately if anything happens."

Xavier nodded. "Will do."

"Sir?"

Doc Elliott spun to face the security officers and snapped out his orders. He followed everyone out of the cubicle. Along the way, he gave Annie the correct orders to administer the medication to the teenager.

"Wow… Feel good…. Wheeeee…." Gavin called out in a loopy, carefree tone. "Good stuff." He went straight to the tipsy, relaxed easy state created by the medication. "What did that lady give me? I feel gooooood."

"She gave you a shot of Demerol. It was meant for someone else with a broken bone and twisted knee." Xavier returned to Gavin's bedside and sat on the edge of the bed.

"Uh-oh. Somebody in trouble." Gavin sing-songed the words in a tipsy tone.

"The nurse? Yes, Doc Elliott is on the case."

"Go get 'er." Gavin pumped a raised fist.

"Doc Elliott will respond to the situation. Any kind of screw-ups piss him off, especially if it happens in his ER under his watch." Xavier tilted to stare down at Gavin. "Guess you're staying here a little bit longer."

"Stay with me?"

"Not going anywhere."

"Good. Don't want you to go." Gavin snagged hold of Xavier's scrubs shirt and tugged him down.

Xavier bent in half under the constant pull. He held still while Gavin stared, his pupils close to full-blown from the drug. "Gavin?"

Gavin sniffed along Xavier's jaw, breathed in Xavier's scent and rubbed his cheek against Xavier's face. Their rough growth caught, bristled and dragged against their skin.

"Feeling the high?"

"Hmm. Good scent. Bit of the ocean, sweat and something else. I like." Gavin rubbed their cheeks again. "Definitely like."

"Yes, you're high."

"Don't matter. Still...like you since the first time I saw you."

"When was that?"

"A 9-1-1 call brought you and your partner to the Charm to help an elderly man who had collapsed. I watched how compassionate and skilled you were. Then I saw these—" Gavin traced his fingers down Xavier's inked arm, following the multiple lotus flowers against a tangle of Celtic labyrinth vines, koi fish, a flirting dragon and other designs.

"You like my ink?"

"Fascinating. All different designs flow together to echo beauty, sadness and pride." Then he tapped the special multi-pointed star at the top. "Then this star to proclaim what you do to the world. You're proud of your job, your work and you show it off."

"Do you have ink?"

"Nope. Stupid. Afraid of the pain and swelling. Sensitive skin that reacts weird."

"Too bad. I'm sure you would look wonderful with some ink."

"Wanted to check out your tattoo, see what is hiding under your sexy paramedic uniform and lick it all over to see if it tastes different than the rest of your skin."

Xavier focused on one part of the rambling words and heated statement. "My sexy uniform?"

Gavin tapped Xavier's butt. "Shows off your fine booty."

There was something adorably sexy about a tipsy Gavin Hartfield. Underneath the bow ties, suspenders and crisp appearance lurked a sexy, desirable man— one Xavier wanted to spend more time with and not for talking.

"Wanted to strip it off ya and see your fine booty up close. Yup, I did." Gavin grinned and scratched at his side. "Still do." He scratched at another spot.

"Are you itchy?"

"Nope. Me. In trouble."

"What kind of trouble?"

"Just remembered something." Gavin wiggled against the sheets. He scratched at his other side. "Allergy."

"Are you allergic to Demerol?"

"Something in it." He flipped open the suspenders at his waist and tugged up on his shirt.

Nasty red hives covered his pale skin.

"Hives?"

"Itchy. Ick. Itchy." Gavin unbuttoned his shirt and yanked it off. With free access, he scrubbed both hands all over his irritated skin. He coughed hard a few times. His breathing became rougher. He clawed at his throat.

"Oh, shit!" Xavier grabbed the oxygen mask and secured it on Gavin's face. He punched the levels up higher. "Breathe, Gavin. Relax and breathe. I'll get help." He hit the call button, yanked on the curtain and looked around the hallway. "Annie! Kelli! Get Doc Elliott! Gavin is allergic. Anaphylactic reaction! Reddened skin around his throat. Hives. His airway is closing."

Annie grabbed the phone and paged Doc Elliott. "I need to get to the dispensary."

Xavier returned to Gavin and went to his side.

Gavin struggled to breathe.

Annie returned to the bay with two syringes. "We have to give him the epinephrine and a corticosteroid to counteract the effects." She opened the EpiPen, punched it into his thigh and held it until the medicine dispensed. Then she followed it up with the shot of corticosteroid into the other thigh.

Gavin gasped behind the mask. His eyes widened at the needles punching his skin, but he couldn't say anything.

Xavier remained close to Gavin's other side. He caressed Gavin's arm. "Breathe, Gavin. Breathe in the oxygen. Feel it open your lungs. Give the medicine time to counteract the effect. Listen to me count out the timing. Follow my count with your breaths. Inhale, one, two, three... Good."

"What the —?" Doc Elliott entered with others.

Annie mentioned what had happened and what she'd administered.

Xavier didn't pay attention while Doc Elliott barked out orders and took charge to save Gavin from the possibly fatal allergic reaction. He remained out of the way, kept Gavin's focus on him and reminded him to keep breathing.

* * * *

Two hours passed before Gavin was out of danger. The reaction was far more severe than anyone had anticipated.

Soon, Gavin slept easily, on oxygen assistance and with the hives under control. The nurses helped change him out of his outfit and into a patient gown. Then they tucked him under the blanket but kept his ankle wrapped, propped and with a fresh ice pack.

Samuel rushed back when Doc Elliott allowed him to sit by Gavin's bedside.

"I need to get out of here. I have an exam for my lab class and a shift in the afternoon," Xavier said to Doc Elliott.

"I couldn't do anything about the exam, but I called in a doctor's note. You're excused from the shift. I want you to relax and get some sleep," Doc Elliott said.

"You did *what*?"

"Doctor's orders. You heard me. Take care of your exam and go home."

"There was no need —"

"Don't give me that shit. You've been here longer than anticipated or expected. Then you're stretching yourself further for the exam. You need the sleep."

Knowing he couldn't change Doc Elliott's mind or orders, Xavier stopped arguing. "Thank you."

"Welcome." Doc Elliott gave him a smile. "If you weren't here, we might not have been in time to help Gavin. What happened?"

"He was only loopy at first, riding the narcotic high. Flirtatious."

"Really?"

"He admitted a few things."

"Things you liked hearing?"

"Yeah, I think so."

"Good. He's a good man — strong, quiet and with a determination to match yours. Give him a chance. His schedule can be as crazy as yours, so he understands."

"Playing matchmaker?"

"Gavin created something wonderful for Jude and me. If it works, then I'll admit to it. Until then…" Doc Elliott shrugged.

"I'll take my chances but will see what happens."

"All I can suggest is take a chance."

"Hard to do that."

"You deserve it." Doc Elliott motioned to the scrubs. "Keep the scrubs. Do you need a ride home?"

"It's a quick jog across the street to the apartment complex. I'm okay."

"Stay safe. Thank you for everything tonight." Doc Elliott held out his hand.

A little confused, Xavier shook it. "Was a little scary, but I would do it for anyone."

"I know. Good luck with your exam tomorrow. You'll be a wonderful nurse. I'll be honored to have you working here."

"Thank you, Doc. I wouldn't want to work with anyone else. Each class gets me closer to that piece of paper."

"You'll reach your goal. We're signed up as an internship hospital with your college. I'll make sure the connection happens when you start your mandatory clinical rotations."

"Appreciate the support." Xavier stepped back to glance through the curtain. He peeked at the sleeping Gavin.

Samuel looked up to meet his stare. "Hey. Not going to say goodbye?"

"Let him sleep. I need the same."

"He's going to be pissed you left without saying anything."

"He'll get over it. Small town, so we'll bump into each other. Tell him I said 'bye'."

"Right. Sure, but there's something else going on," Samuel said. "Thank you, Gray, for helping him."

"I caused the accident, so—"

"You didn't have to help him get here or stay so long. Shut up and take the thank you."

"Okay. Okay." Xavier held up his hand.

Walking away from the sleeping man in bay five, Xavier popped the earbuds back in place, turned on the music and jogged away from the clinic. It was way past his bedtime.

Chapter Six

Miffed after the late-night encounter and the dramatic ER visit, Gavin felt off balance after getting home. Thanks to the nurse's ineptitude, he fought through the allergic reaction on top of his usual intolerance to pain medications. Anything stronger than OTC knocked him for a loop.

Stuck in bed with his bandaged ankle raised on multiple pillows and an ice-pack draped across, Gavin tried to get some sleep. His mind spun and he tried to figure out what he had said and done with Xavier.

Throughout the day, Samuel and Victor stopped in to check on him. Victor drove his Soul home while Samuel followed in his Lexus. They tag-teamed in helping him out. Victor dealt with housekeeping, ran what errands Gavin needed and became his gopher. Since he wasn't much of a cook like his partner, Samuel brought him food Dakota created at the chef's insistence. Following Doc Elliott's orders, Samuel passed out the ibuprofen as required. The pills didn't make him too loopy. Samuel helped Gavin hobble to the bathroom. Doc Elliott gave him a pair of crutches but with strict orders to not use them until the first forty-eight hours had passed. They exchanged out the ice-packs and watched the timing.

After yet another nap, Gavin dialed Arthur's number.

"Hello?"

"Arthur, it's Gavin. Umm…something came up."

"Hi, Gavin. Didn't see you the last two mornings at breakfast. Samuel mentioned you were hurt and recovering but couldn't tell me more. Are you okay?"

"Ran into a bit of trouble on the beach." Gavin offered him a brief explanation of what had happened late Tuesday night and ended with his hospital stay on Wednesday.

"That's unexpected. At least you had a gorgeous rescuer."

"He also caused the accident."

"Look at the bright side of things. You got to meet someone."

"Arthur! You didn't travel here for me to sit on my butt the entire time."

Arthur laughed across the line. "Relax about the change of plans. My flight isn't until Saturday afternoon, but I can change it if we need more time. I don't mind rushing through things to get all the appointments done by then. You know I don't need much time to decide. The same with Neil. We both have a good idea of what we want, and we're keeping things simple and modest…like us. It's a party for twenty-five people or less. Nothing major."

"Thanks for understanding, Arthur."

"No reason for me to get all upset over an accident. Now, relax and get some rest."

"It's all I've been doing. Daytime television sucks."

"Not a Kardashian fan?"

"Not a talk show fan or reality shit."

"Hopefully, you can find a marathon of *Say Yes to the Dress*. That would be right up your preference."

"Maybe."

"I'm going to enjoy another unexpected beach day, and I might poke my nose around town. See you tomorrow."

"See ya, Arthur," Gavin said and hung up.

With Arthur confirmed, Gavin texted the stores to alter the appointments.

Ignoring the order to completely rest, Gavin worked on his laptop—cleared up any remaining issues, spoke with clients and reviewed notes and changes. It wasn't how he wanted to spend his time, but there wasn't much choice.

* * * *

Waking up the following day, Gavin noticed the swelling had decreased in a considerable fashion. Nasty colorful bruises covered the entire joint to reveal that not everything was healthy underneath the skin.

Needing to continue his plans with Arthur, Gavin didn't consider staying home. After wrapping the ACE bandage around his ankle, Gavin placed the stirrup air-brace over his bandaged foot and tightened the straps. The combination worked enough to keep the joint stabilized. He balanced himself on the crutches and went through his regular morning procedure. The only thing missing was his daily trip on his Peloton bike.

"About as good as I'm going to get it."

Dressed in comfortable shoes, Gavin exchanged his regular leather messenger bag for a backpack. He moved over his laptop and daily stuff to help keep his weight balanced.

At least, with the injury on the left foot, he didn't need someone to drive him around. Gavin climbed into his Soul. He had a lot of work to make up for from sitting on his butt the last two days. As Dakota and others had pointed out, to his chagrin, he hated not being able to do something.

Parking, Gavin figured out how to get out without face-planting. Balanced, he headed inside, using the ramps instead of trying to figure out the stairs. Hungry, he swung to the restaurant for the morning buffet.

"Gavin, over here." Samuel waved from his table.

Gavin managed to maneuver around the tables. He dropped hard into the chair and groaned. "I hate these damn things," he complained while he rested the crutches against the table. Then he dragged off the backpack and lowered it to the floor.

"It's only for a few days, Gavin," Samuel said. "What would you like to eat?"

"What do you have?"

Dakota listed the items.

"I'll take some French toast, bacon and the hash-brown casserole, along with a large coffee. One cream. One sugar," Gavin requested. "Appreciate it."

"Anytime," Samuel said.

"How are you feeling today? How's the ankle?" Dakota asked while Samuel left to fill a plate for Gavin.

"A little uncomfortable but not in much pain. Less swollen today, so that's a good thing. I'm using the ACE bandage with the air-brace to get around," Gavin said.

"Samuel mentioned you had an unusual allergic reaction."

"A bad case of hives from a Demerol shot I shouldn't have received, thanks to an incompetent nurse. Started to close my throat."

"Yikes."

"Yes, the whole incident pissed off Doc Elliott big-time. I don't think she'll be working there if he has his way. She might not even be able to keep her license. It all depends on what action he takes with the hospital board. It might even go to the sheriff."

"Oh, I'm sure he'll get his way. Doc Elliott runs the ER and could operate the entire hospital if he desired, but he'd rather care for patients."

"Here's breakfast and your shot of caffeine," Samuel said. He set a full plate and mug of coffee in front of Gavin.

"Thank you," Gavin said and dug into the food.

"Pills?"

Gavin grumbled.

"Gavin—" Samuel warned.

"Okay. Okay. I got them. Relax." Gavin pulled out the bottle of ibuprofen from his backpack. He shook out two and swallowed them with coffee. "Done, Nurse."

Dakota snorted.

"Since I have the two of you here, should we talk about the wedding?" Gavin asked after taking the edge off his hunger.

"Which wedding?" Dakota asked.

"Yours." Gavin narrowed his gaze on Dakota. "Did we settle on a date? That's important, because everything else I need to do will revolve around that date. We pushed it back multiple times."

"Something in September...perhaps," Dakota said.

"September? Oh, I thought we considered an autumn wedding," Samuel said. "The weather is great. It's in the hurricane season, so hopefully we're not going to get smacked with one. We love the colors. It's before the holiday season kicks in and we're packed to the brim."

"Autumn could work," Dakota ventured.

"Is there a reason to hesitate in selecting one date?" Gavin asked.

"A lot to figure out," Dakota said.

"Do we want it to happen this autumn or next?"

"Is there time to work in a wedding within the next few months?" Samuel asked.

"There are openings, especially if you're not planning on something big."

"What about the tropical storm?" Dakota said.

"What tropical storm?" Gavin asked.

"It's not going to turn into anything major, let alone curl around the state," Samuel said.

"What tropical storm?" Gavin asked again.

"After the last hurricane season, I wouldn't put anything past Mother Nature's power to do what she wants with the weather," Dakota said.

Since neither one answered him, Gavin checked the weather app. He learned to keep a closer eye on the tropical updates during hurricane season. More than once a storm had altered the plans. It sucked and terrified a couple when all their wedding plans were about to be blown away, but that was what happened when you had outdoor weddings in an area prone to tropical weather.

"Oh, crap," he muttered.

Three different clusters of storms had rolled off the African coast. There were two larger storms swirling and named, but they predicted one would curl up into the Atlantic and the other heading for Central America.

"Busy season," Gavin said.

"It worsens from late August to September because the water reaches their warmest temperatures, which feeds the storms," Dakota said.

"There isn't a prediction or path for the newest storms. The others aren't coming near us. No danger yet," Gavin said.

"No excuses to not make a decision," Samuel muttered.

Dakota looked at Samuel. "What was that?"

"You never made a decision."

"I said September was good."

"September what?"

Dakota shrugged.

"Why are you acting this way?" Samuel smacked his hand on the table. "You never want to talk to me about the wedding. *Never*."

"Samuel, there are —"

"I know. I know. Reasons." Samuel wiggled his fingers as invisible quotation marks. "Always some unknown reason or excuse that you never give me. I'm tired of it. Forget I asked. Forget I said anything." He shoved his chair back and stood. "Excuse me, Gavin. I need to get to my office." He walked away, not saying another word to Dakota.

"Samuel! Wait —" Dakota cursed. "I'm screwing this up, aren't I?"

"Unless this is an extended engagement that never ends in a wedding, you could screw things big-time. I've seen it happen, and it never ends well." Gavin focused his attention to Dakota. "Placing a ring on his finger meant something to Samuel, especially since the

Supreme Court ruling allowed us to have the same privilege and rights as any married couple. It's something some men and women have dreamed about forever but never expected it could happen to them because they were gay. You made a promise, Dakota, and now, by stalling, you —"

"Are breaking the promise."

"Pretty much."

Dakota lowered his head.

"Hey, Gavin, how are you doing? Crazy accident," Malcolm said when he walked up to their table.

"Eeh, I'm dealing with it. Uncomfortable, but I'm here," Gavin said.

"You always push through, no matter what happens." Malcolm tapped Dakota on the shoulder. "Dakota, sorry... We need you back in the kitchen. We got a delivery and something isn't right between their shipping list and our order. The guy isn't listening to me, and I'm ready to deck him."

"Crap. Which company?"

"The new produce one you thought we should try. So far, it's not worth the discounted prices or hassle."

"Crap." Dakota glanced to Gavin. "We'll talk later."

"Talk to Samuel. Clear things with him. He's far more important than anything I want," Gavin said.

"Keep a weekend in September open for us. I'll...narrow down a date with Samuel." With a nod, Dakota followed Malcolm.

"A weekend in September. Right. Great. There are four of them. That doesn't help me." Gavin scrambled to his feet with the crutches. One of the waiters waved him off while they moved to collect his dishes. He hobbled back to his office. There he spent a few hours speaking with clients, suppliers and vendors to pass the time until he needed to meet with Arthur.

When it got close, he gathered his backpack, balanced back on the crutches and found Arthur enjoying a late breakfast. His skin was colored a little pink from his two days of beach-time.

"Looks like the sun got you," Gavin said.

"Didn't realize how strong it was, and my sunblock wasn't enough," Arthur said. "I'm okay. Got some aloe to cool things off."

Gavin dropped into a chair, set the backpack down and rested the crutches next to his chair. "Sorry about bailing on you the last couple of days. It wasn't my intention to leave you hanging."

"I don't mind the extra quiet time. This is a beautiful place to chill out. What happened?"

Gavin told him a quick version of the crazy accident story and the dramatic hours that turned into a full day in the ER. He held out his propped ankle in the air cast and crutches. "This is the result. I'm in this get-up for at least a week, perhaps longer."

"What about the upcoming weddings and events?"

"I'll be fine. What running around I can't do, I'll have Victor and maybe Samuel and Chandler. Either way, everything will go smooth. Everyone pulls together to help out during emergencies."

Arthur pushed away his plate. "What's the plan for today?"

"Meetings to check out your options. First, we'll start at Flowers in the Breeze and meet with Jude. He designs all the floral arrangements and will give you the final three options for your chosen colors. I prefer to start there, because you can get a sense of colors and how things come together. We can build everything off what Jude designs."

"But I can share the pictures or a video with Neil via the phone."

"Exactly. Cell and WiFi coverage is strong across downtown. I hope Neil will enjoy giving his feedback and choices. It's also his wedding. After flowers, we can figure out our next stops. I contacted all the vendors and they'll be ready throughout the day for our visits."

"Sounds like a plan. Go through the checklist and get things done."

"Exactly."

"At first," Arthur said, "I hoped we could enjoy a walk along the beach trail, but..."

"Not quite an option this time." Gavin flicked the crutches. "Stupid, annoying things."

"A necessary evil. Would you like me to drive?"

"No need, I can drive. It's my left ankle and I drive an automatic." Gavin pushed to his good foot and balanced the crutches. He dug his key out of the backpack's front pocket and slung the strap over his shoulders. "Off we go."

* * * *

The drive took a few minutes and he parked in one of the lots by the cinema.

Gavin balanced his weight on the stronger ankle, the left one twinging a little more often than he appreciated, but he got out of the Soul. Then he adjusted the balance again when he pulled his backpack in place. His pace remained off while he placed the crutches and swung through.

"Damn freaking crutches are going to drive me bonkers. Definitely not what I needed to make me feel graceful."

Arthur snickered at Gavin's good-natured complaints. "I missed your wry attempts at humor. Definitely an odd way at looking at things."

It was one of the first times Arthur had mentioned their time together.

Flushing, Gavin tapped his shoulder against Arthur's arm. They continued down the sidewalk. Gavin suggested some memorable shops and restaurants, perhaps places Arthur could take Neil when they returned. He indicated the gallery and studio of the artist, Wyatt McBride.

"If I was less challenged in my movements, we could swing in and check out things," Gavin said.

"No need. I don't mind window-shopping to get ideas. We'll be so busy with the wedding, and I don't know if we'll have much free time."

"I can build it into the schedule. We can adjust anything you want to give you to make it your special day."

"I'll think about it." Arthur pointed to an outdoor sitting area by one of the popular cafés. "He's quite handsome. Look at all the colorful ink."

Gavin glanced over to find the man sitting on the patio, a laptop and books strewn across the table, his head bopping while he sang to whatever music played in his ears. Then he spotted the lotus blossom-covered arm. He rocked back on the crutches.

"Holy crap!"

Arthur raised an eyebrow. "What?"

"That's the guy."

"What?"

"The grumpy EMT who mowed me over on the beach...Xavier Grayson. Most call him Gray."

"Are you kidding me? You got hit by *him*."

Gavin nodded.

Arthur studied the man. "He's gorgeous. Just your type with all the ink."

"There's more happening than the ink. Believe me."

"What happened? Other than being run over by him."

"He didn't remember that we'd met multiple times. Me! Not even with the suspenders and bow tie." Gavin snorted. "'The wedding guy'. That's how he recognized me. Can you believe that?"

"The wedding guy?"

"That's what he called me."

Arthur muffled laughter behind a raised hand.

"Arthur!"

"Sorry. Sorry... Can't help it. That's priceless."

Gavin *harrumphed* but couldn't even cross his arms since he needed to prop himself on the damn crutches.

"Anything else happen at the hospital?"

"After the Demerol shot sent me into a high, before the hives, I may have flirted. I think I touched him more than once."

"Did you trace the tattoos?"

"Think so. Might have done more."

Arthur burst out laughing.

Across the street, Xavier lifted his head and looked around. He smiled and winked at Gavin.

Gavin stumbled and miscalculated where to plant the crutch.

"Whoa, hold up there. Watch yourself." Arthur caught Gavin with a hand on his elbow to save his balancing act. "Okay, there had to be more than a little flirting and tracing a tattoo between you and sexy grump over there."

Gavin kept his mouth shut. He wasn't going to say another word about his Demerol-induced behavior. It wasn't his fault.

"Not saying anything?"

Gavin glanced back across the street. Xavier continued to watch them.

"What happened?"

"Nothing. I'm not in the mindset to find anyone. What happened between Xavier and me doesn't mean anything."

"You said everyone calls him 'Gray'."

"He told me to call him Xavier."

"Any reason why?"

"Nope."

"Perhaps it could mean something more."

"Don't think so."

"Were you ever in the mindset to find anyone? You witness so many wonderful moments between couples. Don't you want to experience that for yourself?"

"I don't think I could ever be in a relationship. I'm unsure and unsettled whenever I'm in one. The entire time I was with you, I always felt something bad would happen. I expected it. It kept me on edge."

"Gav…"

"Our break-up was never your fault. You did nothing wrong other than putting up with me."

"Did you always feel this way?"

Gavin nodded. "Did you know not every moment I witness in weddings is wonderful?"

"What went wrong?"

"When I worked in Atlanta, there were many times when I assisted one bride through her wedding, then two years later she returned with a new fiancé — and another, and another. You get the idea. She married five times. Each one was more extravagant than the last to override any lingering shadows in her mind or her guests' memories. Each wedding ended in pain, anger and divorce."

"That's the nature of some people."

"True. There were far more couples who stayed the course and remained together than those broken and divorced. Either way, I don't know what it means for me or my future."

"Yet you remain in the wedding business."

"I don't want to do anything else with my life. There are far more wonderful and exciting moments than the awful ones." Gavin stopped at the Flowers in the Breeze store and waited for Arthur to catch up.

An exiting customer opened and held the door for Gavin, who nodded his thanks. He limped inside the store that was filled with lovely blossoms and overwhelming fragrance.

* * * *

Inside the shop, Jude stood with a pair of handsome men in front of the main counter that separated the area from the workshop and storage area. Dawson sat at attention by his feet. Throughout their friendly conversation, all three men were free with smiles and laughter.

"Gavin, hello! I wasn't sure you were going to show up today. Get on — " Jude called out, waved at him and beckoned them closer. "Oh my God! You're on crutches. What happened to you?"

Gavin swung over to them, cautious on the tiled floor. "Hello, everyone. Before we get into all the craziness about my ankle, let me introduce one of my upcoming grooms. This is Arthur Carlton from Atlanta. Arthur will marry his fiancé, Neil Bardon, in two weeks. Arthur, the first man is florist extraordinaire, Jude Sebastian. The other man knows everything there is when it comes to landscaping, Reece Simpson. The last man is a brilliant carpenter and contractor, Sullivan 'Sully' Tarleton, who completed all the renovations on the Charm and is creating the new event building."

"Hello and welcome to Flowers in the Breeze, Arthur. I hope you enjoy the creations I have waiting for you," Jude said.

"Hello, and nice to meet all of you," Arthur said and shook hands.

"Okay. What happened to you?" Jude pounced on Gavin with the questions.

Once again, Gavin explained what had happened.

"Wait. Who ran you over?" Reece asked.

"Xavier Grayson."

"Gray? That can't be true—"

"I know darn good and well who hit me, Reece," Gavin interrupted with a snap. "I saw his tattoos. He helped Samuel take me to the ER. Samuel, Malcolm, Dakota and Doc Elliott all called him by name. I'm not an idiot."

"Okay. Okay. I'm sorry. I didn't mean it like that." Reece held up his hands. "Gray is a caretaker and careful when running, even late at night. He's seen the absolute worse shit that can happen to a human body."

Gavin tugged up his pant to reveal the stirrup air brace supporting his ankle. "Do you want me to hit you with my crutches to make the point that he slammed into me?"

Sully snorted and laughed.

"By the way, Mr. Grayson is sitting at the café's patio table with his laptop and books. He looked over and winked at Gavin," Arthur said.

"Arthur!" Gavin gasped, then hissed, "*Traitor.*"

Arthur grinned and nodded toward Gavin. "Something else happened between them. He refuses to answer my questions."

"None of your damn business, traitor. Tattletale. Sheesh. Like I'm going to help you anymore," Gavin said and stomped a crutch.

The noise startled Dawson, who got to his paws and sniffed at Gavin's crutches.

"Sorry, Dawson. Didn't mean to bug you," Gavin said.

"Easy, buddy, don't tip him over," Jude said to his furry companion.

"That's some way to treat a client," Reece said.

"He's my ex. I give him some leeway," Arthur said.

"Wait... You two—?" Reece moved a finger between them while he figured out the connection.

"Back in Atlanta, yes, we dated for a couple of years. Then we split and I met Neil," Arthur said.

"He's better with Neil," Gavin added.

"Why would you go to your ex to plan your wedding?" Sully asked.

"Gavin is the best. Why would I trust anyone else with my special day?" Arthur said.

"Good answer," Sully said. He glanced to Gavin. "I like him."

"Yeah, I still like him, too," Gavin said. He elbowed Arthur's side.

About to tag him back, Arthur stopped quick because it would have toppled Gavin on the crutches.

"It was good to meet you, Arthur. Sorry, but I need to get out of here and get to work," Reece said.

"Same here," Sully said.

"Please do that. I really need my event center to be finished," Gavin said.

"Working on it," Sully said.

They shook hands with Arthur again, and both men gave Gavin a light hug.

"If you need anything, especially on event days, call me. I'll head on over to help," Sully said.

"Same with me," Reece said.

"You want to try whatever delicacies Malcolm creates, you glutton," Gavin teased Reece.

"Gotta have a taste tester. I happily offer to take that role," Reece said with a crazy grin.

"Good thing you do manual labor or you would be a roly-poly by now," Gavin said.

"Good genes. Fast metabolism," Reece said. He rubbed his flat belly.

"Get out of here, you two. I need to show off my fabulous creations." Jude waved his hands to shoo them.

Laughing, they walked out.

"Crazy people, but you gotta love them." Jude rubbed his hands together. "Ready to see my floral beauties?"

"Show them to me," Arthur said. "I'm going to show everything to my fiancé via text and FaceTime."

"Ooh, I love this moment. It's the first time you get to see your choices come to life." Jude brought them back into the workshop area.

Dawson trotted ahead in a path straight for the fluffy bed. He turned three times and curled up. He kept his attention on Jude, even while he rested, however.

Jude pointed to the stool. "Go sit, Gavin. Do you need pain meds or something?"

"Samuel is already mothering me. I don't need another one." Gavin took advantage of the stool. He rolled his shoulders and wrists, because both sets of joints were tight and uncomfortable.

"You didn't answer the question."

"He's been doing that," Arthur said while he stopped next to Gavin.

"Hey. We're not here to discuss my problems," Gavin said.

"He can be such a brat," Jude said in a soft tone to Arthur, though everyone could hear him. "Okay. Flowers. Flowers. More flowers. Just what I love to talk about. Who chose the sunflowers?"

"Neil. They're his favorite, since he grew up with them."

"All I got from your initial request was sunflowers. You gave me freedom to play around with other options—just that sunflowers needed to be prominent."

"Exactly. Sorry for not being more forthcoming."

"No. No. I love it. I see these moments as challenges to figure out if I can tune in on the clients." Jude went to a cold storage container and removed three different trays. Each tray had a collection of arrangements. Each one was different, but the sunflowers remained prominent, as Arthur had requested. "I went in three different directions—rustic, silver shine, elegant. Each tray has sample arrangements for the ceremony and reception. Which would you like to see first?"

"Rustic."

"That's this tray." Jude pulled the third one closer and rearranged the options. "For rustic I selected empty glass wine bottles, Mason jars and other clear-glass options. I wound neutral twine around the tops and bottoms and kept the arrangement simple with the sunflowers, a couple of yellow roses, smaller white flowers, and natural greenery. Everything can be placed on wooden slabs with smaller jars arranged into bigger groupings. Both the ceremony and reception space would have similar options. I can hang small jars of flowers from the gazebo with fairy lights tucked into the bottom for a flickering effect."

Arthur studied the arrangement and glanced at Gavin. "I can manage this on my own."

"What? Umm. No. Not leaving. I'm the wedding planner. I'm supposed to be here."

"No, you need to go across the street and speak with Xavier."

"No, I don't. He's probably not even there. Besides, I can't leave you alone. I'm here to offer my help and assistance."

Jude hooted at the quick change of topic and back to the flowers.

"Shut it," Gavin said. "You're not helping."

"What is going on between you and Gray?" Jude asked.

"Nothing. He was nice and helped me after he knocked me over. Nothing happened."

"He sat with you all night at the ER," Arthur said.

"Because he felt bad about what happened."

"Gray doesn't do anything he doesn't consider multiple times. Nothing is done by chance with him. He keeps his life fairly structured," Jude said.

"I think Doc Elliott mentioned ADHD to him."

"Gray has it. Diagnosed as a teenager. He also has some OCD tendencies."

"Oh, that must be difficult. Anyway, it doesn't change anything. I need to remain here with you, Arthur — my groom, my client," Gavin said.

"Would you stop with that," Arthur said to wave off his concern. He took hold of Gavin's hand. "Gavin, I found love and happiness with Neil, and I wish you could find the same for yourself. Perhaps it could be with Xavier, but you'll never know if you sit here with me."

Gavin dropped his jaw.

"Go and talk to him. It'll take a bit for Neil and me to discuss options with Jude. Now, I need to take pictures, send them to Neil and get him on a chat program. Let Jude, Neil and me work."

"This is my work and my job," Gavin protested.

"Not this time. I'm in good hands with Jude. He knows his flowers."

"But —"

"Gavin…"

Gavin glanced to Jude with a pleading look. "Help me out here."

"Nope, I'm with Arthur. Get on those crutches and go talk to Gray. Both of you deserve a chance."

"There isn't a freaking chance."

"How will you know if you remain here?"

"Unbelievable. Keep an eye on my damn bag." Gavin grumped about the entire idea. He snagged hold of his crutches, shoved them under his shoulders and hobbled away from them. "See if I help with anything else. I swear." Still muttering under his breath, ignoring the twinges in his ankle, he continued his path across the street.

Xavier remained at the table, concentrating on the laptop and books.

"This is a stupid idea."

Chapter Seven

After finishing his lab exam on Wednesday and a double-shift on Thursday, Xavier was grateful for some free time on Friday. He should remain home and get some sleep. He cleaned his already-immaculate apartment and rearranged an orderly pantry to calm down his impulses. When none of his regular coping strategies worked, Xavier decided sleep wasn't going to happen. Either way, he couldn't remain inside. He tried to study for the next exam, but he couldn't get in the right mindset to absorb the information. His mind continued to jump beyond the test information.

Knowing he had to focus on the next two exams, he decided to leave the apartment and find an outside spot. Xavier gathered the books, notebooks and laptop into his backpack. He dropped headphones in for music, a water bottle, the activity planner to adjust his scheduling and a bag of snacks. Then he left the apartment.

A piece of his mind remained a bit uncomfortable about the encounter with the effeminate wedding planner, who could turn bits and pieces into something spectacular.

Perhaps all this retrospect and feeling reverted to his childhood and how his father had sworn that Xavier would never become anything after he'd come out to his family in high school. It wasn't by choice. A neighbor had caught him kissing his boyfriend and told his parents. Straight out of high school, Xavier had changed his career plans from a business degree and pushed himself hard to complete his training and classes for his EMT certificate. Graduating top of his class, Xavier had learned how his achievement didn't make a difference to his father. He remained his father's faggot son and a disappointment. That was it.

A few years later, with his rise in the EMS department, Xavier had tried to see if he'd achieved his father's respect. Nothing had happened. His father had never contacted him. Xavier had stood in the background at his mother's funeral and never returned.

Wanting to shove his foot up his father's ass, Xavier decided to go further. No one in his family had bothered with a higher education degree. He would become the first.

With this decision, he kept his Ford and minuscule apartment to scrimp and save. He splurged on a few electronics, like a large TV, a gaming system and a laptop. Thanks to his OCD tendencies, he preferred to not add decorations. He maintained a decent kitchen with a stocked pantry and fridge, along with utensils and cookware. He didn't waste money on take-out. Thanks to extended shifts and college, he didn't date or hang out. Everything was a choice to save money, even after finding the tuition reimbursement program.

While he never desired to leave the EMS job, he wanted to do more with his life. He chose the Paramedic-to-RN Career Mobility Option Associate in Science degree to prepare him for the RN exam. With the new degree, he could assist in larger hospitals, serve on Medivac helicopters and work in acute ER cases instead of leaving the patients at the doors. He planned out budgets for the next few months, expecting a severe cutback of funds until his reimbursement came through from the county.

In between fiddling with the numbers, studying his microbiology notes and listening to music, Xavier checked out the action around him. He kept multiple jobs moving through his mind, able to focus on each one long enough to accomplish something. It was the only way he could study for his classes without aggravating his ADHD.

When he felt someone staring, he discovered the pair of men checking him out. The bow tie and suspenders stood out...along with the crutches.

"Gavin," he muttered. *There's something about that man, especially when under the influence of drugs. Why do I want to know more about him? To see if he meant his need to taste my ink? I could give myself a few precious minutes of pleasure or companionship.*

Unable or unwilling to stop himself, he winked at the cutie.

Gavin stumbled his next step, faltered on the crutches and looked away. His friend managed to halt his fall with a hand on his arm.

Xavier smiled since he knew he'd gotten to the man. *Would that be all it took to start something?* It's been a while since he'd stepped into the dating scene. He didn't even dare try to check out Grindr or one of those crazy dating apps.

While they disappeared into Jude's shop, Xavier studied Gavin's careful progress with the crutches. Grateful the injury wasn't worse, he returned to studying his homework and multiple tasks.

* * * *

Some unknown time later, he heard his name being called.

"Hello, Xavier." Gavin stood by the table, balanced on his crutches, and appeared a bit nervous.

"Gavin. Hi." Xavier looked around him. "Where's your friend?"

"Friend… Oh, you mean Arthur. He's a client. He's finalizing details of his wedding and is still with Jude." Gavin motioned to the chair. "Could I sit? I hoped we could talk."

Xavier closed and stacked the books. "Sure. Please sit. I know those crutches are uncomfortable."

"Annoying *and* uncomfortable. They pinch skin under my shoulder and my wrists are screaming."

"Hopefully, you can soon begin to put weight on your ankle and less on your hands."

"Eeh. We'll see when that happens." Gavin nudged one of the books. "What's all this?"

"Trying to study for my upcoming microbiology exam, the lecture part of the class. Then I need to study for my philosophy exam. And I want to review my Intro to Nursing course. I completed that class back in spring."

"All three classes…at the same time?"

"Yup."

"But you have exams in two of them? Why not concentrate on those? Why would you look through the books if you finished the course?"

"To prepare for my next course, Adult Health Nursing. I want to refresh the basic information. I'm kind of anal that way."

"Are you studying for a nursing degree?"

Xavier explained his specialized degree study.

"That's interesting. Good luck with completing all the courses."

"Did you study for a degree to get your job?"

"Yes, I have a bachelor's degree in business and hospitality management with a concentration in special events management. Then I accepted an internship with an Atlanta event company that ended up hiring me. There were online wedding event classes offered, which the company paid for us to study. It helped a lot, but I never considered going for a higher degree."

"Too much studying?"

"Not sure. What are your reasons for doing this?"

"First, I wanted to prove I could accomplish this goal to someone who never believed in me. Now, I want something better. I love being a paramedic but know I can do more. I'm giving myself the chance to prove what I can do…for me."

"That sounds awesome," Gavin said.

"Thanks. What did you want to talk about? I'm guessing it's not about my books."

"I wanted to apologize for my behavior at the hospital."

"Your behavior?"

"I stepped over the line—"

"You were given a medication that wasn't prescribed. It set off a series of events you couldn't control."

"But—"

"Forget about it."

"I can't," Gavin admitted. He glanced over at Xavier. "It forced me to admit my attraction."

"Do you regret that?"

Gavin shook his head.

"Good."

"Good?"

"We know where we stand."

"Where *do* we stand?"

Xavier grinned at the simple back and forth session between them, neither one obviously quite ready to forge forward into the unknown. "What made you step out of the store and leave your client?"

Gavin mumbled something about Arthur and Jude trying to set him up.

Xavier raised an eyebrow. "What was that?"

"Arthur insisted I leave him with Jude and the flowers and talk to you. He hopes I can get a date."

"A date with me?"

"Well, yeah, I'm not talking to anyone else—or admitted I like them."

Xavier grinned.

"So…"

"You need to ask correctly."

Gavin mumbled again, then let out a breath. "Will you go on a date with me, Xavier? Dinner, when you have a free night. I know your schedule is chaotic between EMT and—"

Xavier's phone buzzed and interrupted them.

Xavier checked the screen. "It's the station. I'm sorry, but I must answer it."

"Of course."

Xavier swiped the screen. "Gray here."

"All-call emergency. Multi-vehicle wreck on bridge. Need everyone to respond," the dispatcher said.

"On my way." Xavier looked at Gavin. "I apologize, but the station called me in for an emergency. Looks like I'm going to run on espresso and coffee tonight."

"No worries. It's to be expected with your profession." Gavin scrambled to his feet and balanced on the crutches.

"My answer is yes."

"Pardon?"

"I'll go to dinner with you. My next night free we can go out. I'll call you when I know the night."

"Really?"

"Yes, really, I wouldn't lead you on and ditch you at the last moment," Xavier said. "Could I have your personal number? I only know the Charm's info."

"That would help. Duh," Gavin said and recited his numbers.

Xavier entered them as a new contact and texted Gavin.

Gavin got the ding and added Xavier to his phone.

"Now you have my contact info," Xavier said.

Gavin wiggled his phone with a grin. "Good luck with your exams. Please stay safe on your run — and no more speed bumps."

"I'll keep a look out."

"Text me anytime. Talk soon, Xavier." He swung around and returned to the store.

Xavier watched him for a moment. Then he packed his things to race to the station.

Chapter Eight

With a smile on his face, Gavin returned to the flower shop. Perhaps being lost on the drugs had lifted a veil for him to truly see Xavier beyond the grump. Now he hoped his past issues wouldn't screw up his potential future.

"Still in the back?" he asked.

"Lots of laughter and conversation going on, so I'm going to assume... yes." Lucy, the new assistant, looked him over. "Something good happened to make that quirky grin. Did you get lucky?"

"Not *lucky* lucky, but a possibility."

"Possibilities are good."

Gavin hobbled into the back.

"There you are. We thought you'd abandoned us," Jude teased.

"Hey, you kicked me out." Gavin dropped onto a stool and stretched out his sore ankle. Bending over, he rubbed the side of his calf.

"Overdid things?" Arthur asked.

"Eeh. I'll be okay."

"Should take some ibuprofen to help the swelling."

"Good idea." Gavin scooped up his bag and dug through until he found the zippered pouch and found the pill box.

"Need some water?" Jude asked.

"Please."

Jude went to the small fridge and pulled out a bottle of water. He cracked open the top and set it next to Gavin.

"Thanks." Gavin tossed a pair of round tablets into his mouth. It took a couple of swallows, but he managed it before the pills went down. He hated taking medication. "Okay. Where are we?"

"I added more options or alterations while we talked about different preferences." Jude pointed out the additional decorations. "We narrowed it down to this main grouping, but we're refining things."

"Looks good to me. Simple, but elegant with the natural colors you prefer. Is Neil with us?"

"Still here," Neil called over the speaker on Arthur's phone.

"Hello, Neil. How are you today?"

"Decent and kicking," Neil said.

Arthur rolled his eyes at his partner's twist of saying.

"Good to hear it."

"Oh, don't even think you're getting out of explaining what happened," Jude said.

"What?" Gavin asked.

"Spill it. All of it. What happened with the handsome EMT?" Arthur said.

Gavin blinked. "I don't—"

"Nope. Spill the goods, mister," Jude said.

Gavin muttered something about the dinner plans.

"Come again?"

"We made dinner plans on Gray's next night off but need to figure out what day that will be," Gavin said. For some reason, he didn't want to use Gray's true name. It felt like something special between him and Xavier.

Arthur whooped with joy. He did a little dance.

Jude performed a butt wiggle booty shake.

Dawson barked in perfect doggy agreement.

"May I ask what is happening? I don't think we're talking about floral arrangements," Neil called out.

Arthur explained what had happened to his confused partner.

"Oh, how wonderful. Congratulations, and I hope you enjoy your dinner date," Neil said.

"Thanks, Neil." Gavin took another few swallows of water to get over the embarrassment of having his dating agenda spread across town.

"Okay. Fine. Back to business. We've embarrassed Gavin enough for today." Jude patted Gavin on the shoulder. "Neil, did you look at the pictures from the last arrangement changes?"

"I did and think I've made my choice. Arthur, check your text to see what you think," Neil said.

Arthur's phone dinged. He opened the different app to read the message.

"I agree, hon. Good choice," Arthur said.

"Excellent. I'll let you finalize things."

"Keep close to the phone for our next stop."

"Will do. Love you, hon," Neil said and hung up.

"What's your final answer?" Jude said.

Arthur pointed to their chosen set of displays. "The third version will be perfect."

"Excellent choices. Personally, I like that version, too. Not over-the-top and in your face." Jude altered the different displays to the chosen version. He pushed aside all the discarded ones. "This set is for the ceremony. Each one of these will be at a table. This collection will be at the head table. These small ones are for the wedding party."

"Perfect."

"Wonderful!" Jude made notes of the finalized version. He snapped pictures of everything. "I'll send all my notes, pictures and final invoice to you, Gavin. Delivery remains the same."

"Appreciate that. Yup, usual set up and delivery," Gavin confirmed.

"Then we're done."

"On to the next stop," Gavin said. "Thank you for everything."

"You know I love doing all this for events," Jude said.

"Thank you for your patience," Arthur said.

"Oh, trust me. You're not the worst, not by a long shot."

"Thank God for that."

After securing the backpack, Gavin balanced and hobbled toward the front. Arthur stayed by his side.

When they reached the door, they stepped aside when a man in scrubs entered.

"Elliott! What a surprise," Jude said while he rushed toward him. He flung his arms around Doc Elliott's neck and planted a playful kiss on his mouth.

Gavin and Arthur laughed at Jude's antics and enthusiasm.

"One would think you haven't seen him in days," Gavin said.

"He's been on a forty-eight-hour shift, so, no, I haven't seen him in days." Jude stuck his tongue out at Gavin.

"Oh, well, pardon me," Gavin said.

Doc Elliott snuggled Jude close. "Be nice. He's injured."

"Bah! His injury didn't affect his tongue," Jude muttered.

"Hey!" Gavin said.

"Don't start." Doc Elliott faced Gavin and assessed him. "Please tell me you didn't walk over here from Charm."

"Nope. I drove."

"Are you taking it easy?"

"No, he insists on taking me to all these stops," Arthur said. "Hello, I'm one of the grooms for an upcoming wedding. Arthur Carlton."

"Dr. Elliott Sheffield, good to meet you, Arthur." Doc shook hands with Arthur and glared at Gavin. "Didn't I tell you to take it easy?"

"I don't listen well to orders or sit still for long moments. I laid around at the hospital and the entire day after. Isn't that enough?" Gavin said.

"I don't know if that's enough, given the situation."

"Arthur traveled here to finalize his wedding plans. I didn't want him to waste the trip because a stupid accident knocked me around."

"Fine. Fine." Doc Elliott waved off Gavin's reasoning. "Give the crutches to Arthur. Let's assess your balance."

Gavin handed over the crutches and balanced on both feet. He leaned to his bad side and winced a bit.

Doc crouched and tested Gavin's ankle. "Healing, but you need to give it time. You're doing better. Did you take anything for the swelling?"

"Just took some ibuprofen."

"Good. Finish up your day here, return to the Charm or your home and stay put. Keep following the RICE procedures and medication. Got it?"

"Yes, Doctor," Gavin said.

"Could you please put the doctor away? Just for a tiny bit. I haven't seen you in two days. I'm hungry for my lover and food. Perhaps not that order, but I can adjust." Jude tugged on Doc Elliott's arm to pull his attention away.

Elliott chuckled while he stood. He kissed Jude's pouting mouth. "I came here to take you to lunch, wherever you want. Then I need to get back to the ER."

"What?"

"I'll be home tonight. I promise."

"For how long?"

"Twelve hours. Maybe a bit less if there are no emergencies."

"Yippee!" Jude whistled for Dawson.

"Good to know I made you happy."

"Oh, you'll never guess what happened." Jude wiggled his eyebrows at Gavin.

Gavin shook his head.

"What?" Doc Elliott asked.

"Gavin has a dinner date with Gray, whenever Gray has a night off," Jude said.

Doc Elliott's eyebrows rose high. He grinned while Gavin flushed. "Nice. Good for you. Enjoy."

"We'll see. Come on, Arthur. We need to continue. We have a date with tablecloths and other linens," Gavin said.

"Don't push yourself too hard, Gavin," Doc Elliott warned while they left the floral shop.

"Gotta love small-town life," Arthur said.

"Meddlesome folks."

Arthur laughed.

* * * *

They continued the tour with a pit-stop for Arthur to make a final decision for the linens. They used pictures of the floral arrangements to help.

"Now for the fun part." Gavin opened the door for Katie's Kakes and Kookies. "Cake!"

"Oooh." Arthur rubbed his hands together. "Hit me with the sweets."

"Katie will do that and more." Gavin hobbled inside and waved to the pretty baker. "Hey, Katie. This is our groom, Arthur Carlton. Arthur, this is baker extraordinaire Katie Murphy."

"Hello and welcome, Arthur. Ready for some samples?" Katie asked while shaking hands.

"Best part of this wedding craziness," Arthur said.

"Hey, there's other parts that are awesome." Gavin hitched himself into one of the barstools.

"Cake, Gavin. She's giving me cake."

"Right. Damn. Cakes win over everything else."

Katie disappeared into the back and returned with a tray. She placed it in front of Arthur. Then she settled near him where a tablet and pen waited. "First, we taste. Then we design."

"Oh, the design is simple. We both love sandcastles," Arthur said. "It's our favorite thing to do whenever we go to the beach. The rest of our theme is beachy. Would you call it that, Gavin?"

"Pretty close to it."

"Oh, I would love to do a sandcastle." Katie sketched on the tablet. "Still, try the flavors. Those are our most popular cakes and fillings. Gavin gave me a short list of what you and your fiancé preferred. There's something about no nuts?"

"Neal has a nut allergy."

"Will make a note of that. Can he have marzipan? It's made from ground almonds."

"I don't want to chance it."

"Not a problem. There's other confections we can use to create the details." Katie pointed to the six small plates. Two mini cakes waited on each plate. Each cake had two layers with a filling in between. A small handwritten label explained the different layers and tastes.

Taking his time, Arthur sampled each cake combination. "Gonna step away from the chocolate. We wanted something light, fun and unique."

"What did you choose?"

"How many choices do I get?"

"How about two or three? I can alternate the layers in the sandcastle."

"Let's go two. I don't want to go too crazy."

"You can never be too crazy with cake," Gavin said.

"Oh, I disagree. I had someone go with ten different combinations for one party," Katie said.

"Yikes. Not one of mine?"

She shook her head. "Oh, no, I wish, because you would have pulled them back."

"Hell, yes. That's crazy."

"Ahem? The cake?" Arthur said.

"Sorry. Go ahead," Katie said.

"Champagne cake and strawberry preserves. Spice cake with the brown sugar salted caramel filling. Perhaps a champagne or brown sugar fondant," Arthur said.

"That is unique and sounds like heaven," Katie said. "I'm always impressed with what clients choose."

They discussed a few more details, but Arthur gave Katie plenty of leeway in final design and details. He signed off on the sketch and the cake flavors.

"Thanks for everything. I can't wait to see and taste it." Arthur sent an update to Neil about the cake.

"Same here," Katie said. "Gavin, I'll email everything, including the finished sketch. Like always, I'll wait to post the final creation on my social media until the ceremony is finished."

"Appreciate it."

With a wave, Katie gathered the tray and her things.

Gavin flipped through his folder and ticked off the last item. "We're done. Just need to review the wedding spaces. Malcolm will cover the catering plans."

"Sounds good to me."

"How about we grab something for lunch?"

"Please," Arthur said.

"There are a couple of good spots." Gavin tucked the folder back into his backpack. He got back to his feet and crutches.

On their way back, Gavin stopped off at the pita place. Arthur carried the bag for Gavin.

At the Charm, Gavin headed around to the back via the wooden paths. "Here's the porch. There are multiple levels. That path takes you to the gazebo, and beyond it is access to the beach. How about we eat out here and we can review layouts?"

"Sure." Arthur sat when Gavin chose a table. "Perhaps we could use the lower level and gazebo. Keep a view of the ocean."

Gavin separated the pitas, napkins and bottled drinks. "It's the most popular, plus you don't have a large party, so it's the perfect size. We could spread out a bit on the beach, but I don't see a problem." While he enjoyed the late lunch, he pointed out the different options on a layout page.

"There's no need for a seating chart. I'd rather have our friends and family mingle." Arthur finished his lunch and kept checking his watch.

"Is something wrong?"

"I'm anxious to get home. Neil had another doctor appointment today. I'm waiting to hear from him."

"I hope everything comes out in a positive way."

"I hope the same, but I'm not sure this time. He has always had a heart condition, but it's been managed with medication and lifestyle changes."

"When is your flight?"

"Tomorrow afternoon. I leave a little after two. I scheduled an early check-out tomorrow so I can leave around eleven to get across the bridge and to the airport. You never know how airport security will go, so I don't want to take the chance." Arthur shoved his trash in the bag. "Anything else we need to do?"

"Just the catering menu with Malcolm."

"Oh, okay."

"We can schedule it for your later return."

"I don't want to inconvenience him."

"How about I have Malcolm send a few different menus to you? We could have a quick talk to give him some ideas of where to go?"

"That'll be good."

Gavin texted Malcolm to see if he could join them for a catering consult. His phone beeped back. "He'll be right out."

Within minutes, Malcolm walked outside, carrying a tablet and folder. "Hi there. You must be Arthur. I'm Malcolm or Mal, the assistant chef at Delights. A pleasure to meet you," he said.

"Hello, Mal, thanks for meeting us out here," Arthur said while they shook hands.

"Happy to get out for a bit," Mal said while he sat. After spreading out menus, he turned on the tablet. "How about you tell me about the wedding, your fiancé and what you both would like to eat? This is for a Saturday brunch after a morning beach wedding. It's a beautiful time on the beach."

Arthur went through the simple beachy atmosphere. He mentioned about Neil's nut allergy, heart issues and that he desired a light, easy meal.

Malcolm went through a few menu options until they narrowed them down. He jotted down the final version. Arthur signed off. With the meeting over, Malcolm returned to the kitchen.

"Anything else?"

"Nope, that was the last piece," Gavin said. "I would go with you for tuxedo choices and fittings, but you mentioned handling that in Atlanta."

"Yes, now that we've selected the colors, we can narrow down ties and stuff. I can text you pictures. I'm excited for our upcoming wedding and how it all comes together," Arthur said while standing.

Gavin hugged Arthur. "Thank you for choosing me."

"Couldn't think of anyone else to guide us," Arthur said with another quick squeeze. "See you soon."

"Bye, Arthur. Tell Neil I said hello and wish him well."

"Will do," Arthur said. "Enjoy your dinner date with the sexy EMT. Don't talk yourself out of it."

Chapter Nine

Exhausted from the additional shift he'd accepted, Xavier felt ready to drop by Sunday afternoon. Then he signed off on the supply checklist and headed inside to work through the stacked paperwork.

While moving through the pile, he tried to figure out what to do with the rest of the evening. He needed to study for the last two exams. Though he felt, if he tried, he would end up forgetting everything. After several semesters, he'd learned when to push himself and when to step back.

He pulled out his multiple calendars. While he flipped through the pages, Gavin's face popped in his mind.

The quiet question...or was it a request? No, more of an offer.

Xavier couldn't figure it out.

Still, there was the possibility of a date.

"Shit. I haven't texted or anything. Stupid. Stupid." Xavier tapped a pen against his forehead.

The lean form of his partner appeared around the doorway. "Why are you beating yourself up with a pen? I don't think it did anything to you, other than squirt ink," Norman said.

"I have a possible date."

"Possible date? How do you end up with a *possible* date?"

"Someone asked me out, but we didn't solidify the plans, due to our crazy schedules."

"Well. Yeah. Guess that could happen. When is this *possible* date supposed to occur?"

"There's a problem with that. We don't have a set day." Xavier waved over the calendars.

"Right, the calendars are out. Hard to set a date without them." Norman understood the reason. "How could that happen? You didn't even go on the date...yet."

"I didn't call, text or email him."

"Oh." Understanding that this could be a lengthy conversation, Norman dropped into a chair. "Since when?"

"Friday."

Norman's dark chocolate eyes widened a touch at the soft admission. "Umm...ouch."

"Yeah." Xavier grimaced when he realized the hole he'd dug himself. "Did I totally fuck up my chances?"

"Don't know. It depends..." Norman tapped his fingers along the chair's wooden arm.

"Like what?"

"Okay. To start with. Who is it?"

"Gavin Hartfield."

Norman's eyebrow winged up. "The wedding consultant at the Charm?"

"The one I sort of ran over on the beach."

"I met him. Gavin created my sister's wedding." Norman wagged a finger at Xavier. "Umm, you were there."

"Well, yeah, the wedding was wonderful. Your sister looked gorgeous. Gavin did all that?"

"That's his job with Charmed Occasions. He took her through everything, listened to her bridezilla moments, calmed her down, held her hand and built the wedding of her dreams within her budget. She can't stop raving about him to anyone who listens. She pushes all her engaged friends toward him."

"I thought he only did LGBT weddings."

"Nope." Norman shook his head. "He'll do anything for the Charm's event planning. The LGBT is their specialty, but he'll help everyone create their special event. I think he does some smaller things on the side but not all the time. Either way, he's damn good at what he does."

"Didn't know all that about him."

"He's a great guy. Friendly. Easy-going but can get pissed off when a situation calls for it. Sis saw him chew out a vendor for trying to screw over an order. You don't want to get on his bad side," Norman said.

"I might already be there. Remember?"

"Ahh. Right?"

"Hey, Chief, Norm. Why are you two still here? Thought you would hit the road," Ryder Marshall, another EMT, said when he appeared in the doorway. His shift partner, Aiden William, stood behind him.

"Paperwork." Xavier pointed to one of the stacks. He pushed his planner books to the side, but the team knew why he had them.

"Yeah, that stuff can pile up on you," Ryder said.

"Don't let him fool you. He's contemplating how badly he screwed up with a potential date. Hence all the planners out to help him figure out how to fix it," Norman said, ratting him out. "Dum dum *dum*."

Xavier rolled his eyes and groaned.

"Chief has a date?" Ryder let out a low whistle. "Wow. That's unexpected."

"Only the goombah didn't call, text or email his potential date for almost three days," Norman added. "Nada. Zip. Zilch."

"Ouch. Chief, man, way to drop the ball." Ryder helped nudge the dig deeper into Xavier's pride.

"Who asked him out?" the quiet one of the pair, Aiden, asked.

"Gavin Hartfield," Norman said.

"No way. I enjoyed a dinner date with Gavin at Breezy Lagniappe. It was an awesome night," Ryder said.

"And?" Xavier asked.

"Nothing happened. We remained friends since nothing sparked. He's a great guy. I wish you luck," Ryder said.

The alarm rang.

Ryder and Aiden listened for the information over the loudspeaker.

Dispatch called for the EMTs to respond to a private residence. According to the code, the request appeared to be a possible heart attack.

"Gotta go," Ryder said and motioned to Aiden.

Within precious seconds, the ambulance had powered up with sirens and rolled out. Ryder's voice on the speaker alerted the dispatcher to their response.

When things quieted down, Norman nudged the phone back toward Xavier. "Call him." He encouraged him to get them back on the subject.

Xavier flicked the phone's corner to send it spinning. "Do I even have a chance?"

"You'll have a better one if you explained what happened, Xavier," Norman said, using his first name possibly to make the point. "You deserve to have a life outside of work and school. Take the chance." He got to his feet. "Take advantage of the downtime. You don't know how long it'll last around here. Look through your planners. Figure out a time...then call him." He closed the door to give Xavier some privacy.

Hoping the offer for a date could be open, Xavier selected Gavin's personal number. He heard it ringing.

"Hello, this is Gavin Hartfield. How can I help you?"

"Hi, Gavin, it's Xavier Grayson."

"Xavier, hello. How are you?"

"Been on schedule for the last few days. I apologize for not getting a chance to text or call you until now. Please excuse my screwy memory. According to Norman, I'm a goombah."

"It's okay. I understand about crazy schedules. Mine has been up and down, too."

"I was hoping that offer for dinner is available."

"It can be."

"According to my planner, I'm thinking about Tuesday night." Xavier crossed his fingers, pushed back all his ADHD nagging about screwing with the schedule and hoped.

"Planners?"

"It's part of my coping mechanisms. I have OCD and ADHD."

"Right, I heard about it."

"I know it's last minute and a strange night for a date. I don't have a shift on Tuesday but do have my last two final exams. I should get out by four. How about it? I didn't want to wait until the weekend, since I know those are your busier days."

Please. Please. Please say yes.

"What time?"

"Could I pick you up around six? We can go across the bridge to Pensacola."

"Six? Yeah, that sounds good."

"We might eat a little late. It all depends on if there's a wait."

"That's fine. I'm used to eating at odd hours since I don't know if I'm dining with a client or have to figure out something on my own."

"Great."

"Need my address?"

"Oh, yeah, guess that would help," Xavier said.

Gavin snickered and recited his address.

Xavier jotted it down. Then he made multiple notations in the different planners, including his phone to secure it in his brain. "I'll see you on Tuesday."

"Looking forward to it. Bye," Gavin said and hung up.

Someone whistled the 'Wedding March' outside his door.

Xavier glared when he recognized Norman. "Norm!"

Unrepentant, Norman opened the door. "Got the date?"

Xavier rolled his eyes. "Yes. I'll see him Tuesday night for dinner."

"Good. Go get him, Gray. Luck on the date!" Returning to whistling the tune, Norman walked off before Xavier could smack him.

"Unbelievable," Xavier muttered. Smiling at securing a date, he packed his planners into his backpack then found it easier to get through the final batch of paperwork. When he left his office, the firefighters echoed Norman's teasing and wishes of luck.

Bunch of idiots. I swear.

Back home, he pulled something together for dinner and sat down with his planners and textbooks. When he learned the philosophy exam was scheduled right after the microbiology lab, he cursed about the double shot. Still, it would be an early end to the semester. He decided to study for the philosophy exam, since he was overloaded on microbiology. The humanities one was a little more foreign to his science-based mind. It took him longer to remember the chapters and notes.

Flicking the TV on, he picked up on the binge-watch of the Marvel's *Agent Carter* series. The background noise helped him concentrate while he jotted reminder notes on a new pad of highlights that appeared on previous tests and quizzes.

Chapter Ten

With a scheduled brunch event to happen, Gavin arrived early Monday morning. At least he didn't have to bother with the blasted crutches. The ACE bandage and air cast remained in place, but his ankle was more stable. He couldn't go for his usual morning ride on his Peloton bike, but he hoped to return to his exercise routine soon. It was the best gift he'd ever given himself.

Shifting his bag, Gavin stopped in by the kitchen. "How early did you get in?"

Moving around the space in a crazy coordinated way known only to chefs, Malcolm waved after checking something in the stove. "Almost two hours ago. Around five-ish. The sky was fairly dark when I left the house."

"And you left Reece in bed?"

"Yeah. Lemme tell you how super hard it is to do that when he's all warm and cuddly. All your fault for scheduling this event so early. Make me miss cuddly time with my Reece-bear," Malcolm said with a playful pout.

"Reece-bear?"

"Don't tell him."

"Playing around with nicknames?"

"Trying, but he's always so darn serious. Gotta shake him up when he least expects it." Malcolm shrugged. "Why would someone request a Monday brunch? Of all days."

"Something about an anniversary on this specific date, but the ladies didn't give me the details. I let them have their wish. The client—"

"Is always right," Malcolm finished. "Believe me. I know that saying all too well after years in this business."

"There you go—"

"What are you doing on your feet after that insane weekend? That was a crazy, wild fiftieth birthday celebration then the sweet sixteenth celebration. I think those are worse than weddings. Either way, what's the part of staying off your feet? Do you not want to heal?"

Wincing at Samuel's sharp reprimand, Gavin turned to face his boss. "Morning, Samuel. How are you this morning? I'm doing great," he said to tease about the greeting as Samuel swept past. "The celebrations went great. Hopefully, it'll create a whole lot of business for Occasions."

Malcolm swallowed a chuckle behind him.

Samuel glowered at him. "Morning, Gavin. Why are you on your feet?"

"Honestly?" When Samuel's expression didn't change, Gavin grumbled. "Okay. Okay. My ankle is doing better. No twinges. The air cast and bandage are in place. Don't even need my crutches."

Samuel crossed his arms over his chest. "Why do I not believe you?"

"I'm being honest. I'm not feeling any sharp pains. There hasn't been any significant swelling or bruising."

"You should still take it easy."

"I understand my limits."

"Chill out, Samuel. He's not your baby boy," Malcolm said.

Samuel's jaw dropped. "I—"

"We know. We know. You mean well." Malcolm shoved a cup of coffee in Samuel's hands. He flicked his fingers. "Now shoo. Back to your office. I got things to discuss with our wedding planner."

Samuel gaped his mouth like a fish, but he didn't say anything. He sipped on his coffee and disappeared down the hall.

"He's going to plan his revenge on you," Gavin said.

"I'm sure he is. I'll deal with it later, or I'll get Dakota to distract him." Malcolm placed a cup of coffee and a fresh scone next to Gavin. "Now, eat your breakfast and we'll go over the details."

Gavin took a few bracing sips of the delicious coffee. He plucked a corner of the cinnamon scone. "What's the status? Drinks?"

"Fresh coffee is brewed. I have hot water for anyone wishing tea. Two cocktails to bring in a little booze. I worked with Zak to create a strawberry and chamomile punch with a splash of bourbon. It's a bright pink, feminine and sweet drink. The other one is a champagne punch with an aromatic mixture of sage, lemon and ginger. It creates a refreshing and light drink to counteract everything else. I had a taste, and you could drink it all day without feeling a thing. A little dangerous but should be fun for the ladies."

"Both sound delicious. What about the food? I don't see anything."

"Everything is finishing up in the oven. The ladies kept things simple but delicious and filling to satisfy the morning hunger. No samples. Just your scone."

"Come on."

"Not all the time. Sorry."

"You're not sorry."

"Nope. I'm the chef."

Gavin grumbled. "Cake?"

"The cake was delivered earlier and is chilling in the cooler."

"Guess you don't need me here for anything else."

Malcolm ticked off a few items on his list. "Nope. I got this one covered."

Gavin scooped up his scone and mug. "Gonna take this to my office." He scurried out to Malcolm's laughter.

While nibbling on the scone, Gavin worked through his emails.

After getting some caffeine in his system, he went to the library.

As usual, Jude was already there with his beautiful flowers. A couple of other vendors had also arrived.

"Morning, Jude," Gavin said.

"Hey there, how are you feeling today?" Jude twisted a vase of flowers into a different spot on the bookshelf. "Nice combo today."

Gavin glanced at the simple navy mini dot suspenders with brown leather fasteners, matched to a plain navy bow tie. The combination set off against the herringbone white shirt and charcoal pants with brown brogues. "Went for something a bit simple today. Ankle is stronger."

"Simple is good. Nice news about the ankle."

"Good morning, Gavin," Claudia, one of the ladies who created the event, said while she entered the room. "Oh, those pink roses are perfect. Thank you, Jude!"

"Welcome, Claudia. Hope I found the right shade."

"They're wonderful," Claudia said.

"What exactly are we celebrating today?" Jude asked.

Gavin hid a smile, since he never could get it out of Claudia.

"Guess I can let the secret out of the bag."

"Does this mean I'll finally know?" Gavin teased.

"Yes. Yes. Sorry for all the secrecy, but I couldn't dare let it get out. My dearest friend, Melanie, is a breast cancer survivor. That's the reason for the pink colors. This is the anniversary of her remission news after a three-year battle."

"That's wonderful," Gavin said.

"There's more. She found out she's pregnant!"

"What?"

Claudia nodded with a wide smile. "With a baby girl! She saved her eggs after her diagnosis and before the treatment. When she felt stronger, she tried IVF treatments with her husband, and one finally took. She's five months pregnant. She's under close care by her OB-GYN, but all looks good for a healthy delivery."

"Holy crap!"

Claudia waved her hand around the room. "She believes we're giving her a party to celebrate the remission anniversary, but..."

"It's a surprise baby shower," Gavin finished.

"Bingo!"

"That's an awesome surprise. Well done," Gavin said.

"It's a doozy," Jude said.

"It's been difficult keeping it from everyone." Claudia inspected the space. "There's something bugging me about the opening. It's there...for everyone to see, especially Melanie. Can we figure out something to disguise it?"

Gavin checked the area. "We have the metal standing frames. I have several sets. I'll get Victor to bring them up and stretch them across. We can add votive candles and tuck in whatever leftover roses and greenery Jude has, along with decorations."

"Perfect! We have a few extra pieces to add."

"Sure, bring in whatever you need and work them into the design. I can find more..."

"Oh, there's no need for you to stay. Go on. We've got this covered," Claudia interrupted.

"Seems to be the case this morning. I'm going then." With a smile, Gavin returned to his office.

On his return, Samuel appeared and followed him. He carried a fresh pot of coffee.

"Don't start on my ankle again. I promise I'm doing fine. I don't need to take a couple of days or anything else," Gavin warned.

"Am I that predictable?"

"Since I got carried in by Gray, yeah," Gavin said.

"Why do I get the idea you haven't had many people concerned about your personal well-being? Like they only care about what you can do for them."

"Part of being a wedding coordinator. It's my profession to care and worry for others over all the minute details," Gavin said.

"Doesn't sound right."

"What is when it comes to life?"

"Too damn philosophical for a morning conversation." Samuel placed the pot on the warming stone. Then he dropped into a chair. "Not enough caffeine."

"You started it."

Samuel waved him off. "I still say you should take time off. You've got the days."

"And do what? Sit at home? On the beach?" Gavin shook his head. "Nah. I'm happier when I'm busy."

"You could go on a date. The last one was with that EMT, Ryder. You haven't been on a date since. That's a long drought, especially if nothing happens at the clubs."

"I've done the dating scene in Atlanta. Flirting with the hot brothers, best friends or other wedding guests? I've done it."

"Before or after Arthur?"

"Both. Ended up with someone I regretted and that caused complications." Gavin shrugged. "After that, I gave up on dating. Those scenes are tiring. Ryder ended up being a friend, someone to hang out with. I'm always on and upbeat during consults and events. I didn't want to keep it up during personal time."

"So...what? Did you shut it all down?"

"Took a break. Reset my life when I came here. It's a completely different lifestyle and speed down here. So different from a big city."

"I know. I came from New York. I lived in downtown Manhattan with access to everything, no matter what time of the day or night. Then I came here..."

"Outside of certain seasons, the sidewalks roll up and the lights darken by ten."

"Even on Friday."

They laughed at the differences that former city-dwellers pointed out to the locals.

"Though I might have heard something about you talking with Gray outside the café. Small-town grapevine," Samuel said.

"Oh gawd." Gavin leaned forward to fill his cup with fragrant coffee.

"So, this little nugget is true."

"Yes. We talked."

"And?"

"I might have asked for a date. Possibly. Don't know."

"Umm. What?"

"Crazy busy schedules don't always line up. I wanted to give it a try with him, see if something was there. I left it up to him," Gavin explained.

"That sounds awesome. I hope things work out and you can line up dinner—"

"Well…"

"What?"

"He called me yesterday."

"And?"

"We're going to dinner tomorrow night. He has two final exams and he's free. So…"

"What did you say?"

"Yes."

Samuel squealed with his happiness. "I hope you have a wonderful night. You two deserve something good to happen. You've been nonstop since you joined our B&B. Gray is nonstop between his EMT job and going to school. He has a few more semesters to go before he gets that all-important piece of paper. His final must be for this summer session. I think the fall semester starts mid-August."

"He mentioned that he's taking a nursing class for the fall semester. I know his time will be even more limited."

"If things connect between you, though, I wouldn't give it up, no matter how much you need to fight for a few minutes together."

Wise words from Samuel. Gavin fell silent.

"Just saying."

Gavin nodded.

"Back to business stuff? Shouldn't be as heavy," Samuel said.

"Yeah," Gavin said.

Clearly seeming a little relieved, Samuel steered them back to their regular morning business discussions.

Over a fresh cup of coffee, Gavin explained this morning's event, along with upcoming ones. He pulled out a graph and report from a different pile.

"What's that?"

"The latest marking report from the various websites we chose, our website, newsletters, and advertisements with different agencies. We're getting the word out about the Occasions, the Charm and all the B&B offers for weddings and other events. I don't know if it's enough."

"We're busy every weekend."

"Yes, but with the new area Sully is building, there's potential for more growth. I think we need to connect with someone who knows all about advertising and marketing — not with someone from the hotel home office."

"I agree. The home office is concerned with the main lines, not the small boutiques."

"And not all of them with specialized options like the Charm."

"I'll look through the budget with Dakota and Chandler. We'll see what we can do to move that part along. We can't let it go, no matter what. To keep the event business, the marketing is a must."

"Exactly. Word of mouth is great. A good-looking website is a start. Other social media is a definite plus with the younger crowds. Same with a newsletter, but we need more," Gavin said.

"Anything else?"

Gavin pulled out the folder of Samuel's wedding. "Your wedding. Lot of things are still in the air. The finalized date. A guest list. What's happening?"

Samuel groaned.

"What?"

"Most of my family can be uptight snobs. My father can easily go over the edge into obnoxious and privileged. I worked on him, but..." Samuel shrugged.

"You can only do so much. What about Dakota's family? I thought he said something about his parents being in Chicago, but they're not talking."

"Can't believe he's going with that cover story."

"What?"

"There are issues with his parents—issues going way back to his childhood. His siblings are better. But when you mix the entire family together..." Samuel shuddered. "Yikes."

"Have you met them?"

"His parents? Nope." Samuel shrugged. "I met his brothers and one of his sisters. He has a few more. I was looking forward to meeting all of them, even his parents."

"This is one of the sticking points between you."

"Starts an argument every single time. I don't know what—"

Dakota staggered into the office.

Samuel twisted in his chair. "Dakota, what is it?"

Dakota waved the cell phone, but he couldn't get the words out.

Samuel brought Dakota to a chair. He placed a hand on Dakota's cheek. "Dakota, hon?"

Dakota dropped into the chair. He lowered his head in one hand. Tears shimmered in his eyes.

"What happened, Dakota?" Gavin asked.

"Bad news. Expected...but..." Dakota faded off. He moved his hand over his mouth.

"What happened? Just talk to us," Samuel said.

"Penelope Stewart slipped into unconsciousness. Her day nurse called 9-1-1. She's been moved to intensive care. She's in late-stage multiple sclerosis with aspiration pneumonia, multiple pressure sores and a nasty kidney infection. Her body might be shutting down from all these complications," Dakota said.

"Oh, shit," Samuel said. He moved to the other chair and took Dakota's hand.

"How bad is it?" Gavin asked.

"Penny has been on the far end of the Expanded Disability Severity Scale for some months," Dakota said. "She prepared for what the complications could bring her."

"No one can prepare for all this," Samuel added. "Where is she on the scale?"

"High nine to nine point five. She's totally helpless, bedridden and unable to communicate or effectively eat or swallow."

"Next level is..."

"Death." Dakota dragged his fingers through his hair.

"Does Dorian know?" Gavin asked.

"Yes, they contacted him, pulled him out of class to give him the news. They also spoke with Reece," Dakota said. "Reece called me to help spread the word."

"Can Dorian get away from CIA?" Gavin asked about the Culinary Institute of America, where Dorian studied at the Hyde Park campus for a Bachelor's in Food Business Management with an Associate in Culinary Arts.

"Dorian is trying for an emergency absence," Dakota said.

"What does Reece need from us?" Samuel asked.

"Reece hopes we can contact the others to tell them what happened. He'll concentrate on helping Dorian get out of class, find a flight home and he'll coordinate healthcare at the hospital, according to Penny's wishes." Dakota spun the phone. "She has a DNR. Reece hopes she'll hold on until Dorian can come home to say goodbye. The rest of us will coordinate visiting, perhaps help clean their apartment and whatever else Dorian might need. He's strong, but I don't think he'll hold up under all this pressure. It's a lot for anyone to take, even after a long illness."

"Okay. Let's go to my office. We'll alert the others," Samuel said while he assisted Dakota to his feet. "Gavin, we'll continue this conversation later."

"Whatever help you need, let me know."

"You have enough with the upcoming events."

"But—"

"Gavin, I promise. We'll let you know what is going on when we learn."

"What about Malcolm?"

"Reece will—"

"Dakota, Samuel, Reece just…" Malcolm stopped in the doorway. He looked at all of them. "You know…about Penelope."

They nodded.

Dakota moved and took Malcolm in his embrace.

"This is gonna destroy him," Mal muttered.

"We'll get Dorian through this. He's not alone," Dakota said.

Samuel helped move them out of Gavin's office and across the hall to his slightly larger office.

Gavin didn't want to be alone. He couldn't believe what was happening. Since his arrival to the Charm a couple of years before, he'd become fast friends with Dorian and Malcolm. They'd brought him into the fold, showed him around town and introduced him to everyone. They'd even dragged him to their favorite clubs in Pensacola for nights of dancing, drinking, and he'd discovered how Dorian had gotten the nickname 'Tigger'.

Dorian had gotten his acceptance notice into the Culinary Institute of America the summer of his arrival and had begun classes in New York. Through all the hardships he'd faced in his young life, Dorian had kept a wonderful attitude and confidence through everything. He hadn't allowed the darkness to pull him down.

Gavin had missed Dorian these last couple of years but knew that Dorian had followed his dreams to attend the CIA and achieve a degree he didn't think possible until he'd met Reece, Dakota and their circle of friends.

"Morning, Gavin," Victor said moments before he knocked on the frame. "I didn't see anyone in the kitchen."

"Hello, Victor. Yes, sorry about that. Umm…"

"Is everything okay?"

"No. No, things are…bad." Gavin swallowed back the hurt. "We received some news about Dorian's mom."

"Oh no, what happened?"

Gavin explained the situation.

"Is Dorian coming home?"

"They're working on it." Gavin opened the current binder.

"Do they need help?"

"No, not right now. They want us to concentrate on today's event. It's a simple brunch in the library. Please retrieve the three silver metal screens with the decorative filigree from storage, along with the box of glass votive holders and tea-lights. We'll use that as a barrier from the hallway and entrance area. Also add in another dozen chairs. The ladies mentioned there will be twenty guests, but a couple more could arrive."

"Gavin—"

"We need to concentrate on this event. Please." Gavin held out the list. "Please do this part for me."

"Okay."

"Thank you. The ladies are there with their decorations. Jude dropped off his flowers. Please help with final preparations. I'm still not cleared for heavier things."

"Okay," Victor said.

After Victor scurried off, Gavin composed himself, hooked up his earpiece and prepared himself. He covered his internal pain for Dorian and Penelope while he went to coordinate the event.

At odd moments, thoughts of Xavier entered his mind. He thought about their upcoming date.

Should he cancel?

He didn't know what would happen if Dorian did come home. They would all need to be with him at the clinic.

Not sure what to do, Gavin figured to keep his date tomorrow. If things changed, he would call and cancel.

Chapter Eleven

It was a double shot of exams for this crazy Tuesday. After the first exam, Xavier called his favorite Pensacola restaurant to secure a table for dinner. Then he went off to the philosophy exam that didn't take the full three hours. His ADHD issues threatened to knock him for a loop multiple times during the philosophy final, but he managed to calm himself and focus. After finishing the last test, Xavier returned home, changed and went running to burn off the leftover energy and buzz from sitting for so long.

After the four-mile run, Xavier checked the timing. He was cutting it close. He showered to remove the sweat and stink.

Xavier changed into a white checked oxford, navy trousers and a caramel-colored belt. He dug through his closet to find his favorite caramel leather ankle boots. A touch of styling product through his hair and a splash of cologne and he called himself done. It was a little better than his regular uniform.

Arriving on time at Gavin's home, Xavier climbed out of his old truck, walked up the walkway and hit the doorbell. He smoothed a hand down the shirt and rolled the sleeves up his forearms. Then he undid the top two buttons because he couldn't stand having the cloth pressed against his throat. He rolled back on his boot heels while he waited.

The door opened to reveal Gavin. Always smartly dressed in a crisp outfit, Gavin didn't fail Xavier tonight. He'd selected deep maroon slacks with a pale gray oxford with a bow tie and suspender combination to highlight the maroon color. He'd finished it off with a pair of suede gray brogues.

"Wow, you look great," Xavier said.

Gavin smiled at the simple compliment. "You look wonderful, too."

"Better than my jogging shorts or scrubs."

"I don't know. The jogging shorts left things wide open to my imagination."

Xavier chuckled.

"Would you like to come inside?"

"We should get going. I managed to snag a reservation, but I'm not sure of the timing across the bridge. We need to hurry if we're going to make it."

"I'm amazed you were able to get something." Gavin left the door open while he gathered his personal items.

"Got lucky. One of my favorite places had a table open. Depending on bridge traffic, I'm hoping we make it in time."

"I'm moving. I promise." Gavin hurried to the door, set the alarm and locked it.

Xavier led him down the walkway and helped him into the old truck. "Old Blue doesn't look the best but gets me to where I need to go. Always reliable."

"Hello, Old Blue," Gavin said when he patted the console.

With a grin, Xavier fired the engine and they drove away.

"I feel I should apologize again for not even bothering to type out a quick 'hi' in a text or something," Xavier said while he drove.

"There's no need. I know what you do for a living. Plus, you have school. How were the exams?"

"Grueling, but I got through. The philosophy one went faster than I thought."

"Good to hear. What's next?"

"Fall semester starts in a couple of weeks. I only have one class, but it's a doozy."

"How bad?"

"Eight hours in one classroom."

"Ouch."

"Plus a four-hour lab."

Gavin winced. "Double ouch."

"Did I mention I have ADHD?"

"I remember overhearing Doc Elliott mention something about it," Gavin said. "I take it being stuck in a classroom isn't a good combination with your ADHD."

"No, these classes I dread, but they're the important ones. It's one of the nursing requirements. Can't get out of it if I want my degree. No options to take them at home."

"Did you talk to the professors?"

"When I signed up for the first nursing course, I tried to see if there were options." Xavier shrugged.

"There isn't any other choice, but I can get extended time for my exams and finals if required."

"How does that help?"

"Sometimes having an exact time frame messes with my ADHD. Instead of concentrating, like everyone else, my mind wants to wander and push my body into overdrive and movement. With the extra time, I can do my best to relax and focus. If it's a bad day, I'm allowed to have a private room."

"Has it been helping?"

"For the last few courses, yes. I'm grateful for that bit of help. Most of my classes can be taken online, especially anything outside of the nursing degree. Guess it's something about the materials that you need to be in a classroom to understand. I don't know. I ended up not needing the extra time for these last two classes, since I understood and recalled the information."

"What made you interested in returning to school?"

"I'm tired of leaving my patients at the ER doors and walking away. I want to go beyond the initiation of a crisis. Being a nurse, I can continue to care for a patient."

"Sounds like a wonderful plan."

"One I'm hoping to put into action soon."

"Would you continue to work in Breeze?"

"If there's a position at the clinic with Doc Elliott, that would be my dream job. I know the area, the people and the clinic. Doc Elliott mentioned he wanted to have me on his ER team." Xavier shrugged. "That's my hope."

* * * *

After snagging a space in the parking garage, Xavier figured they'd gotten a bit of luck. "Sorry about the walk. We're over by the Plaza Ferdinand."

"Don't mind the walk. It's pretty nice outside."

"How's the ankle?"

"Healing. Twinges if I overdue things, but for the most part, it's fine."

"Good." Xavier headed toward Seville Square and Plaza Ferdinand VII. Then he led them down Palafox Place. He stopped and opened the door to O'Riley's Irish Pub Downtown. "We made it. Hope you like Irish food."

"Love it. I like the choice. This place is one of my favorites."

"Wonderful. Up for a pint of Guinness?"

"Yes," Gavin said.

"Great," Xavier said and went over to the hostess stand to give his name.

They didn't wait long for their table not far from the bar. When a waitress appeared, they each ordered a pint of Guinness and a glass of water. Then they took a few minutes to look through the menu while waiting for their drinks.

"I'm hankering for old-fashioned classic Irish," Gavin said.

"Which is?"

"Shepherd's pie...and they make a good one here. You?"

"Their classic burger is my favorite," Xavier said.

The waitress dropped off their drinks and took their orders.

Their easy conversation from the car continued across the table.

Until one of the stations on a television disrupted a baseball game with a severe tropical weather update. Some of the patrons grumbled about the interruption. One of the meteorologists appeared on the screen. The report broke through the low hum of conversation and noise around the bar.

"Please excuse our interruption for this severe tropical weather update. We'll return to the scheduled baseball game in progress. We're keeping a close eye on Tropical Depression 88," the meteorologist said. He pointed out how the massive depression swirled north of Haiti and the Dominican Republic while continuing its westward trek through the Caribbean Sea and toward the Gulf of Mexico. *"All the models expect the depression to reach tropical storm status within the next couple of days. It could potentially be a powerful hurricane with the name Katia. Some models are pulling the storm toward the Florida coast."*

After the update, something typical during the hurricane season, the television flipped back to the baseball game in progress.

"Looks like the season is heating up...again," Xavier said.

"I mentioned the same thing to Samuel and Dakota since I'm trying to get them to agree on a wedding date. Dakota said most of the activity is next month. How do the storms alter your EMT schedule?"

"It increases them, obviously. We're first responders, so we're on call twenty-four seven. If evacuations are announced, we'll be one of the last groups to leave Breeze."

"What happens when they don't impact our area?"

"If there's a need for volunteers, I'll go whenever I can leave. I volunteered for a few weeks in New Orleans after Katrina. I spent time in Houston after

Harvey. Then I went to the harder hit areas of Florida after Irma. If someone needs help, I pack up and go." Xavier paused and nodded when the waitress placed their dinners down. "Thanks. Appreciate it. Smells delicious."

"Enjoy, gentlemen. Do you need a refill on your pints?" she asked.

"Gavin?" Xavier asked.

Gavin shook his head. "Oh, no, one is good enough for me. Thanks."

"Same here. I'm driving," Xavier said. "Could we exchange them for glasses of iced tea?"

"Of course. Enjoy, then. I'll check in on you later," she said and cleared their empty glasses. Then she went off to assist another table. She returned with two glasses of iced tea.

They dug into their meals with a hungry need to fill their empty bellies.

"Mm-m. This is so good," Gavin said after a few bites. "Do you volunteer to help for other natural disasters?"

"Sure. It's not always about the disaster itself but the remnants and chaos left behind. I've helped out with everything from twisters to floods, to forest fires and anything else that crops up."

"I know you love being an EMT, but why?"

"It's who I am and what I love. Another reason I want my degree is to be able to go beyond the basic EMT level of help. I can jump in and volunteer more as a trained RN."

"But your base would always be Breeze?"

"If possible, yes. I love the town. It's home."

Gavin smiled at the answer. He sipped at the tea, though he had to admit the Charm's tea was better.

While they finished dinner, Gavin's phone buzzed from his pocket. "I'm sorry. Do you mind?" he asked when he pulled out the phone. "It's a call from Samuel. Oh no, it could be about Dorian and his mom."

"Answer it. I don't mind. We know mine can go off at any time and mess up plans," Xavier said.

Gavin answered the call. "Hey, Samuel, what's happening?" He listened and curled a hand against his mouth. His eyes widened and misted with glistening tears. "Dorian's home? Oh, wow, he got a good flight. Okay. Okay. Yes, I'm in Pensacola now. Yes, on a date with Gray, like I told you yesterday." He glanced over to Xavier. "Where's Dorian and — Oh, the clinic." He glanced back to Xavier.

"I'll take you there now, but it'll take some time to get across the bridge," Xavier said and waved to the waitress to get her attention.

"We'll be on our way shortly and meet you at the clinic. Give Dorian a hug. Okay. Bye," Gavin said and hung up. He offered a partial smile to Xavier. "Thank you. I'm sorry to cut things short."

Xavier shook his head. "Don't worry. May I ask what is happening? Norman mentioned that one of our teams went on a run to her home. I didn't hear anything further about her condition."

"From what I've learned, Dorian's mom, Penelope, slipped into a coma sometime yesterday. I'm not sure about the timing. From what Dakota and Reece shared, Doc Elliott explained she's in the end stage of her disease and recommended her transfer to a hospice. She's not responding to treatment. Reece got in touch with Dorian at his culinary school to help set up a medical leave from his classes and fly him home. They worked on it all day, and I guess it worked. Sully and

Mal picked him up from the airport and took him straight to the clinic to see Penelope and speak with Doc Elliott. I'm sure Reece is there, as his guardian, to help him figure out their choices." Gavin dragged his fingers through his hair. "Losing her will devastate him."

"Dorian is a strong young man with an entire family supporting him. I met Penelope during a couple of runs. All of us know about her illness." Xavier accepted the black booklet and slipped enough cash to cover their bill and tip. "Okay. Let's get back to the truck and over the bridge. They'll be waiting."

"Thanks, Xavier. Oh, I was going to help—"

"I got the bill covered tonight. Next time—"

"You sure?"

"Yes. We need to go."

Gavin rose from his chair and accepted Xavier's comforting embrace.

It wasn't how he wanted to end their date, but Xavier wouldn't let Gavin face things alone at the clinic.

* * * *

The situation became emotional from the moment they stepped into the clinic. There they found Samuel and Dakota pacing the waiting area.

"Samuel, Dakota," Gavin said when they entered.

Xavier fell back when Samuel embraced Gavin upon their arrival.

"Hey, you made good time across the bridge. Everyone else is upstairs in the ICU waiting area," Samuel said. "We wanted to wait for you."

"Hey, Gray, sorry about disturbing your date," Dakota said and offered his hand.

Xavier shook hands. "It's okay. We'd finished dinner when Samuel called. I planned on meandering around Palafox Street to keep our night going and walk off our meal but left it all open. Should I leave Gavin with you?"

"No, please don't go," Gavin said and held out his hand. "Stay?"

"Of course." Xavier took Gavin's hand.

Samuel smiled behind Gavin's back.

Xavier noticed Samuel's response to Gavin's request but didn't say anything. Instead, he followed everyone else to the elevator up to the ICU.

It intrigued him how the Charm family circled around one another to protect them. Even though he was a newcomer, they treated Gavin like family and had brought him into that special inner circle. While Xavier had his own EMT family, he wondered what it would feel like to be part of the Charm circle.

When they reached the waiting area, Dorian walked down the hallway from his mother's room. Doc Elliott joined him. Exhausted with dark circles under his eyes, Dorian smiled and greeted everyone with an embrace. "Hey, Gavin, thanks for coming." He went to hug Gavin but paused for a second at Xavier's presence in their tight little family. "Gray?"

"The EMT, yes," Xavier said. "I'm sorry to hear about your mom."

Dorian glanced from Xavier to Gavin to their joined hands. He repeated the movement until he raised an eyebrow toward Gavin.

"We were on a date when Samuel called," Gavin said.

"Wait! Do you mean you stopped your date to run to my side? What the hell? Man, you should have enjoyed your night out. There's nothing you two can do here. It's a waiting game—and not the best kind," Dorian said. "I've been too crammed with classes, an internship and work to even think about a date. Mom wouldn't want me to rush away from a date to sit by her bedside. She'd want the same for you two."

Gavin smiled while Xavier chuckled.

"Don't worry about it. We both wanted to be here," Xavier said.

Doc Elliott stopped and cleared his throat. "Hello, everyone, Dorian and Reece agreed to share the news about Penelope."

"What's happening?" Dakota asked while he wrapped his arms around Samuel.

Doc Elliott glanced at Dorian.

"Mom isn't going to come out of the coma. I understand this and can't slip into childish hopes and dreams for a miracle—" Dorian paused when his voice thickened with tears.

Reece and Mal stepped over to rub his back.

"I...umm..."

"Take your time," Reece murmured.

Nodding, Dorian pulled in a breath.

Gavin leaned again Xavier while they waited him out. Xavier wrapped an arm around Gavin's waist.

"I agreed with Doc Elliott, the neurologist and Reece. Mom will be moved to a hospice. The closest one with a bed is in Pensacola, which makes visiting or staying difficult, but we'll figure it out." Dorian rubbed the back of his neck. "Mom has a signed DNR. She fought for so long..." His voice thickened again. "We suspect she won't have long. She's not responding to the medication for her pneumonia."

"How long do you think?" Samuel asked.

"A couple of weeks. Maybe less," Doc Elliott said while he placed a hand on Dorian's shoulder. "No matter what. We'll keep her comfortable until the end."

"She fought against MS for so long. To be taken out by pneumonia..." Dorian's words drifted off.

"Dorian—" Reece murmured. "It'll be okay. She made her decision."

"You're right, Reece. It's her time. I understand. I do," Dorian said, "but I need to help my heart understand."

"Whatever you need from us, you'll have it," Dakota said. "I believe I speak for everyone."

The others nodded their agreement.

"Thank you, everyone. I love all of you," Dorian said.

The group took turns saying their goodbyes to Dorian. Most of them then slipped into Penelope's room for a kiss and whispered a few words. No one planned on leaving Dorian alone, either here at the clinic or the hospice.

"Lemme say goodbye," Gavin said to Xavier.

"Of course. Take your time."

"You can—"

"No, I'll take you home. You shouldn't be alone," Xavier insisted. He nodded to other members of the Charm family.

Gavin squeezed his hand and went over to where Dorian stood with Doc Elliott, Reece and Mal. He listened when Dorian insisted everyone head home. He planned to stay at the clinic for a little longer then would go to Reece and Mal's home for some sleep.

"Dorian?" Gavin said.

Dorian turned and said, "Thank you for coming, even if it disturbed your date. Don't let it happen again." He winked at Gray and hugged Gavin. "Where's Victor?"

"I wouldn't want to be anywhere else, you silly goofball," Gavin said and shrugged. "I'm not sure what he's doing. Should I have him call you?"

Dorian nodded. "Wouldn't mind talking to him."

"I know he misses having you around."

"I miss him, too. Could you ask him, though? I don't want to… With Mom and all…"

"I mentioned to him what happened, but he didn't say much. I'll check with him again, explain what is happening and let him make the decision," Gavin said and hugged him again. "Take care of yourself."

"I will. Promise."

With those words, Gavin returned to Xavier's side. "Okay. Good to go."

"This isn't how I thought things would end up for our date," Xavier said while leading Gavin out of the clinic and back to his truck.

"Yeah, same here."

"Would you like me to stick around? Nothing…sexual, I promise. I don't think either of us is up for sexy stuff. I can be a good snuggle buddy, though. Watch a marathon on Netflix. I keep a change of clothes in my truck and could use them tonight."

"I would like that. I don't want to be alone."

"I don't want to leave you alone," Xavier said and turned on the truck's engine. He drove the short distance to Gavin's home. After he parked, he pulled a duffel bag from the backseat. "At least I don't need to bring in my books."

"Which means I get all your attention. It's different from knowing it was going to happen and physically facing the inevitable. Her life is going to end soon.

Days. Not weeks. Months. Days. I don't know her as well as the others, but she's a sweet lady. So kind and giving, so proud of her son."

"That's the way she has always been, before the MS stripped away her strength and freedom. It couldn't touch her heart or her mind, though. I've known her as a paramedic but also outside of calls." Xavier studied him. "There's no magical cure or treatment."

"I know. Mentally, I know. Emotionally?"

"It'll take time for the news to settle, which is why I don't want to leave you alone," Xavier said.

"How about we head on in?"

"Sounds like a plan." Xavier pulled the keys and climbed out of the truck. Walking around, he opened Gavin's door, since it was a being a touch sticky.

The door creaked and groaned.

"Hmm. Needs a spray of oil on it...perhaps something more." Holding up a free hand, he helped Gavin climb down from the truck's cab.

"Always something with good old trucks," Gavin said.

"Always." Xavier locked up with a key.

Then he followed Gavin to the front door where Gavin used his key to enter then stepped farther inside to press a code into his security system. After Xavier closed and locked the door, Gavin reset the alarm.

"If you need to go out for any reason, hit this button to deactivate the alarm and this one to set it again," Gavin said. "Otherwise, it'll start screaming, my alarm company will call to verify and contact the police and fire if needed."

"And we definitely don't want that."

"Nope. Don't want to disturb Sheriff Robin and his deputies for nothing." Gavin flicked on a few lights. "Welcome to my home."

The house was warm and friendly, with wooden floors with an open floor plan. Nothing fancy or overwhelming, cool colors on accent walls. The furniture was dark, either gray or black-brown, with clean, simple lines that Ikea was known for. Nothing fancy, but a beginner's basic. Simple silver and blue accents complemented the dark colors. The kitchen had granite countertops with high-end stainless-steel appliances and rich cabinets that were dark on the bottom and a complementary lighter color on top.

"Do you like to cook?"

"Yes, I love to cook and bake. I don't have as much time now, and I have Dakota and Malcolm offering breakfast and often sending me home with meals. So, I'm being…"

"Spoiled."

"Yes…*so* spoiled."

While Gavin led Xavier around to reveal the layout and upstairs where the different rooms were, his phone rang. Pulling it out, Gavin frowned and silenced the device. After a few minutes, the phone rang again…three times then silence. Then it repeated the rings and Gavin the hang-ups. By the third time, Gavin rubbed his temples.

Xavier dropped his bags on an armchair. Then he cupped a hand around Gavin's arm and led him to the sofa. After helping him sit down, he removed Gavin's bow tie and laid the strip on the coffee table. A couple of pats, he pulled out the wallet and phone. Then he placed the wallet on the table and held out the phone. He settled on the cushion next to Gavin.

Gavin stared at the phone.

"Gavin, please, that was a strange set of calls."

"Work phone. Cell phone. Doesn't matter. Can't change it. Can't block all of them."

"Is it spam calls?"

Gavin shook his head.

"Robocalls?"

Gavin shook his head again.

Xavier flipped the cell phone between his fingers. "Then who is it? Do you know who it is?"

Gavin lifted his gaze to find Xavier. Fear shone in the baby-blue color.

"Gavin? Talk to me."

"Atlanta. The calls are from Atlanta," Gavin finally said.

"Where you used to live and work."

"I didn't leave on the best of terms. My boss resented me leaving and starting my own company, even if it was out of state. I tried to smooth things out, but there were issues."

"Is that who is calling you? Harassing you?"

Another negative shake.

"Then who?"

"My ex. A co-worker. I made the mistake to get involved with someone I worked with, and my position grew while his sank. Clients requested me for their events. Even when they were assigned to my ex, within weeks—even days—the clients called and demanded to be moved to another coordinator. Most of them brought up my name, again and again." Gavin clasped his hands and rubbed them together. "He hated it. Yelled at me. Argued. Screamed. Hollered."

"Did he hit you?"

"Eventually, yes. Always in the privacy of our home and never in places that would show. Still there was domestic abuse. I can admit that now."

Xavier cursed under his breath.

"It took six months, but I managed to quietly pull my stuff out of the shared condo and into storage. I shuffled my finances so he wouldn't realize I was saving more than giving him. Then I got the chance to leave, left my key and drove away. Thanks to a friend, I rented a small apartment on a short-term lease on the opposite side of the city."

"But you still had to go in and work with him."

"Every single day. I made sure if he confronted me, it was in front of others, and I was never alone with him. I made sure that he and everyone else knew that I'd left and wasn't planning on going back. It was an extremely tense time."

"I bet. When did the calls start?"

"Within days of my leaving. He knows I wouldn't change my cell phone because my clients needed access to me during their events."

"Even speaking to him and HR?"

"HR was little to no help. They documented it, but unless it changed to a physical event..." Gavin shook his head. "Same with the cops. I couldn't put in a restraining order because we were in the same office, and it would reveal my home address to him. There wasn't enough of a basis, according to one of the officers after I explained the situation."

"There should be levels put in place for domestic violence..."

"But it doesn't always work the way it is proposed."

"Messed up shit," Xavier said and shook his head. "I'm sorry if the system failed you."

"Me, too, but it works for those who are in more physical trouble than I was. My ex kept it mostly verbal and mental but went to physical at rare times. Not at the level where I was scared for my life."

"Yet. Not yet."

"No. Not yet. I don't know what degree he could be pushed to."

Xavier rubbed his hand over Gavin's closest knee. "How did you end up here?"

"Within those last six-to-nine months and a friend's encouragement to get out, I found the advertisement for an event coordinator to create a new company within the Southern Charm B&B. I worked up my resume, showed it to one of my clients who was in HR, saw several of them for advice and changes then submitted it."

"How did you get away?"

"Used the excuse of meeting a potential high-end exclusive client in Miami. Instead, I got a flight to Pensacola, rented a car and drove here to interview with Samuel, Dakota and Chandler. As soon as I walked in, I could envision everything they mentioned happening within the elegant setting and the potential for something bigger. Within a week, I got the offer and accepted immediately. My dream was coming true. I had a way out, and I could be safe. I just had to figure out how to leave." Gavin rubbed his face with one hand. "Somehow, Samuel could hear the stress and worry in my voice without me telling him what was happening. He assisted me with ending the lease and moving expenses after I gave my old company the official notice. I had to get through that time of completing the immediate events, transfer my clients to a new coordinator, dealt with whatever shit my ex threw at me and changed my entire life. On orders from my boss, I couldn't tell the other coordinators that I was leaving, only training a new person. Hiding secrets and lies didn't help the situation, but I couldn't stop my boss from trying to give me new assignments, even though I was leaving."

"In a few months, you came here and..."

"The calls continued. The rings. The hang-ups. Sometimes a nasty voicemail. Emails. I couldn't hide my presence on the Internet or my contact information. That had to be out there to promote Charmed Occasions and for me to do my job. He used it to his advantage to locate and harass me."

"Does he know this address?"

"I don't think so. I don't know if he understands how to search property records in a different state. At the Charm..."

"It's out there on the Internet. But there, you're not alone."

"No. After the first series of calls, I finally sat down with Samuel and Dakota and explained about my ex harassing me with calls and emails. I wouldn't let it affect my ability to do my job and that I've tried to find ways to make it stop but I'm unable to do so."

"I wonder if Sheriff Robin could figure out some way to help."

"It would be the same answer — and now there is the issue of states."

"Robin goes deeper and further than other officers. It's what helped him achieve his position and multiple elections. Domestic violence, especially among the LGBT community, is one of his strongest points to fight against, to protect the survivors and properly prosecute the abusers before it escalates to death."

"Really?"

Xavier nodded. "Whenever any one of the EMTs comes across a domestic violence call, we quietly alert the sheriff's station. They'll begin an investigation, but most of the time they must wait for the victim to make it official. Still, they'll keep an eye on reported addresses." He tightened his grip for a moment on Gavin's knee and released it. "Nothing is wasted or lost if you speak with someone. Perhaps they could give you options — since what you're doing isn't working, and he refuses to stop."

"He can't stop."

"Because there's no incentive or threat to make him stop. He still has his position at the company, the home you left and can do whatever he wants. That's how he sees it. And you left him."

"Without his permission or knowledge."

"Twice."

Letting out a groan, Gavin dropped his head in his hands.

"Shit. I'm sorry. I didn't want to make things worse this evening." Xavier placed the phone on the table. Then he gathered Gavin into his arms and leaned back to snuggle the man.

"No, it's good to get it out, to share the truth with someone," Gavin said. He toed off his boots and picked his feet up and off to the side.

Xavier held him close, offering quiet support.

"Thank you…for everything," Gavin said.

"Anytime. I'm just offering a different perspective and choices."

Gavin smiled. "I suggest we take showers, change into something comfortable and binge-watch something on TV for the rest of the night."

"Good plan."

"You can take over the guest room and bathroom. We can take showers at the same time."

"Okay," Xavier said while he rose with Gavin and gathered up his overnight bag.

Gavin grabbed his bow tie and suede boots. Then he led Xavier back upstairs and pointed out the bedroom and bathroom. He disappeared into the main bedroom.

Xavier watched him go into the room but not completely close the door.

There wasn't any tension between them — nothing sexual or any craving for more — just a simple need for companionship.

Sometimes Xavier craved that more than a night of okay sex with someone handy.

To his surprise, his ADHD and OCD were quiet. Neither one was humming in his brain, nagging him to do something, change something or pushing him. It was a quiet relief.

Smiling, he went into the room to shower and change into comfortable clothes.

Within a half-hour, he wandered back downstairs and saw Gavin on the sofa with a remote in hand. A bowl of fresh-popped popcorn and two glasses of water were on the table. The glasses were even on coasters.

"Is this okay?"

"Perfect."

"I was watching *Lucifer* on Netflix."

"I can watch that handsome devil charm his way through LA," Xavier said while he dropped next to Gavin. He tugged Gavin down to curl back against him.

Gavin started the next episode. Then he pulled the bowl closer while it started.

Throughout the rest of the night, it was comforting to be with another person.

Chapter Twelve

Gavin couldn't forget all that had gone on with Xavier. He didn't know what was happening between them. Could things work between their crazy schedules? Of course it would take more dates and time together to know.

An early call had woken them up. Xavier mentioned something about leaving for an extended shift to cover for another EMT who was down with some nasty virus that was going around. The symptoms didn't sound pleasant. Xavier had left with promises to text, plan another date night and gave him a kiss on the lips that curled Gavin's toes.

After Xavier had gone, Gavin pushed his body through a grueling Peloton bike routine. He'd taken time off to let his ankle heal, but now he wanted to get back into the morning workout. While he pedaled and fought his way through the climbs, his mind wandered, since he couldn't focus on the schedule. The upcoming weekend was quiet.

Exhausted and sweating, he dragged himself off the bike and into a shower. Memories of Xavier stimulated him but not enough for a full erection. The beginning tendrils of a romantic relationship were there, and it stirred his sexual response. Since his broken relationships in Atlanta, he'd learned how important a close relationship was when it came to his sexual needs. It was frustrating, but he let himself go through the motions. After the horrible lessons and truth he'd learned from Maury, he wouldn't force himself into anything sexual and end up with pain and heartbreak. No orgasm was worth that shit.

Dressing and picking out the day's bow tie and suspender combination, he double-checked his reflection. Knowing he looked good and wondering if he would get a smile or whistle from Xavier, Gavin shook his head.

"Get your head out of the clouds."

Gathering his belongings into his messenger bag, Gavin drove to the Charm. A lingering smile remained. Starving, he went to the simple buffet set for the few guests and other morning visitors. Multiple members of the Charm family were gathered around a table.

This was the first time he'd seen everyone since their late-night gathering at the clinic to support Dorian and Penelope.

"Morning, everyone," Gavin said while he stopped by a chair. He lowered his bag next to it.

Samuel and Dakota looked up from their conversation first. Samuel smiled over his cup of coffee.

"Hello, Gavin. What's got you in such a good mood?" Mal asked.

"Could it have something to do with a certain EMT spending the night?" Sully teased while he leaned back. He slung one arm along the back of Chandler's chair.

"Leave him be, Sully." Chandler nudged an elbow straight into Sully's side. Then he pointed to the silver carafe of coffee. "Would you like some coffee?"

"Nothing happened. We...curled up on the sofa. That's it," Gavin admitted. "Still, it was wonderful to have someone there. He left this morning to cover a shift." He nodded to Chandler. "Yes, coffee would be wonderful. I'm going to get something to eat." With those words, he walked off to fill a plate. Then he settled and accepted the cup from Chandler.

"Are you going out with him again?" Mal asked.

"I hope so. I would like to. Our schedules are crazy, but it's probable," Gavin said. "Where's Reece?"

"Watching over Dorian back home. I left to help get the morning's buffet finished, but I'll stay with him later when Reece has to oversee some clients and projects this afternoon," Mal said. "I didn't see anything on the books for this weekend. Am I right?"

Gavin paused in his eating. He flipped open the bag's top, pulled out his tablet and opened it to the calendar program. "You're correct."

"We can't have a crazy weekend every single time," Samuel said.

"Can I open the entire restaurant all weekend?" Dakota asked.

"Yes. The restaurant is all yours."

"That's rare. What about next weekend?"

"The wedding happens Saturday morning in the gazebo and on the beach. The reception is on the porches and scheduled to end around one-ish.

So…with clean-up and reset for the restaurant, I'd say, yes.

"Two rare weekends for me," Dakota said. "How does that happen?"

"Sometimes you get lucky," Gavin teased him.

"Wait! We don't have that weekend free," Samuel said.

"What? Why not?" Dakota asked.

"Gavin, did you forget?" Samuel asked.

"Forget what—" Gavin flipped through his planner. "Oh, shit! The Expo!"

"Oh, damn, we gotta leave on Thursday with Victor, don't we?" Dakota said.

Samuel nodded. "To cover the table until Gavin arrives after the wedding. We arranged all this after realizing the double-booking."

"Crap. No second full weekend for me. The restaurant might have to close," Dakota muttered.

Samuel nudged Dakota's side. "Chill. As soon as Sully and his crew finishes the reception building, you'll have your precious restaurant all to yourself. Right, Sully?"

"Hmm?" Sully looked up with a mouth full of bacon.

"Really, Sully?" Chandler scolded him.

"Sorry. Good stuff," Sully said after he chewed and swallowed the mouthful.

"The reception building?" Samuel asked.

"We're getting close. Another few weeks if the weather holds and we run into no complications…sometime in late September. You'll have it for all the holiday events," Sully said.

"Can't wait to get my hands on the place. Speaking of events—" Gavin pointed his fork at Samuel and

Dakota. "Let's get around to your wedding. I need a wedding date—a firm one, something more than 'a September weekend'. Then we can move forward. I have no theme, colors, flowers and not even a menu. Come on, fellas. Something has to give if you want to marry this year."

Samuel poked Dakota in his side. "Well? You're the one who said September."

"Don't know..." Dakota mumbled. His eyes widened when he looked away. "Hey, Ray, turn up the television."

Everyone turned to the television that was set up in the corner during the mornings for news breaks. One of the young waiters, Ray, reached for the clicker and turned up the volume when the tropical weather update broke.

The most recent update didn't appear promising. The depression had become Tropical Storm Katia, while pressure continued to fall and the wind speed increased. A clear eye had defined itself overnight. Hurricane hunters had flown into the storm and predicted it would continue to increase in strength, size and winds until it reached hurricane status. The storm was six hundred miles east of the Leeward Islands and moving along a westerly track. The current models kept the tracks north of Cuba, but it could shift. Everyone in Florida and the Gulf Coast region was encouraged to keep a close eye on the storm, because future tracks maintained a course across or around the peninsula.

"Okay, umm, perhaps there could be a slight delay?" Sully said. "Guess Mother Nature wasn't finished with sending us Hurricane Irma, so she wanted to give Florida a little extra."

"Not funny," Chandler said.

Sully rubbed Chandler's back.

No one enjoyed the crazy hurricane experience Irma had given them.

"I can adjust any plans. This doesn't have to change anything," Gavin said.

Dakota pointed to the television. "What the hell about the storm? That changes everything. We should change the date to October. That way we'll avoid the height of hurricane season, and you'll still get the autumn feeling you want."

"Really? That's your answer. Delay the wedding...again." Samuel slapped down his napkin and glared at Dakota. "What the hell does it matter? It's been two years since the proposal. Fine." He pushed to his feet. "Perhaps you should call it all off. Why marry me at all? I don't think you give a shit." Then he glanced around the table and dropped his gaze. "Excuse me." He stormed out.

"Oh, shit," Dakota muttered. He scrambled to follow Samuel. "Samuel! Wait!"

"Holy Moses!" Mal's mouth dropped open.

"Samuel is pissed. I've never seen him this bad. This isn't going to blow over easy," Chandler said.

"Did I screw it up?" Gavin looked around the table.

Chandler shook his head. "No. This confrontation has brewed for a while between them. You helped it erupt. They needed to release this pressure and face the problems."

"What should I do?"

"Give them a few minutes alone. Then I suggest you take them back to their home. They'll be more comfortable there and will talk, I hope," Chandler said. "Go with the suggestion of an October wedding. The invitations weren't sent, so you have the flexibility. Some of Dakota's siblings will be there—same with some of Samuel's family. The attendees will be us, our employees and folks from Breeze."

"I agree with Chandler. It'll be a good way to smooth things over and help open up Dakota," Sully said. "His family life was crap, and he holds what happened in a sealed jar. He needs to crack it open before he can settle on anything with Samuel."

"Sounds like I have my work cut out for me."

"You do, but it'll help them. This could be just what they need, and you're the perfect one to crack the seal."

Gavin wrapped his fingers around the coffee cup while he turned over the situation and words in his mind.

* * * *

Taking Chandler's advice, Gavin first went to his office, checked his emails and settled a few disputes. Then he calmed down a few upcoming couples regarding the weather and assured them that he kept a close eye on reports. Their precious day would be saved or moved, but nothing would be ruined.

Since there were no weddings or events happening, Gavin realized he wouldn't see Victor. He called Victor and explained everything about Dorian and Penelope. He relayed Dorian's request to see Victor if he wanted. He mentioned they could do a full clean-up and inventory this weekend since nothing else would be happening.

Finishing the conversation, Gavin gathered his bag and headed to Samuel's office. He knocked on the closed door and entered at Samuel's soft call. Samuel sat stiff behind the desk.

Perched on the corner, Dakota shifted to speak to Gavin. "Now isn't a good time, Gavin. Samuel and I need to—"

"I'm sorry, but I believe now would be the perfect time," Gavin interrupted. "Perhaps we could go to your home and talk through everything. Mal and Chandler can manage things here. There is nothing else keeping me on site other than helping the both of you. My whole attention and concern are about you." He glanced between them. "Please let me help."

"Samuel?" Dakota asked his partner.

Samuel nodded and stood.

"Okay. Guess we're going home," Dakota said.

"Thank you," Gavin said.

Following the couple across the short path, he studied the renovated owner's home perched on stilts to avoid any potential floods or surges. Sully had worked on the house during the Charm's renovation. Gavin adored the home that suited the couple.

Inside the living room, Gavin settled in an armchair while Dakota sat on the sofa.

Samuel returned from the kitchen with a pitcher of the Charm's famous iced tea and glasses. After he placed the tray on the coffee table, Samuel sat on the sofa, but kept a cushion between them.

"Really?" Dakota said.

"Don't push me. I'm really upset with you, Dakota." Samuel opened and clenched one hand on the armrest in a rhythmic fashion that revealed his inner turmoil and emotions.

"Sam—"

"Dakota, no. Hold up a minute," Gavin said.

Dakota dropped his head back.

To give everyone time, Gavin placed his tablet, a thin binder and a pen on the coffee table. Instead of opening the binder and getting right to work, he studied the couple. "Okay. Do you want to tell me what is happening? What set all this off? Is there a problem with having a wedding? We don't need one. You can go in front of a judge, say a few words, sign a piece of paper and it's done. We'll have a party. Is that it?"

Leaning forward, Dakota rubbed his hands between his knees. "There's more to it than a wedding or party or anything."

"What is it then, Dakota?"

"The problem with the commitment remains squarely with me—in my hands and mind," Dakota said.

Gavin tapped his fingers on the armrest. *How do I go forward with this?*

"*Why?*" Samuel's voice cracked with emotion. He continued to plead to Dakota, "Why? Why are you doing this? Is it *me*? Did I do something wrong?"

"No. No, baby." Dakota shifted his position to face Samuel. He reached across the cushion to touch Samuel's hand. "My delays and avoidance don't have anything to do with you, Samuel. Nothing with you. You *are* my heart, my life and my love." He lifted his gaze to lock onto Samuel's gaze. "I love you with everything inside me, Samuel Ashford. The happiest and proudest moment of my life was when you said yes to my proposal."

"Then explain to me why you are doing this to us?" Samuel moved his hand away from Dakota, apparently not willing to touch him until he learned everything. "Tell me. Tell us. Get this pressure or darkness off your back. Our wedding could become our new start, our step into the future without the pull of the past. I can't help you if you don't tell me anything. Is it...your family? You never talk about it and freeze whenever I mentioned meeting anyone beyond your brother, Cal."

"It's all about my family and past. It wasn't the best." Dakota sighed and rubbed his hands again. "I'm wary of committing to anything. The story about my parents is a complete lie — something I created to avoid telling the truth." He held up a hand before either of them could ask questions. "Let me get through this. My parents were leftovers of the sixties. They were restless, rootless and dropped out of college. They experimented with LSD, marijuana and alcohol. No matter the difficulties, they remained together, travelling the country in a modified RV where they birthed and raised six kids. Since they barely bothered to watch my sister Carolina and me, we ended up taking over the positions as parents by the fourth kid. In between minimum-pay and cash jobs, my father lost himself either in a cannabis high or in a bottle. My mother chose to spend her time in multiple forms of arts and crafts, sometimes selling them to raise a few dollars. She enjoyed a cannabis smoke or brownie since she swore it opened her 'third eye' and made magic in her art. It was all bullshit. In worst cases, I stole the government checks to cash them for food and supplies before my parents could spend it."

Samuel gasped.

Dakota pushed forward in the story. "When I was old enough, I got a job whenever I could to help Carolina make ends meet. While we weren't physically abused, we were mistreated, malnourished and mostly abandoned." His hands shook. "In the end, we all left our parents at the earliest possible moment. My two youngest siblings escaped to Carolina's home instead of being left alone with our parents — though it took some work on Carolina's part to get Cal out, because he's the youngest. While we bounced around between jobs and tried to figure out how to live a regular life, we all put down roots. Only Cal remains a bit restless with his music."

"Oh my God, Dakota." Samuel shifted across the cushion to embrace Dakota.

"What about your parents now?" Gavin asked.

"I don't talk to them anymore," Dakota admitted. "After all the shit they pulled with us kids, I haven't forgiven them for screwing around with our lives. The last thing Carolina told me was they settled on a cannabis farm in Colorado. Dad grew cannabis to sell to local stores while Mom used the hemp to make her 'crafts'. They traded the RV for a manufactured home but remained off the grid."

"Jeez, Dakota, why didn't you tell me any of this?" Samuel asked.

"I never wanted to face what happened to me as a kid. It's the total opposite of how you grew up."

"In wealth and privilege, yes, but we were ignored in our own way," Samuel said. "Our father left us to nannies and private schools. Our mother gave us attention, but it wasn't a typical family. Only when we became useful did we get attention."

"You never said that."

"Like you, I didn't want to admit my family isn't perfect. No one has the perfect family situation." Samuel rubbed Dakota's shoulder. "We both came from rough backgrounds. Somehow, we've managed to find each other. Our love is strong, and it belongs to us." He captured one of Dakota's hands and held it tight. "A wedding will show our love is strong. We'll share it with our friends and family—the family we built around us, around the Charm."

"You were always the smooth talker," Dakota said.

Samuel chuckled. "Babe, we can forget your parents. You want to see your siblings. Right?"

"Yes, I want my brothers and sisters there. Two sisters are married and the youngest is engaged. Del and Cal are still single."

"That's okay. We can invite all of them. There's enough room at the Charm for our families. Most of the other guests are local, so they don't need rooms."

"That helps."

"Exactly. The rest we leave up to Gavin." Samuel glanced over at Gavin and winked.

"What? No. That's not how that works," Gavin said.

Dakota chuckled. "What do you need from us?"

"Do you want to go forward with planning your wedding?"

Both men nodded.

"Due to the growing issues with the weather and the late start of planning, I agree with Dakota's off-hand decision to move the wedding to October." Gavin opened the tablet to the calendar. He flipped it around to show them. "The first weekend of October is wide open. There are no reservations at the Charm."

"I know it's not our original plan," Dakota said.

"No, no, I agree. Let's go for Saturday, October sixth. I hope it'll be better weather. I enjoy fall," Samuel said.

"That should be the theme. 'Fall at the Beach'."

"Good. Deep golden shades plus the rich reds and dark greens against the pale sand and beautiful ocean. I like it." Samuel looked at Gavin.

"This is awesome," Gavin said while he scribbled notes. He passed over some paper and pens to each man. "Write down a list of family guests. We'll figure out the locals later."

Both men jotted down names.

"I want a small wedding on the beach. Simple. Our selective family members, the Charm family and other local friends," Samuel said.

"Then we'll have a large reception where we can open the restaurant and all the porches," Dakota said.

"What?" Gavin asked.

"A large reception where anyone else could attend and celebrate with us. We'll set up for one of Charm's famous BBQ dinners. Some size of a cake to feed the crowd or a cake with cupcakes — whatever Katie would prefer to create," Dakota said.

"Are you sure about that?" Samuel asked.

"Of course. We can treat the reception the same way as our big BBQ days. We'll set up a certain amount of food and once it's gone, than that's it for food. I have a few chef friends who offered to create and serve the dinner for my wedding. They wanted to gift it to us," Dakota said.

"Oh, wow, that'll be…awesome," Samuel said.

"They're some of my oldest friends before I met the guys here. They taught me things during school about how to live and survive. I wouldn't be as grounded if I didn't have them in my life."

"What's next?" Samuel asked.

Over the next couple of hours, they continued to work their way through Gavin's checklist. Based on the theme and colors, they selected the invitations, fabrics, possible flowers for Jude to pick through and create his designs and other decorations. They'd go shopping for tuxedos or suits once they settled on the numbers for the immediate wedding party. They'd go to the bakery and speak with Katie. Dakota would purchase the food and connect with his friends to cook for the BBQ.

"We'll figure out the rings," Dakota said at the end.

It was one of the easiest planning sessions Gavin had ever overseen.

It was clear to Gavin that everyone felt better with the decisions by the time they'd finished in the late afternoon.

Exhausted by the long session, Gavin packed up his things and headed home instead of returning to the Charm. He could easily enter all the information on his laptop. For now, he wanted to be home. For some reason, home called to him — a feeling like he needed to be there. It was an odd sensation, and he hoped to figure out why.

Chapter Thirteen

During the last call of his shift, Xavier heard a familiar address called over the radio of a man complaining of shortness of breath and unresponsive to his medication. Over the years, they'd visited the man multiple times. It was the home of a flirtatious older gay bear, Thomas Donaway, who had lost his partner to cancer over a year before. The friendly bear never failed to flirt with Xavier, who always played along with him, which always got Norman cracked up laughing.

"Uh-oh. That's Mr. Tommy," Norman said.

"Let's get over to him."

"You got it." Norman hit the sirens and pressed the accelerator.

"*Rig 3232, on our way,*" Xavier said over the radio. Then he tugged on a fresh pair of blue gloves.

Norman hit the brakes and parked the ambulance in front of the bright yellow cottage-style home north of Breeze's downtown area and close to the schools. Xavier remembered Mr. Tommy was a retired schoolteacher, who had taught history to the middle school students for almost thirty years. He turned off the sirens but kept on the lights.

"*Rig 3232, responding on site,*" Xavier reported on the radio. He jumped down with his go bag. He rushed up to the door with Norman following and knocked on the door. It opened under his touch.

"Must be waiting for us," Norman said.

Xavier opened the door and looked inside. The big man sat in an ancient armchair.

The man waved to them. "Get on in here, boys."

Smiling at the man, Xavier entered the house. He moved over to where the old bear rested on his cushioned throne. "Hey there, Mr. Tommy, what's happening?"

"There's my handsome tattooed man. Boy, where have you been? Been needing your help and company," Thomas said between harsh coughs that shook his barrel chest. He held a mask against his face and breathed in the oxygen. His breathing created a wheezing sound that told the paramedics he couldn't move the air. In the late stages of COPD, the man often called for assistance when his home treatments stopped working.

"You know I'm waiting for your calls, Mr. Tommy," Xavier said. "What's happening? You don't sound so good."

"Don't feel so good, boy. Oh, my lungs are giving me all kinds of trouble. Can't suck a damn thing."

Norman cracked up laughing.

With the flirting and playful bantering continuing, Xavier concentrated on gathering Tommy's vitals. When Norman returned with the stretcher, they helped get him onto it and secured him. At Tommy's insistence, they locked the door after wheeling him outside. Xavier placed the keys, wallet and cell phone in a plastic bag to remain with Tommy.

"Not much time left. Docs told me this last appointment," Tommy said while they pushed him into the back.

Norman glanced at Xavier before he secured the doors and got in behind the wheel. He clicked the radio to report, "*Rig 3232, on route to the clinic – male, sixty-two, late-stages COPD.*" He hit the lights and gas on the way.

"Mr. Tommy –"

Tommy shook his head. "Knew it was coming. I could feel it. My lungs are shot. I get to see my love, my Lyle, again…my heart. We always thought I would go first with this stupid lung issue. Didn't expect brain cancer to take my Lyle. He was brilliant. One of the finest lawyers who could sweet-talk a jury into following him wherever he wanted them to go. Damn tumor grew and never let go. Miss him so damn much. Now I'll get to be with him again where I belong…in his arms."

"Damn. Don't want you to go out like this, Mr. Tommy."

"Nothing you can do for me, tattoo-boy. You gave me some smiles and laughs, letting this old bear flirt with a pretty boy. I needed that," Tommy said while he stroked Xavier's tattooed arm.

"You're a good man, Tommy. The world will be less without you," Xavier said.

"Don't go through this world alone. Find someone to love. Promise me."

Xavier smiled and thought about Gavin.

"I know that smile. Who is he?"

"Gavin."

"Gavin who?"

"The event planner at Southern Charm. He built Charmed Occasions from scratch with Samuel and Dakota. He's..."

"Got a picture?"

"Yeah." Xavier tugged his phone from his pocket, clicked over to the gallery and the picture he'd had someone take for them after leaving the restaurant. He wanted something to help remember their first date. He turned the phone to show Mr. Tommy the photo.

"Oh, my, such a dapper fellow. I adore the bow tie and suspenders."

"That's a thing with him. A little like Nate Berkus, right?"

"Hmm. I can see the resemblance. He's adorable."

"He likes my tattoos."

"See? Perfect fit. Good choice for you, my boy. Hope it all works out. You need someone to spend your life with and don't be alone. Alone is no fun." With those words, Tommy smiled and fell quiet while he struggled to breathe.

Xavier glanced at the picture and hoped the fledgling relationship could work. He slid the phone back into his pocket.

Norman reached the clinic and killed the sirens. He raced around back and opened the doors. Together, they whisked Mr. Tommy inside.

"What do we have?" Doc Elliott said when he reached them.

Xavier snapped out all the relevant details regarding Mr. Tommy's extended case and time with them. "Hang in there, Mr. Tommy. You're in good hands with

Doc Elliott. He'll get you some relief and support. Don't give up on me."

Tommy waved to them while Doc Elliott and the nurses whisked him farther into the ER.

"Damn, that's a bad turn for Tommy. Gonna miss him," Norman said after the doors closed. "I'll take care of the gurney while you do the casework?"

"Yeah, it's real bad for him. I'll finish the chart. Give me a few minutes here."

"Sure." Norman pushed the gurney to another hallway where he'd exchanged the sheets on it for a fresh set then moved it to the ambulance.

Xavier stripped the gloves off and tossed them into the container. He opened the small laptop they carried on the rig to track all their cases. He leaned against one far end of the nurses' central desk and opened it. He searched for Mr. Tommy's name and clicked into the file, notating the call number, date and time. It didn't take him long to tap in the information and sent it to the various file managers.

"Oh, Gray, glad I caught you here," a pediatric ICU nurse said when she walked over to him. "Do you have a minute?"

"Hey, Nurse Holly, yeah, finished with the last run. Got some time. How's my young friend Adam? I found a new pony for his collection and hope to bring it to him."

Holly looked around and back to him. "Can we sit down?"

Xavier didn't like that change. "What happened?"

"It isn't good." Holly motioned him to an empty room and closed the door.

"What happened to Adam?"

"I'm so sorry. There was an unexpected turn in Adam's condition. A bleed started near the injured section. His brain swelled. Before the surgeons could take him in for surgery, the alarms went off. His little body crashed." She shook her head. "We couldn't save him. The doctors tried everything for over an hour, but we couldn't bring him back. He was gone. I'm so sorry, Gray."

Xavier dropped into a chair. He lowered his head to his hands. "No. It can't be." Tears fell from his eyes. "We didn't get him here soon enough. No one kept watch for a bleed. He was talking to me — "

"You do everything possible to get to the patient and bring them here. This was a rare occurrence." Holly crouched in front of Xavier and placed a hand on his knee. "Please listen to me, Gray. This wasn't your fault. I thought you would want to know. I'm sorry."

Xavier met Holly's gaze. "Thank you for telling me, Holly."

"I'm so sorry. You're a wonderful EMT, Gray. Remember that." Holly walked away.

"Oh, God, I'm so sorry, Adam," Xavier whispered to the sweet little boy.

It hurt like hell whenever he couldn't save someone.

The hurt increased by tenfold when the victim was an innocent child.

He felt his self-confidence in his job take a nosedive…steep. He couldn't save sweet young Adam. He couldn't save Mr. Tommy from his failing lungs. His role was to be a savior, a healer and one who fixed things, yet he couldn't save that child.

It felt like something kicked him hard down in the gut.

He exhaled a breath as the emotions hit him hard.

Why does it hurt so much?

"Hey, Gray, where—?" Norman stopped in the doorway. "Hey, there you are. Got the laptop. You left it out there. Good to go? This is our last run."

Xavier wiped his eyes and forced himself to stand. "Yeah, let's close up the shift."

"Hey, you okay?"

"Bad news."

"Wanna share?"

"Can you drive us back?"

"Yeah. Sure. No problem."

Quiet, Xavier took the laptop and followed his partner out of the clinic. They climbed into the rig and Norman drove them away.

Xavier glanced in the mirror and caught sight of the clinic.

I'm so sorry I couldn't help save you, Adam. You deserved better. Hope you're running with all the ponies in Ponyville. Say hi to Rainbow Dash and Fluttershy for me.

* * * *

Xavier went through the motions of restocking the inventory, going over the checklists and cleaning the rig.

"Hey, you doing okay? Not like you to be quiet," Norman asked.

"They lost Adam. He started bleeding in his brain and crashed...hard. He's gone."

"Shit. That's not right."

"No. No it isn't—not for a sweet boy who wanted to enjoy a summer movie with his friends." Xavier cursed under his breath. He tapped his head against the headrest. "Drive the rig back into place. I'm heading inside."

"Got it."

Grabbing the final list, Xavier forced himself to sit at his desk. He slid the list in the proper folder then he signed any necessary paperwork. He felt lost in a fog.

A choking sensation overwhelmed him when the pain and grief hit. Xavier pressed a fist against his chest. "Holy crap. What the...?" He coughed a few times and felt the odd feeling dissipate. *Why is this happening? This wasn't the first patient I've lost on the job.* He'd only known the boy for a few minutes, but they'd connected. "Back to work. Do the job. Keep moving forward." Running his hand through his hair, Xavier continued to methodically clear the paperwork. It was part of the job he needed to do. It was always the job. It ruled his life.

Finally, Xavier signed the last form. He headed for the exit of the combined fire and EMT station.

"Hey, all done?" Norman called out.

Stopping short, Xavier looked over his shoulder. "For tonight."

"Want to go out for drinks? You look like you need a break."

"Not for something like that. No. Sorry. I'm bushed. Need some sleep."

"No problem. Did you check the schedule for us?"

"Yeah, umm..." Xavier dug out his phone and checked the calendar he'd updated. "We're off tomorrow and Friday—back in on Saturday and Sunday shift."

"Right. You're all done with school."

"For a couple of weeks. Then the fall semester only has the one big nursing class with a lab."

"Right." Norman leaned against the doorway. "You're really not looking good, buddy. Sure you don't want to go out?"

"No. Not good company."

"Okay. I'm sorry about the boy's death." Norman looked at his hands then at Xavier. "It might be forward of me, but try to call Gavin."

"Gavin?"

"Talk to someone...someone who doesn't see the world like we do. He seems to be good for you," Norman said. "You're good for him."

"We're not that..."

"Don't even go there. Don't talk yourself out of a chance. Call him. If you need me for anything else, call," Norman said.

"Thanks. I'll think about it. See you Saturday."

"Bye." Norman hollered at some firemen who were coming off shift. "Yo, fellas, do you want to go out for a drink? I'm itching to get a beer in my hands. Don't want to drink alone. That's a bad country song."

The firefighters laughed and taunted Norman with all kinds of lyrics.

Xavier slipped out of the building without talking to anyone else. He climbed into the old truck. When he went to put the key into the engine, he stopped and sat back. Then he tilted his head back. His mind rambled through the tangled mess of emotions and horrible news.

"Oh, please, let go. Please. Just give me some peace and quiet."

Only his request wasn't heard. For some reason, this loss continued to hit him hard. Exhausted from the extended shift, he craved some quiet time, something decent to eat and sleep. He desired a night of undisturbed sleep.

Something stopped him from cranking the engine and driving to the apartment.

That was the main problem.

The apartment was empty — of life, of anything resembling a home...unlike Gavin's place. He'd felt comfortable the moment he'd entered Gavin's home.

Gavin.

Perhaps Norman was right. He should call Gavin.

He closed his eyes to bring up memories of his time with the man. Instead, Adam's face haunted him. The memory shifted to the accident scene and the panicked look in his young face, the pain darkening those pale-blue eyes and quiet pleas for Xavier to do something to help him, the noises of the chaotic scene and the hysterical desperate cries of the mother slammed his ears.

When he opened his eyes, he let out a long breath and shook his head. Hard.

"Damn it all to hell. I can't do this. I *can't.*"

Xavier lowered his gaze to the phone. He didn't want to go out for a drink. He didn't want to go to his empty apartment. He wanted Gavin. No, not wanted, but needed. There was a desperate need to have Gavin wrap his arms around him and blanket him against the barrage of pain.

"Please be free. Please."

Grabbing the phone, he opened the messenger app and connected to Gavin's name.

Gray: *Hey. U free?*

A couple of minutes passed.

Gavin: *Yup. Hey there. Was driving home. U?*

Gray: *Just off shift. Don't want to go to my place.*

Gavin: *Why?*

Gray: *Bad stuff. Lost someone. Brain crazy.*

Gavin: *Oh. U shouldn't be alone.*

Gavin: *Come over to mine.*

Gray: *U sure?*

Gavin: *Yup. My turn.*

Gray: *For what?*

Gavin: *Take care of u.*

Gray: *Really?*

Gavin: *I insist. Come over.*

Gray: *Thanks.*

Gavin: *Of course.*

Gray: *On my way.*

Gavin: *Drive safe.*

It was exactly what he needed to soothe his battered soul. He shoved the key in the engine and cranked it. Old Blue returned to life with a few croaks.

Xavier shifted gears and drove away.

* * * *

Parking in the driveway, Xavier climbed out of Old Blue after grabbing his duffel bag and backpack. He spun the key around his finger while he stood next to the old truck.

"Are you going to stand there all night or come inside?"

At the tender tone, Xavier felt a bit of bright energy break through the darkness and bring him hope. He looked up to see a barefoot Gavin leaning against the front doorway.

Gavin wore loose sleep pants and a T-shirt—not the prim, proper and respectable look he normally portrayed. His dark caramel hair was tousled from its normally stylish perfection.

Needing to hold that gentle warm man to push back the darkness, Xavier faltered on the first step. Then he caught his balance.

"Xavier..."

Hurrying forward, Xavier lowered his bags to the ground. Then he captured Gavin and held on to him. He buried his face between Gavin's neck and shoulder.

"Oh, Xavier," Gavin said while his arms went around Xavier to embrace him back.

A long breath escaped him when he felt Gavin's hold tightened.

"Steady. Steady yourself. I've got you now. I've got you."

When those soft, gentle words had been whispered into his ear multiple times, Xavier felt himself settle back inside his trembling body. The darkness and pain of losing that sweet boy lingered. It would always remain with him, like all the other patients he couldn't save. There would be more horrible situations he would face as a nurse and more losses he would have in between the good times.

Gavin removed his arms, only to bend and grab Xavier's bags. He returned one arm around Xavier's waist and tugged him inside. While he dealt with the locks and alarm, Xavier removed his work-boots.

"The first steps are the easiest—upstairs, shower, change into comfortable clothes then I'll get some food and water into you. After that, we can curl up and binge on a show or anything else you want to do." Gavin rubbed a hand around Xavier's back. "Sound good?"

Xavier didn't want to think about anything at this point. Part of him wanted to just follow Gavin like a zombie and not respond or react.

"We'll get you through this. I promise."

With gentle touches, Gavin led Xavier upstairs to the main bedroom. He dropped the bags on the end of his bed.

Xavier remained standing there, barely holding himself together.

Gavin cupped Xavier's face. "I need you to move, baby. You need to help yourself and push through what happened. Talk to me."

"It was the boy from the crash...the afternoon I saw you by the scene."

"The one by the movie theater?"

Xavier pulled away from Gavin's touch and sat down hard on the end of the bed. His hands dropped between his knees.

"The victim was a little boy?"

"Adam. He went to a summer movie special to see *My Little Pony* with his best friends...on his bike. His mom was getting her hair done at the salon. Crossing the street to return to where she was, he was hit by a series of cars started by one drunk driver. He—" Xavier's breath hitched. He cleared his throat and swallowed multiple times. "Adam wasn't wearing a helmet."

"You got him to the hospital. You made sure he got the help and support he needed."

"There were complications—swelling, bleeding. The surgeon and doctors tried everything. His little body crashed. He didn't come back," Xavier said.

Gavin dropped to a crouch between Xavier's legs and took hold of his hands. "This wasn't your fault. You're a wonderful paramedic and did everything you could. The fault lies with the driver who caused the accident that hurt Adam…not you."

"All he wanted was to see his favorite pony in the movie. Instead, that choice caused him—"

"No. Not *his* choice." Gavin squeezed Xavier's hands. "The *driver's* choice to drive drunk. That's what caused all this."

"I know. Mentally, I know. Physically, I know."

"Emotionally, you're all messed up because you have a wonderful big heart and care about every single patient you touch, because that is who you are. Deep down inside this strong tattooed body, you are a big teddy bear."

"A teddy bear?"

"Yeah, my tattooed teddy bear. Got a problem with that?"

Xavier shook his head. A smile tugged at one side of his mouth. No one had ever dared call him that before.

"You loved that little guy in your own fashion and cared for him while he was under your watch. You put him in the absolute best of hands. Complications happen. We can't stop them. No matter the tools, the medicines, the operations, nothing, they happen. A family is hurting. You're hurting."

"And that bastard—"

"Will face the justice of karma and the law. I'm sure the sheriff and his team are on top of the investigation. With the boy's death, it changes things."

"Yes, I know Sheriff Robin wouldn't let this one disappear without looking into everything."

Sliding his hands up Xavier's forearms, Gavin tugged on Xavier's shirt. "Leave it in his hands. You know he's capable of taking care of that little boy."

"I know. I hear you."

"Then how about we get you into the shower?"

"Join me?"

Tilting his head, Gavin looked at him.

Xavier stroked his fingertips down Gavin's cheek. "Please. Give me something else to focus on—on you, on us."

Gavin smiled. "Yes." He tapped his finger against Xavier's shirt.

"Help me?" Xavier lifted his hands. They noticeably trembled.

Gavin wrapped his fingers around Xavier's hands and squeezed. "Every single time you need me, I'll be there."

"Same here." Xavier studied their joined hands. Then he lifted his gaze to stare into those intense baby-blue eyes. "There's something here...between us."

"Since the moment you ran over me on the beach."

"There was the image of you in a White Rabbit costume. That little fluffy tail..."

Gavin's jaw dropped. "You said..."

"Might have fibbed…a touch. Couldn't admit I was looking, not then."

Moving a hand free, Gavin used it to playfully bump Xavier's shoulder with a soft fist.

Xavier rocked more than he needed in response to the gentle hit.

"Come on, big guy," Gavin said while he rose to his feet. He pushed at Xavier to straighten his back. Then he unbuttoned his shirt with slow, deliberate movements. Along the way, he brushed his fingers against the chest he bared with each freed button.

Xavier sucked in his belly when Gavin reached his waistband. His skin shivered underneath Gavin's tender touches. He was almost ticklish.

Gavin tugged the lower half of his shirt free from Xavier's waistband and finished the buttons. Then he slid his hands back up Xavier's chest, flicking both nipples in a light teasing fashion with his thumbs and pushing the shirt off his shoulders. Xavier moved his arms to help the shirt fall away. "Stand up," Gavin ordered while he unbuttoned Xavier's pants.

While Xavier stood, Gavin kept his hands on the pants. Then Gavin slid down the zipper. He was careful around the bulge of Xavier's cock pushing against his underwear. Pushing his hands inside, Gavin moved the material around Xavier's hips and ass then helped them drop to the ground. It left Xavier standing in socks and his gray boxer-briefs with a damp spot from his growing interest.

Gavin rose to his feet, trailing his fingers up Xavier's legs, dancing them across his boxer-briefs and cupping the bulge in a deliberate fashion. He patted his other fingers on Xavier's lower belly. Then he brushed his lips against Xavier's chest, neck and bristled jawline.

"Follow me to the bathroom." With that whisper, he walked away.

Xavier let out a breath he didn't know he was holding from Gavin's touch. "Holy shit," he whispered. The sensuality ran through the man's simple caresses and words. It jolted him back to the present and got him moving. He hopped on one foot to the other to remove the socks while he went to the bathroom.

At the same time, he heard the water starting and the multiple shower heads opening. Entering the room and staring at the corner shower stall, he watched the water flow from the rainshower head in the ceiling, two pivoting body sprays and a multifunction hand shower. Gavin controlled everything by the wall controller panel. Steam began to rise and fog the glass walls.

Straightening, Gavin turned with a smile. He pulled off his T-shirt and tossed it to another corner. Then he pulled a couple of towels from the small linen closet and hung them on the towel warmer bar.

"Did you set all this up?"

"Nope. This was created by the previous owners — an up-sell point to the entire home. I'm a sucker for a gorgeous shower. They also chose the clawfoot tub and shower in the hall bath with the wrap-around ceiling rail for the shower curtain."

"I saw that. Enjoyed it the last time."

"Now you can enjoy this one," Gavin said while he loosened his pajama pants and let them drop to the ground. He was bare underneath but not erect.

Xavier glanced down and stepped forward. "You're not…"

"I'm demisexual. It takes time for me to" — Gavin waved a hand around his crotch — "respond." He finished in a quiet tone.

"Do you...?"

"Yes. I can rise to the occasion. Give me time to connect. I need the deep connection between us to fulfill me." Gavin stepped closer and rested his palm against Xavier's cheek. His other hand slid inside the boxer-briefs and wrapped around Xavier's hardened shaft. "Doesn't mean that I don't want this, don't want you, don't enjoy making you feel better." He circled his fingers around the shaft and used the early droplets to slick things. "Because I do want...all of it."

"Gav..."

"Ssh. My turn to take care of you. Time to get rid of these," Gavin said while he snapped the waistband against Xavier's ass.

"Ouch. Hey..."

With a grin, Gavin pushed at the boxer-briefs until they dropped to the floor. After Xavier stepped out, Gavin kicked them away. Then he opened the glass door and sent Xavier inside. He followed him and closed the door.

Warmth and steam filled him, along with a slight eucalyptus scent.

"Eucalyptus?"

Gavin pointed to a small cheesecloth ball hanging from the rail by the hand shower. "There's Epsom salts and essential oil inside. When the water and steam hit the ball, it releases the scent. Thought it would be soothing."

"I like it."

"Good." Gavin moved them forward until they were hit by the rain shower and pivoting body sprays. He moved his hands around Xavier's skin to spread the moisture. Then he gently turned Xavier until his back faced the dual sprays and stopped water from splashing on his face. Leaning in, he kissed along Xavier's neck, then down his chest. He lingered around both nipples while he drifted his fingers lower.

While kissing and licking his way down Xavier's body, he crouched until he lowered to his knees onto the tiled floor. He wrapped his fingers around the hardened shaft for a few long pulls then lifted his gaze to take in Xavier's reactions.

Xavier dropped his stare to watch this beautiful man arouse him in a slow sensual fashion. He moved his fingers through Gavin's hair and threaded them through the wet strands.

"Don't tug hard or shove your cock into my mouth. That..." Gavin licked his lips. "I can't tolerate it — any type of force or power."

"We'll go at your pace. Promise. I'm just... enthralled by you," Xavier said. He wiggled his fingers. "Is this okay?"

Gavin smiled. "Touch me all you want. I can handle you threading fingers in my hair. Just no — "

"Yanking or tugging. Got it."

"May I...?" Gavin slid his thumb along the thick vein in Xavier's shaft.

A moan escaped. "Hell, yes."

Wrapping his fingers, Gavin gave the shaft a long stroke and altered the pressure along the way. He paused, stood and went to a corner shelf. There he pumped a shot of waterproof lube into his palm. Returning to Xavier, he dropped back to his knees and took hold of Xavier's cock. With the lube's slickness, his movements were easier.

Leaning in, he licked around the purpling mushroom head. When he enclosed within his mouth,

Xavier moaned louder. He rested his free hand on Gavin's shoulder and tilted over his lover.

Working in opposite motions, Gavin continued to meet his hand and mouth together in the middle. He hummed and vibrated against the thickened flesh for another sensational moment.

"Oh, shit, Gavin..."

While he deepened and worked the shaft and head, Gavin used his free hand to caress Xavier's balls. Xavier rocked a couple of times but kept it light and shallow to Gavin's movements.

"Oh, shit, yeah... There..."

Gavin placed his hand at the base of Xavier's cock. He applied firm pressure while he rubbed back and forth in that area.

That pressure was enough to intensify everything in Xavier's body. When Gavin sped up, Xavier responded with more moans and groans, then clutched at Gavin's shoulder and neck. Though cautious with his touch, he had to reveal how he felt to Gavin.

"Gavin... Gonna lose it..."

Gavin quickened his speed and enhanced his pressure.

The orgasm rose from his lower belly and shot through his body.

"Gavin!" Xavier cried out when he shot his load.

Gavin pulled back and opened his mouth. He let Xavier cover him with strings of cum.

Shaking when he finished, Xavier dropped to his knees. He used his fingers to wipe away his fluids then captured Gavin's swollen lips in a kiss.

When they both recovered, they rose to their feet and finished their shower with long, leisurely strokes of a shower-gel-covered puff. The steamy warmth, the eucalyptus scent and the touch of another man soothed him — and clearly Gavin as well.

Then Gavin turned off the shower when he touched the controller pad. He opened the door and yanked both towels off the warming bar. He handed one to Xavier and used the other to scrub at his hair and his body then he stepped onto the expansive rug.

Xavier followed, using the towel to dry off. He wrapped the towel around his waist. Then he used his fingers to comb back his hair. While Gavin wiggled back into the pajama pants and tugged on the wrinkled shirt, Xavier left the bathroom and went to his duffel bag. He exchanged the towel for sweatpants and a T-shirt. Then he returned the towel to the bar.

Snagging Gavin, he tugged him in for an embrace. "You are a wonderful, fabulous man," he whispered. Then he followed his words with a kiss.

Gavin responded to the kiss and embraced him back. "Time for the rest of the plan."

"Plan? What plan? My brain is mush."

Laughing, Gavin caught Xavier's hand and tugged him out of the room and to the stairs.

Smiling, the darkness no longer lingered within him, Xavier happily followed Gavin's 'plan' for the rest of the evening and the next couple of days.

Chapter Fourteen

Xavier allowed himself to relax. He stretched and rolled until he nudged a warm body. A smile curled his lips.

Gavin.

He was with Gavin.

Xavier played with a few of Gavin's soft curls. He wrapped around Gavin's back, spooned him and nestled his morning arousal against Gavin's firm bubble butt.

"Hmm. I feel ya back there. Too early. Got the day off. Make the most of it. Sleep in," Gavin said while he smacked a hand toward Xavier's way.

"Don't want to sleep. I'd rather tease and play with you."

Groaning, Gavin wiggled until he rolled to his back. "Do you need a morning workout to burn off that energy?"

"Are you telling me no?"

"Yup. I want to take it slow with you. We took the edge off last night. Let's enjoy our time together, see what we can do with this relationship." Gavin stroked his fingers against Xavier's morning stubble. "Please?"

"Okay. I understand what you're saying. No point jumping into things."

"We're compatible. We learned that last night. Let's go deeper."

Xavier rubbed their scratchy cheeks together. He placed a gentle kiss on Gavin's lips. "I'm with you."

"Lemme introduce you to the Peloton. Go put on a pair of shorts you would ride a bike in and sneakers. Meet me in the other bedroom."

"What?"

"You need a way to burn off your energy. Right?"

"Yes, but I could go for a run. It's what I always do."

"Let's change it up. Go find those shorts and sneakers. Got both with you?"

"Yeah, I think so."

"Go." Gavin kissed him and rolled away. He moved to a sitting position and tugged on a pair of sleep pants then dragged fingers through his hair. He snapped his fingers at Xavier to get him moving.

"I'm going. I'm going."

"Good. While you go for a ride, I'll set up the plans for our day."

"We're not going to laze around?" Xavier rolled into a sitting position.

"Like either of us would laze around for an entire day."

"True. Too true. Even when I want to sleep in, I can't." Xavier strolled over to where Gavin left his duffel bag and dug through it. He didn't care that he mooned Gavin the entire time.

"Shake that booty," Gavin teased.

Xavier obliged with a quick shake.

Gavin cheered and whistled.

Xavier did a reverse striptease by pulling on briefs then shorts. He rearranged his balls with a deliberate movement. "Don't want them to get crushed on a bike ride."

Laughing, Gavin left the bedroom. "Get a move on."

Grumbling, Xavier dug through the bag and unearthed the sneakers and socks. He sat and slipped his feet into them. After tying the sneakers, he walked to the other bedroom.

Inside, Gavin stood next to a complex bike machine with a large screen. He programmed something on it. "Come on over. I need to adjust the seat for your height since there's about six inches difference between us."

"I've seen this machine on television. It looked pretty damn cool in the commercials."

"It's even better in person. Within twenty minutes, I'm dripping with sweat and still cycling. Have you gone bike riding? On a bike or machine."

"Both. You can step it up beyond a beginner class."

"You sure?"

"Yeah. Push me. Lemme see what it can give me." Xavier climbed on after Gavin adjusted the seat. Together, they checked the positioning of the handles and pedals. "Okay, let's get going."

"Here you go. This is one of my favorite rides," Gavin said and hit the button to start the program. He chuckled while leaving the room and saying, "Have fun."

Forty-five minutes later, the high-octane endurance ride had almost killed him. Finally slowing down as the program ended, Xavier groaned and wiped the sweat streaming into his eyes.

"Fuck me," he muttered.

Gavin entered the room and a big evil grin curled his lips. "That's what I thought. Wore you out."

"My legs feel like cooked noodles. Do you do this all the time?"

"I do this workout twice a week to keep up my endurance. Then there are other programs I mingle with it for different days. I try to ride up to four times a week. Part of me wants to get an actual bike and go out on a real course for a race, but I'm not ready yet. Only had the bike for a year, one of those crazy pandemic resolutions. I'll give myself another year of training before I attempt an actual race."

"Holy fuck me, Gavin," Xavier said.

Gavin laughed.

"This is better than a run. Things adjust while I went along to increase or decrease the speed and pressure. I even used those little weights." Xavier stretched out his legs to prevent cramps and managed to climb off the bike. He walked around to get his legs back underneath him.

"Want a shower?"

"Hell, yes."

"Come on. I've got it all set up for you."

Moaning at being made to move, Xavier followed Gavin back to the main bedroom. He dropped onto the bed, exhausted.

"You wanted me to push you."

"Hush."

Gavin chuckled. "Would you like to hear the plans for our day?"

"Does it involve another bike ride?"

Laughing, Gavin sat next to him. "Nope. I promise."

"Good. What is it?"

"We're going to play tourist."

"Whaaaat?"

Gavin punched Xavier's shoulder. "Chill. We're going to cross the other bridge to the Santa Rosa Island and relax on Pensacola Beach. We'll be beach bunnies all day and swim in the ocean."

"I don't have anything for the beach with me."

"I figured that. After your shower, I want you to hurry back to your place, change clothes, grab whatever beach gear you have and return. I'll gather my stuff and a picnic lunch in my car and drive us over."

"I like this plan."

"Good idea?"

"Excellent one. Haven't enjoyed a beach day in a while."

"Great. Go take a shower and get to your place."

"What about you?"

Gavin rose from the bed and snagged his sneakers from the closet. "I'm going to take a bike ride—an easier one than you since I biked that program earlier. Then I'll get clean up, get our stuff together and meet up with you."

"Wanna join me? Conserve water."

"Xavier…"

"Just asking. My legs will barely hold me up."

"Then there's no chance to hold me against a slippery wall." Gavin returned to the bed and kissed the sweaty Xavier. "Go get cleaned up. Not that I mind the sweaty you, just under different circumstances." With a wicked grin, he left Xavier in the room…again.

"Damn, that man can turn me on." Xavier toed off his sneakers and yanked off the damp socks. He stuffed them in a side pocket for immediate tossing into the laundry pile. Pushing to his feet, he pulled out a pair of jeans, briefs and a T-shirt from the duffel. Then he went to the bathroom, tossed the clothes on the vanity and stripped off his shorts and briefs.

Gavin had left out towels, an extra toothbrush and a razor.

With a grin at how efficient Gavin kept things, Xavier stepped under the rainfall shower and sighed in bliss. He would enjoy this. Still, he couldn't dally since they'd made plans. After a day at the beach and swimming in the ocean, he would be able to enjoy another turn in the bathroom.

* * * *

Over an hour later, Xavier returned to Gavin's home with a different bag. He'd changed into his favorite Vans Floral Rust boardshorts, a tank top with an opened button-down shirt covering it and ancient Birkenstock slide-on sandals. He'd stashed a beach towel, a charged Kindle and a portable charger for his phone. He entered through the open garage and knocked on the connecting door. "Gavin? It's Xavier." He slid his sunglasses back into his hair.

"Come on in. It's open," Gavin called out.

Xavier stepped inside. "Hey. All ready. I parked off to the side so you can pull your car out."

"Great. Almost done here." Gavin met him by the kitchen. Dressed in gray-and-peach striped boardshorts, a peach T-shirt and flip-flops, he was ready for a relaxing beach day. He'd left his ankle unbound. His hair remained soft and curly instead of the slicked-up style he clearly preferred during work.

Xavier enjoyed checking out this loosened-up version of Gavin. "Hmm. You're looking sexy in those shorts."

Gavin glanced down and back to Xavier. "You're wearing a similar style. No Speedo brief?"

Xavier snorted. "Hell no. I'm not that crazy to go prancing in one of those teeny things. I'll keep my Vans, thank you. Managed to find these on clearance." He posed to show off the shorts.

"Nice color. Good fit."

"I do know how to find clothes that fit. Doesn't mean I can afford them."

"I didn't mean it like that." Gavin touched Xavier's smooth cheek.

"Sorry. Habit. Money goes to school and bills...not many luxuries."

"Which is why I'm treating you to our day. No arguments," Gavin said.

"Gav—"

"No arguments. My turn to treat you."

"Okay. Okay."

Gavin returned to the kitchen. When he came back, he rolled a medium cooler. "Got some sandwiches, snacks, fruit, water, iced tea and Gatorade. I don't have beer."

"Don't want any. I'm good with what you have."

"Great. This is the last part." Gavin tossed his wallet into his beach bag and snatched his keys from the hook. Then he perched his sunglasses in his hair. He checked the front door. "We'll leave out of the garage. This way..."

"I've got the cooler." Xavier took the handle from Gavin and followed him to the garage.

Gavin hit the locks to open the trunk. He placed a large blanket, lightweight sand chairs and an umbrella in the back. He grabbed a battery-powered radio from the shelf and added it.

"Figured this was easier than streaming on our phones. I pulled it from my hurricane prep stash. Batteries are good, but I have extra if one of those storms come near us." Gavin helped Xavier lift the cooler into the empty space and shut the trunk. "Doors are unlocked. I gotta set the alarm."

"The one storm Katia looks like it might swing our way. It's still on the possible future tracks."

"Just what we need...another storm." Gavin armed the house's system and returned to the Soul. He climbed into the driver's seat while Xavier got in the passenger side.

Xavier set his beach bag by his feet and secured the belt. He dropped his sunglasses in place while Gavin pulled out of the garage, hit the clicker and drove away.

"Away we go. Change the station if you want," Gavin said.

They drove across the bridge to Pensacola Beach that occupied most of the Santa Rosa barrier island that helped protect Shore Breeze and Pensacola from incoming tropical storms. Gavin drove to the far side facing the Gulf and located some public parking near a beach entrance. He paid the fee and pulled into an empty spot.

"I thought we could try Casino Beach since it faces the Gulf and not the barrier waters," Gavin said when he turned off the engine and hit the locks.

"I'm good with wherever you want to put down the chairs."

"Perhaps we could have dinner at Crabs, the seafood spot overlooking the beach. We could also go over to Quietwater Beach Boardwalk to walk around, sightsee and enjoy a concert if something is playing."

"Okay, I'm easy and will follow you anywhere," Xavier said while they walked to the back.

"This isn't going to set off your ADHD or OCD? Since this is rather spontaneous."

"I noted all the changes in my calendar and journal at my place. My smaller calendar and journal are with me. If I need to update to soothe things, I will. I'm okay. I wouldn't be here if I wasn't."

"Okay. I didn't want to make things worse —"

"Relax, Gavin. I'm fine…honest."

Gavin smiled and opened the trunk.

Together they unpacked, shared the load and carried everything to the beach. Stepping onto the sand, they looked around to find a spot. In a somewhat empty area, they spread out the blanket, anchored it with the cooler, chairs and umbrella. They dropped onto the blanket after kicking off their shoes and lowered their bags onto another corner to prevent the wind from flipping it up.

"We'd better get some suntan lotion on your pale skin, ghost," Xavier teased.

"Hey, I'm not that bad."

"How easily do you burn?"

"Probably within minutes I'll be pink, so super easy. I can turn into a lobster within a couple of hours. It's why I have a chair under the umbrella. I'll keep my butt in that spot most of the day."

"Hmm. Where's your lotion?"

Gavin pulled out a bottle of the highest SPF. He yanked off the T-shirt and tossed it toward the bag. Then he found the radio and clicked it on to a classic rock station. After adjusting the volume, he placed it on the cooler.

"Give me your back." Xavier squeezed lotion in his palm.

Shifting on the blanket, Gavin faced his back toward Xavier. He leaned forward to give Xavier space to work.

When Xavier turned the application of sunscreen into a sensual motion, Gavin held back a moan at the rising sensations of Xavier's hands skimming over his skin. He laughed when Xavier hit a sensitive spot, and he wiggled away from the fingers.

"What did I find here?"

Gavin giggled and shifted away. "Hey, no, stop…"

"Hmm. Ticklish spot?"

"Yes. No more." Then Gavin leaned back against Xavier to stop him.

Xavier helped Gavin tilt his head a bit more and captured his lips in a kiss. Their mouths moved together in the lingering moment. The scent of coconut from the lotion wafted around them.

"Thank you for getting me outside," Xavier said.

"You're welcome."

After finishing applying the sunscreen across Gavin's arms and chest, Xavier stripped off his shirt and let Gavin return the favor. They each took care of their face, chest, arms and legs, then Gavin tossed the bottle back into his bag. They stretched out for a bit on the blanket, relaxed in the warm sunshine and people-watched.

Playfulness remained between them while they created stories for various families and groups. Laughter rang high.

When the heat got to be too much, they raced to the water and waded through the incoming waves. Diving in, they swam, teased and played like a pair of playful otters.

Leaving the water, they returned to the blanket. As promised, Gavin dropped into the chair under the umbrella after drying off.

Xavier stretched out in the sunshine to dry. "This is a perfect afternoon—a perfect idea," he said while pillowing his head on his arms.

"Wish I could do this more often. At least here, I can totally relax. If I was on the Charm beach, I would want to check into something or worry about work."

"Close proximity."

"Yup."

It was a picture-perfect day with a brilliant blue sky with a few fluffy clouds. Low ambling waves rolled in across the beach.

To his enjoyment, Xavier lounged around under the sunshine and dove into the Gulf's waters to splash around with Gavin. After drying off, he dug through the cooler to enjoy sandwiches, chips and drinks. To work off the meal, Gavin suggested a walk along the shoreline. Xavier smiled when Gavin picked up shells.

"Whoa, that's an impressive castle, kids," Xavier said when they returned after the latest walk.

About six kids of different ages were constructing what looked to be a massive sandcastle complex. They worked diligently by gathering wet sand in buckets and building up their base.

"Wanna help?" one little girl asked. She held up a small shovel.

"He's an adult. He don't wanna help," another boy said, his words a little off, thanks no doubt to missing his two front teeth.

"Hey, I love building sandcastles." Xavier settled down on the sand and glanced at Gavin. "Wanna help?"

"I'll oversee the decorations," Gavin said. He set down his collection of shells by the blanket. Then he brought his chair and umbrella closer to watch and remain protected.

"Okay. What do we need?"

"The water circle thing around a castle," one boy said.

"That's called a moat. Let's trace out the size of the castle and we'll add the moat," Xavier suggested.

Over the next couple of hours playing with the kids, Xavier constructed an epic sandcastle with multiple tiers, towers and an impressive moat. A couple of fathers joined in when their kids demanded even more add-ons during the construction.

"I'm impressed. Now it needs decorations," Gavin said when they finished.

"Really? What kind?" a girl asked.

"Pick from our collection of shells. We can use the small ones as windows. The bigger ones can be doors," Gavin said and spread out the pile of shells. "I got an idea." He got up and walked along the beach. This time he returned with several pieces of driftwood, reeds and seaweed. Then he constructed a drawbridge from various debris.

"Oh, wow, that's cool," one boy said. "Daddy, look at that."

"I see, son. I see it."

Gavin smiled at Xavier while he laid the drawbridge in place. He used a bit more seaweed to create 'chains' back to the castle's walls.

Other parents wandered over to take pictures of the massive project, congratulating everyone on a good job. Other beachgoers stopped their walk to admire the castle.

Xavier went to the water to wash off most of the sand and cool off one last time. Returning to the blanket, he picked up the towel and dried off, then he glanced over at Gavin. "Uh-oh."

"What?"

"You're looking a little pink on your legs and arms."

"Oh, no, I reapplied sunscreen…twice." Gavin checked out his skin and groaned.

"How about we clean up and hit the boardwalk?"

"Yeah, we better. Otherwise, I'll be hurting even more later if this burn gets worse."

They gathered up their belongings, schlepped back to their parking spot and deposited everything in the back. They used the boardwalk's fountains to clean off the lingering sand and shoved their feet into sandals.

"To the boardwalk?" Xavier slid his wallet and phone into the somewhat-dried shorts.

"Sounds good." Gavin placed his phone, wallet and keys into his pockets. He grimaced when he checked out his lower arms.

"It's not too bad. Got aloe at home?"

"Yeah, and a couple of other things. It'll be okay."

Xavier took Gavin's hand and led him to the boardwalk. They walked down to the laid-back beach eatery, Crabs. "Table for two?" he asked the hostess.

"Any particular spot?"

"Upstairs balcony? Outside, but covered."

The hostess checked and gathered menus. "We've got a spot. Follow me." She led them to an outdoor table on the upstairs balcony. A live band played near them.

"Here you go." She laid the menus on the table. Then she adjusted the umbrella to provide a bit more shade. "Enjoy."

After checking out the menu, they ordered a snow crab and shrimp boil to share, along with the fixings. They added a pair of ice-cold longnecks of McGuire's Irish Red beer.

"To a perfect day," Xavier said when they received the longnecks.

Gavin smiled and clinked their beers together. "Perfect day."

Xavier picked up Gavin's arm. He checked it out against the shadow from the building instead of the bright sun. "You're going to need some aloe."

"I know. I know. Stupid evil UV rays."

Xavier chuckled. "Can I stay tonight?"

Gavin flushed underneath the sunburn. "Yes. Are you off tomorrow?"

"Yup. Need to do laundry and groceries. Figure I'll do that tomorrow."

"I can take off again. We don't have any events scheduled." Gavin moved to lace his fingers with Xavier's. "You could bring your laundry over and use my machines."

"Nah. Don't want to keep you from anything or get in the way."

"Not keeping me from anything, and you're not getting in my way. We'll keep the option open."

"Yeah, we'll do that," Xavier said and took a long sip from the bottle.

When the waitress returned, they dug into the massive pile of shrimp, crab, potatoes, corn on the cob and used biscuits to collect all the juice and sauce. It was heaven after a long day in the sun.

Chapter Fifteen

Days after his day on the beach with Xavier, Gavin welcomed Arthur and Neil to the Charm. By late afternoon, most of the guests had arrived for the weekend wedding, ready for a week of fun and relaxation in the sun. It ended up being a mini vacation, along with a celebration—something they all claimed to want after Arthur and Neil chose their wedding location and they checked out the B&B.

Gavin gathered everyone in the wedding party by the gazebo. He sent the rest of the guests to the upper patio where Victor helped the restaurant employees set the tables for the rehearsal dinner. The rest of the restaurant remained open for regular diners. The hostess, Cecilia, knew not to seat anyone on the patio.

Though the officiant wasn't available, Gavin took the wedding party through the rehearsal. He directed them through the different walk-on sites and locations to stand. Then he explained the ceremony Arthur chose, but the grooms weren't sure if they wanted to create vows or use standard ones. The decision would need to be made so Gavin could tell the officiant.

After the ceremony, Gavin explained how the rest of the morning would go, from signing any paperwork to photographs, a cocktail time and, finally, the brunch reception.

"Okay. That's it for me. Does everyone know what they need to do?"

The couple nodded and glanced around at the family.

"Just need to figure out your vows," one of their friends teased.

Everyone chuckled.

"Yeah. Yeah. We'll figure out something," Arthur said.

"Make it a true Hallmark moment," Neil added.

Everyone laughed.

With everyone happy and aware of what they need to do, Gavin motioned for them to move. "Everyone ready for a delicious meal?" Then he led them back to the upper patio where the rehearsal dinner waited.

The rest of the guests rose with cheers and applause for the soon-to-be-wedded couple. Gavin stepped back during the moment.

Victor moved in next to him.

"Is there a menu for everyone? What was set up?" Gavin asked.

"Relax, boss. Malcolm is on top of everything. He created a mini menu for the dinner, since they didn't pre-select options. He chose from what Dakota had planned for the week because they had everything ordered and waiting in the pantry and fridges. A couple of waiters are dedicated to the party and took orders. We're waiting for the wedding party to bring out the food."

"Good work."

"Welcome, boss."

"Let's get the party seated."

Victor pointed to the empty table. "They're all at the one table in the center. The couple is in the middle with their groomsmen on either side."

With a nod, Gavin moved to the wedding party. He motioned toward the table. "Could everyone please take a seat at the center table? Arthur, Neil, you're in the middle with your groomsmen and family on each side. There is a menu for your dinner options. Waiters will take your choices."

"Are you staying with us?" Arthur asked.

"This night is for you to enjoy with your families and guests. I'll stop by later and check-in," Gavin said. "I hope everyone enjoys their time at the beach and in Shore Breeze. If anyone needs anything, please don't hesitate to find me."

"Thank you for everything, Gavin," Arthur said.

"Yes, everything is wonderful. Perfectly planned," Neil added.

"You only got a teaser tonight. Wait till the grand reveal this weekend. There will be far more than a simple walk through an empty gazebo. Trust me. There will be much more to see. Enjoy your dinner." With a wave, Gavin walked away. There was still work for him to figure out before he could close his evening.

* * * *

About an hour later, Victor dashed into Gavin's office. He almost tripped over his own feet before he got control and clung to the door.

"What on earth is wrong with you?" Gavin asked.

"You'd better come. *Now*. Something bad is happening outside — something with the older groom, Neil."

"Why? What's happening?"

"Don't know." Victor shook his head multiple times and leaned back out of the door to look down the hall, but they were blocked from seeing anything. He licked his lower lip. Then he curled his hand to beckon Gavin to get moving. "Come now. You gotta. It looks bad."

Gavin rushed out of his office after Victor. They headed down the halls toward the back patio, but shouts for help redirected him toward the front entrance.

"Help! Please! Someone help us!" Arthur cried out.

Gavin skidded to a stop with Victor banging into his back. "Arthur, what is... Oh my God! What happened?"

On the ground by the staircase, Neil was collapsed along the lower steps and floor. His face was pale while his eyes remained closed. One hand was pressed to his chest. Then he moaned low under his breath.

"Neil, please, stay with me." Arthur dropped to his knees next to him. He moved his hands over his partner's face and shoulders, caressed him. Tears fell down his face.

Samuel stood nearby them, cell phone in hand. "I'm on the line with 9-1-1. They're sending an ambulance now. Arthur, can you give me the details? Is he breathing?"

Gavin crouched next to Arthur to help calm him down and get him to focus. "Come on, Arthur. You know everything about Neil. They need that information now to help save him. We have one of the best hospitals to treat him, but they need your knowledge."

With a nod, Arthur pulled in a deep breath. "Yes, you're right." Then he relayed the details about Neil's heart condition, his doctor's contact information in Atlanta and the medication in their room.

Gavin patted Arthur's pockets and found the keys. He tossed them to Victor. "Go to their room. Bring down the medication. The EMTs and clinic will need it. Go. *Run!*"

"Okay. Okay." Victor raced up the stairs.

"Our clinic is one of the best. They'll do everything possible to help Neil," Gavin said. "We call it a clinic, but it's really a strong hospital."

Arthur's and Neil's families had rushed into the area, but Dakota, Chandler, Malcolm and Elise kept them back.

"Neil! Let me through. That's my brother," Neil's sister called out. "Neil!"

"Please. Keep back and remain calm. The EMTs are on their way. They will need room to work on Neil and transport him. Please, we're doing everything we can to help him," Dakota called out.

Sirens grew closer and louder. Red and blue lights filled the windows.

Victor raced down the stairs with the medicine bottles. He dropped the wallets, bottles and key next to Gavin. Then, without anyone saying something, he opened both front doors while the ambulance parked.

Xavier and Norman climbed out with their bags. Xavier ran straight up the steps while Norman wheeled the gurney up the side ramp.

"Hello, my name is Gray. I'm here to help you," Xavier said while he crouched next to Neil. He went through his initial assessment of Neil.

"This is Neil, my partner and fiancé," Arthur said. "I'm Arthur."

Xavier looked over. "I remember you. You were with Gavin in town."

Arthur nodded.

"Tell me what's been happening with Neil."

Arthur went through the details and the medication Victor had retrieved. "He complained about some stomach discomfort and was a bit nauseous."

"Did his doctor warn him of the possibility of a heart attack or stroke?"

"Yes. His heart is weakening, and he's high risk. Was this because of our flight? Could that have done this?"

"Don't know the reasons. The doctors will figure that out." Xavier went through his complete head-to-toe assessment. He reports the vital signs to Norman. "BP is eighty-eight over fifty. Pulse ninety-four. Respiratory rate eighteen. I'm administering a hundred percent oxygen via a non-rebreather mask, applying an ECG monitor and performing a twelve-lead ECG." He attached an SaO2 monitor and checked the blood with a quick prick and swipe on the machine. "Glucose is one hundred twenty-five mg/dL. Let's transport him to the truck. He needs two intravenous lines of normal saline and a fluid bolus. We need to get his blood pressure up."

"Arthur. Come. Stand up." Gavin drew Arthur back while Xavier and Norman worked to lift and transfer Neil to the gurney. They strapped him onto the bed and gathered their gear.

"Can I go with him?" Arthur asked.

"Of course. You can ride up front with Norman," Xavier said.

Arthur scooped up the wallets, medication and key. He squeezed Gavin's hand. "Thank you, Gavin." He raced after the paramedics. Then he waited until they'd loaded Neil into the back before he went to the passenger side.

The rest of the group gathered around them and some quietly spoke.

Neil opened his eyes.

"Hey there, Neil. Good to see you awake. I'm Gray. I'm here to help you. How are you feeling?"

"Hurts. Dizzy. Bad heart."

"Okay, I understand, and we're here to help you. I need to poke you for a few moments, Neil, but it'll help you out. Bear with me," Xavier said while he strapped Neil's arm to force up a vein and slipped the needle into the skin. "There. Not too bad." He hooked up the first intravenous line with a bag of normal saline and bolus. After he repeated the procedure on the other arm, he administered something underneath Neil's tongue that Gavin assumed was nitroglycerin. "Let that dissolve, Neil. It'll help you feel better." He snagged the print-out from the ECG and relayed the details to the clinic's ER team for their preparations. He rechecked the blood pressure. "Norm, BP is going up. Increased to one thirty-four over seventy-eight."

Neil perked up a bit more under the treatment.

"Okay. Stabilized. Let's get out of here, Norm," Xavier called out. He looked back at Gavin.

Offering a small half-smile, Gavin waved. Then Xavier hitched a wave back before he closed the door.

With sirens and lights, the ambulance raced back up the road. The rest of the family scrambled to get to their cars. They all planned to follow the ambulance.

"I gotta go with them. Arthur will—" Gavin moved to rush off for his wallet and keys.

Samuel stopped Gavin by grabbing hold of his arm. "Don't go after them, Gavin. Best leave it to family. Arthur and Neil are in good hands. Let the clinic staff do their job. Find him in the morning."

"But Arthur…" Gavin looked at the doors and back to Samuel.

"I know you want to help. That's your heart talking. Right now, Arthur's heart is with his Neil and needs to remain there. You're a friend, not his lover."

"Samuel…I wasn't thinking that. It was as his friend."

"Was it?"

"I should have stuck around. Made sure things went perfect with no—"

"Don't go blaming yourself. No one could have predicted this would happen tonight. Neil was sick, yes, but he wanted this week to happen. He wants to share this time with Arthur, give him the wedding celebration he desired. You gave that bit of light to him." Samuel drew his hand down Gavin's back to calm him.

"What should I do then?"

"Nothing but shut down your office and go home. It's all you can do. Perhaps Gray will give you a call and an update. He's good at doing that, right?"

Gavin nodded a couple of times.

"Victor, same for you," Samuel said. "Head on home."

"I promised to meet up with Dorian. He needs a break," Victor said.

"Go on. Samuel is right. Cheer up Dorian," Gavin said.

With a small smile, Victor hugged Gavin. "It'll be okay."

"Thanks, Victor. Say hi to Dorian for me."

"Will do." Victor raced off to Gavin's office to collect his stuff and leave.

"Your turn," Samuel said. "We'll take care of clean up."

Without anything else to do or say, Gavin headed to his office to shut down and gathered his things into the messenger bag. Then he pulled his keys and headed outside. "What a freaking night," he muttered while he climbed into his Soul. His phone buzzed and he answered it. "Hello?"

"Gavin, it's Xavier. Doing okay? That was a few rough moments back there."

"Oh, Xavier, so damn good to hear your voice. I don't know – " Gavin rushed through the words.

"Ssh. Hold up, baby. I need you to calm down," Xavier interrupted. "Breathe, Gavin. Breathe with me."

Following the soothing tenor of Xavier's voice, Gavin calmed down and leaned back.

"Better?"

"Yes. Thanks."

"It's okay. I'm used to the chaotic scenes, not you. Okay. Where are you?"

"In my Soul in the Charm parking lot. I'm not driving...yet."

"Okay. Good. You sound a little shaky."

"Can you tell me what is happening?"

"We left Neil with the cardiac team and Doc Elliott. They're talking to his Atlanta doctor. It was a heart attack. Okay? But he's going to be okay. He's been monitored for his heart condition, and we responded in time. Arthur is with him and mentioned contacting you when he learns more about Neil's prognosis."

"Oh. Good. Umm... Guess there might be changes or cancellations—"

"Quiet that busy mind. You don't know yet," Xavier said with a light chuckle. "I'm the one with the ADHD, not you."

"No, just overactive and used to multi-tasking."

Xavier's warm chuckle soothed Gavin's frayed nerves.

"Thank you for calling me," Gavin said.

"Anytime, baby. Now, I want you to take care while driving home. Take a warm shower then curl up with your favorite TV show or movie. I would say grab some ice cream, but you said you can't have it."

"Yeah, it sucks being lactose-intolerant at these kinds of moments."

"Find another way to indulge. I wish I could be there with you, but I need to finish up my shift. It'll be another twelve hours before I'm off."

"Wish you were there, too. Why so long?"

"That's how shifts run around here. Small town. Not a lot of EMTs or firefighters."

"Wish things were different."

"Me too, sometimes. Now, be careful driving home. Settle your mind," Xavier reminded him.

"Thank you."

"Of course. Anytime. Night, baby."

"Night," Gavin said. The soft nickname in Xavier's tenor gives him all kinds of fuzzies and thrills.

When Xavier clicked off, Gavin turned on the car and pulled away, his mind soothed by Xavier's calming words and nature.

Chapter Sixteen

The following morning, Arthur returned with dark circles under his eyes from a restless night watching over Neil. He walked over to where Gavin sat with the Charm family.

Gavin rose to his feet. "Arthur! What are you doing here? How are you? How is Neil?" he asked while walking toward his friend and embraced him.

Arthur returned the hug. "Hello, exhausted, but there are so many things to take care of here and decisions to make. Neil is stable...for now."

"Would you like some coffee? Breakfast?"

"Coffee, please."

"Black. Two creams. Right?"

Arthur nodded. "Could I speak in private with you and Samuel?"

"Sure. Hang on. Lemme get your coffee." Gavin poured coffee and cream into a fresh mug. "Samuel, could you speak with Arthur and me in your office? He wants some privacy."

"Sure. I'll grab a pot of coffee, some food and meet you there," Samuel said.

"Okay." Gavin picked up his messenger bag, returned to Arthur and handed over the cup. Leading the way through the halls to Samuel's office, he offered Arthur one of the chairs and took another for himself.

Entering a few moments later, Samuel carried a small tray filled with coffee, supplies and a few scones. "Thought you might want something to eat. How are you holding up, Arthur?" He set the tray down and settled into his chair.

"Thank you. I do love the scones here." Arthur cradled a scone in a napkin but picked at one of the scone's corners and worried it into crumbs.

"It's okay. You can tell us whatever you need. We'll figure out something," Samuel reassured the man. He glanced at Gavin, who nodded for him to continue leading the conversation.

"It isn't the best of news. His heart is failing faster than expected. Neil needs further care and requires a medical transfer home to get under his cardiologist's care. The doctors at the clinic agree with the decision. We planned the transfer for Friday. It's the soonest we could get everything together and he's not considered critical — not at this point."

"What about the wedding?"

"While I would rather cancel everything and move the wedding to a different date, Neil doesn't want that. He wished to marry me before we return home, but he's unable to leave the hospital. Neil is too weak, recovering from the heart attack and connected to multiple machines. Even with all this, he still insists on marrying me. He doesn't want to lose a single possible minute of calling me his husband." Arthur shook his head. Tears glistened in his eyes. He lifted a fresh napkin to soak up the tears. "I can't believe him…this crazy man of mine. Before he goes in for complex surgery, he wants to marry me. Can you believe him?"

"I believe he loves you so much and wants to take care of you before he can concentrate on himself."

"I don't know how we could grant his wish. It's impossible," Arthur said.

"Oh, darling Arthur, nothing is impossible with me around. I know our small town and can get everything figured out. I will grant Neil's wish," Gavin said and rubbed his hands together. A smile curled his face.

"What are you planning?" Samuel asked.

"The answer to all the problems."

"Which is?" Arthur asked.

"Simple. We move the wedding to the hospital's chapel. Give me a couple of days to set up everything. You're leaving on Friday?"

"Yes, early Friday afternoon via a private ambulance," Arthur said.

"Instead of a morning wedding by the beach, you will have a late-morning wedding on Thursday in the clinic's chapel. It's a lovely little spot, and I can decorate it. Then we'll have the reception in a section of the cafeteria. We can easily block off an area with screens and curtains." Gavin held up his hands. "I know this isn't what you planned, but…" He shrugged. "I don't think your families and friends would care about the change. They can still be there to help you enjoy your wedding day. We'll remain in the hospital where Neil can receive his care. Everything will fit into place. You'll be married on Thursday and leave on Friday. Only the honeymoon will be delayed."

"Which we've already planned. Gavin—" Arthur's jaw dropped while Gavin explained his plan. Tears flowed from his eyes. "Oh my God. Can we do this?"

"Unbelievable," Samuel muttered.

"How about it?" Gavin asked.

"Ohmygod. Ohmygod. Ohmygod," Arthur repeated.

"I think you broke him," Samuel said with a chuckle.

"You are brilliant!" Arthur leaped out of the chair and tackled-hugged Gavin. Luckily, neither one held coffee cups. He squeezed and thanked Gavin over and over. "If you can pull this off—"

"I'm pretty damn good."

"More than good. Brilliant. Brilliant. Brilliant." Arthur sat back in his chair and clasped Gavin's hands. "Can you do this? In two days' time?"

"Let me work my magic. I promised to give you a wedding, and I will deliver. Overall, it's a minor change. It's not the biggest problem thrown my way, but no matter. That's my problem. You go back and worry over your Neil. Tell him to work on those wedding vows. His wish is coming true."

"Oh my God, Gavin, you..." Arthur shook his head. "I don't have the words."

"Don't need them. Honest. Do you agree to the changes?"

"Yes. Yes. Yes."

"I promise you'll have your wedding when I'm finished." Gavin popped out of his chair and rubbed his hands. "I need to get started. Finish up with Samuel and lemme do my thing." He kissed Arthur's damp cheek, finished his coffee and snagged his messenger bag. He rushed out and made a beeline for his own office. At the same time, he hollered, "Victor! I need you. Emergency!"

* * * *

With a new plan of action and a little over forty-eight hours to pull it off, Gavin raced into his office with Victor following him.

"We're changing the Carlton-Bardon wedding. It'll be Thursday morning at the clinic. Can you go there and speak with whoever runs the chapel and cafeteria?" Gavin said.

"Umm. Yeah. Eep…" Victor sneezed hard. "Wow. Excuse me. Sorry." He snagged a tissue and blew his nose.

"Are you okay?"

"Yeah, cleaning the inventory room. Too much dust." He sneezed again into the tissue. "Sorry. Jeez."

"Bless you?"

"Thanks. Anyway, back to the wedding. What do you want me to say?" Victor blew his nose again and cleaned up after himself.

"Umm. Hang on. You'll need more than words. Lemme get something official for the request. If this works, they might let us do it again in the future if needed." Gavin pulled up a program. He tapped out a simple but earnest request. After a quick check of spelling and grammar, he printed it on the Charmed Occasions' letterhead and signed it. He folded the letter and stuffed it into an envelope. He scribbled a list of locations Victor would need to find within the hospital. "Here. Give this to whomever you need at these locations." He tapped the list. "I need an exact range of time we can have the chapel and section of cafeteria to prep, decorate and hold the ceremony and reception on Thursday. It must be sometime Thursday since they're leaving Friday. My preference is a late morning with the reception following it. The reception will be a couple of hours, maximum, with a minimum number of guests. We'll need one corner of the cafeteria."

"Don't you remember how I'm supposed to leave on Thursday afternoon with Samuel for the Atlanta Wedding Expo? We were going to set up and cover until you arrived on Saturday," Victor said.

"Oh, shit," Gavin said and smacked his fingers on the desk.

"Well, I guess we can adjust who goes." Victor snatched another tissue before another violent sneeze hit him. "Damn dust. Really. Sheesh. Anyway… Figure you can go instead or something, since this wedding is happening early."

"Perhaps you should take something for the sneezing?"

"If it gets worse, I'll grab something. What about the Expo?"

"We'll figure it out…later." Gavin waved his hand to dismiss the problem. "Let's get through this wedding. I need that time so I can prepare the vendors for this radical change."

"Okay. I'm on my way. I'll text you as soon as I get the answer." Victor took the envelope and snatched a couple of more tissues.

"Good idea. Go. *Go.*"

Victor took off running.

Gavin pulled out the binder and opened the online file. He wanted to call everyone but couldn't give them exact information until he heard from Victor and the clinic. Everything depended on the time.

"Eeh. At least I can give them the head's up about the change and that it'll definitely be Thursday."

Decision made, he began to call the vendors.

* * * *

Hours later, Victor texted him the confirmed time for Thursday, guaranteed for the chapel and cafeteria.

"Woohoo!"

Wiggling a happy dance, Gavin went back through the list to alert everyone to the confirmed times. With everyone agreed, even Katie would push hard to get through the delicate cake decorations, Gavin checked off more on his list. He pulled over the different layouts and redesigned everything.

"Gavin. Gavin. Gavin!"

At the third repetition of his name, Gavin blinked and looked up. "Xavier? What are you doing here?"

"Gavin, baby…"

"That's the second or third time you've called me 'baby'."

"Gavin, it's almost nine…at night."

"What? Impossible…" Gavin blinked and stared at the clock on the screen. Then he double-checked it on his phone. "Oh. Crap." His stomach gurgled and growled.

"You haven't eaten."

Gavin shook his head.

"Shut it down and pack it up. I'm taking you home."

"Taking me… My Soul is here."

"I know. I walked over here after ordering a pizza. Mal is keeping it warm until I get you out of the clouds." Xavier waved toward the chaotic mess on Gavin's desk. "Pack it up. No more work."

"I can't. I need to get—"

"Sweetheart, you did everything possible to get this wedding together. You have tomorrow to finish."

"How did you hear?"

"I have my ways. Forget about that. Pack it up. I'm hungry and picked up a pizza. Now I want to curl up with you on the sofa. We need to see what happens next on *Grimm*."

"Still can't believe they finished it. At least, I heard the writers wrapped up the loose ends." Gavin packed a laptop and some paperwork in his messenger bag. He logged off the system. Then he tossed his keys toward Xavier, who snatched them out of the air with an easy grab.

Xavier hit the light when Gavin reached him and led him down the narrow hallway. "Hey, Mal, got him. Pizza?"

"Good job, Gray. Record time. Here you go," the chef said with a grin.

"Yeah. Yeah. Yeah," Gavin grumbled.

"Gotta feed him. It'll help the rough break from his work." Xavier balanced the box on one hand and led Gavin away with his other.

They went to Gavin's Soul and Xavier unlocked the doors. He gave Gavin the box to hold and climbed into his seat. Within moments, they drove to Gavin's home.

After entering, Xavier tossed his now-familiar duffel bag on the sofa and carried the pizza box to the kitchen. He glanced over his shoulder to Gavin. "Go shower and change. I had one at my place before I left to get you."

Without arguing, Gavin left his messenger bag on an armchair and headed to his bedroom. He took a quick shower and changed into a pair of crazy panda-covered sleep pants with a black T-shirt. He tugged on fuzzy black-and-white socks since his feet were cold. Running his fingers through his damp curls, he yawned and returned to the main area.

There he discovered Xavier had set up their pizza and drinks on the coffee table. He'd also fixed up a simple salad. Then he'd cued up the next *Grimm* episode. Between all that, Xavier had changed into sweatpants and a gray tank with the SBFD logo. He had the overhead light on low.

"Wow. You went all out," Gavin said and sat on the floor next to Xavier. He let out a long sigh. "Man, what a day. Still not over. Most of the changes are done. Just need some more work to finalize the layout and look."

Xavier tugged him over to let him lean against his side. Then he handed a plate to Gavin. "Eat before you pass out. Hey, I know how to put together a decent meal sometimes."

Gavin bit into the still-warm slice of Via Pizza's special basil chicken pizza. He groaned when the homemade basil pesto sauce, marinated chicken, fresh mozzarella and sliced Roma tomatoes mixed in his mouth. "Oh, this is my favorite," he murmured.

"I remembered," Xavier said while he hit Play to start the episode.

"This one is going to freak me out, isn't it?"

"Don't know. I'll be here to catch you if it does."

"I like that part the best." Gavin lifted himself a bit to press his lips against Xavier's mouth. A soft kiss lingered between them.

With a groan, Xavier responded and pressed back a little harder to deepen the kiss. It turned passionate and filled with longing. He slid his tongue against Gavin's mouth.

Gavin tasted the pizza's flavors on Xavier's lips. He returned the gesture, then pulled back to lighten the kiss. Then he nuzzled his cheek against Xavier's shoulder.

Xavier kissed Gavin's temple.

Neither one moved to push things between them. They were enjoying taking time to learn more about their relationship.

During the next couple of hours, they watched two episodes of *Grimm*, polished off the pizza and most of the salad and curled close, snuggled under a blanket. Xavier cleaned up everything.

When Gavin could barely keep his eyes opened, Xavier turned everything off. Then he led a sleepy Gavin to the bedroom where they spooned under the covers.

"'Night, Xavier," he whispered.

"Sleep well, hon."

With a smile on his lips, Gavin snuggled back and slid deep into sleep.

* * * *

The sound of Xavier's phone chirping with his alarm brought him out of the deep sleep. Gavin blinked open his eyes when he felt Xavier move. At some point, their positions had changed, and Gavin was spread out across Xavier's front and side. He knew that sound. Part of him hated it intruding on their quiet time together. It was Xavier's alert to get to the station.

"Hmm. Don't want you to go," he murmured.

"Sorry. There are times I hate it, too, but this is part of my life — an important one."

Gavin rolled until he faced Xavier.

Xavier smiled at him. "Got about an hour before they need me. I set it early."

"What? Why would you do that?"

"Wanted a little more time with you. Can I take a spin on your Peloton and have a shower?" Xavier asked.

Gavin buried his face in his pillow. "Really? That's it? You're addicted."

"Sorry, but yup, I really enjoy that bike. I get a better workout than running along the beach. Please?" Xavier drew his fingers through Gavin's soft hair. "Can I use it?"

Gavin tilted his head to look at Xavier. "Yeah. Just using me for my bike. I see how things are."

Xavier chuckled and nuzzled Gavin's cheek. "That and other things — waking up in your arms, having you drape yourself across me, our quiet conversations, eating together."

"I enjoy all that, too."

"Somehow you ease the craziness happening inside my mind. You quiet the ADHD tendencies."

"Really?"

"Yeah. Don't know the reason why that happens."

"Perhaps you feel safe and comfortable here...and with me. You don't have to be on alert or ready to go at a moment's notice."

"Less noise here than at the apartment. I like your home."

Gavin yawned and stretched against Xavier's solid frame. He lowered his chin on his hand and rested it on Xavier's chest. "I like it, too. It's better when you're here with me. I don't feel so lonely."

"Same here."

Blinking, Gavin gave him a sleepy smile. "Want something to eat before you go?"

"Nah. You don't have to get up."

"Nope. I want to. Lots to do today to get ready for tomorrow's wedding." Gavin stretched against Xavier's warm body—not really because he needed to, but he wanted another feel of the solid frame before he lost him for a long shift.

"Okay. Whatever you want to make, I'll eat."

Pushing up, Gavin kissed Xavier's mouth. "Morning."

Xavier smiled. "Morning."

With an answering smile, Gavin rolled away. Humming soft under his breath while his mind worked, he wandered to the bathroom for a piss, brushed his teeth and took a quick shower. He had a revised wedding to finish planning, and there were lots of holes to fill and smooth.

"Already lost you to the wedding, didn't I?" Xavier said while he appeared next to Gavin. He added his own stream to the toilet.

Gavin glanced down at their cocks then glanced up at Xavier.

"What?"

"What?"

Xavier lifted an eyebrow. "Is this a problem?"

Gavin glanced down again. "No. No. Not a problem." He finished his stream, shook off any leftovers and tucked himself back into his pajama pants. Then he washed his hands while listening to Xavier finish and flush the toilet.

Normal couple stuff for getting ready in the morning.

He'd been through it before with Arthur and Maury. There was an easiness here — nothing overtly sexual, just comfortable.

It was…wonderful.

"I'll use the other shower." Xavier pressed a few kisses from Gavin's cheek to his neck and shoulder, drew his fingers down Gavin's spine and slipped out of the room.

Gavin smiled. The deep sexual stirrings swirled within his lower body. The connection strengthened and enlivened his need for this man.

This guy was a keeper.

Chapter Seventeen

Like he promised, Gavin rearranged everything for the Thursday morning wedding at the clinic's chapel. A couple of times he didn't think he could make it happen, but problems smoothed out and cleared up.

Now tying a ribbon around a bouquet of flowers, Gavin secured the bundle to the pew's side.

Nibbling on his inner lip, he continued to second-guess himself. He wanted everything to go perfectly for Arthur and Neil today. It must make up for not having their planned wedding on the beach.

"Would you relax? They'll love all of it," Jude reassured him. He handed over another bunch of flowers he'd rearranged. "It remains their colors, flowers and requests for wedding decorations. Pieces of their original wedding remain in these bundles and the other embellishments. I think it's sweet how they still want a wedding."

"This isn't what they wanted, though. I'm doing a work-around to give them something."

"Can't get around health issues when they crop up their ugly heads."

Gavin glanced over at Jude. "Something you know about all too well."

"Yeah. Way too much."

"Thank goodness you're sleeping with a doctor."

"One of the good things about keeping him around," Jude said.

Gavin shook his head at Jude's teasing. There was far more to their wonderful relationship. He'd caught a slice of it when he helped to plan Doc Elliott's Valentine's surprise for Jude. When he looked around at the supplies, he realized he'd run out of ribbons. "Damn. Where's Victor with the ribbons? He should have been back by —"

"*Aaaaaaaaaah-chooooooooooo!*"

The violent sneeze rattled and echoed.

Gavin jumped in surprise.

Dawson lifted his head and whined.

"Holy crap, what the hell was *that*?" Jude asked.

"Gabin? Don't feel so good. Dis is more dan dust," Victor said. His face was pale with some feverish pink spots. He leaned hard against the wall. Then he snagged a tissue from his pocket and blew hard.

"Who rattled the walls?" Doc Elliott turned the corner. Dressed in his mint-green scrubs, he held a large cup of fresh coffee and a stethoscope dangled around his neck.

Gavin pointed to his assistant.

Doc Elliott studied the young man. "You look like you're not feeling so hot. What's going on, Victor?"

"Sowwby, Doc. Was sneezing earlier, thought allergies. Rest came on yesterday. Didn't want to mess up plans for webbing and leab Gabin in a lurch," Victor said in between deep sniffs, snorts and a clearly stuffed-up nose.

"Victor, you should have mentioned something. I could manage this on my own. It's not a big wedding. You should have stayed home…in bed…with your germs." Gavin moved to step closer but Doc held up a hand to stop him.

"Keep your distance, Gavin."

"What? Why?" Gavin asked.

"Why? Dis bad?" Victor asked. "You got the convention to go to this weekend. Can't get sick. All paid."

"I know. I know. I'll figure out something. Things opened up because of this wedding change." Gavin fiddled with his bow tie.

"Convention?" Doc Elliott asked.

"A wedding expo for engaged couples, consultants, businesses and everything else related. It's in Atlanta for three days. We're going to represent the Charm," Gavin said.

"You're going to lose your assistant," Elliott said.

Gavin grumbled.

"Sowwby, boss." Victor pushed away from the wall and wobbled. "Whoa. Room tilted. I feel dizzy."

"Best sit down, Victor. Come on…over here." Doc Elliott set his coffee down and helped Victor to the closest chair.

"Didn't geb ribbons. Dizzy hit. I couldn't grab the bin." Victor dropped the keys on another chair.

"It's okay. Forget the ribbons," Gavin said.

Elliott pulled a radio from his pocket and hit a button. "Melanie, it's Doc E. I'm in the chapel. Looks like I found another case. Can you bring a full work-up kit to me? We'll need to transfer him back to the ER."

"On my way, Doc."

"Another case? Case of *what*?" Gavin said.

"There's a nasty cold-bug going around. It spread throughout town from kids to seniors and everything in between. Looks like Victor tangled with it and is on the losing end," Elliott said.

"Someone coughed and sneezed when I visited Dorian," Victor admitted.

"That'll do it."

Victor bent over during a harsh coughing spell. He moaned and pressed a hand to his chest. "Ow. Feels like someone is sitting on my chest."

"With an added touch of bronchitis. Double whammy of hell. Wonderful."

"Someone doesn't sound good," Melanie said when she entered the chapel pushing a small cart. She handed over a mask and gloves to Dr. Elliott, who quickly donned them.

Once protected, the doctor began a quick exam to confirm his suspicions. Melanie assisted and kept the record.

"Temp is 101.4," she said when she pulled the thermometer from Victor's ear.

"Set up a chest X-ray. We'll need a bed in ER and a wheelchair."

"I'll call in for help and get him in line. There are a couple other patients ahead of him. X-ray machine went down earlier and things are backed up," Melanie said and stepped away with the radio to contact others.

"Just our luck. Oh, can you shoot some disinfectant on those keys? I don't want the germs to spread," Dr. Elliott said.

Used to the request after the pandemic, Melanie used the Lysol to spray the keys to disinfect them and the chair.

"Thank you." Gavin scooped up the dried keys and tucked them into his pocket.

Elliott crouched to address a groggy, flushed Victor. "Victor, you're going to stay at the clinic. This bug can get nasty real fast if we don't treat you with antibiotics and fluids, especially when you add in a case of bronchitis."

"Dis bad, then?"

"Yes, but you're in good hands. Luckily, you came to work today, and it was at a healthcare center," Elliott said with a smile.

"Sowwby, boss," Victor said.

"Get better, Victor. That's the main thing," Gavin said.

"'Kay." Victor slid into another nasty coughing and hacking spell.

"Yikes, that sounds like a whole lot of folks Norman and I transferred during the last couple of days," Xavier said when he entered the chapel. Dressed in his EMT uniform, dark circles under his eyes and a large cup of coffee in hand, Xavier looked rumpled and exhausted.

"Looks like young Victor caught the bug, Gray," Dr. Elliott said. "We're transferring him to the ER for further testing and treatment."

Victor hacked and coughed a few times. "Not how I wanted to get outta going to Atlanta. Looked forward to it." Then he sniffed hard through plugged sinuses. "Stupid bug."

"Someone call for a transport?" an ER tech asked.

"Over here," Elliott said.

It took a few minutes to transfer Victor to the wheelchair.

"Do you need his healthcare info?" Gavin asked.

"I'll have one of the nurses contact the Charm. It's not the first thing on my personal to-do list for patients. Stupid paperwork is the bane of my existence, along with insurance companies," Elliott said.

"Hi, hon. Bye, hon. See you later," Jude teased.

Elliott blew him an air kiss behind the mask. Then he picked up the cup of coffee he'd set aside. "Sorry, babe. Doctor's life. Make sure you stay safe from this bug."

"I know. I know." Jude twirled a flower between his fingers. "Flowers are easier. You can't get sick from them."

"Unless you're allergic or brush up against poison ivy. Then...well... Come and see me." Chuckling, Elliott followed the others out of the chapel.

"Always gets the last word," Jude said. "Dawson, go bite his butt."

Dawson whined but didn't move.

"Fine. Fine. I know he slips you treats when I'm not looking," Jude said.

Dawson whined.

"Traitor."

Dawson flipped positions to give Jude his back.

Xavier snorted. "Love that dog."

Jude shrugged.

"Oh, man, this is *so* not what I planned. Oh, man, oh, man, oh man," Gavin said and paced the aisle. He tugged on the bow tie then loosened the loops to release it.

"Umm. What did I miss?" Xavier looked between them. "What isn't what you planned?"

"I'm going to let you deal with him and the questions," Jude said. "I'll finish the flowers and get out of the way." He glanced to Gavin. "The wedding happens in an hour."

"I know. I know." Gavin waved his hand. "I'm not going to let them down. I can't."

"What is happening? I'm running a bit on fumes here since my shift is finally over. Need to take the rig back with Norman and hose it down, along with other stuff I don't want to think about right now. Anyway, my brain is a little slow. I'm missing part of the conversation," Xavier said while he dropped into a chair, making sure it wasn't near the one Victor had used.

"Lemme get this germy thing out of the way." Jude grabbed leftover paper that protected the flower stems and used it to drag the chair into a far corner. He poured a liberal dose of hand sanitizer on his hands for protection.

"Damn, I forgot. I still need the ribbons—" Gavin said.

"I'll get them," Jude interrupted to calm him down. "In the back of your car?"

"Yes," Gavin said and tugged the keys out of his pocket.

Being extra cautious, especially with his fragile health, Jude sprayed them again with the sanitizer. Then he used the paper to protect his hands. He whistled to Dawson and left the chapel.

"Okay. Start talking," Xavier said and pointed to a nearby chair. "You weren't this upset when I left you. What happened?"

"Oh, things are a mess and it's not about the wedding. That's fine," Gavin said and dropped into a chair. "With Samuel's encouragement, I signed up the Charm as a vendor for the Atlanta Wedding Expo and Bridal Show this weekend. It's the first big one happening after the pandemic."

"But you had a wedding planned."

"I know. Samuel and Victor planned to leave tonight and set up for Friday. Then I'd fly over there after the wedding and join them. We'd all drive back together."

"And..."

"Now Victor is sick. The wedding is moved to today. We'll need someone to sign in tomorrow morning to make sure we don't lose our place. I can't leave until the wedding and reception are over." Gavin checked his phone. "It'll be a little after two—maybe earlier, maybe later—depending on how Neil's feeling. It'll take a little over five hours to drive to Atlanta and I'm hoping I can check in late."

"Okay. Hold up. Hold up. What is Samuel doing for this thing?"

"Don't know."

"Call him."

"What? Now?"

Xavier nodded.

"Oh. Okay." Gavin thumbed across his phone's screen and dialed Samuel. He put the phone on speaker.

"Hello, Gavin, what's happening over there? Need any help?" Samuel asked.

"Samuel, we have a problem—but not with the wedding."

"Oh, what's wrong?"

"Victor is sick. Bad sick. Like Doc Elliott swooped in and took him to the ER sick."

"Oh, crap," Samuel said.

"Yeah, my whole schedule is thrown for a loop, and I didn't even consider the expo until now."

"Relax. I'm loading up my SUV with everything you pulled out of storage. Got Sully and Dakota helping me with the heavy stuff," Samuel said. "Now I can't command the table alone. I don't know all the packages and options like you and Victor do."

"Thanks to the wedding change, I don't have to fly out. If we can wait until I finish up the wedding and reception, make sure Arthur and Neil are happy with everything, I can run home, pack my bag and head to the Charm. We can drive up together and I'll be there for the entire weekend," Gavin said. "It'll be late when we arrive, but it's doable since the expo doesn't start officially until Friday morning."

"Sounds like a plan. I'll have Chandler cancel your airline tickets since the Charm booked them," Samuel said.

"Would it help if you have a third person?" Xavier asked.

"Who's that?" Samuel asked.

"Oh. Xavier is here with me. He's helping to calm me down and figure out this mess," Gavin said.

"Oh, hi, Gray. Umm. That would be up to Gavin. I haven't been to one of these expos before."

"It would be nice to have a third person. I wanted to have someone walk around to check out the other vendors and their options to see how we compare or where we could improve. Samuel has the advantage to look at things from a hotel point of view, while Victor and I covered the wedding side," Gavin said.

"I wouldn't know what to do other than be a go-fer," Xavier said.

"Perhaps function as a potential client," Samuel said. "But a go-fer would be good, too."

"What about your schedule? Aren't things hectic for you? What about school?" Gavin asked.

"There's some wiggle room, and I'm already off this weekend since I put in a few double shifts this week. The fire chief ordered me to take it easy before the chaotic mix of school and work begins again. Norman can cover my position as chief. School starts Monday morning, so I'm in the clear." Xavier looked over to meet Gavin's gaze. "Do you want a third? I could help with the driving, the set-up and the expo."

"Samuel, would you mind?" Gavin asked.

"Nope. You would be alone in your room since Victor isn't coming. Dakota backed out earlier after the wedding change to open the restaurant, but I might be able to sweet-talk him into joining us again. I'll pick up a day pass for him. There's enough room for all of us to drive back, since we're not over-packing the SUV."

"Then it's a plan?" Xavier asked.

"Sounds good to me," Samuel said.

"Okay. Then we'll meet up at the Charm around three? That'll put us in Atlanta between eight or nine with some wiggle room for traffic, stops and food?" Gavin asked.

"Sounds about right," Samuel said. "How about I send over a couple of the housekeeping staff to oversee the clean-up in the chapel and cafeteria? I know a few folks who wouldn't mind the extra hours and pay. That will give you a little more time to get free."

"That would be awesome. If they worked previous events and know the procedures, it would be even better, since I wouldn't need to supervise them. I figured the flowers could be spread out to other patients and nursing stations. I'm not using any supplies from my collection. The other vendors will manage their own clean-up."

"Perfect. I'll find and send them over about an hour after the ceremony starts. Which was…" Samuel rattled off a time. "Right?"

"Yeah. That's good."

"Okay. Then it's set."

"See you later, Samuel," Gavin said.

"Bye," Samuel said and hung up.

Gavin rolled the phone between his hands. "Are you sure— Wait! What about your ADHD? It's a long drive. Won't that drive you bonkers?"

"I wouldn't have offered if I didn't want to do this, and I can manage my ADHD symptoms. It wouldn't stop me from helping you. Besides, I get to hang out with you and see you in action. Plus" — Xavier offered a mischievous grin full of promise and decadence — "we'll have a private hotel room."

Gavin hugged Xavier. "Thank you…for everything."

Xavier returned the embrace. "Anytime." He pressed a kiss to Gavin's temple.

Gavin placed a hand on Xavier's stubble-rough cheek. "Okay. You need to go home, shower, pack a bag and take a nap. You look exhausted."

"I'll be okay. What should I pack?"

"Business casual, since we're representing the Charm. We can snag you a few shirts with either the Southern Charm or the Charmed Occasions logo."

"You're representing the Charm, and I'm the hired hand."

"Nope. You're coming, so you're gonna help, too. I can explain everything about what Charmed Occasions offers to engaged couples along the drive."

"There better not be a test at the end," Xavier said while he stood.

Gavin chuckled. "I thought a college boy would be used to tests."

"Hmm...nope. I'm on break for four more days," Xavier said. "Get back to prepping this wedding. I'll see you in a few hours. I'll grab some munchies for the road. Anything you desire on a road trip?"

"Doritos Cool Ranch. Big bag. Love them."

"Doritos? Huh?"

"You asked," Gavin said.

"Okay. I'll pick them up and call Samuel to see if he wants anything." Xavier captured Gavin in a light embrace. "Should I add in some other supplies?"

A flush colored Gavin's cheeks.

"I'll take special care of you. Promise." Xavier lowered his head to kiss Gavin.

Gavin lifted on his toes, wrapped his fingers around Xavier's neck and returned the kiss. The man could kiss like a dream.

"Errmm. Perhaps save that for later?" a voice said.

At the interruption, they glared at Jude, who'd returned with the ribbon box. Dawson sat, his ears cocked.

"Really?" Gavin asked.

"What? If I can't, you can't." Jude dropped the box on the chair. "We're on the clock. I'll set up the centerpieces in the cafeteria area."

"Slave-driver," Gavin muttered.

"Heard that," Jude said while he walked away.

With a wag of his tail, Dawson followed his human.

Gavin rested his forehead on Xavier's shoulder. Xavier chuckled at the florist.

"Make it perfect for Arthur and Neil." Xavier tied Gavin's bow tie and twitched the loops to make them perfect. "All fixed. I'll see you later."

Gavin tilted his head back. "Fine. Fine. Sheesh."

"You wouldn't want it any other way. Work your magic." Xavier kissed Gavin again. Then he left the chapel.

Sauntering back over, Jude asked, "Well? What's happening?"

"I thought you were going to work on centerpieces."

"They can wait. Tell me all the gossip."

"Road trip to Atlanta will happen right after the reception. Samuel is sending some housekeeping staff to deal with the clean-up. That way I can rush home, shower, pack and get to the Charm." Gavin snagged a few ribbons and picked up where he'd left off.

"And Gray?"

"He offered to join us."

"Really?"

Gavin nodded.

"Hmm. I see things are improving on the love affair side."

Gavin felt heat rise up his neck. "Nothing happened."

"Yet?"

The flush darkened.

"Would be perfect timing. Just saying... Go for it, my friend."

"I can't jump into physical things. I don't function like that."

"Then take your time and so will Gray. Either way"—Jude finished with his flowers and looked straight at Gavin—"don't give up."

Clearing his throat to push back his embarrassment, Gavin checked over the chapel, transformed with a few flowers, ribbons and fabrics. It was perfect. A faint echo of the planned wedding.

"Looks good," Jude said.

"Thank you for your help."

"Anytime. Let's finish the cafeteria. Then you can go check on the eager couple."

"That's the plan. Wanna be my new Victor?"

Laughing, Jude gathered his boxes of flowers on the cart. Gavin hurried to add his things to the bottom levels. "Nope." Then Jude whistled to Dawson and left the chapel.

"Aww. Come on. I need a Victor. Mine is sick," Gavin whined while they moved through the hospital.

"Don't even try it," Jude said.

Gavin stomped off to speak with the vendors. The clinic's administrator gave Gavin free rein. One of the wonderful things about working with a smaller hospital was less red tape and bureaucracy.

They had used a couple of rolling screens to cordon off an area and turned it into a reception. The couple's chosen linens covered the tables and chairs. Jude placed the centerpieces on the different tables with the elaborate ones around the couple's place.

Though he hadn't requested it, the local lighting company set up a few spotlights and a display of Neil and Arthur's initials intertwined against the wall. It was an exquisite touch and offering.

The DJ had set up his boards and speakers and kept the music low. He assessed a few things and gave Gavin a thumbs-up.

Going around the area, Gavin set up a few finishing touches with flowers, ribbons and other bits and pieces.

Natalie from Blissful Cloths handed him a folded chocolate brown piece of draping fabric. "I thought this would be appropriate for Neil's wheelchair to drape over his legs. I don't think the doctors wanted him to completely change."

"Oh, wow, this is wonderful, Natalie. Thank you so much. Yes, they allowed him to take off the gown and wear scrub pants with a different version of a top. This will help him feel a little better," Gavin said.

"I hope so. Just have him leave it on a chair and we'll pick it up. No extra cost," she said.

"Thank you, Natalie."

"With that, we're all done. I'll send a clean-up crew later." With a wave, she returned to her helpers.

"I'm going to find Arthur and Neil," Gavin said. "Time to get this wedding started. Thank you, everyone, for helping me create this emergency wedding. It came out even more wonderful than I imagined."

"Oh, here. Take this box." Jude placed a box with flowers on top of the folded cloth.

"What's all this?"

"Tie these around Neil's wheelchair. Bring some ribbons to help decorate them. The four smaller flowers are the boutonnières."

"You're beyond awesome."

"They deserve it."

Gavin left the cafeteria in good hands. He adjusted the precious gifts, then texted Arthur. That was when he learned they were in Neil's room, along with their chosen best men and a few family members. Other guests made their way to the chapel.

"Crazy out of control and I don't like it," Gavin muttered while he raced up to the room. He waved to the nurses and skidded to a stop by the door.

The crowd of people all turned around.

"There's our wedding event coordinator extraordinaire. Gavin created all of this within the last forty-eight hours. He swore he would get us married before we left Shore Breeze," Arthur said. He walked over and embraced Gavin. "Thank you for doing all of this."

"Both of you deserve the best. You came here for a wedding, and I'm going to give you a wedding. Might not be on the beach, but we'll make it special," Gavin said while he returned the embrace with one arm.

"I know you will." Arthur released Gavin and stepped back. "How do I look? I thought I'd drop the jacket and just go with the vest and tie."

Gavin set the box and fabric down and walked around Arthur. "Perfect. One more touch." He went to the box and selected a boutonnière. Then he pinned it to Arthur's vest. "There. Which one is your best man?"

"My brother, Aaron," Arthur said and pointed to the man who appeared similar in coloring to Arthur.

"Of course, I remember Aaron, and not just from the rehearsal dinner. How have you been?" Gavin asked Aaron while he selected another flower and pinned it to Aaron's chest. He adjusted Aaron's tie a notch and smoothed his vest, a few shades darker than Arthur's sand-colored one. "There. Perfect."

"I'm doing well. My wife and boys are down in the chapel. Thank you for doing this," Aaron said.

"I'd do anything for them. I'm happy to hear your family is here. I hope they enjoy the visit to our small town."

"We will," Aaron said. "What do you need me to do? Since we didn't quite rehearse this."

"Nope. Not this one, but we'll start the same. Take your brother downstairs to the chapel and stand in the front by the minister. Do you know where to go?"

"Yes, I checked it out before coming up."

"Great. Could you find someone to stand in the different doorways and direct any guests looking around?"

"I've got a pair of teenagers who can do the job. I'll put one by the outside door and one by the chapel." Aaron pulled out his phone to text his family.

"Perfect. I'm a bit lost today because my assistant Victor got laid low. He's in the ER, so I'm doing everything," Gavin admitted.

"Oh no. What happened?" Arthur asked.

"A nasty bug knocked him out. Lucky Doc Elliott swung by, heard Victor and whisked him right to the ER."

"I'll take care of downstairs. You take care of Neil," Aaron said.

"Thank you so much."

"Welcome." Aaron laid a hand on his brother's shoulder. "Come on, bro. Next time you see your fiancé, it will be at the altar. No. No kiss. Not yet." He tugged on Arthur's arm.

"Good luck," Gavin said while Aaron pushed and pulled Arthur out of the room.

Neil laughed.

Except for a man and woman, the rest of the guests left, following Aaron and Arthur.

"You remember my brother Dan and his wife Renee from the dinner?" Neil said.

"Hello again. Renee. Could you pin this flower on your husband? I'll take care of our handsome groom," Gavin said while he picked up the last two boutonnières from the box.

"How lovely." Renee took the flower and pinned it to her husband's fawn-colored vest. She fixed his tie to help it lay better.

Neil adjusted his position in the wheelchair. He'd changed into a loose shirt with a chocolate brown vest. Due to the various leads and IVs, he couldn't get into the entire outfit he'd planned for the wedding. He tugged on the pale-blue scrub pants and scuffed the pale slippers against the chair's footrests. "Not quite what I wanted to wear."

"You look wonderful, Neil. Arthur doesn't care what you wear. He just wants to see you roll down the aisle to be at his side."

"Listen to him, Neil. You look wonderful," Renee said. "What should we do with the rest of those lovely flowers?"

"They'll get tied to different parts of the wheelchair and the IV stand. I was given this chocolate fabric to drape across Neil's legs." Gavin picked up the fabric, shook it out, then folded it in half and placed it over Neil's lap. He tucked in the sides and made sure it covered the scrubs and slippers. "There we go. A few finishing touches and we'll get you to your groom."

With Renee's help, Gavin decorated the rest of the wheelchair and the IV stand. Then Dan pushed the wheelchair and stand on their journey to the chapel.

After kissing the brothers' cheeks, Renee slipped inside and took her spot.

Gavin waved at the DJ to start their chosen music and motioned to the minister and the photographer. He waited a couple of bars and sent Dan and Neil into the chapel. Then he remained by the doorway to watch his former boyfriend marry the true mate of his heart.

When they finished, Neil tugged Arthur down and smacked a kiss on his lips. Then he did a quick spin to everyone's delight. Arthur laughed while he hung onto Neil. After Arthur got to his feet, they walked down the aisle, now a married couple. Dan and Aaron followed and made sure the IV followed close, while Dan pushed the chair.

Outside in the hallway, Arthur hugged and kissed Gavin's cheek. "Thank you so much. It was wonderful—the flowers and colors…everything."

Neil shook Gavin's hand. "Perfect."

"Oh, we're not done yet." Gavin grinned. "Dan, could you drive our groom's chair to the reception?"

"Of course."

"Reception?" Arthur asked.

"You set up a reception?" Neil asked.

"What's a wedding without a reception? Sheesh. What kind of wedding planner do you think I am?" Gavin winked. "The photographer will capture a few outdoor pictures after I show you."

Within a few minutes, they reached the cafeteria. Gavin got the couple to close their eyes. He gestured to the guests to head inside and find their places. The DJ hurried by to return to his station and turned on the music and lights. After Dan positioned the chair, Gavin pulled open one side of the screens.

"Welcome to your reception," he said. "Open your eyes!"

The newly married couple stared around the transformed area. Their guests let out a cheer and soft applause.

"Ohmygod!" Arthur said.

"Not quite—"

"No. No. Gavin, it's perfect," Arthur interrupted and embraced Gavin. "Thank you for doing all this!"

"You're more than welcome," Gavin said while he hugged him back. He smiled down at Neil, who had a few tears. "Okay. We're going out of this door into the courtyard for photographs. We'll get your license signed to make it all official. Then you can enjoy the reception."

For the next two hours, Gavin kept everything flowing. He kept his eye on the time and on Arthur and Neil. When he noticed some weariness appearing on Neil's face, he shortened the reception. Everyone waved and cheered Arthur and Neil when they left. Instead of a honeymoon, they would return to Atlanta the next day.

With Aaron and Dan as back-ups, they pushed the guests to return to the Charm, their homes, a visit to the town or the road. Then he welcomed the clean-up crews that allowed him to make his escape.

Chapter Eighteen

While the clean-up started, Gavin gathered his personal things and left the hospital. He texted Samuel and Xavier that everything had finished and he was free. A few minutes at home to shower, change and pack, and he would be on his way to the Charm for their road trip.

The whole thing took almost an hour until he pulled up at the Charm and wrestled his suitcase and backpack out of his car.

"More than a few minutes," Dakota teased while he left the Charm's kitchen.

"Yes. Yes. I know. Shush," Gavin said. "It takes a while to get all this styling in place."

"Missing your bow tie and suspenders."

"Too uncomfortable on a long road trip, but I did bring plenty for the expo. Gotta look my best."

"Lemme get the suitcase," Dakota said while he pointed to the case. "Leave the keys with me. Someone will check your house and mailbox while you're gone. I'll figure out where to put the bag."

"Thanks, Dakota," Gavin said and tossed him the keyring.

"No problem." Dakota snatched the keys in midair and pocketed them. He took hold of Gavin's suitcase. "Gray is inside with Samuel. I packed you guys a small bag of goodies and drinks for the trip, along with whatever Gray picked up."

"Appreciate it," Gavin said while he raced inside with his backpack.

"There you are. We've got a bit of a problem," Samuel said when Gavin entered the kitchen area.

"Oh no. I don't like the sound of that," Gavin said and glanced at Xavier.

"Not my fault. Honest," Xavier said.

"The fault lies with my family. I need to fly to New York and deal with a troublesome acquisition my brother is trying to oversee. Since that was my previous position, my brother requested I join him. I tried to get out of it, but it's a multi-billion-dollar deal and since my family's company helps pay for things here – " Samuel shrugged.

"Go. Go to New York," Gavin said when Samuel paused. "I can manage the expo. If you get the chance, join us in Atlanta. If not, I can work the weekend with Xavier's help."

"I'm so sorry about this unexpected issue, Gavin."

"It happens. Can we still use your SUV?"

"Of course, Dakota will drop me off at the airport. I don't think those supplies will fit in your Soul. I added seashell stress squishies and pens with the Charm's logo and contact info for extra giveaways."

"Oh, wow, that's wonderful. Thank you."

Samuel handed Xavier the clicker. "Registration and insurance are in the glove-box. Please don't have a need to use them."

Gavin chuckled. "No, we'll behave ourselves."

"I'll get Dakota to remove my bag. Oh, he's going to enjoy undoing part of that Tetris puzzle," Samuel said. "You two get ready for your trip. I texted you the information for the rooms and the expo, Gavin."

"Got it all set up on my phone and printed stuff in my bag." Gavin let the backpack swing around.

"Good to have a back-up. You can use the on-screen navigation." Samuel left the kitchen to find Dakota and rearrange the SUV's baggage compartment...again.

"I'm done with changes. No more. Why is it so hard to adult?" Gavin leaned back against the nearest counter.

"Yup. Good thing I thought about joining you. I wouldn't want you to travel alone to Atlanta," Xavier said. "As for how to adult, I stopped trying to figure it out a long time ago."

"I lived there for years. I know exactly where we're going. I went to this expo many times with my Atlanta company." Gavin glanced over. "Though I'm happy you're sticking with me. I didn't want to make this trip alone."

Xavier bumped their shoulders. "Now you're not."

Samuel returned with Dakota following and pulling on a suitcase handle. "Okay. Everything is ready to go. If possible, Dakota and I will join you and help with the drive home. At this point, I can't guarantee we'll make it."

"If you don't, we'll drive home," Xavier said.

"It's what I figured." Samuel glanced at Gavin. "Do you have all the check-in information?"

Gavin smiled and shook his head. "Yes, Dad, I have everything. Again…we'll be fine. I did live in Atlanta for years. Remember?"

Dakota snorted.

Samuel smacked the back of his hand against Dakota's belly. "Have a good trip. Enjoy yourselves. Hope you make Charmed Occasions a star among the vendors."

"Bring in lots of clients," Gavin said.

"That, too. Gotta pay for that new event building."

"I might need another assistant or a dedicated team if that happens."

Samuel laughed. "If it happens, we'll discuss the options."

"Guess we hit the road," Xavier said.

"Thanks for jumping in and helping Gavin," Samuel said.

"Get to spend some time with him. Gonna enjoy myself." Xavier grinned at Gavin, who bumped their shoulders again.

"Still gotta do some work," Dakota reminded them. He handed over an insulated bag. "Bottles of water, iced tea and some munchies—to go with the junk food."

"Appreciate everything," Gavin said when he took the bag.

"Be nice to my baby," Samuel said.

Gavin waved while Xavier dangled the clicker. "Bye!"

"Bye," Samuel said while they left the kitchen.

"Let's hit the road," Xavier said while they headed to the rich blue Lexus GS SUV. He passed over the clicker.

Using it, Gavin slid into the driver's seat. He plugged in his phone, placed the printed map on the lower console and tucked his backpack and cooler behind his seat. He pressed the button to start the engine and adjusted the seat, mirrors and steering wheel.

Xavier slipped into the passenger seat and closed the door. "Was Dakota driving?"

"Yeah, gotta hike it up a couple of inches to reach the pedals." Gavin pulled on the seatbelt and waited for Xavier to settle. "Can you figure out the screen and the map thingy? I know how to get across the bridge and over to the first highway."

"Will do. Have you driven this before?"

Gavin nodded while he backed the SUV, complete with the screen. "Yeah. We went on a road trip to an expo in Jacksonville. I drove a couple of times. It's easy to handle, even loaded down."

"Good to know."

Gavin fell quiet while he followed the road away from the Charm.

Xavier fiddled with the screen and map. He hit a button and said, "Let the road trip begin."

The feminine voice offered the first direction.

* * * *

Gavin sang along when the Tom Petty's *I Won't Back Down* came up on the classical rock satellite channel. He hummed a few lines and went back to the chorus. All the while he tapped away with his fingers on the steering wheel.

"You have a nice voice."

Realizing he wasn't alone since he was lost in the music and the drive, Gavin flushed and hunched his shoulders. "Oops."

"Oops?"

"Forgot you were there."

"How did that happen?"

"Lost in figuring out the drive and the music. I love classic rock when driving. Plus, we can get this channel throughout the drive, thanks to satellite radio. Love this car!" Gavin patted the dashboard. "Pretty shiny Lexus with all the bells and whistles. A few more luxuries than my baby Soul."

"And you often break out in singing?"

"Yup. Is that bad?"

"Since you can actually carry a tune and not sound like you're strangling a cat?" Xavier paused and shook his head. "Nope."

"Ha!" Gavin smacked Xavier's arm with his hand.

"You're not bad at all. I enjoy classic rock almost as much as I love country."

"Country?"

"Yeah. I'm an old cowboy at heart. I can wear cowboy boots, tight blue jeans and a faded Stetson with the best of them and knock out any song you want."

Gavin glanced at Xavier and knew the man could sinfully fill out a pair of faded denim. "Can you country line dance?"

"Maybe."

"Learn something new about you every day."

"Same way I learned you have a good singing voice and should do it more often." Xavier swiveled his head to check out Gavin. "Tom Petty is awesome. It hurt when I heard about his death."

"Big-time sucks to lose him like that. Awesome singer and songwriter. One of the best." Gavin wiggled in his seat when Boston's *More Than a Feeling* played next and hummed along when the guitars started.

Xavier chuckled while he picked up the printed map. "Do we take this highway to I-65 North?"

"Yeah. There are construction zones, like everywhere else, but it's the shortest route to Atlanta. We'll switch over to I-85 N. That will take us straight into downtown and Peachtree."

"About five hours?"

"Give or take, due to construction and traffic. The navigation system might switch us around if it's bad. We're leaving at an odd time on a weekday, so that'll help, I hope."

"Unless we hit rush hour in Atlanta."

"Crap," Gavin said.

"Want me to drive that part?"

"I know Atlanta and the crazy traffic. I lived there for fifteen years. How about taking over for the drive on I-65?"

"I can do that. Perhaps we can find someplace to eat."

"Sounds fine unless we wanna make a push for it." Gavin whispered the last few chorus lyrics. "No, I can't get that high."

Xavier laughed. "Don't want you breaking any glass trying."

Gavin laughed and shook his head.

Later down the highway, Gavin whooped and tapped the steering wheel to the drums. He sang along to the Bachman-Turner Overdrive song about taking care of business.

Xavier joined in with the next few stanzas while he air-rocked the guitar.

"Oh, yeah," Gavin said while they rocked through the song. "Sweet air guitar, man."

"Running Rockstar champ at the firehouse."

"All of you play Rockstar?"

"It's something that's quick and easy to drop when you have a call. Not like you could lose your life or someone else's spot."

"That's something I didn't expect. Figured all you tough guys would be working out, cooking or chilling."

"We do all that. Depends on how the day's calls are going." Xavier twisted and tugged the sack of munchies closer. "Want your Doritos?"

"Did you get them?"

"Of course."

"Awesome. Yes! Crack those babies open."

Xavier rolled his eyes in amusement while he popped open the bag and wedged it between the console and seat. "Remember. This isn't our car. No crumbs. Don't smear stuff all over the steering wheel and buttons." He snatched a couple of napkins and tucked them between the bag and the console. "Wipe your fingers."

"I know. I know. Otherwise, I'll be vacuuming and detailing for days. Don't piss off the boss by messing up his pretty car," Gavin said and popped a chip into his mouth. He said something around the mouthful.

"What was that? Couldn't understand the chip mumbling."

"Got it. I got it."

"Good. This is a sweet ride," Xavier said while snatching a chip from the bag.

"Hey. These are mine."

"Shush. I got two bags. You can share. Water? Iced tea? Soda?"

"Tea, please."

Xavier reached into the cooler and pulled out a bottle of the Delights' tea. He cracked the top and set it in the holder.

"You're handy to have around on a drive."

"Shush or I'll put it all away."

Gavin gasped in a playful fashion. He clutched the Doritos bag and whimpered.

"Addicted?"

"They're my crack." He lowered his voice to a throaty mimic of Gollum. "*My precious!*"

"That was bad."

"I know, but you enjoyed it."

Xavier snorted and settled back with his own bottle of tea. Then he pulled a small medicine holder from a backpack pocket. After selecting a pill, he popped it in his mouth and followed it with a few gulps of tea.

"What's that?"

"Hmm? Oh, an extra med to calm me down... Relax. Don't worry about my screwy brain. I've lived with this condition since I was a kid. The doctors diagnosed me in college since I was always moving around with sports, but I kept up my studies. I confused the doctors." Xavier dropped the holder back into the pocket and zipped it. Then he pulled out a small diary and pen and made a notation. He selected a different journal and made a few more.

"Is that...normal? All those journals?"

"For me...yes. I need to keep things organized on paper and my phone since I can't rely on my brain. Things get a bit more complicated when I'm taking classes. There's a third journal that deals only with my classes, homework, exams and other lessons that pop up." Xavier clicked off the pen, clipped it in place and tucked the journal back inside the bag. He rearranged to make sure things fit in a certain position that satisfied him.

"Anything I can do to help?"

"Nope. Just need to satisfy my brain and urges." Xavier turned to watch the boring highway scenery pass the window.

"My Kindle is in my backpack. You're welcome to check it out."

"I have my own, but thanks for the offer. What about you?"

"I'm doing okay," Gavin said in between crunches of Doritos. "Go ahead and chill out with a book or take a nap. You don't have to talk to me the entire time."

"I'll take a nap. Still catching up after the crazy-long hours. This med makes me a little sleepy, so it'll help knock me out." Xavier pressed a button to tilt the seat back. He snagged a ball-cap from the backpack resting by his feet and tugged it into place. Then he lifted it for a moment. "Wake me when you want a break from driving."

"Will do. Enjoy your nap. Should I lower the music?"

Xavier readjusted the cap to cover his eyes. "Nah. I can sleep through anything. You get used to sleeping through noise at the station."

Gavin lowered one of his hands to touch Xavier's forearm. He squeezed and felt Xavier tap his hand back. Then Gavin returned his hand to the wheel and hummed along to a Fleetwood Mac song.

* * * *

Almost three hours later, Gavin pulled off at a rest stop and found a parking spot. By the time he'd turned the engine off, Xavier woke from his nap and stretched.

"Hey. Stopping to change spots?" Xavier asked on the edge of a yawn.

"Yup."

"Where are we?"

"Just past Montgomery and about to enter Georgia."

"Oh. You made good time."

"We're about two hours out from Atlanta. Traffic moved along, so I felt fine continuing. Shit, I know you wanted to stop somewhere to find a place to eat. I'm sorry—"

Xavier waved off his concern. "Wasn't hungry. Needed the sleep more. We can eat when we get to the hotel."

"Okay. Felt the same way." Gavin bounced in the seat. "Need to pee."

"Same here."

Gavin clicked the locks. Then they made their way to the bathrooms for a quick break.

Leaving the restroom, Xavier walked around to stretch out his legs.

"Feeling any better?" Gavin leaned against the SUV to watch Xavier.

"Much. I'm good to drive." Xavier held out his hand for the clicker and Gavin tossed it over. "Get on in. You can move my backpack behind the seat." He hit the button to open the locks. Then he slid in, turned on the engine to gain control over the buttons to alter the seat and mirrors to accommodate his longer legs.

"Tall people. Sheesh," Gavin teased while he climbed into the passenger side. He moved the backpack behind the seat as Xavier had suggested.

Then he switched their bottles of iced tea and the bag of Doritos.

"How much of a dent did you make?" Xavier tugged on the bag to check it. "Halfway down. Are you kidding me?"

"What? I like to snack while I drive."

"And sing."

"And sing."

"Where do you put all those calories?"

"Fast metabolism?"

"No wonder you weren't hungry for dinner." Xavier chuckled while he clicked the belt into place and put the car in gear. The map screen flicked over and resumed tracing their path to Atlanta.

* * * *

Within a couple of hours — made a bit longer thanks to traffic — they located a parking spot. Xavier insisted on finishing out the drive.

Gavin twisted to grab his backpack. "Need to check in and register for the conference, too. We'll have to set up tonight since things kick off early in the morning."

"How about I go with you? I'll take our personal stuff to the room and return to help you with the rest of the gear."

"Splitting the load works for me."

Xavier snagged his backpack and followed him out. He hit the locks and alarm and pocketed the clicker.

Inside, the check-in process went smooth. Gavin explained about Samuel's room and hoped the hotel could keep the reservation open. There would be a price, but the room could be saved for forty-eight hours. After that it would be released. Gavin texted

Samuel while Xavier accepted the keycards and listened to instructions. After another quick conversation, Gavin learned where to find registration. They went there next and stepped in line.

"Hello. Welcome to the Atlanta Wedding and Engagement Expo. Vendor or attendee?" the lady asked behind the table.

"Hello. Vendor. Charmed Occasions at Southern Charm B&B. Gavin Hartfield," Gavin said and spelled his last name.

"And guest?" she asked while she pulled out his lanyard and badge.

Gavin slipped the lanyard over his head. "I had a change of helpers, thanks to a last-minute attack of a cold-bug. The original name is Victor MacArtney. This is Xavier Grayson."

"That's been happening a lot. We'll have to give Mr. Grayson a handwritten sticker over Mr. MacArtney's badge."

"That's fine. I don't mind." Xavier spelled his name for the lady and accepted the lanyard with the expo's name, main sponsors and the plastic-covered badge and access level.

"There are two more on the list for Southern Charm—Samuel Ashford and Dakota Mitchell."

"Yes," Gavin said, "I hope they will be here by Saturday. Can they still check in?"

"Yes, we have day passes, so we'll be open throughout the expo."

"Good to know. I'll make sure they understand."

The lady picked up a bag with the expo's name and sponsors and placed it on the table. She pulled out a single piece of paper. "Here's your vendor bag and packet, but it's only one per vendor, Mr. Hartfield. This is the map of the vendor area where your table is located. The table is here…" She paused while searching a list and the map. Then she circled a table by the wall. "This one."

"Oh, that's great. Are we allowed to put a standing display banner? How about posters on the wall?"

"Yes, you can, since it's not going to block another vendor. You can post what you want as long there are no marks or holes. The room is open until eleven tonight. Then it reopens at six a.m. for vendors to finish set-up before the doors open to attendees at eight."

"Brilliant. Thank you so much," Gavin said while he scooped up the map and bag.

"Have a wonderful expo, and I hope you gets lots of visitors. We had a high registration since this is the first big event. Lots of interest and need out there for wedding assistance beyond knowing how to set up a Zoom meeting room or a Discord chat."

"Thanks!" Gavin walked toward the hallway that led to the massive rooms. He found the door with the matching name on the map. "We should be in this one. We'll figure out the table location first, so we know where to go before splitting up."

"Lead the way."

Gavin slung the bag's straps over one shoulder and entered the massive room. He whistled low. "Big event. Lots of vendors. Hope folks can find us." He pointed to the stage. "Those are for fashion shows, DJ performances and local music groups. The consultants are along the back wall and corner. That corner has photographers, honeymoon destinations and everything in between."

"Everything you collected and organized into one package is spread out in total craziness in these two massive rooms," Xavier said.

"Yup."

"*Dang*. You do more than even I expected."

Gavin chuckled while he moved through the pre-determined aisles and paths toward the consultants' area. He counted off the tables and pointed to theirs with the number and name on the placard. "Here we are." He figured out their generalized location. "We're along major paths, not lost in some corner. We should get plenty of traffic."

"What now?"

"Get the gear from the SUV. Set up. Get some sleep." Gavin dropped the bag on one of the chairs. "Unless you want to eat first?"

"Nah. Let's at least get everything inside. Then we'll figure if we want food. I spotted a couple of decent places to eat within the hotel, or I can always get takeout or room service." Xavier checked the key-card holder. "We're on the tenth floor. Not too bad. I'll find it. This is your card."

Gavin slipped his card in the back of the badge holder. "Can't lose it that way. I'm wearing this for the next three days."

"Good idea." Xavier tucked his card into his holder. "To the car?"

"To the car."

"Dakota added the hand truck—the one that opens and folds out to a flat bed. You don't have to wait for a free cart." Xavier led the way back to the parking lot. He nodded toward the overflowing carts filled with boxes being used by other vendors. "You would wait all night for one to get free."

"Thank you, Dakota," Gavin said.

"Someone painted the Charm's name on the side, so it won't get lost."

"I can collapse it and tuck it under the table. It'll be covered by fabric and a banner."

"Even better. Here we are." After opening the doors, Xavier managed to unearth and set up the flat-bed cart.

Together, they transferred the bins, boxes and bags onto the cart. Somehow, they managed to make it all fit on the first trip.

"Now that's a game of Tetris. Oh yeah!" Gavin wiggle-danced in place.

"Now, hope nothing topples along the way." Xavier dropped their suitcases on top and slid his backpack onto his shoulders. After making sure they were in the right parking area, he clicked the alarm. Then he handed the clicker to Gavin, who tucked it into his backpack.

"Let's get all this to the ballroom first. I'll take our personal bags upstairs. There's no way you'll maneuver all this on your own," Xavier said.

"I might…"

"Not taking a chance. That's why I'm here. The muscle…" Xavier playfully flexed his biceps to show off. "Remember?"

"Oooh. Be still my fluttering heart." Gavin tested Xavier's hardened muscle. "Can you show these guns off all weekend? It'll draw in the crowds, especially with those colorful tattoos. Damn, I forgot to ask about the shirts —"

Xavier pushed the laden cart through the parking lot. "Relax. Samuel shoved a few Charm shirts into my backpack. I think he chose a couple of short-sleeved ones."

"Yay! Oops, go to the right. Right. Right!" Gavin said while he steered the front.

They bumped into the curb and scrambled to save anything from toppling off.

"A little more notice, please," Xavier said while they turned the cart.

Gavin giggled while they continued to maneuver. He nodded to a doorman who held open the doors. "Appreciate the help."

"Good idea to bring your own cart," the doorman said. "Enjoy your stay and the expo."

"We will," Gavin said.

"More moving, please. Hard to keep this thing going from my end," Xavier ordered.

"Sheesh. So impatient."

"I would like to eat before we hit the bed. Now I can figure out how you stay so damn skinny. You do everything but sit down and eat. You need a keeper."

"Grumble, grumble, grumble." Gavin tugged the cart to get it moving across the main floor. He directed the way back toward the convention room.

Once inside, they wound their way to the table.

Gavin stopped the cart directly in front and bounced on his toes. "Made it! See? That wasn't too bad."

"*Oy vey*! Can you unload? I'll take our bags up to the room," Xavier said while he slung his duffel bag strap over one shoulder. He hefted Gavin's larger suitcase down and pulled the handle up. Then he dropped the smaller matching bag on top and figured out how to connect them.

"Yup. I got everything labeled and numbered. Just gotta put them in order and off I go."

Xavier pinched his fingers together and teased, "Just a touch of OCD."

"Chandler must be rubbing off on me. Though it does help keep things organized and prepared. Go. I'll be fine until you return."

"I might have to visit the gym later and burn off some energy."

"Whatever you need to do, go on and get 'er done. I'm not keeping you chained to my side—at least until the expo opens."

"What? You didn't pack the handcuffs?"

Gavin laughed and shooed him away. "Nut case," he muttered while Xavier left him alone. "Time to figure out this Tetris pile."

First, he pulled out his cell phone and flipped to his music app. He chose an upbeat play-list. Of course, it was more classic rock. Then he placed the phone and the expo's bag on the chair. He tugged out a water bottle and added it to the mix. All the while, he hummed along when The Who's *Who Are You* played first.

Humming and singing, Gavin unpacked and set up the tall standing banner since it was on top. He set it so the entire image could remain in full view and draw in attention.

It took a few lifts and drops, but he located the first plastic tub and opened it to reveal the table's drapery and banner. Then he pulled out a small box of tools he might need during set-up. He spread out and smoothed the ocean-blue cloth. With a combination of tape and clips, he centered the horizontal banner. Since he had the available wall, he taped a couple of larger pictures with advertisements and list of packages. To make sure everything was positioned how he wanted, he backed away to double-check. With a grin, he pulled out the various stands and baskets to corral all the giveaways. Then he tucked the banner's holder inside the tub and closed it.

"Where are you, Tub Number Two?"

Grumbling, Gavin re-stacked the tubs according to their numbers and contents. He left the boxes of new giveaways on the cart.

"Okay. Here we go." He pulled the second tub closer.

"What are you doing here? I thought you scurried away from Atlanta for good. Scurried like a little scared mouse."

Gavin closed his eyes at the harsh tone. While he'd known his former company, Mosaic Events, would be here, he'd hoped to avoid them. He'd prayed his ex wouldn't be in attendance, but just his luck... Straightening, he composed himself before he turned to face the trouble.

Standing in front, the instigator was his biggest rival within the firm and ex, Maurice 'Maury' Hirschinger. The ladies, Hillary and Patricia, who stood behind Maurice, had been friendlier.

"Good evening, Maurice, Hillary and Patricia," Gavin said. "Good to see —"

"Cut out the niceties, Gavin," Maurice cut in. "You lost that position when you left." He stepped closer to invade Gavin's personal space. "When you left *me*."

"Don't go there — not here, not now."

"You left us without a word, Gavin. Nothing. We scrambled to spread out all the events you were supposed to create and oversee," Hillary said.

"I thought we were friends. How could you leave without a goodbye?" Patricia added.

"I didn't leave in an abrupt fashion. Carole Ann understood my decision six months before I left."

Gavin glanced at Maury when he didn't mention any specific reason for leaving. "I gave her the proper notice."

"She said nothing to us."

"I didn't know. She told me it wasn't my place to say anything. While I didn't agree, I followed her request."

"That's ridiculous. That's no way to leave a place where you worked for almost fifteen years," Hillary said.

"I didn't have a choice, Hill. I tried to send out a company email, but Carole Ann blocked it."

"She didn't really accept your leaving—not if she held such a grudge," Hillary said.

"I don't know what was going on with her. I explained my reasons and need for a change to my—"

"Screw that shit," Maurice interrupted again. "You left like a fucking coward without a word. You left me."

"No, our relationship had ended before I left. You just didn't accept it."

"No one leaves."

"I did. Accept it, Maury, and move on."

"Move on? Like how you left me, the company and dumped all your shit on us?" Maurice said. "Yeah, no, it doesn't work like that."

"No, I didn't leave any work behind," Gavin said.

"Try again. Our work tripled because we took on all your clients."

"I didn't accept any new clients the last three months. I finished the preparation for my last four weddings and transferred them to Clara to oversee the actual events. I prepared Clara to take over my position."

"Carole Ann fired Clara a week after you left," Patricia said.

"What?"

Patricia repeated her words.

"Oh, shit. Are you kidding me?" Gavin leaned back against the table. "Why?"

Patricia and Hillary shrugged. "Carole Ann didn't tell us. One day Clara was there. The next day she wasn't."

"Which left all her work on our desks," Maurice said.

"Why are you complaining? More work meant more billable hours. Isn't that what you wanted, Maurice? To pull in the most money and biggest clients and make a name for yourself in high-society weddings," Gavin said.

"And my weddings were the best."

"Screw that shit," Gavin said while he straightened. "I forget how many times I had to bail out your ass because you promised more than what you could deliver. How many times did you put out shabby shit and over-used designs? How many times did Carole Ann have to placate and calm down your clients because they were so distraught?"

"You sonofa —" Maurice grabbed Gavin's shirt in a fist.

Gavin froze at the escalated move.

"Maurice!" "Stop!" the ladies called out together.

"Excuse me. Could you please remove your hand from my boyfriend's shirt?"

Almost collapsing in relief, Gavin stared at Xavier when he appeared behind Maurice.

Maurice didn't remove his grip but shifted his position. He looked over his shoulder and tilted his head back to take in the height difference. Plus. Xavier was overall wider in his frame and more muscular.

"Let go of Gavin."

"I don't think so. Gavin and I have some things to discuss," Maury said.

"I don't want to talk to you, Maury," Gavin said.

Xavier was clearly about to repeat the name but visibly stopped himself. "You heard him. Release him...*now*. I'm not going to ask again."

"Another time. We'll be here all weekend." Maurice released his grip.

"You're not going to come near him again." Xavier shoved his arm between them. "Step away."

Maurice raised his hands. "No problems here." He backed away a few steps.

"Thank you." Xavier brushed past the smaller man, smacked him hard with his shoulder and stopped in front of Gavin. He smoothed the wrinkles in Gavin's shirt. Then he brushed his fingers along Gavin's chin. "Are you all right?"

Gavin managed to nod but slid his eyes to the side.

"No. Keep that pretty gaze on me."

Gavin returned his focus to Xavier.

"Calm down. You're safe," Xavier whispered.

Gavin nodded.

"How do you know these people?"

"Used to work with them. Here. In Atlanta. Mosaic Events. Then I left for the Charm," Gavin said in small sentences. The unexpected confrontation had knocked him a bit more off balance than he'd wanted. He lowered his voice to a whisper. "Maury. That's..."

"The ex? The nasty one."

Gavin nodded.

"Okay. Let me deal with this." Xavier shifted his attention to the trio. "Is there anything else you need to speak with Gavin about? We've had a long day and still have some work to accomplish."

"No. Nothing else. Wanted to make sure he's okay. We didn't know the reasons behind his departure. Our boss doesn't like to share the news with us," Hillary said.

"Right. He's fine — the leading event planner in the area. Everyone is thrilled to have him with us in Shore Breeze, and we're not letting go. What happened when he left is done and can't be changed. It's not his fault, and there's nothing left to discuss. Good night," Xavier said. "Enjoy the expo."

"I'm so sorry, Gavin. I didn't know you dated…" Hillary glanced over her shoulder at Maurice.

Gavin shrugged. "It's over. He hasn't accepted it."

"Of course. You've found a good one," Hillary said. She added a smile to Xavier.

"Come on, Hillary. We need to go." Patricia shoved Maurice to get him moving. "We'll keep him away from the table."

With a nod to Patricia, Xavier placed his hand against Gavin's waist.

"Bye, Gavin." Hillary motioned to the others to leave and followed them.

Gavin let a long breath escape. He rolled his shoulders to shake off the lingering fear of what could have happened if Xavier hadn't returned. Then he pressed his forehead against Xavier's shoulder. "Holy shit. What happened?"

"Someone tried to threaten you. Why?"

"Called him out on his shit after he tried to accuse me of a few things when I left."

"He didn't take it well."

"Nope."

"Just like he didn't take it well with the end of your relationship."

"No. No one had ever left him. He always did the leaving."

"Then you left Atlanta, which really —"

"Pissed him off. It's been over two years. He holds a freaking grudge," Gavin said. "I don't know what to do."

"Has anything happened since those phone calls?"

"No. Not a peep." Gavin looked over his shoulder at where his ex had walked away. He returned his attention to Xavier. "I don't know. He could be planning something."

"Then we'll deal with it together."

"I'm happy you're here. I knew I would see some of my co-workers but didn't think Carole Anne would send him. He's horrible at these things."

Xavier embraced Gavin and rocked him. He slid his fingers through Gavin's hair to smooth and comfort him.

"Thank you for being here."

"Anytime, but don't make a habit of getting into trouble," Xavier said.

"I'll do anything possible to stay away from him. Trust me." Gavin smacked Xavier's side at the playful dig. He stepped back and resettled his shoulders.

"You're not going to be alone. Promise." Xavier touched Gavin's cheek. "Doing better?"

"Getting there." Gavin glanced at the stack of tubs and found his phone. He groaned at the time. "Damn. It's getting late and I'm barely ready."

"Easy. Calm down." Xavier placed his hands on Gavin's shoulders. "What do you need?"

"For this to get done. Food. Sleep. A little bit of luck."

"Good. I checked out the available restaurants. There's a café downstairs. How about I grab sandwiches, chips and drinks? You keep working and I'll bring back dinner and help." Xavier glanced between the tubs and empty table. "Just take it one step at a time. Whatever we don't finish, we'll get done before the expo opens. You can get back here in the morning while I grab us some coffee and breakfast."

"Sounds like you figured everything out."

"That's why you got a go-fer—food, supplies and muscle."

"And extra hugs when I need them," Gavin said.

"Anytime. What do you want to eat?"

Gavin gave him a couple of options since he didn't have a menu. With a nod, Xavier kissed him and left him alone. Gavin turned to look across the vast room but didn't see any sign of his former co-workers. Hopefully, he would be left alone to finish his set-up in peace.

Chapter Nineteen

The following morning, Gavin woke early with Xavier and enjoyed some morning snuggles.

Xavier traced a finger along Gavin's nose. "Tonight I was thinking we could try to get a table at the restaurant or order in room service, take advantage of the hot tub and enjoy some sexy times."

Gavin flushed under the touch and Xavier's words. "Okay."

"Can't wait to see you in action."

"What action?"

Xavier laughed. "While I prefer the sexy Gavin, I'm talking about the wedding-planner Gavin."

"If it's the wedding planner Gavin, then we need to get going. I hope it's going to be crazy busy with lots of potential clients stopping at the table. While we mostly support LGBTQ+ couples, I'm not turning away heterosexual ones. That's not how you run a successful event planning company. Samuel and Dakota agree."

"I know. I'll have to wait for sexy Gavin…somewhat patiently. At the same time, I'll make sure we guide all types of couples to our table for you to wow them with all the wonderful options." Xavier kissed him again before he rolled away.

Racing through showers, dressing and gathering their things, they hustled downstairs.

"I'll get coffee and breakfast. Meet you at the table," Xavier said and kissed Gavin's cheek.

Gavin paused and glanced at him. He kissed Xavier's cheek back. "Yay. Caffeine. See you soon."

With a chuckle, Xavier headed off in a different direction.

At the door, Gavin sighed while he watched Xavier leave.

"That is a good-looking man," the lady at the door said.

Chuckling, Gavin grinned. "Oh, yes, he is. There's more to him than looks."

"Yours?"

"Working on it."

The lady laughed. "Good for you. Badge?"

Gavin held up his badge for the lady to scan with her little device.

"All good to go. Good luck with the expo."

"Appreciate it." Gavin headed straight to the table, removed the protective covering and was grateful to realize that no one had messed with the displays. He wouldn't put it past Maury to sink low and either destroy or steal items. Then he folded the cloth covering and dropped it on a chair, along with his backpack.

"What to do? What to do... Ahh. Display. Giveaways. Got it."

Gavin organized, stacked and adjusted the display filled with folders of information regarding the different packages and options to build-their-own-event, business cards and flyers filled with highlights about Shore Breeze and Southern Charm. He collected a bunch of the squishy seashells and grouped them in a basket along with a pair of rainbow flags to stand in the corner. Then he piled a bunch of pens between the basket and a stack of small notepads. He tucked a couple of pens into the holders on the back of his badge.

"That should be everything."

After stuffing the tubs and boxes underneath the table and double-checking to make sure he'd used everything, Gavin stepped into the aisle to check out his work. He took a few pictures and sent them across the social media accounts he'd created.

"Looks wonderful, baby. Not too busy, but full of information and goodies. I like the simple rainbow touch to promote our equality. Here's your coffee," Xavier said and handed him a cup.

"Oooh, blessed caffeine. Gimme." Gavin sipped multiple times to get the black nectar into him.

Xavier chuckled while Gavin sighed over the large cup. "You're welcome."

Gavin sent him a couple of air kisses.

"Do you need any more help here?"

"Nope. All done. Will need to restock when things get low, but everything is organized underneath the table."

"Want to check out the other tables? You got another half-hour-ish. I'll cover things and eat my breakfast," Xavier said while he walked around the table and dropped the small bakery bag behind a display.

"You don't mind?"

"Nope. I'm good. I'll need a walk later to burn some energy, but right now I'm good," Xavier said. "The place that shall not be named is about ten tables down on your right and tucked in a bad corner. That way." He pointed off to the side.

"Okay. I'll be right back and avoid that area. Is he there?"

"Not yet."

"That's a good thing. He was never a morning person, even when we had to do these conventions together." Gavin kissed Xavier. "Thank you."

"Stay safe. I'm not going anywhere."

"Silly man." Gavin scooped up a small stack of business cards, tucked them in a pocket and left to take a circuit.

Most of the tables and displays were finished and gave him an idea about the competition within the event-planning section. He needed to beef up options regarding the music side. There were a few he used, but he could always check out new ideas. It was the same with photographers and videographers. After a few stops to chat, he passed on some business cards and pointed out his table's location. With the draw of Pensacola and all the beaches, he could bring in additional options.

After his circuit, where he did everything to avoid the table of his previous employer, Gavin returned. He pulled out the last of his cards and added them to the holder. Then he tugged out the other cards, flipped through them and tucked them into his backpack. Then he settled in a chair. "Still not there."

"That's a good thing. Screw him. Our table looks awesome."

"Yeah. Screw him. We're gonna knock this outta the park."

"First…food." Xavier handed him a breakfast sandwich with egg whites, bacon and cheese. "Enjoy, before anyone catches you with your mouth full of food."

"Ooh. Still warm." Gavin scoffed down the meal and finished the coffee.

"Need another cup? They set up a coffee station. I need a refill myself," Xavier said.

"Yes. Always need caffeine."

"Coming right up." Xavier scooped up their cups and walked away. He nodded to their neighbors. "The doors are opening. I'll make it quick."

Gavin smiled after Xavier. He couldn't have picked a better assistant.

"He's cute. Taken?" the lady at the opposite table asked.

"All mine," Gavin admitted. He finished his sandwich in a few bites. Then he brought out a tablet, a notebook and a paper planner that went out five years. All he needed now was prospective clients.

"Lucky man."

Throughout the rest of the day, Gavin smiled and greeted everyone. According to compliments, his bright cheery blue bow tie and suspenders combination helped draw their eye, along with the beautiful photographs and wall displays. Even the little rainbow flags brought same-sex and trans couples to them. Xavier complimented Gavin's look with dark brown pants and the bright-blue shirt with the Charmed Occasions embroidered logo.

Gavin engaged the visitors, answered questions and explained the packages and options. Xavier handed out the different materials. Sometimes Xavier even commented on the Charm and the town.

They worked excellently as a promotion team.

Xavier kept them hydrated with refilled water bottles and snacks to boost their energy.

They left the table during the lunch break and returned for a full afternoon. From their vantage point, they watched the various bridal shows and DJs playing on the stage.

During a lull, they dropped into the chairs.

"Holy crap. Are all expos like this?" Xavier asked. "It's exhausting to always be 'on' for anyone walking over."

Gavin chuckled behind the water bottle. "Yes. When it's a big expo with plenty of advertising and attendance, it can truly be worth having a table."

"Do you have any more of these?"

"Yes. Samuel and I registered for expos in Orlando, Tampa, Miami and are discussing whether we should go to New Orleans. We're trying to draw in more traffic and guests from outside the local area. I might travel farther up the coast or out west to bring in destination events. Once the new center is finished, I can accommodate much bigger events. While not everyone can stay at the Charm — we try to limit it to the wedding party — there are enough hotels across the different bridges for guests either in Pensacola or the beaches. So...bonus. Come to a wedding and enjoy the beach and ocean — all in one trip."

"According to the sign-up list, you have lots of interested couples. A good mix of equality too," Xavier said and waved the clipboard. "I made sure to tell everyone to sign up for information."

"Perhaps next time Samuel and I can come up with a prize. Gotta figure it out."

There was another rush after the final bridal dress show finished. With a sigh, Gavin got back to his feet and finished strong.

When the doors closed, they re-stocked everything and covered the table.

"I managed to get a reservation at the restaurant during the last break. If we leave, we can get ahead of the crowd," Xavier said.

"Really?"

"Hmm, a stroke of luck on my part. It's a nice one. I want to make tonight special as a reward for all the hard work you put in this week." Xavier trailed his finger down Gavin's nose.

"I would like that."

"Excellent." Xavier took Gavin's hand and led him through the crowds.

* * * *

"Your pathetic little company will never survive...nor will you." The harsh words were a scant warning before Maury brushed hard against Gavin in the jostling crowd by the restaurant. He shoved an elbow hard into Gavin's side.

Gavin hissed in pain but revealed nothing.

"Give up. Leave him. Return to Atlanta. You might stick around a little longer." With the nasty threat, Maury disappeared into the crowd before Xavier returned to his side.

"Ten minutes for a table. Even with the reservation, there's still a wait," Xavier said. He brandished the slim restaurant pager. "This will go off for us. Also, I scanned in the QR code so we can view —" He dropped his words and narrowed his gaze. "What happened?"

"What? No. Nothing—"

"Gavin."

"Maury. More threats. Nothing. Honest, I'm fine. I don't want him to ruin our night," Gavin said. "What about the QR code?"

"Gav—"

"No. I don't want him to ruin our night," Gavin repeated.

"Fine." Xavier slid the pager stick into his pocket. Then he stood next to Gavin, pushed him closer to the wall for protection and held his phone between them. "Here's the menu. Want a cocktail or wine?"

"Not tonight. I don't like drinking at these events. If a planner gets too tipsy, it can put out the wrong impression. I saw it happened."

"Good to know. We can celebrate back home with a private one."

"Much better."

"I can scroll past that section. Appetizers?"

"Please…starving."

They scanned the options, discussed potential ones and almost made it to the entrees.

The pager buzzed in Xavier's pocket.

"Always hated these things." Xavier grabbed the device and slid his phone into his pocket, took Gavin's hand and led him to the hostess station. "Two for Grayson." He handed over the pager.

"Thank you. Sorry about the delay. Please follow me," the hostess said and led them to a table by the windows. "Your waiter will be with you in a few minutes."

"Thank you." Xavier helped Gavin sit down before he walked around for his chair. Then he mumbled and pulled out his phone and set that off to the side. "Always gets in the way."

"Kept mine in the backpack." Gavin tucked the pack on the ground by his chair. Then he opened the menu.

They continued their discussion on their options until the waiter arrived.

After a cheery exchange, they ordered everything to not delay the meals. Within a few minutes, the waiter returned with a breadbasket, an olive oil-based dip and their drinks.

Soon their sharable appetizer of lump crab-cakes with a lemon mustard aioli sauce was placed between them.

"One of our most popular appetizers. Enjoy," the waiter said after giving them a small plate.

"This looks wonderful," Gavin said. He snapped out the napkin and laid it across his lap. Then he scooped one of the thick cakes onto his plate and drizzled some sauce on the side.

"To a successful expo," Xavier said while he held up his glass.

"And a wonderful weekend with you," Gavin added and tapped their glasses together.

After the delicious appetizer, they received their main entrees. Xavier had chosen a ribeye with fingerling potatoes, patty-pan squash and house-made steak sauce. Gavin went with the salmon plate with an edamame succotash, potato au gratin and a citrus vinaigrette.

Both declined dessert.

There was a slight tug over the bill.

"I suggested it."

"This is a business trip," Gavin countered. He snatched back the leather holder, added the tip and signed it to the room with his name. "Samuel made sure I sent everything to the room's bill if we did anything within the hotel. He's covering all the main expenses. We were going to eat somewhere."

"Not because you think I can't afford dinner," Xavier said.

"No, I wouldn't think that. I invited you to join me this weekend at the Charm's expense. You're working with me, and you should be rewarded, too."

"It was hard work. I didn't think it would be so difficult, though not crazy insane like an EMT shift."

"We're on our feet almost all day and constantly on point. Just keeping up the cheery upfront personality is exhausting, even for me." Gavin set aside the billfold. Then he picked up the backpack. "Ready to go?"

With only a smile, Xavier rose and assisted Gavin to his feet. Then he wrapped an arm around Gavin's waist and led him back toward the entrance-exit.

"Have a good evening," the hostess said in between assisting new patrons.

"Night," Gavin said.

"Want to walk around or head upstairs?"

"Upstairs."

"To the elevators," Xavier said.

After catching one of them, Xavier hit the button and maneuvered them toward a corner.

While the elevator rose through the multiple lighted buttons, Gavin smiled when he remembered something. He whispered in Xavier's ear, "Remember when I told you that I will rise to the occasion?"

Xavier grinned. "Yeah. Right before a really spectacular beej in a shower, if I recall."

"Guess what?" Gavin brushed his hardened erection against Xavier's leg. "It's that time. Whatever shall we do about it?"

"Everything and anything you want." Snatching Gavin's hand, Xavier bounced on his toes while the elevator counted the numbers. Soon as the doors slid open, and he almost dragged Gavin down the hallway to their room.

Laughing, Gavin broke into a jog to match Xavier's speed.

At the door, they fumbled with the card and lock, but managed to get the door open — then it closed shut behind them.

Xavier pressed Gavin back against the door and captured his lips in a hard kiss.

When they broke to breathe, Gavin stared at Xavier. He framed the handsome face between his hands. "Did you bring stuff?"

"Stuff?" Xavier quirked a smile.

"You know what."

Xavier smiled while he moved his hands over Gavin's hips.

"Fine. I'll say it. Lube. Did you bring some lube? Condoms?"

"I got lube. I tested clean at my last physical."

"Me, too."

"Don't need the condoms." Xavier caught one of Gavin's hands and kissed the back of it. "I'm not planning on straying once I have you."

"I can...do that. Never did it bare before."

"Not even with...?"

Gavin shook his head. "Never trusted him."

Xavier leaned even closer, if it were possible. There was no such thing as personal space right now. He dropped his focus to Gavin's lips.

After popping the button and zipper on Gavin's slacks, Xavier rubbed Gavin's swollen cock through the soft fabric of his boxer-briefs and his thumb against the damp spot and head. Sliding his fingers inside the waistband, Xavier took Gavin's length in his hand. While he stroked his length, he stared down into his baby-blue eyes. He twisted his wrist and moved in a slow, silky motion.

Leaning his head back, Gavin let out a liquid moan while Xavier stroked him. It felt so damn good to have another person touching him. Not any person but Xavier—the man he was connected to.

"I can't wait to feel this inside me," Xavier whispered, his voice thick with need and arousal.

Gavin's eyes widened. He put his hand on Xavier's hand to stop him. "Say that again."

The corner of Xavier's mouth tilted up. "Didn't think I liked it that way?"

"I don't question anyone's desires."

"Did you top?"

"Once or twice."

"Will you top me? Will you make love with me?"

Gavin lifted his gaze to meet Xavier's stare. "Yes."

"Then come here," Xavier said. He gave Gavin's cock another silky stroke. Then he walked back into the room. With each step, he began to strip his clothes.

Smiling, Gavin followed and removed his.

Pausing only to grab the bottle of lube from his suitcase, Xavier dragged down the hotel quilt and blanket. Then he rearranged the pillows before he dropped back onto the mattress. Setting the bottle to the side, he held up a hand.

Gavin took Xavier's hand and went to his knees next to Xavier. Threading their fingers, he bent over and kissed Xavier. Then he trailed his lips down Xavier's neck and chest. Freeing both hands, he moved them ahead of his lips while he learned every part of Xavier's body. Leaning up, he took the thickened length of Xavier's cock in his hand and stroked it. He used the pre-cum to lubricate his touch. He kissed Xavier while he worked his cock.

Moaning and moving against Gavin, Xavier clutched at the sheets. "Lube. Now. Inside me."

When Gavin moved back to grab the lube, Xavier shoved a pillow under his lower back. Gavin shifted between Xavier's opened legs. With care, he worked lubed-up fingers in Xavier's warm channel. Their bodies pressed close while he loosened the tightness. He kissed along Xavier's neck and shoulders.

"Okay. Okay. Good. Want to feel you stretch me," Xavier said.

Gavin lubed his cock and gave himself a few strokes. Shifting in place, he pulled one of Xavier's legs around his hip, and he lined himself up. Leaning forward, Gavin kissed Xavier while he pushed forward. Xavier's channel gloved his cock while he slid deeper inside.

Working his hips, Gavin focused on Xavier's face and emotions.

"Oh, yeah. There. There. Keep it up. There…" Xavier muttered and moaned. He planted his hands on Gavin's hips and rocked up into each stroke.

They connected while Gavin stroked deep inside him.

Xavier's cheek flushed as he clearly approached his orgasm every time Gavin pegged his prostate. He wrapped on hand around the back of Gavin's neck and kept their sweaty foreheads touching.

"Oh, God, Gavin, keep going. There... There... So good... Love it so damn much," Xavier said. He gasped when the orgasm rocked through him and fluttered his eyes shut when it took over his body. His channel clenched around Gavin's cock, and Gavin's name ripped from his throat.

Gavin sucked up a hot spot on Xavier's neck and groaned when the orgasm rocketed down his spine and shot through him. After a last hard thrust, he spent himself deep inside Xavier. Harsh breaths moved through him as he shuddered and shivered through the lingering orgasm.

"Holy shit," Gavin said.

"Putting it lightly," Xavier said.

They kissed hard and lingered through multiple kisses and the soft strokes along their bodies that shivered from the emotions and sensations riding through them.

"Lemme go get a cloth to clean us up," Gavin said while he carefully disengaged and knelt back. "When I can feel my legs again."

"Having the same problem," Xavier said while he rolled his ankles and wiggled his hips.

It took a few moments longer, but Gavin finally got to his feet. A little wobbly, he continued to the bathroom, wet a cloth and cleansed himself. After a few rinses, he wrung it out and carried it to the bed. There he carefully wiped Xavier. Part of him was thrilled to see his cum dripping out of Xavier's ass. That was the most personal bit of possession he could imprint upon Xavier.

"Hmm. Feels good. Thanks," Xavier said.

"Welcome." Gavin kissed him again. "Oops. I marked you." He tapped his fingers on Xavier's neck.

"You gave me a hickey."

"Sorry?"

"Nope. Don't be." Xavier chuckled. "I'll show it off at the expo."

Gavin went to the bathroom and tossed the rag onto the tub. He stared at his image in the mirror. His eyes were bright and dark with emotions. Thoughts raced through his mind, though there was no hidden regret for the act, not with Xavier. His connection with him held true and firm. It was what had been missing from all his earlier relationships.

Internally satiated, he hit the light and left the bedroom.

Xavier was sitting up in bed, had rearranged the pillows and drawn the sheet and blanket over his hips. "I didn't think you were going to come out. Is something wrong?"

Gavin smiled and lifted the sheet and blanket. He slid underneath and didn't stop until he was pressed against Xavier's side. "Everything is perfect. That's the best thing. It's never been like this before for me." He pressed a kiss to Xavier's chest. "Thank you for tonight."

Xavier kissed Gavin's hair. "Thank you. I need to read for a bit before I sleep. Okay?"

"Hmm. I'm going to sleep, then," Gavin said and worked down until he used both a pillow and Xavier to rest his head. He wiggled and stopped. "Nope. Can't free ball when I sleep." He got out and pulled on his pajama pants. Then he returned to the bed. When he placed a hand on Xavier's leg, he felt the extra layer of fabric. "You too?"

"Yup. Definitely can't do the nude thing in bed."

Chuckling at learning something new about his lover, Gavin returned to his cuddling spot to sleep. He hummed when Xavier hit the light, but a soft glow emanated when he opened his Kindle to read. Closing his eyes, his body warm from Xavier's natural heat, he slid into sleep.

Chapter Twenty

By Sunday morning, Gavin was ready to pack it in and head home. As expected, Samuel couldn't get away from New York to join them.

"Oh my God, Gavin! Is that you?"

Gavin recognized a familiar face. It was one of his favorite high-end Atlanta brides. "Rosalee? What are you doing here? Oh, please don't tell me you and Griffin..."

"Not quite, dear Gavin." Rosalee broke through the crowd and revealed a very round belly. She rubbed a hand over it.

"Wow, that's a belly," Gavin said while he moved around the table. He kissed her cheeks. "So wonderful to see you again, Rosalee."

"Same here. I stopped by your company, and they told me you'd left."

"I did. Needed a change. I found a wonderful B&B that needed an event planner and created a new company with them." Gavin waved a hand toward the table. "Charmed Occasions. What are you doing looking for me if you're—"

"Very pregnant?" Rosalee laughed. "Not for me. One of my bridesmaids, Vanessa, is getting married and loved what you did for Griffin and me. She wanted the same, but when we looked for you—"

"I wasn't there," he finished.

"Exactly. So I brought her here."

"Oh my God, that guy was horrible. What a sleazeball. Rosie, did you hear him?"

Rosalee glanced to the side and smiled. "That would be Nessa." She lifted her voice. "Vanessa, over here, I found Gavin. What happened?"

"That sleazeball promised me the moon and stars. Unbelievable. I heard all about him from Jenny and Rachel. He didn't give a damn about what they wanted and ruined their days because he couldn't plan crap. How could he even be called a wedding planner?" Vanessa moved around a small crowd. "Wait? What? You found Gavin—?" She stopped and turned to face them. Her eyes widened.

"Vanessa Radden, this is Gavin Hartfield, my wedding planner," Rosalee introduced. "Who were you talking about?"

"Maurice, that horrible guy a few tables down."

Rosalee glanced at Gavin.

"Yes, I know him all too well. He can be worse than a sleazeball and, yes, he would promise the moon and stars then deliver a pile of rocks," Gavin said.

"Screw him," Rosalee said.

"Yeah, screw him. Gavin, I can't believe we found you." Vanessa studied the table. "You're not in Atlanta."

"Not anymore, no, but perhaps I can still help you," Gavin said. "Tell me about your fiancé and wedding."

"Oh, wow, really?"

Gavin smiled. "Yes…really."

Vanessa talked all about her fiancé, Keith, a marketing VP with an Atlanta company, and their plans. "Unlike Rosalee, I wish for a simple wedding — simple, but elegant. I wanted something by the water or the beach."

"Would you prefer it to be in Atlanta or somewhere else?"

"We're open to a destination wedding."

"Wonderful. Let me explain about my new company. It's in a beachside town called Shore Breeze, south of Pensacola." Gavin brought her closer to the table, picked up the main folder and explained everything about the B&B and the company.

When he finished, Vanessa danced in her spot while she flipped through the packet. "Yes. Yes. Yes. It's perfect." She grabbed her phone and dialed. "Keith. Keith, oh my God, Rosie and I found Gavin, the wedding planner. Yes, we found him at the expo. He went to a new company on the beach in Florida. No. Not Daytona…over by Pensacola. Yeah. The Gulf. I can't believe it. It's perfect! Everything is right in our price range. Should I book it? I can bring home all the details." She nodded and paced. "Okay. Okay." She looked at Gavin. "Would you have Memorial Day weekend available next year? We want the wedding on Saturday."

"Umm. Wow. Let me check our calendar." Gavin snagged his tablet and opened the application.

"Hello, ladies, Gavin. Sorry, I would have gathered more snacks and drinks," Xavier said while he returned. He carried a box filled with two coffees, a couple bags of hash-brown patties and French fries and a bag of Cool Ranch Doritos.

"Xavier, hello, this is Rosalee, one of my Atlanta brides, and Vanessa, a new bride-to-be." Gavin glanced at the Doritos then at Xavier. "I'm not driving."

"Looked like you could use a boost." Xavier popped open the bag and shook it a little.

"He's mean to me, giving me useless calories," Gavin said while he first grabbed the coffee. He took a few sips. Then he snatched a chip and crunched.

"Your weakness?" Rosalee asked while she also grabbed a chip. "Hmm. This baby makes me hungry all the time. I swear I could live on greasy pizzas and strawberry milkshakes."

"Would you rather have the fries?" Xavier held out the bag of fries.

"Oh, wow, really?"

"I don't come between a pregnant lady and greasy fries."

"Thank you!" Rosalee snatched the bag and munched.

"Rosie," Vanessa said and chuckled.

"It's okay. I don't mind," Xavier said.

"I have good news. The entire week before and the weekend of Memorial Day is open," Gavin said.

"Can I reserve it?" Vanessa asked.

"Of course." Gavin tapped a few things on the tablet's surface with his stylus. "Done. The B&B has enough rooms for the immediate wedding party and some family. Eleven rooms. The last is our honeymoon suite that we reserve for after the wedding. How many in the party?"

"I'll have Rosie and two bridesmaids. Keith will have three men. My parents are divorced, and my mother remarried. Keith's parents are together. He'll have his grandmother, who lives with his parents."

Gavin added up the names. "So that's eleven...just at the limit. There are hotels in the city of Pensacola and Pensacola Beach." He brought up a map to show Vanessa. "Each area is located on either side of Breeze. Depends on how far they want to travel and what they wish to spend."

"The beach would be best. My family and friends prefer either the Hilton or Marriott and don't mind the prices."

"That makes it easier. I can ask to reserve a block."

"Do it. We'll cover the reservation costs. I can't believe this is working out."

"A few months before the wedding, I'll need you and Keith to visit the B&B. We'll go through the packages and options. While we can have the wedding on the beach, the new event center will be finished and ready for a reception. Then I usually like to have you return to the B&B a month out to confirm everything."

"Fabulous. Keith and I will talk, and we'll set a date for each appointment." Vanessa grabbed his hands. "Thank you. Thank you."

"You're more than welcome —"

An announcement over the loudspeaker mentioned that the expo was closing.

"Oh, damn," Vanessa said.

"Don't worry. We've accomplished what we needed," Gavin said. "You have my number. The folder includes all the information. Go over it with Keith and give me a call. Plus, here are some squishies, pens and notepads." He added the extra giveaways to both ladies.

"Oooh, I love this squishy," Rosalee said while she played with the seashell. "I'll use it during the birth instead of squeezing Griffin's hand."

Gavin chuckled at Rosalee's reaction.

"You're silly, Rosie. That's why I adore you." Vanessa stared at Gavin. "I will call soon. Thank you."

"You're more than welcome. I can't wait to create the perfect wedding for you and Keith."

"This is going to be fabulous!"

"We need to get going, Nessa," Rosalee said. "I'm thrilled we found you, Gavin. I'll let my friends know how to find you if they need an event planner." She scooped up more business cards and flyers to tuck into her large bag. "I'll pass all these out to anyone who asks about you."

"Can always use more business." Gavin hugged both ladies. "It was so wonderful to see both of you. Have a safe drive home."

"Same to both of you," Rosalee said after the hug. "I'll let you know when this little one comes. Perhaps you can create her first birthday party for us."

"I would love to do that for you. Would be like going full circle with one of my couples."

"Perfect. I'll call you," Rosalee said.

With waves and more byes, the ladies finally walked away. They were among the last of the crowd leaving the massive room.

* * * *

"And it's all over," Gavin said. "I can't believe that we actually scheduled a wedding. I didn't expect that to happen. This is fabulous!"

"Ended on a high note." Xavier pulled out the cart and empty bins. "I packed up our things and need to finish the check out."

"I'll pack up all this. The sooner we get out of here, the better."

"Oh, I don't know about the getting back is better part. I've got school in the morning — my marathon day of sitting in a classroom."

"That starts tomorrow? Oh my God. Did I ruin something for you by bringing — "

"Stop. Stop." Xavier pressed his fingers against Gavin's lips. "I wouldn't have offered to come if it screwed up anything."

Gavin kissed Xavier's fingers and smiled. "Guess you're going to need a grueling ride on my Peloton before and after class."

"Yeah, I'm staying with you just for your bike."

Gavin tapped Xavier's shoulder with his fist. "Go check us out. The room is paid for on my business card. Just sign the bill. I'll get started on packing."

"I'll be right back. Don't get into trouble."

"Trouble finds me. I don't find it."

"Either way. Avoid it, please," Xavier said.

"Promise. Go. The sooner we pack up, the sooner we can go."

"I'm going. I'm going." Xavier held up his hands and walked away.

Smiling, Gavin studied the table to realize that they'd given away more than half their items. He walked around to finish the now-cold patties and coffee. He set the empty box on the chair and kept the bag of chips handy. After setting up some music on his phone, he began breaking down the display.

"Your table was pretty busy, stealing potential clients. With your smile and bow ties, of course you would," Maurice said while he walked over. "Gavin the perfect coordinator. The wonderful salesman. The charmer." He flicked at a stand and knocked it over.

"Your attitude certainly doesn't help attract the clients." Gavin stayed behind the table. "I'm sure you scared more away than I could ever attract."

Maurice flicked over another stand. "This little company of yours will never work."

"Not only does it work, but it's also succeeding. With every event, the company grows in status and reputation. Not even a worldwide pandemic could shut us down. Nothing you say or do will ever mess with my company."

Flicking another stand, Maurice shrugged. "You never know what could happen. Good to see you again. I'll see you around."

"Stay away from me."

"Oh, such a silly one, that's no fun. You'll never get rid of me. I'm everywhere. I chose you, and you belong to me—"

"Fuck you." Gavin curled his hand against the table to hold back his fear and anger. "I'm never going to be with you again...*ever*."

"I'm sure I can change your mind. No one ever leaves me without it being my decision. I'm definitely not done with you. Not even your muscle-bound friend can stop what I desire. No. There is too much I want from you." Maurice wiggled a single finger. Then he dropped it to the table, traced a weaving finger along the top and swung close to Gavin's fingers, though he didn't try to touch him. "Far too much I want from you.

No, my dear, perfect Gavin, we're not done. I'll talk to you soon." He air-kissed and walked away.

Not sure what Maurice was going on about, Gavin shook all over to get rid of the heebie-jeebies. He would need to remain on guard when he returned home.

"That guy is bad news."

At the different voice, Gavin looked to see it was the lady from the nearby table—the one who had admired Xavier on the first day. "Yeah, not the best."

"Dated him?"

"Unfortunately made that mistake. Bad time. Real bad time."

"Oh, honey, I'm sorry, but you got yourself a good one now."

"Yeah, he's one of the best."

"Keep him around," she said. "He's much better than that…thing."

Chuckling, Gavin continued to break down the display. He stacked and packed things into the different tubs.

"All checked out. Got the invoice," Xavier said. "Did I miss something?"

"Nothing I couldn't manage. Sent Maurice running again."

"What—" Xavier turned to look down the area, ready to go after the man.

"Relax. I took care of it."

"Gavin—"

"Don't make an issue out of it. Please. Let's go home."

"Okay. If he tries anything…"

"You have my permission to hit him."

"I'll do more than hit him if he gets near you."

"Ooh, so vicious." Gavin handed over a stack of leftover folders. "Use that energy to pack and stack the cart."

"Yes, sir," Xavier said.

Together, they cleaned up everything and rolled the cart back outside.

"Now to figure out how Dakota did this Tetris thing," Xavier said while he studied the back.

"Always the main issue when it comes to packing and moving."

Xavier snorted but got to work.

Somehow, they figured out how to stack everything inside. The last piece was sliding the cart back into its spot.

"And the door even shuts," Xavier said when he hit the button to drop the trunk. They both heard the satisfying click. "Who gets first shift?"

"Can you?" Gavin dug the clicker out of the backpack and held it out.

"Need a break?"

"Yeah. A bit overwhelmed. Need to come down for a bit."

"No problem." Xavier took the clicker and hit the button. "We're on our way."

Gavin kissed him. He slid his fingers through Xavier's hair while the kiss lingered. After Xavier responded to his touch, Gavin pulled back with a smile. "Thanks for staying the weekend with me."

"I had fun…learned a lot."

"Don't want it to end."

"Some of it doesn't have to. We'll figure out how to combine our crazy schedules. Get on in. Let me take you home."

Gavin climbed inside the SUV. He leaned back and closed his eyes. Xavier reversed the navigation system and started their journey home.

* * * *

During a rest stop visit, Gavin heard his phone ringing. He rushed back around the SUV to lean inside and grab the call. He managed to answer it in time. "Hello, this is Gavin."

"Gavin, it's Dakota. Where are you?"

"Hey, Dakota, we stopped at a rest stop outside of Montgomery to stretch our legs. We'll be back in Breeze in a few hours," Gavin said. "How's Samuel?"

"We just got home from the airport. There's..." Dakota paused.

"What's happening?"

"Mal called."

"Oh no."

"Yeah, it's not good news. The pneumonia didn't respond. Dorian refused further treatment because it went against her last wishes. Penelope died sometime this morning."

"Oh God. She's gone? Oh, sweet Penelope. I hope her passing wasn't difficult."

"She slipped away in her sleep, sedated to ease her breathing, pain and passage."

"That's good to know."

"Anything else?"

"There isn't a funeral. She'll be cremated. Half of her ashes will be entombed outside of Pensacola. That'll be done by Dorian and Reece. He doesn't want any fanfare. The rest of her ashes will be placed with a baby tree and planted by Southern Charm. She loved the place as much as her son and wants to watch over him…in a fashion."

When Dakota paused to steady himself, Gavin waited him out. He knew this news hit all the Charm men hard, especially the ones who truly knew and loved the sweet lady.

"We'll have a celebration of life with a unitarian preacher. It'll be on the lower balcony overlooking the ocean. I'm trying to get Cal to fly over and sing one of Penny's favorite songs. She loved to hear Cal sing. That's about it. During the ceremony, or after it, the ashes will be moved to the tree. Then Dorian and Reece will place the urn where needed."

"Do you want me to set up something to decorate things? Flowers? Candles?"

"No, Dorian doesn't want anything. Samuel and I will pull out chairs and a small table to hold the urn. We'll use one of the small tablecloths to cover it. Wyatt is bringing a portrait and stand."

"That's it? Are you sure?"

"Following Penelope's and Dorian's wishes."

"How's Dorian?"

"Broken, but accepting her death. He's with Mal and Reece. Victor is heading over. Doc Elliott mentioned he's recovered enough to not spread germs. He remains on medication for the bronchitis."

"Okay, we're heading back."

"Good to know. We didn't want to call sooner and ruin the last day. How did it go?"

"The expo went wonderful. Everyone who stopped it became interested with the Charm and the company. We have a definite wedding for Memorial Day weekend next year. I'm sure there will be multiple calls."

"Can't wait for the event center to be finished to get you all out of my restaurant."

Gavin chuckled. "We'll call when we cross the bridge."

"Talk later."

Gavin turned off the phone.

"What happened?" Xavier asked while he walked over.

Gavin nibbled on his lower lip. "Penelope died sometime this morning. She was never transferred to hospice."

"Oh, shit, no."

"We need to get home."

"On our way."

Hours later, they crossed the bridge. Gavin checked in with Samuel and Dakota. With the call, they went first to the Charm to return the SUV and unload the back.

"Hey, welcome back. You made good time," Samuel said.

Gavin welcomed the embrace from Samuel. "How was New York?"

"Crazy, but things are straightened out and pushing forward. The deal should finalize at the end of the month."

"Sorry to hear about Penelope."

"Yeah, me too, but it's what was best for her," Samuel said. "I wish I'd known her better."

"Me too."

"Hey, Samuel." Xavier hit a button to open the trunk. He pulled out the suitcases and set them to the side. He dropped his backpack on his duffel bag. "We took good care of your baby. It's a sweet ride." He tossed the clicker to Samuel.

"Hey, Gray, thanks," Samuel said.

"The travelers are back," Dakota said when he joined them.

The group made simple small talk while they unloaded the SUV's contents onto the cart. Dakota teased about the lightness of the boxes and bins.

"That's a good thing. That means they gave stuff away and drew interest to the Charm," Samuel said.

"Which is exactly what we did," Gavin said. "Wait until you see the sign-up sheet. It's immense. I hope it generates even more leads and bookings. Perhaps, next time we should think about doing a giveaway."

"I hope it all works out," Samuel said. "That's a great idea. Perhaps money off a package or the honeymoon suite for free or something else."

"Where do you want all this?" Dakota asked.

"Just inside the inventory room. Victor and I will restock and put them away. I have to put in a couple of orders." Gavin stopped and smiled at Samuel. "Oh, the seashell squishies were a hit."

"Thought they would be. Everyone loves a good stress ball." Samuel glanced at Dakota. "Told you."

"Really?"

"What?"

"Oh, boy," Dakota muttered while he pushed the cart away. "Head home, Gavin. I can put this in the room."

"Oh, come on," Samuel said while he chased after him. He paused only to close and lock the SUV.

"Should we follow them?" Xavier asked.

"Nah," Gavin said. "Like Dakota said, he can push it into a room. I'm ready for home. I should find Dorian, but I know Mal and Reece have him. Besides, you have class tomorrow."

"Don't remind me."

"Do you wanna stay with me?"

Xavier smiled. "Yeah, I would like that. I need to get some clothes and things from my place."

"Okay. Meet you at my house?"

"Want me to pick up pizza?"

"That would be wonderful. Bring your laundry. I'll wash everything together."

"Appreciate it. I enjoyed the trip," Xavier said. Then he leaned in to kiss him.

Gavin met Xavier's lips. He responded and leaned against the taller man while the kiss lingered between them. Until he pulled back and smiled. "There will be more of that later."

"Good to know." Xavier grabbed his backpack and duffel and headed to his ancient truck.

With a smile, Gavin grabbed his bag and suitcase handle to head to his Soul. Soon, he drove away behind Xavier's blue truck.

Chapter Twenty-One

On a sunny Wednesday morning, the Charm family gathered around Dorian on the lower balcony overlooking the ocean. Due to another note, no one wore black. Penelope Stewart was adamant that she didn't want everyone to be so dark and sad. This was a celebration of her life, not a mourning.

Standing with Xavier, Gavin wore a dove-gray shirt, charcoal-gray pants with a blue-charcoal pin-stripe bow tie and suspenders. He chose his favorite gray suede boots, the ones he'd taken off the night Xavier had tripped over him. He adjusted his sunglasses.

Xavier chose to wear a warm blue shirt with chocolate pants. He borrowed a pair of Gavin's suspenders with a chocolate and blue pattern. They rolled their sleeves up their forearms. Xavier opened the top buttons in deference to the summer heat. Leaning against the railing, he kept a hand against Gavin's lower back.

"The portrait is beautiful. It was my favorite picture of her," Dorian said when he walked out onto the balcony. He touched his fingers along the edge of the frame. Then he glanced over at the artist. "Oh, Wyatt, this is wonderful. I didn't know you could paint."

"I had a bit of help from some other artists," Wyatt said. "Acrylics aren't my forte, but I did create the frame."

"It's beautiful. Perfect." Dorian turned and hugged Wyatt.

Wyatt hugged him back. "I'm pleased you love it. It's what every artist wants to hear. I'll tell my friends you loved it."

"Did Mom ask you to design her urn?"

"She did. Simple, but it includes a bit of her story."

Dorian touched one of the wheelchair wheels etched into the urn's sides. Wyatt had colored everything an ocean blue. "Mom's favorite color. She loved staring at the ocean for hours." Tears welled up. Then he rubbed his fingers against the sapling tree's leaves. It stood in a temporary container, placed there by Reece. "Is this Mom's tree?"

"It is. A local hardy one that will stand up against any hurricane. Not as well as a palm, but she wasn't fond of them. Do you approve?" Reece asked.

Dorian nodded. "Her ashes?"

"We'll place some in the dirt and transfer it to the spot you selected yesterday. Sully and I have already dug a hole and prepped it. We'll plant it after the celebration. Wyatt created a small plaque that we'll place in front of the tree."

"Sounds perfect. A bit of her will always be here with the Charm—just what she always wanted," Dorian said. "Then we'll take her urn to her final spot at the Pensacola cemetery. It doesn't overlook the ocean, but it's peaceful."

Dakota and Samuel walked out with the Unitarian minister.

"Dorian, may I introduce you to the minister?" Dakota asked while leading the lady over.

"Of course. Hello, I'm Dorian Stewart," Dorian said.

"Please accept my condolences on the loss of your mother, Penelope. I'm Minister LeeAnn Scott," she said and clasped both of Dorian's hands. "I'm honored to be here. I met Penny during her visits. During some conversations around some difficult moments, we got to know each other."

"I didn't know."

"That was her wish."

"Just like Mom," Dorian said. He glanced over at the urn.

"Is everyone here?" Dakota asked Reece.

Reece looked around and nodded. "Yes. Everyone we called and invited."

Dakota stepped forward and cleared his throat. "If everyone could take a seat, we'll get started for the celebration of life services."

Gavin took Xavier's hand and followed the others to the chairs. They sat next to each other and in the same row with Doc Elliott, Jude and a quiet Dawson.

Reece and Dakota led Dorian to the front row and helped him sit. Reece sat next to Dorian with Malcolm on his other side. Dakota sat across the small aisle with Samuel and Cal next to him.

* * * *

The minister bowed with reverence to the urn and whispered a blessing. Then she placed a case on the floor. She set a small wooden box along with a silver chalice and candle on the table. Pulling out a book, she faced the quiet gathering. "Good morning. Today we have gathered to celebrate the life of Penelope Emma Stewart. My name is LeeAnn Scott and I'm a minister from the Legacy Unitarian Universalist Church of Shore Breeze. I welcome all of you to our home on the Southern Charm's patio, overlooking the beach and ocean.

"Sorrow and joy weave a tapestry as death gathers us today to bid one we have known and loved farewell and welcome to her new path. Our feelings and source of strength come from a deep well within all of us. Together we join in a harmony of memory and celebration.

"As we share our thoughts and memories, we may feel like laughing. Penny gave us joy and love throughout her life. She also got great joy from her beloved son, Dorian, and her Southern Charm family.

"At times we'll feel like crying. There is grief in losing someone whose life we hold dear. Penny was precious to our lives and to Dorian, but we all understand it is a blessing in her death. She's released from the pain of a life-long illness, after a valiant fight. Our tears today help us begin to learn to live without Penny.

"This is what we shall do together while we begin a new way of appreciating Penny's life, memory and all it has meant.

"We will not let the shadow of death obscure the living person who touched us many times, in many ways, filling our lives with memories, meaning and love," LeeAnn said. "At this time, I would like to call upon Dorian and Reece to step forward to light the chalice. It shall remain lit throughout the celebration and guide Penny's soul."

Reece guided the younger man across the patio.

LeeAnn took out a long match, which she set to flame. Then she handed it over for them to hold together. She pointed to the candle resting inside the chalice. "We light the chalice, a symbol of faith in the power of love. May the spirit of the divine, the powerful presence of love, be with us. May this candle's flame guide our friend Penny's soul to the light." She sang a hymn while Reece and Dorian lit the candle together.

Then Reece helped Dorian back to his chair.

"We have come together to remember and celebrate Penny's life — because we need each other in empathy and consolation, and because we need each other in courage and wisdom. We show our love and support to her beloved son, Dorian, and all the loved ones of her Southern Charm family.

"Penelope Stewart was born on June third in Savannah, Georgia. She died on Sunday, August nineteenth, in Shore Breeze, her home for the last twenty years. In between those two dates and those places was a life well lived. Penny was a sweet, kind person with a beautiful spirit, open to the ideas of caring. I met her shortly after she moved here with her infant son. She forged a new future and home for herself and her son. Even after her diagnosis of multiple sclerosis at the young age of twenty-four, caring for her five-year-old son, Penny never lost that sweet spirit and hope of a better future.

"She strived to be the best in anything she started and worked. She helped Southern Haven Landscape & Design become one of the top landscaping companies in Florida by being the executive assistant and keeping its owner, Reece Simpson, in line," she said.

There were lots of chuckles while Reece held up his hands.

"It's true. I owe her everything. Sharon, Emmy and I would all be lost without her various systems," Reece said.

"Penny loved her position there until the debilitating MS symptoms arrived. No matter how bad those symptoms became, she vowed to live her life. Her only regret was how Dorian had to grow up faster than she'd wanted while her condition worsened and he took on more responsibility. She marveled at how her son grew from a precocious boy to a strong, brilliant young man, gifted in his chosen culinary field and surrounded by a wonderful family of his choice. She supported him the moment he mentioned something about liking boys more than girls. While we all knew she dealt with this disease, it's not why we all love her and come together today. There is far more to our beloved friend.

"Penny loved music and mentioned how lyrics could take her away from her pain and discomfort. She would hum or sing various lyrics from The Beatles, her favorite band. Though she fell in love with the band after their break-up, they were her go-to artist for the rest of her life—even singing to soothe baby Dorian to sleep.

"Let us listen now to her favorite Beatles song, *Let It Be*, sung for us today by Cal Mitchell. Take comfort amid our grief as we let the memories of Penny singing this song to Dorian and the light of her spirit fill our minds and hearts," LeeAnn said while she motioned to Cal.

Cal lifted his acoustic guitar and rose. He slipped the strap over his head and plucked a few strings. Then he faced the small congregation, cleared his throat and smiled. "Dorian, this one is for you, straight from your mom. I hope I do her a bit of justice." He strummed his callused fingers against the strings and slipped into the familiar bars of music and sing the first verse. Soon the last notes of the guitar hung in the air. With a bow of reverence to the urn, he nodded to Dorian and returned to his seat. He placed his guitar back in the case.

"Thank you so much, Cal," LeeAnn said. "Let us bless her ashes, to carry her spirit upon the wind, while they help enrich the life of a young tree to be planted on Southern Charm's land. She will forever live in our hearts, and our love for her will never disappear. Now we pray." She bowed her head.

"Whispering Breath of Mystery, rattling the windows of our spirits with tears and sorrow, draw us back to the wonderful, the loving, the beautiful times we had with Penny, whose ashes we now hold. Recall to us Penny's inspirational actions, caring and commitment. Together we shall be again, as together we came out of the stars and earth, stardust and mud, extraordinary and mundane. These ashes are blessed, because Penelope Stewart's life was worthy and meaningful. These ashes are blessed, a reminder of the gift of Penny's life, a gift of return to this earth, a gift of renewal. And from such blessing, we give thanks for the life that has gifted our own.

"We must now say our goodbyes to Penny. Give us the strength, so that each day yet to come we find more compassion, understanding and the loving kindness that fills our world with joy and laughter. Give us the courage to cherish one another so that we use our lives to heal instead of forget and lead us to the possibility of forgiveness. And we give thanks for Penelope Stewart. Let her memory live on in the great Spirit of Life that surrounds us, and her memory, cherished by us, dwells deeply within us by the person she was and still is in our hearts. We have celebrated the cycles of life in which we find ourselves, celebrating life at its beginning and its end, both always present among us.

"Spirit of Love and Life, remind us to love life as fully as we are able. And even though we must bid our beloved friend farewell, the gift of her life is a treasure that cannot be ungiven. We celebrate the life of our beloved who lived among us, and now her soul is at rest.

"With our celebration closed, thank you to everyone who joined us this morning as we say goodbye to our friend, Penelope Stewart. Dorian, you may come up and blow out your mother's candle," LeeAnn said.

Dorian struggled to his feet and shuffled over. Tears streamed down his face. He blew out the flame, held a hand toward the urn and collapsed to his knees when his grief overwhelmed him.

Victor was the first to reach Dorian's side. He gathered him close and rocked him. "Go ahead and cry. Don't hold it in. Go on," he whispered.

Cal dropped close to the other side to help soothe Dorian.

While they protected Dorian, LeeAnn helped pour some ashes into the soil around the sapling tree. She added an extra blessing. Then she closed and handed the urn to Malcolm.

"Thank you very much for the wonderful words and memorial," Reece said.

"It was sincerely my pleasure to stand for Penny. I hoped I could offer a bit of comfort to everyone," she said.

"I'm sure you did—more than anyone could have expected," Sully added.

"Do you have a spot for Penny's tree?"

"Yes, Dorian found a spot for the tree yesterday. Our friend, Wyatt, created a small plaque and stand. We'll add that later," Reece said.

"Then I'll take my leave and let all of you remember her," she said, while removing her sash and robe. She placed her things back inside the case and closed it up. Then she crouched next to Dorian. "Please know you have my love and prayers, Dorian, supporting you. Come find me at the church if you wish to talk…about anything. Know my door is always open for you."

"Thank you…for everything," Dorian said past the lumps in his throat. He didn't brush away his tears.

"My sincere pleasure. Know you're safe and loved in this wonderful gathering. Find comfort in their presence," she said and rose to her feet. With those final words, she took her leave.

Gavin wandered over to the others with Xavier and other lingering friends.

"Shall we go plant Penny's tree? Then we'll enjoy a light lunch Dakota prepared," Reece said.

With a nod, Dorian rose to his feet, supported by Cal and Victor. He let them lead him away.

* * * *

After planting the sapling, they all entered the closed restaurant.

Dakota, Mal and a couple of waiters had created the simple buffet. They offered water, iced tea and soda.

Dorian sat and let Victor fill a plate for him. After accepting a couple of tissues to dry his face, he picked at the meal, barely eating a bite.

Gavin and Xavier chose spots on the far side of the table when they got their plates.

Light conversation filled the room. Shared memories and stories of Penny reverberated through everyone.

Then Dorian shattered the quiet when he spoke. "I'm going to return to New York for school next week. I'm not going to redo the semester. It'll mess up the path and timing."

"Dorian, stop. This isn't something you need to decide now—"

"No, Reece, I'm going back to New York next week and finish the semester and my internship."

"Dorian—"

"*No*, Reece, I know where I need to be to get through this. If it's too much, then I'll come home." Dorian paused, his eyes widened. "Home... Where is home?" Tears welled again.

"With us, baby, with us," Mal said. He walked around chairs to hug Dorian from behind. "That guest room is yours. We'll set it up however you want."

"The apartment..."

"After we inter Penny's ashes into the wall, we can head over there and decide what to do with all her things. Whatever time you need, you can take. Nothing has to be done right away," Mal said and reassured him. "Then Reece, Sully and I will box up everything. Move and donate what you want. We'll put some stuff in storage if you're not sure what to do with it. We'll bring your personal stuff back to the house. I promise. We'll clean up the apartment and close the lease."

Dorian nodded. "I can stay…"

"With Reece and I for as long as you want. When you're ready, we'll help you find your own place…if that's your decision."

"Okay. Mom's stuff…"

"We'll figure it out starting tomorrow. Put it off until then."

"Okay."

Kissing Dorian's temple, Mal returned to his seat. He accepted a long embrace in Reece's arms while he tried to hold off the tears.

Gavin rubbed his chin on Xavier's shoulder, needing some extra touch.

"Doing okay?" Xavier whispered.

"Weddings are so much easier. It's about a beginning, joy…" Gavin shook his head. "This…"

"Is another beginning for Penny and all of you who loved her," he said.

"But so sad."

"Part of life."

"Something you've witnessed."

"More times than I care to count." Xavier pressed his lips to Gavin's temple.

"What about your wedding, Samuel, Dakota? Are you having it this year?" Dorian asked. "We need something to celebrate. I can't think of anything better."

The couple glanced at each other and over to Gavin.

"We decided on October. Right, Gavin?" Dakota asked.

Grumbling at how Dakota threw the issue at him, Gavin sighed and lifted his chin from Xavier's shoulder. "Yes, the first weekend of October. The ceremony will be held on the beach. The reception here. We selected the invitations, and the printer should send them out within the next week."

"Then I'll plan to be here that weekend, too. I'm not missing your wedding," Dorian said. "It's something I can look forward to during exams and classes."

Keeping up with the cheery turn of events, the conversation turned toward the wedding with Samuel, Dakota and Gavin fielding questions through the rest of the repast.

Chapter Twenty-Two

All attention returned to the tropics where Tropical Storm Katia continued to increase in size and strength a week later. It slammed the Florida Keys, caused some destruction and entered the Gulf of Mexico. Forecasters predicted a curve to the north. Thanks to the warm waters, the storm could increase into a powerful hurricane. The cone of prediction and tracks kept the storm pointed toward a new landfall along the Panhandle.

The storm worried Samuel and Dakota so much that they called an emergency meeting.

Over the next day, Gavin contacted clients who had planned weddings throughout September. With every call, he updated them about the changing tropical weather, then requested they also keep an eye on reports. While Occasions would do their best to honor all promised dates, he explained how everything depended on Mother Nature. If the storm came anywhere near them, the county would be under a weather advisory that could cause them to evacuate.

The weddings could change, depending on damages and clean-up.

"Yes, yes, I know you requested this date over a year ago, Felicia, but please remember I mentioned the possibility this could happen. The hurricane season runs from June first to November thirtieth. Nothing can change that, not even a wedding planner. I'm hoping nothing happens, but there's always the possibility. The storm remains too far out for any official track toward us." Gavin wanted to thump his head. "I understand, Felicia. I apologize for this happening, and I'll do everything possible to save your wedding. Okay?" He paused while he listened to the bride. "Understood. Goodbye."

Gavin hung up the phone and checked off the name.

"Last one on the list. Thank you! Thank you! Thank you!"

Then his cell phone rang.

"Oh, no. Please. No. No."

The phone continued to ring. The number flashed with the ID of the hospital.

That intrigued him.

Gavin hit the button to place the call on speaker. "Charmed Occasions. This is Gavin. How may I help you?"

"Afternoon, Gavin, it's Doc Elliott. Do you have a moment to talk?" Doc Elliott said.

"Doc Elliott, hey there. Yes, I finished my last call to my upcoming events. This storm is causing a mess. How are you?"

"Doing okay. Increased number of patients with heat-related illnesses flooding the clinic, but that's typical for late summer. Got a question for you."

"Fire away."

"Are you dating a certain stubborn, pain-in-the-ass EMT?" Doc Elliott asked.

Confused by the question, Gavin stared at the phone. "Umm...if you're talking about Gray, yes. I haven't heard much from him since he started the fall semester. I understand about his crazy busy schedule, though I hoped he would return my messages or texts."

"Stupid stubborn idiot," Doc Elliott muttered. "Why haven't you called Gavin?"

Gavin couldn't make out the entire conversation on Elliott's end. He barely made out Xavier's voice, but not the words. "Doc?"

"Complete and utter idiot. He didn't charge his phone because he's been going nonstop. The man can't say no."

"He didn't charge his phone."

"Multiple times. Battery kept dying on him. It's why he didn't get back to you."

"Okay. Umm... Good to know."

"I'm calling because Gray worked himself into a case of severe fatigue, heat exhaustion and passed out during an EMT call."

"Wait a minute. He did *what*?"

Elliott repeated the diagnosis.

"Who is watching over him?"

"Other than Norman while on the job, I don't think anyone else. That's the problem. I don't want to release him on his own recognizance because the dumb shit will keep up his insane pace. I can't rely on Norman, who can never say no to Gray. No matter what, he needs a break," the doctor said. "With the possibility of a hurricane landfall, we need him healthy. Gray isn't going to sit still unless someone sits *on* him...like a freaking elephant."

Gavin laughed at the doctor's exasperating attitude.

"Damn it, Doc, leave him alone!" came a faint voice. "I don't need a babysitter."

"And there's Xavier's answer," Gavin said.

"Shut it or I'll shove a needle in your hip and knock you out on your ass, Grayson. Don't think I won't," Elliott threatened and returned to the conversation. "Xavier? Oh, yes, his first name. Sorry. He's always been Gray over here."

"Why are you calling me?"

"I'm hoping you can come get him and sit on his ass for the next forty-eight hours."

"What?" Xavier squawked. "No! I have a lab—"

"Shut it, Gray. Forty-eight hours. I'll give you a damn doctor's note."

"What—"

"Needle. In. Arm. No, better idea. In your ass," Elliott snapped. "Did you hear me, Gavin? Rest, food and light activity." He grumbled when Xavier interrupted him. "Yeah. Yeah. I can allow some sex, you horny idiot."

Gavin laughed at the back and forth.

"Can you help me? If you're pissed at him, I understand and will find someone—"

"I can help, Doc. Good thing I finished my hurricane alert calls. There's no wedding this weekend, so my time is open. I need to tell Samuel, but I don't think it'll be a problem."

"He can follow you to the Charm but must chill out somewhere. No helping with preparations or anything. I don't want him left alone where he'll try to go for a ten-mile run or something stupid."

"Already had a meeting with the rest of the Charm team. For the most part, I can manage from home.

We're meeting again to discuss further preparations depending on future weather reports. Lemme find Samuel." Gavin scooped up his phone and headed to Samuel's office. He stuck his head through the doorway. "Got a minute, Samuel?"

"Hey, Gavin, any problems with the clients?" Samuel tapped on the keyboard.

"Nothing so far. Everyone understands but don't want to accept it. Anyway, no. This concerns something else."

"What's up?"

"Doc Elliott is on the other side." Gavin wiggled his phone.

"Oh no. Anyone we know in the clinic? Who's hurt?"

"Hello, Samuel. No, relax, it's not a major accident or anything," Elliott said.

"Oh, okay. Good to know. What is it?"

"It seems Gray has worked himself into a case of fatigue and heat exhaustion," Gavin explained. "Doc needs someone to sit on him for forty-eight hours."

"Are you kidding?"

"Nope. Idiot would work himself into a coma if we let him," Elliott said over the speaker. "Mind letting Gavin off to babysit our favorite paramedic?"

Samuel laughed. "Go ahead. We're covered. Dakota and I decided to close everything down. Unless there's a drastic change in the track, we're going to concentrate on preparing for the storm. I don't want to take any chances after all the renovations. I don't want to have reservations, only to tell our guests they need to retreat in a mass evacuation instead of chilling out on the beach. Not the best of impressions."

"Appreciate it, Samuel," Elliott said.

"Welcome. This should be interesting," Gavin said.

"Tell me about it. Thanks, Samuel," Gavin said. "Doc, I'll be there in about fifteen minutes."

"I'll have him ready for you."

"This is ridiculous. I'm a grown-ass adult," Gray shouted.

"Don't push me, Grayson," Elliott snapped. "Hurry, please, otherwise I'm shoving a needle in his butt and knocking him out. I'm not kidding." He hung up.

Gavin and Samuel cracked up laughing.

Chapter Twenty-Three

Stripped to scrubs and parked on an ER bed, Xavier couldn't begin to understand what was happening. "I can't believe you're doing this to me, Doc."

"I'm not the one who passed out during a call and ended up on the gurney instead of the patient being there."

"There's no need for me to go home with Gavin."

"Why not? You stay over there all the time."

"By choice, not by orders. There's a difference."

"Don't you want to be with your boyfriend? You seem to be avoiding him."

"I've been busy between classes and work shifts. Not avoidance. He knows what I do and understands my crazy hours. His schedule can also be insane." Xavier waved a hand. "Screw this. I'm pissed about your orders. Let me go home...alone. Please? I'll get some sleep. Chill out."

"Riiiiight. Cause that's what got you into this mess in the first place. No possible way I'm letting you leave without supervision." Doc Elliott glanced over. "You'll end up right back in that ER bed."

"No, I won't. I know better than trying to pass out again."

"I truly doubt that."

"Thanks for the vote of confidence...really." Xavier dropped back to the gurney with a loud huff.

"Patient still grumpy?" Norman asked while he walked over.

Elliott grumbled. "He's ramping up the need for a sedative."

"Yikes. Well, I packed up some things like he wanted." Norman dropped a packed duffel bag on the bed. "I grabbed your backpack." He lifted the other bag.

"Not that one. Not yet. Let me look through that," Doc Elliott said. He snatched the backpack and yanked it open. "I need to make sure there's nothing too taxing for Gray."

"What? Are you kidding me? What the hell are you doing? Get your grabby hands out of my personal stuff. You know I can't deal with that with all of my issues," Xavier hollered.

"I'm making sure you don't end up in my emergency room as a patient. Who knows what the hell you have in here that can cause all kinds of trouble."

"Nursing books and notes. My laptop. Please. Real dangerous."

Norman smacked Xavier on the side of his head.

"Hey! What the hell?" Xavier cried out. "Attacking the patient?"

"Umm. Did I come at a bad time?"

Xavier looked to the side and discovered Gavin had appeared in midst of all the abuse. Gavin's eyes were wide.

"Oh, come on," Xavier said, "I don't need a babysitter. Gavin, go home. Honest, the doc is messing around."

Norman smacked Xavier's head again. "Would you please try to behave around Gavin? May I remind you that he's only here to help with your sorry ass. He didn't have to show up."

"Or agree to babysit your sorry ass, as cute as it might be," Gavin said. "What's happening here?"

"Oh, a certain paramedic being a royal snarky pain in the ass. I'm trying to protect him and all he does is holler and complain. I'm ready to shove a certain instrument in his butt." Doc Elliott wiggled a loaded hypodermic needle. "Just give me a reason, Grayson."

Nurses chuckled.

Eying the needle, Xavier clamped his mouth shut.

"Will you behave?" Doc Elliott asked.

Xavier rolled his eyes. "Yes."

"Even when you're away from the big scary needle?" Gavin asked.

"Really?"

Gavin shrugged. "Have to ask."

"Yes, I'll behave myself."

"Promise?"

Xavier lifted his pinkie finger. "Pinkie promise."

Gavin shook his head but smiled. He stepped closer, placed his hands on the edge of the gurney and leaned over. Then he pressed his lips against Xavier's mouth in a gentle kiss. "Promise sealed with a kiss. Better keep it."

Xavier cupped one hand against Gavin's face. He returned the kiss and nuzzled Gavin's cheek. "Hey, there. Missed you."

"Missed you. No call. No text. Nada. What happened?"

"It's my ADHD messing with me — and sometimes the OCD interferes. I hyper-focus on course-work, then on my EMT calls and my inner gears — " Xavier shook his head. "It overrides everything. I messed up. I'm sorry."

"We'll figure out something to help you." Gavin glanced around them. "How about we continue this back home? Can't get much rest here, unless something knocks you out."

"Probably best." Xavier leaned around Gavin to stare at Doc Elliott. "Can I go now?"

"Got your ride right here," Doc Elliott said. "Let me remove the last leads." He disconnected the final pieces to free Xavier. Instead of bothering a nurse, he secured a bandage to the back of Xavier's hand after removing the IV needle. Then he waved over the orderly and wheelchair.

"What the hell?" Xavier smacked the gurney. "Are you kidding me?"

"Get your butt in the chair. Not a word."

"Move, Xavier." Gavin scooped up the duffel bag and backpack.

"Aww, hell," Xavier said. "At least my ass isn't hanging out." He climbed off the gurney.

"Any dizziness? Disorientation?" Doc Elliott asked.

"No, I'm fine." Xavier lowered himself into the chair. "Ready to roll."

"You heard the grumpy patient, orderly. Wheel them out." Doc Elliott pointed to Xavier. "Rest. Relax. Chill out. At least forty-eight hours. Plenty of water. Don't eat anything too heavy."

"Yes, Doctor, I understand."

"Don't go against my orders. I mean it. Your system went into overdrive. Please understand how bad this was," Doc Elliott said. "You need a break."

"I'll make sure he gets one," Gavin said. He rested his hand on Xavier's shoulder. "Time at home to rest...then perhaps a beach day. We did good on our last one."

"Anything other than long hours of studying and an EMT run," Doc Elliott said.

"I promise. I won't screw it up," Xavier said. "I'll listen to Gavin."

"Thank you." Doc Elliott nodded to the orderly.

After driving to Gavin's home, Xavier followed Gavin inside. Neither one spoke much on the short ride. Though, Xavier allowed Gavin to help him out and to the garage entry door.

Gavin set the bags on a chair and unloaded the rest of his things.

"I'm damn sorry all this happened," Xavier mumbled while he dropped onto the sofa. He lowered his head in his hands.

"Do you have a headache?"

"A bit. Leftover from whatever the doc gave me. Haven't been sleeping well."

"Is your ADHD driving you to do all this?"

"Don't know. I think that's the main issue." Xavier leaned back to rest against the cushions. He dragged one hand down his face. "Yeah, I overdid things. I admit it. I pushed myself so hard to get through this course, to get to the next one and the clinical hours."

Gavin lowered himself next to Xavier and took his hand. "Why would you push yourself so hard?"

"To succeed when my father swore I wouldn't amount to anything when I left his house for the last time," Xavier said. "His words continue to haunt me, to drive me, and I'm afraid they might destroy me."

"I will never let that happen." Gavin cupped a hand to Xavier's face. "You mean too damn much."

"I hate feeling so lost."

"Then let me be your guide. I'm sitting right here for you."

"For now."

"Then we'll take the next step."

"Next step?"

"Yeah. There's always another step in these relationship" — Gavin tick-tocked his head — "things."

"Things? So says the wedding planner."

"I prefer 'event coordinator'."

Xavier chuckled and yawned until his jaw cracked and popped.

"You need a nap."

"What? I'm not a chil —" Another yawn cut off his words.

"Lay back and take a nap. No arguments," Gavin said while he snagged the blanket from the back of the sofa. He shook it out.

Grumbling under his breath, Xavier stretched out along the sofa's length and punched the pillow into position.

Gavin draped the blanket over Xavier's lower half. He slid his fingers through Xavier's hair. "Sleep. I'll keep watch over you. We'll talk more later."

Xavier grabbed Gavin's hand before he pulled it back. "Thank you for sticking around, even after all my shit."

"I'm not going anywhere."

Chapter Twenty-Four

By the end of the prescribed rest time, Gavin woke up with Xavier. Together, they made their way to the kitchen.

"We're about done with your break," Gavin said while he got coffee and breakfast going.

"I know. Not sure what to do next. Guess we should check with the doc."

"Are you feeling better?"

Xavier smiled at him. "Always, when I'm with you."

"It's when I let you out of my sight that I don't want things to turn bad again."

"Again, something we need to figure out, plus a call with the doc. I'm gonna see what's happening out there...unless you want me to join you."

"Nope. Go and sit down. Check the weather."

Dropping onto the sofa, Xavier located the remote and turned on the television.

"*This is an emergency tropical weather report for Hurricane Katia,*" the local meteorologist said.

"That doesn't sound good. Hey, are you seeing this?" Xavier called out.

Gavin leaned around the tower separating part of the kitchen from the main area. He raised his eyebrows toward his sleep-tousled hair. "Oh, crap."

"*Good morning, folks. There's a lot to get to with our tropical weather,*" the local meteorologist said. His shirt sleeves were rolled up, his tie loosened. "*A strong front altered the previous track. After leaving the Keys and entering the Gulf, Hurricane Katia continues to follow the edge of the front and curled to the north and the northeast. The computer models now place the eye's landfall between Mobile, Alabama, and Pensacola, Florida. At current speed and strength, the models predict a landfall within the next couple of days. The cone includes all areas of Santa Rosa County.*" The meteorologist shifted to face the news desk. "*For information about preparations, evacuations and other news, I'll turn it back to you, James.*"

"*Thank you for the update, Tom.*" The anchor looked at the camera and his notes. "*We have new evacuation orders by the governor. The entire barrier island of Santa Rosa is under a hurricane warning. A full evacuation is ordered for the barrier island. Fairpoint Peninsula is under a hurricane warning. This includes the towns of Shore Breeze, Oriole Beach, Tiger Point and Navarre. A partial evacuation is ordered for all waterfront properties and low-lying areas. Hurricane shelters are being set up in the schools. Except for emergency disaster response personnel, everyone in the vicinity must secure their home and business and evacuate to either a shelter or other safe location by ten a.m. The Three-Mile Bridge will close by two p.m. unless the wind speed rises faster then the bridge will close earlier. Anyone evacuating with pets is encouraged to stay in the pet-friendly designated elementary school shelters. Please visit our website for specific details. We encourage everyone to finish their remaining preparations by tomorrow. Remain close to a television, computer, phone or radio for the latest updates on any evacuation orders, preparation changes and changes regarding the hurricane. Our meteorology team is keeping a close watch and will update you. We now return you to your regular scheduled programming."*

The television switched back to the daytime morning show out of New York City.

"Crap. Looks like we're going to get hit by this storm," Xavier said.

"Are you considered emergency disaster personnel?"

"Part of my training, remember? I can be sent anywhere there is need."

Before Gavin could answer, their phones rang. It was almost a simultaneous event.

"That's freaky."

"Hello, this is Gavin Hartfield," Gavin said when he answered the call.

"It's Samuel. Did you see the recent hurricane update?"

"Yup. Just saw it with Xavier."

"Can you get to the Charm for an emergency meeting? Say in an hour?"

"Sure, I can get over there. I might have to drop Xavier somewhere."

"Okay."

Gavin hung up and turned to hear Xavier finishing his call.

"I'm to report to Breeze's EOC. Luckily my truck isn't parked far away. How about you?" Xavier said.

"Gotta head to the Charm. Then I'll run to the stores and get the last bit of preparations. Hopefully, I can find what I need."

"It's going to be crazy."

"I've got it. Part of the experience. Will use my elbows to get what I need if I must."

With a smile, Xavier leaned in for a kiss. Gavin lifted on his toes to return the affection.

They went to the kitchen for coffee and a quick breakfast. After showering, they dressed and got into Gavin's car.

They kissed again when Gavin dropped Xavier off at the Emergency Operations Center, a specialized building situated near the schools, the highest point in Breeze. The building was rated to withstand or survive a hurricane, a tornado and a storm surge and keep operations running. The electrical and information technology wires and connections were buried deep underground in specialized covers to maintain energy and connection outside of the town.

"Hey, Gray," the sheriff called out. He arrived with the local IT guru and his partner, Beau Courtenay.

"Hello, Robin. Beau, what are you doing here?" Xavier shook hands with the IT tech guru.

"Gotta make sure everything remains running. Robin only trusts me," Beau said. He nudged Robin Burke's side with his elbow.

"I also want to keep you close," Robin said. He tugged Beau close for a quick kiss.

Glancing back at Gavin, Xavier smiled.

Gavin returned the smile and waved. "Hey, Robin, Beau."

"Hi, Gavin, how are you?" Beau called out.

"Doing okay. Nervous about the hurricane. Samuel called a meeting at the Charm."

"Just dropping our boy off?" Robin asked.

"Yes, had to keep an eye on him. He was under Doc Elliott's orders to rest."

"Yeah. Yeah. Tell everyone. Go on. Get going." Xavier shooed him.

"You're still under Doc's warning. Nothing too strenuous for him, Sheriff. Got it?"

"Understand, Gavin. I don't want to get between Doc and a needle," the sheriff said with a bark of laughter.

"Get outta here before you ruin my rep," Xavier said.

Laughing, Gavin drove away. Once he parked, Gavin headed to the restaurant. He was surprised to discover only the Charm family present, not the employees.

"Hey, Gavin, right on time. Have a seat," Samuel said. He waved him over with his tablet.

"Hello, Samuel, everyone." Gavin took a seat. "What's happening?"

"Already took care of the employees and sent them home until the storm passes. Dakota and I can close the Charm, thanks to all the upgrades Sully added. Only need to press a few buttons to close the hurricane shutters." Samuel snapped his fingers and pointed to Gavin. "Can you give us an update about Occasions' clients?"

"Umm. Yeah." Gavin explained about the phone calls. "Everyone for the next month was notified. I have a couple of brides and a pair of to-be husbands freaking out. We might have to adjust some prices, perhaps extra gifts, but most issues should be smoothed out. They know we can't control the weather."

"Thanks, Gavin. We can cover any changes that you see fit to offer to satisfy those clients," Samuel said while he made notes. "This is one of the first major hurricanes our rebuilt Charm is facing, so I'm freaking out. I know you locals are old hands with these things. As a New Yorker, I got swiped by Sandy but know it's nothing like what you face down here season after season. I'll rely on your requests and recommend-ations."

"Doesn't hurt to update protocols and preparations," Sully said from his spot next to Chandler.

"Fire away," Reece called out.

Samuel glanced at Dakota, who nodded for him to take charge.

"According to the newest models, we know Breeze could be in the path of the hurricane. The top-right quadrant, which I learned can be the nastier edge," Samuel said.

"What? Why?" Gavin asked.

"It's also called the dirty side. The right side of a hurricane rotates counterclockwise and is the leading edge of the storm. This includes the strength and the forward velocity. This edge whips around the winds and creates the storm surge. You'll interact with the most extreme wind, flooding rain, possible tornadoes and the dangerous storm surge. The closer we are to the eye wall, the worse things get," Sully explained.

"The entire hurricane, especially one of this size and strength, is bad. Don't forget that fact. There's more damage when the north-right side smacks against us," Reece added.

"Oh, this sounds so pleasant," Chandler muttered. "Can I fly to New York?"

"No. You're staying here...with me," Sully said while he tugged Chandler in for a kiss.

"Damn. Oh, well, you'll protect me." Chandler lowered his head to rest on Sully's shoulder.

Everyone chuckled.

"Okay. Okay. Back to the problem," Dakota said.

"The Charm is in the evacuation area, along with our home. Most of your homes are on the coast and therefore under the evacuation order," Samuel said.

"Why are we here?" Malcolm asked.

"I thought we could figure out about evacuation and what to do—if we should stick together or go our separate ways," Samuel said.

"I suggest everyone evacuate in from the coastal homes," Sully said.

"To where?" Malcolm asked. "The shelters are uncomfortable and crowded. Hotels are expensive. There's no guarantee for fuel, food and places to go. Even Pensacola is going to get smacked, so we would have to go beyond it—*if* we can make it that far. I'd rather hunker down."

"All good points," Samuel said.

"What about my home? It's situated toward the middle of town and is two stories. The three bedrooms are upstairs with the other rooms downstairs, along with the garage. It's a couple of streets away from the firehouse, so I'm slightly higher. It could be a Hurricane Sleepover Party," Gavin suggested.

"That could work. Your place would better protected than our coastal homes," Reece said.

"Since I don't have enough guest rooms, you'll need to bring a few things. Everyone can bring air mattresses, sleeping bags, personal stuff and storm kits including extra water, food and fuel. I have a standby home generator system connected and it runs on propane. We'll need to do a little rearranging, but we can make room for everyone. What do you think?" Gavin asked.

Sully and Chandler whispered to each other.

"We accept the offer," Sully said.

After a quick chat with Reece, Mal said, "We're in, too."

Samuel and Dakota glance at each other and nodded. "Count us in."

Mal and Sully texted the rest of their friends with the offer.

"Dorian is safe back in school," Mal said.

"Doc Elliott says he'll have to help evacuate the clinic and will make a decision after a meeting. Jude agrees to join us but hopes you don't mind a dog and cat," Sully said after a couple of exchanged texts.

"Both are welcomed," Gavin said.

"Then count Jude and the furry kids," Sully said.

"I believe Beau will be with the sheriff at the EOC. I saw them together when I dropped Xavier there," Gavin said.

"Will Gray join us?"

"He's part of the emergency team, so I don't know. It'll be the same with anyone involved with the EOC and clinic."

"Wyatt, Keegan and Wyatt's nephew are going to stay in the apartment above Wyatt's studio," Mal said. "If things get bad, he asked if the option could remain open."

"Sure," Gavin said.

"Is that everyone?" Samuel asked. After a round of nods, he called an end to the impromptu meeting.

"I need to brave the stores then I'm heading home. Do we know when to expect landfall?" Gavin asked.

"Possibly Sunday or Monday—but keep an eye on the news. The hurricane could speed up, change the path, strengthen and everything else. The predictable thing about hurricanes is that they're unpredictable," Mal said.

"Then I'll expect everyone by Saturday. We can narrow the window when we learn more."

After the last bit of information, Gavin waved to everyone. The group split up to follow the plan and dive into preparations.

Chapter Twenty-Five

Three days later, with the hurricane not changing its track, Xavier remained on duty and took on extra duties where needed. Through texts, he learned that Gavin had invited the Charm group to hunker down at his home. While some had arrived on Saturday, the rest of the group planned to head over that morning. The hurricane center predicted a landfall before sundown, but that could change.

"Gray, got a moment?"

Looking up from the latest text from Gavin, Xavier darkened the screen when the SBFD Battalion Chief Isaac Fromme spoke. The six-foot-plus man in the deep blue shirt and pants uniform was an impressive figure. His dark hair was tipped with silver. Laugh lines at his deep brown eyes spoke of his humor and strength. His SBFD shield pinned on his chest marked his rank with double gold bars upon his shoulders.

"What can I do for you, Chief?"

"This monster is getting closer. Could you do a full circle around the northern neighborhoods along the coast and make sure everyone either took cover or headed for the shelter? Then make your way down and do the neighborhood west of us. The deputies are spread out and the sheriff asked for all hands-on deck. Winds are rising. We're not doing any emergency runs until the hurricanes passes. I know you have a radio in your truck to contact me and the ECO," Chief Fromme said.

"I can do that, sir. My truck can push through this weather."

"Great. Your handle is 'EMT Gray'. Do you need to grab anything from your home?"

"No, sir, I gathered what I deemed important. I have an extra duffel bag and emergency kit if it's needed," Xavier said.

"Keep it with you. You might not be able to get back here in time. The sky is darkening faster than we'd expected. Contact me on the radio if you need to take shelter. Appreciate the help, so does the sheriff. We'll keep one of your teams here. The rest are helping to evacuate the last of the priority patients. The bridge will close after their last run, and they'll remain in Pensacola."

"Understood," Xavier said.

With a nod, Fromme walked off to speak with another group.

"What's up?" Norman asked, while Xavier scooped up his backpack. "Saw Fromme leave."

"He requested I run one of the final patrols. Gonna go out in Old Blue, and I have a radio to connect if the cell phones go down." Xavier walked to his locker and pulled on his storm-weather gear with the hip-length heavy raincoat, hat and rain boots. Leaving the boots off for now, he gathered them in one hand. "Need you to take over here. It's just you and the other team, Ryder and Aiden. Luke and Wendy are helping with the hospital evac and will stay in Pensacola."

"We've got it covered, Gray. We might move to the EOC if things get worse. Take care out there."

Closing his locker, Xavier dug his keys out and twirled them. "Old Blue will get me through. Hope to be back before Katia makes herself known." With a wave, he left the combination fire and EMT station. The increase in the winds was noticeable, along with the darkening sky as the heavy gray clouds filled the once-bright-blue sky.

Climbing into Old Blue, he turned on the engine, the radio to listen to the weather updates and the box that connected him to EOC. He adjusted the knob and picked up the receiver. *"EMT Gray. Private truck. Badge SBG-75214. EOC, come in."*

"EOC here. Good to hear you, Gray. Where ya headed?"

"On patrol to northwest coast and west of the fire station."

"Gotcha. Katia ETA six hours. Could be less. Will update."

"Thanks for update. EMT Gray out."

With that news, Xavier shifted Old Blue into gear and headed out to check the coastal neighborhoods. It was past time for people to get to a shelter and hunker down.

The storm moved faster than predicted. The EOC radio operator kept him updated. Winds whipped into a frenzy while rain bands circled around the eye of the hurricane. Each run of the hurricane hunter planes came back with bigger numbers. Some were getting a bit scary.

At times, Xavier fought to keep his truck centered on the slick roads. After leaving the upper northwest, he worked his way from the coast and toward town. This was where Gavin lived. Watching the road and checking to make sure homes were secured, he kept an ear on the two radios. The weather kept getting worse.

The EOC connection crackled with reports from other deputies clearing their areas and returning to base. Another deputy reported the last ambulance had crossed the bridge and the bridge was now closed. He was heading back along the main road to the EOC for the last check.

"Base to all cars. Base to all cars. The first outer band is reaching us. Make your way to base or the closest safe place. Time to get off the roads."

"Just what I need— What the hell?"

Stopping the truck short, he shifted the gear into Park and pulled on the extra hand brake. He used it to secure the truck and help it fight against the wind.

He couldn't believe what he was seeing.

"Un-fucking-believable."

* * * *

"EMT Gray to EOC Base," Xavier said when he thumbed the radio.

"Base to EMT Gray. What's up?"

"Something stupid."

"Pardon?"

"Ever hear of hurricane surfing?"

"Do I want to know?"

Xavier summed up what he was seeing at the address he gave to the operator. At the same time, he picked up his phone and set it to take a video of what he watched.

There were two couples standing at the end of the driveway. Three of the adults dangled beer bottles from a hand. Multiple six-packs waited on the edge of the patio. To his horror, four small children were huddled within the open garage door and trying to keep away from the squally weather.

From the slightly off movements and beer bottles, Xavier figured the adults were either smashed or well on their way.

One of the females, to his surprise, dropped a skateboard in front of her and placed a foot on it. She opened a child's pink umbrella. With a shout, she stepped onto the skateboard, held the umbrella in front of her and let the winds bluster and push her down the street.

She was 'hurricane surfing'.

Using the umbrella, she turned around and returned. She cheered and shouted, along with the others. When the wind gust hit, her speed increased and almost caused her to fall off the board.

"Holy. Shit."

"I said worse. I got a video of it."

"Hold up. Sheriff—" the operator hollered before he cut the connection.

Xavier watched the lady change places with the other one. She handed over the umbrella.

"EMT Gray."

"Gray here. Second lady is now taking a ride."

"Sheriff says send the video to him ASAP. Then stop them if you can. Holler at them to get the hell inside, close all their damn doors and lose the beer. Make sure the kids are inside *before you leave. He'll send a patrol car when the hurricane clears."*

Xavier tapped on the saved video, tapped another icon and sent it to the sheriff's email. *"Done. Sent to email."*

"Great."

"Should I take the skateboard?"

"No. Don't go that far. You're not a deputy. Still, you're in an official coat. Bluster."

"Will do."

"Good luck."

Pulling the key, Xavier buttoned up the heavy raincoat, slid his phone into a pocket and pushed open the door. It took a little more strength because he pushed against the wind. Climbing out, he closed the door. The wind almost pulled it away from him.

Bracing himself, he walked over as the second lady made her return trip. He stopped her short by stepping into her way.

"Hey, move over," she said, laughing in the way only someone tipsy could and seemingly not giving a shit about the danger.

"Shut up," Xavier snapped. He snatched her umbrella. "Get off the skateboard."

"No way. It's not yours."

"Get. Off. The. Skateboard," he said and raised his voice to be heard over the winds. He reached into his coat, unclipped his shield and held it in front of her face, though he kept a finger over the EMT designation. *"Now."*

"Fine. Fine. Stupid cops." She got off the board, tilting farther to one side before she found her balance. "Whoa. Wind is strong." She laughed again, along with her friends.

"Mommy!" one of the little kids called out.

Xavier flipped up the board and took hold of the deck. Then he slid the shield back in a pocket. He grabbed her above her elbow and forced her back.

"Hey, let go of my wife," one of the guys said.

"He's a cop, Mike," she said.

"Do you idiots have any idea what the hell you are doing? This is a freaking hurricane that's going to hit our shores. We're already getting the outer bands. It's not time to have a 'drink all you want' party and put your lives in danger, along with those of your kids," Xavier shouted. He pointed the board at the shivering kids. He pushed the lady toward her husband. Knocking the nearest man aside, he crouched in front of the kids. Then he gentled his voice when he asked, "Hey there, my name is Gray. Are all of you okay?"

The kids nodded, their eyes wide.

"It's noisy and windy. Don't like it out here. Worse inside. Everything rattles. But it's better than out here," the oldest boy said. "I'm Danny."

"Mommy and Daddy drink...lots," one of the girls said. "Tell us to go play. They created a game outside with my umbrella and Danny's skateboard."

"This is your skateboard, little man?" Xavier asked Danny.

Danny nodded.

"Okay. You keep it and hang onto it." Xavier handed over the board. Then he held the umbrella to the girl. "Same goes for you and your umbrella."

"Thanks, Officer," Danny said and hugged his board.

"Thank you!" the girl said.

"I'm gonna send your parents in, and everyone needs to figure out a better game of staying indoors until the storm goes away."

"When's it going away?" Danny asked.

"Tomorrow."

"Long time."

"I know, but we can't change it. Just stay safe inside. If it gets too noisy, get blankets, pillows, a flashlight, some snacks, water bottles and go hide in a bathtub. Take a game or book. Stay there until you feel safe."

"Okay. I'll get it ready," Danny said.

"Good. Counting on you to keep the others safe, Danny."

"I will."

"Good. Now take them inside." Watching the kids hurry in, Xavier stormed back to the adults. He ripped them all a new one while he yelled about their stupidity, at the bottles and pointed back where the kids had been. He passed on the operator's words about how he'd sent the video of their surfing to the sheriff and a deputy would come by their homes after the hurricane passed. With that threat of potential tickets and jail time for their sheer stupidity, he snapped at them to get the hell back inside, shut the garage door and not do anything else until the hurricane had passed, and that included finishing the rest of those six-packs. He mentioned that they should brew some coffee and sober up, because their kids needed them to pay attention.

Xavier turned to head back to the truck.

"Wait a fucking moment? Who the hell—?" one of the men hollered.

Xavier turned to face the drunken idiot stalking toward him.

The wind whipped up crazy. Rain pelted their skin. The wind almost knocked them off her feet.

Then there was a strange cracking and creaking noise.

Waving off the man's drunken attempt to change things, Xavier was about to yell at him to get inside.

"Xavier! Xavier!"

Hearing his name, his true name, Xavier stopped paying attention to the man.

Then something yanked on his heavy raincoat, the motion causing him to fall to the ground.

When he hit, Xavier looked at where he was standing. He watched a massive oak tree being ripped apart by the winds and the loose soil. Three powerful limbs snapped at their base connections and fell to the ground. A large trunk-like limb dropped across Old Blue's engine and smushed the entire hood. Headlights popped and cracked from the pressure, and the front lowered a foot to threaten the tires. Another branch smashed and dented the cab. Then the third dented the bed of the truck near its connection to the cab. Different fluids pooled underneath the engine and mixed with the water.

"Holy shit, Blue, no. My truck…" Xavier swallowed and realized he would have been crushed by the limbs if he'd remained there.

Glancing over his shoulder, he watched Gavin rolling to his knees.

"Gavin?"

"You didn't hear me with the wind. I tried to call out to you – same with Reece and Sully." Gavin pointed behind his shoulder.

Xavier saw Reece and Sully standing near them.

"Good thing Gavin got to you when he did. Man, that would not have been fun trying to extricate you from that," Reece said. "Poor old tree. It shouldn't have fallen this early."

"What are you doing here?" Gavin asked.

"Fire Chief asked me to do a final round of a couple of neighborhoods to help out the deputies. This was the last road I had to do before I headed back to the fire station to wait out the hurricane," Xavier said. He grasped for Gavin's hand. "Thank you."

Gavin smiled, lifted Xavier's hand and kissed the knuckles. "Anytime."

"Where are those dipshit neighbors? I swear... I would have been gone if it weren't for those idiotic bastards. Did you see that shit they were pulling?" Xavier continued to curse under his breath while he climbed back to his feet. Then he helped Gavin to his feet.

"Skateboarding down the street with an umbrella?" Sully asked. "Yup. Definite idjits."

"You've been watching *Supernatural* again, haven't you?" Reece asked.

Sully narrowed his gaze. "Don't look down on the Winchester boys."

"There was worse," Xavier said. "The kids were standing inside the open garage door."

"With this wind picking up?"

Xavier nodded.

Sully cursed dark and nasty.

"It's why I avoid them whenever I'm home. I'll say hi to the kids, though. They're sweet...Danny and Cassie," Gavin said. "The adults rushed inside by the time I yanked you off your feet."

"Bunch of cowards didn't try to help. That guy stalking you saw the tree begin to sway and didn't do shit to warn you." After talking, Reece raced over to his truck and reached into one of the containers. He returned with a chainsaw and a large pair of pruning shears.

"Of course they would run away." Xavier shook his head. He dragged his fingers through his damp hair and pushed it back. "Poor Old Blue."

"I don't think he's going to come back from this one, Gray," Sully said. "Even an old steel beast like him."

"He needed some engine work before this hit."

"Yikes."

"Shit, the radio." Xavier fought his way through the branches.

"Hold on. Hold on. Let the pro at this, Gray," Reece said. He handed the chainsaw over to Sully. Then he started to clip at the branches to work them down. "Hate doing this before a hurricane but don't have options."

"We can stick them under the bed's cover. That way they can't fly around," Xavier said and went to open up part of the tarp cover. "Just get me close as you can to the passenger door. I hope we can force it open."

"What's in there?"

"The EOC radio and my personal stuff. The radio is the best way to contact them. I gotta let them know what happened and that I'm not dead," Xavier said.

"That's a good thing to alert them," Reece said. "Not dead."

Falling quiet, Gavin took the cut branches. When he reached Xavier, he helped shove them under the tarp. "You're staying here."

"I can't. I need to get back to the station."

"There's no time — not by the time we get your stuff. You'll never make it there. There's another band after this one on the radar. We're getting into a little lull, but it's not going to last long." Gavin shoved in the last branch. "Stay here."

"After I contact the station, I'll make the decision."

"Stubborn idiot," Gavin muttered and went to collect more branches.

Before Xavier could respond, Reece revved up the chainsaw and used it on the heavier pieces of the branch. After the limbs dropped, Reece turned it off, propped it on the flattened hood and helped Gavin drag the pieces to the back.

"Okay. We're through," Reece said.

"Brilliant," Xavier said and went to Reece. He checked the frame and saw it was all bent to hell and back. "This isn't going to be good." He grabbed hold of the handle, made room for Reece to get a spot, and together they yanked back.

The door didn't budge.

"Damn," Xavier said.

"Stuck tight," Sully said. "Hang on. Lemme in with you." He added his weight.

Steel creaked, screamed, screeched and finally the door was released.

All three men did a fast dance backward to regain their balance.

Gavin cracked up laughing.

"Yeah. Yeah," Xavier said. He reached inside for a look around. "Poor baby. I'm sorry, buddy." He patted the crooked dashboard. Then he released the EOC radio from the dash and hit the button.

The radio came back to life.

"I'm going to check out the tree while you contact the base. Then we need to get our asses inside," Reece said. He braced the shears on his shoulder and walked around to check out the rest of the oak tree.

"*EMT Gray to EOC Base. EOC Base, come in.*"

"*EOC is here. Damn good to hear your voice. What happened?*" the operator said.

"*The skateboard surfers are back in their house. A tree smashed my poor truck.*"

"*Were you – ?*"

"*No, EOC. I'm in the clear, thanks to friends.*"

"*Good. Sheriff's call. Too late to head to station. Stay in place and shelter where you can. His orders.*"

"*Will do. I'm with Gavin Hartfield and the Southern Charm men at Gavin's home. Could you alert the FC Chief and my team to my change in status?*"

"*Will do, Gray. Thanks for checking in. We'll contact you on the radio throughout the hurricane for status updates.*"

"*Appreciate it. EMT Gray out.*"

"*EOC Base out.*"

Xavier hung up the receiver. "Looks like you have another hurricane guest."

"The more the merrier," Gavin said. "Can you get your bags out?"

"I think so," Xavier said and reached inside.

"Damn fucking idiots," Reece said while he stomped back.

"What's up?" Sully asked.

"Damn homeowners. The entire tree is dead, down to its core. It should have been leveled months ago. I remember this tree now. I recommended its removal last winter. There are damn rules to follow. I'll take care of the situation after the storm," Reece said. "Basically, if they'd followed through on my recommendation, this wouldn't have happened. All this shouldn't come from your insurance, but the homeowner's because the tree is on their lot. I'll make sure there is a record of everything so you can report it to your insurance, Gray."

"Appreciate the help. Don't know how I'm going to afford a new one. Another problem for a different day—" Xavier trailed off while he reached and tugged. "Ah. Got it. Can someone take my duffel and backpack?"

"Got them," Gavin said. He accepted the bags.

"Here's an extra emergency kit." Xavier pulled out the bigger bag with a large red cross on both sides and handed it over to Sully.

Reece grabbed his tools and returned them to his truck.

Wiggling back out, Xavier pushed and dragged the door back. It wouldn't close completely shut. Patting it in commiseration, he took his duffel and backpack from Gavin. Shouldering both, he followed Gavin and Sully to the house.

Within moments, Reece followed and was the last one in the door. He closed and locked it.

Gavin reset the alarm.

Shaking off the wet, Xavier placed his bags on the entrance shelf unit. Then he removed the heavy EMT raincoat and let Gavin take it out to the garage area to let it drip dry. Along with the others, he tugged off the heavy boots and added them to the collection of shoes and boots and he ran a hand through his damp hair to wick off some of the moisture.

"Hey, Gray, fancy seeing you here," Samuel said while he walked over. "Sorry about your truck."

"Yeah, me too," Xavier said while picking up his bags.

Gavin returned to Xavier's side. "We can take your bags up to my room. Everyone is going to be spread out wherever they can. We have air mattresses and sleeping bags for those guys who can't get a bed."

"Complete with no sex during the hurricane rules, because no one else wants to hear you getting it on," someone called out.

The others all laughed.

"'No sex' rules?" Xavier asked.

"What else are we supposed to do without power and the Internet?" someone said.

"We're not losing power. I have an attached generator. It'll kick in if we lose power. We're not cavemen," Gavin said.

A couple of the guys snapped back with cavemen grunting noises.

Others fell into laughter.

"Idiots, all of you," Gavin said. "Behave yourselves. I'm taking Gray upstairs. We'll be right back."

A few of them made kissy-face noises.

Not giving them anything, Gavin dragged Xavier upstairs and down the hall to his room.

Xavier placed his bags on an armchair and accepted a long embrace from Gavin and a kiss.

"I was so damn afraid when I saw that tree listing and the limbs cracking. I didn't know if I would reach you in time," Gavin said when they broke the kiss. He snuggled against Xavier's chest.

"You did. You saved me, thanks to your quick actions."

"So damn scary."

"Yeah. Even for me...and I've seen a lot." Xavier trailed a hand down Gavin's back to soothe the other man.

After a few precious minutes, Gavin stepped back. "Go on and dry off, unless you want a shower."

"Nah. Just a quick dry of my hair. Then I'll change out of my uniform."

"You have a stash of clothes here. I laundered them," Gavin said and went to the dresser. He opened the drawer where he'd placed everything.

"Oh, even better," Xavier said and tugged out a pair of sweats and a three-quarter raglan-sleeved baseball-styled shirt with Captain America's logo across the front. Then he grabbed some socks.

Not shy in front of his lover, Xavier changed his clothes.

After hanging up the damp uniform in the shower, Gavin grabbed a towel and brought it back for Xavier to make a few cursory swipes through his hair. He gave it a finger-style and left it at that.

"Ready?"

Xavier nodded.

Taking Xavier's hand, Gavin led him back downstairs.

"Make room, guys," Gavin said.

Reece slid from the sofa to a pillow on the floor for Xavier to sit down and relax. "You earned it, man. That was some crazy stuff out there," he said.

"Appreciate it," Xavier said. He dropped with a sigh.

Out of nowhere, a slim gray cat hopped up, walked along the back and dropped onto Xavier's lap. He sat, stared at Xavier and meowed. Then he circled a few times and curled up for a catnap.

"Umm, hello, kitty," Xavier said while he kept his hands out of the way.

Jude was the first to notice the change and laughed. "That's Elliott's cat, Sigi—a rescue who adopted the doc. You can pet him. He's a friendly sort. Kind of a wannabe therapy cat."

"Sigi?"

"Sigmund Freud."

"Well, it is Doc Elliott's," Xavier said.

A couple of others chuckled and agreed.

Xavier stroked the cat's head. He got a rumbly purr in return.

"You hungry, Gray? We fixed up some barbecue to use up a few things?" Dakota asked while he wandered out of the kitchen. "Gavin has a decent grill on the patio."

"Sure. I could go for some food. Whatcha got?"

Dakota listed the options, and Xavier made his choice.

"Be right back. Don't move."

"Can't. I'll get clawed in a bad place."

Puzzled, Dakota leaned over and spotted Sigi. "Gotcha. Be right back."

"Thanks, Dakota."

Gavin settled next to Xavier and leaned against him. He picked up a conversation with Jude, Mal and Samuel.

Xavier tried to follow the news on the television and another conversation with Reece, Sully and Dakota, when he returned with a piled high plate.

This was different from what he'd planned at the fire station or the EOC.

In a much better fashion.

Chapter Twenty-Six

Throughout the day, the bands continued to swirl around the eye of the hurricane and swept around the barrier islands. They grew stronger and more frequent throughout the day and deep into the night. Each one brought higher winds and pounding rain. The winds and rain increased, disappeared and pounded around the house. The sustained winds battered the protective boards.

There was a massive creaking and cracking. Then a powerful sound of something falling and crashing into the ground.

"That would be rest of the oak tree meeting your truck," Reece said. "Sorry, Gray, but I think your truck is truly toast."

"Damn. That's not what I need," Xavier said.

"It'll be okay. We'll figure out what to do," Gavin said while he rubbed a hand over Xavier's arm.

"Hello, this update is for Shore Breeze. You have another powerful band wrapping around. Hurricane hunters reported increased sustained winds around the eye. The

Hurricane Center in Miami now puts Hurricane Katia as a Category Two storm. Good news, though. The eye continues to drift west of Shore Breeze and Pensacola. The cone now places the eye making landfall in Alabama. That doesn't mean Florida is out of danger. We're still getting those dangerous bands whipping around. There are multiple tornado warnings. Please stay alert, stay calm and be aware of what is happening. Until the hurricane passes Florida, stay in your homes or shelters, hunker down and we'll get through the night together," the weatherman said. By now, his sleeves were rolled up and his tie tucked in behind the buttons. His voice was a little rougher, but he kept up his support and optimism.

"Hey, baby, yeah, she's at a Cat Two now, but the eye is going west...away from us. Yup. How's everything at the clinic? Yeah? That's good. Good to put everyone possible in the same area. Good. Plus, there's food and caffeine. I know. Love you, too. Bye," Jude said and hung up after his latest checkup with Doc Elliott, who had stayed at the clinic with the lower risk patients, nurses and other doctors who'd remained behind.

"How are they doing?" Reece asked.

Jude dropped back down on the sofa. When Dawson placed his head on his lap and whined, Jude stroked and scratched around the soft triangle ears. "Everyone is in the cafeteria. They collapsed most of the tables, wheeled in beds and machines and others in wheelchairs. They closed everything else down, including the ER, and kept everyone away from the windows. Some of the cafeteria staff stayed to make sandwiches and other meals, along with coffee, tea and drinks. Other support staff remained, and some even brought their families to the clinic. Elliott said it's okay, doable for a couple of days. The clinic has powerful generators and is connected to the Emergency Operations Center if anything happens."

"Wish you'd stayed with him?"

"If this happens again, I might decide that, though it would be hard on Dawson and Sigi—especially Sigi, who would have to be cooped up in a strange room or a carrier. At least here he can roam around," Jude said.

"Or lie on my lap the entire time," Xavier added and glanced down at the gray cat that had barely left his lap.

"Sigi senses you need him. He's an untrained service cat. He did the same thing when he made Elliott his human," Jude said.

"Smart kitty." Xavier gave the cat an affectionate stroke.

During one thick band, the lights and television flickered.

Multiple guys said, "Uh-oh."

There was another flicker.

Then a third a few minutes later.

Then everything went dark with the fourth one.

"Hold on. No one move. The generator will kick in," Gavin said.

As promised, the outside generator turned on with a click of the powerful machine when it sensed the outage. The lights and ceiling fan oscillated back on, along with the A/C. It took another minute for the cable and Wi-Fi unit to cycle back online. The screen blinked back on after the power-up cycle.

"Sully, can you help me dedicate the power to certain things? I don't want to waste the propane on minimal stuff. Can everyone go around, turn off any lights, ceiling fans and unplug big stuff?" Gavin said.

Everyone went off to follow directions. Gavin, Sully and Xavier, who'd set aside Sigi, went to the generator's interior control panel and figured out the new configuration. Since the drain wasn't too much, they kept on the television and Wi-Fi. They made sure the fridge, coffee maker and countertop toaster oven would work. After the storm, they could make use of the grill. There were other countertop appliances to use instead of the bigger ones.

For now, they chose to keep on the A/C unit, but it was a drain. Gavin upped the temperature. They turned on the standing floor fans and a couple of lamps within the first floor. Outside of the area, they would use smaller fans and lanterns.

"We're done upstairs. Most of it was already off and unplugged," Reece said.

"Thanks. We're done here. To save propane, we're going to rely more on fans and lanterns than the air conditioning," Gavin said.

"Wouldn't the first time we went without the creature comforts. Should I break out the Cards Against Humanity case?"

"Case?"

"A big black one, special-made. I have the master decks, all the extra boxes, packs and expansions. It's the ultimate collection," Reece said with a waggle of his eyebrows.

"Sure."

"Woohoo," Reece said and went back to the living room. He hollered about the CAH game.

Throughout the howling winds and pounding rain, they played the card game. Hilarity ensued with each progressive round as they got deeper into the pile of cards. They kept their spirits high, laughing and listening to Mother Nature go out of control.

Deep into the night, when the eye moved north of the town, they closed the game.

Xavier helped the others pull out the airbeds and sleeping bags. Gavin added blankets and pillows to the sofa. Everyone figured out where they would sleep, giving room to another.

Gavin's 'Hurricane Sex Rules' kept the sexual atmosphere to a minimum. Though everyone chuckled and teased, Xavier could tell the Charm family respected Gavin's decision.

Gavin and Xavier stripped to boxers and adjusted the fans. It was a little sticky and humid, but they could manage. Falling asleep under a single sheet, they made the best of the situation.

Throughout the night, Xavier remained in a light sleep or awake. He listened while the bands continued to whip around the eye and flowing across Shore Breeze. While they wouldn't be a direct hit of the eye, the direction kept Shore Breeze on the dirty right side. From experience, he knew the bands would continue to give the town a good beating of wind, rain and tidal surge across all the beaches. Before they turned off the television, there were reports of some flooding in the sections of Breeze closer to the beaches and power outages throughout the barrier islands. Even without the eye, they wouldn't get a break.

At some time during the late morning, the hurricane made landfall outside of Gulf Shores, Alabama.

* * * *

By the following afternoon, the weather improved as the hurricane continued to head north.

"Florida is in the clear. After landfall in Gulf Shores, Alabama, Tropical Storm Katia is pulling away to the north and east. She continues to weaken into a tropical low. Power outages are reported throughout Escambia, Santa Rosa and Okaloosa Counties. The Pensacola Bay Bridge remains closed, due to a partial collapse and debris. This is delaying assistance to Shore Breeze through Navarre and the barrier islands. It's a balmy day. We're expecting a high of ninety-one with clear skies and a light wind from the south. Take care out there while going through the clean-up. There will be downed live wires in and around the water, so please be careful to avoid shock. Keep hydrated. Use sunscreen. Don't forget those sturdy shoes and gloves," the weatherman said.

"That's it?" Gavin asked.

"Your first hurricane, and that's all we got. Not too bad for your first one. Now is the clean-up, repairs and waiting for the power crews to come through. If there's damage done to the bridge, they'll have to take the Avalon Boulevard Bridge and come west from Tiger Point," Sully said. "We can at least go outside and take a look around."

"I have a pair of hiking boots and thick gardening gloves in the garage. I'll get them," Gavin said. He headed there with a flashlight and located the items. Then he brought them to the main room.

All the other guys located their heavier-styled shoes and pulled them over socked feet. Everyone was eager to get out of the house and stretch their legs.

Gavin opened the front door and stepped outside with Xavier and Sully right behind him. The other guys followed. Only Sigi remained inside.

Dawson gamboled around the front yard.

"You goofy dog. Be careful. You never know what debris is left behind. It could damage your paws," Jude called out after his crazy dog.

Laughing at the dog's antics, Gavin stepped farther out and until he could get a full view of the roof from the front. Reece and Dakota walked around to the back to inspect everything.

"Looks like some shingles pulled away. You might have a possible leak, but I can check your attic before I leave. Looks like everything came from the garage, which is better than over the living area. After you document everything for insurance, I can get a crew over here to fix it, along with the missing fascia and that loose gutter," Sully said while he pointed out the missing pieces.

"Here are the shingles," Xavier said after gathering the missing pieces from the yard. "Don't think this is all of them. I'm sure the winds carried most of them away."

"I can figure out a color match. If it's worse than it looks, I'll switch things over to a roofing contractor I trust. You have coverage for all this, right?"

Gavin nodded while listening. "Got whatever the insurance rep said, even flood coverage."

"Then everything will be covered by them."

There was debris all over the place—branches, broken pieces of roofs, twisted pieces of unknown origins or types.

"Think that might have been a lounge chair or something," Samuel said.

"Good guess."

"Holy shit. I found out why we lost power," Malcolm hollered.

Everyone walked across the lawn to the street.

Malcolm pointed down. "Another oak took out the power line."

"While this one took out my truck," Xavier said while he walked down to where Old Blue rested underneath the old oak tree. All the tires were flat and the entire truck almost brushed the ground. The metal bed was all twisted. "Blue is a lost cause. He couldn't survive being smashed by a tree *and* a hurricane." He pulled out his phone and took pictures of everything to document the damage and situation for his insurance.

"That is not good. Sorry, Gray," Sully said.

"Looks like the rest of your vehicles were spared."

"Sully and I drove everyone over in our big trucks and left the smaller cars in the garages. I grabbed Jude and the animals since Doc Elliott was stuck. Dakota and Samuel drove over in Samuel's SUV," Reece explained.

"We figured we would end up needing the equipment we often carry in our trucks during the clean-up," Sully added.

"Can we try to walk home and see what happened?" Mal asked. "We can check out Sully and Chandler's place, too. Can even swing down the street to Jude and Doc Elliott's home. I know you want to check your greenhouse."

"Do you guys mind if we head over?" Reece asked the others.

"Go ahead and check our place," Jude said.

Sully and Chandler exchanged glances. "Go ahead. We'll stay here to help with the clean-up."

"Grab some water bottles first," Gavin said.

"I've got them," Mal said and darted back inside the house. He returned with two bottles and tugged a ball-cap over his purple-highlighted hair. He tossed another cap with Southern Haven Landscape's logo stitched on the front to Reece.

"Not sure how long we'll be, but we'll check on everyone — well, except for the Charm. Don't think we can get that far right now," Reece said.

"I'm hoping we can get there soon," Samuel said.

"Good luck," Dakota added.

Malcolm and Reece took off to check on the houses.

"Now what?" Gavin said. "I'm at a loss for what to do."

"That's why you have us," Xavier said after pocketing his phone.

"I'll start taking down the boards," Sully said.

"I'll help with that," Dakota said.

"Do you have any heavy-duty trash bags? We can collect all the debris and toss it in them," Xavier said.

"Yes, I have a box in the garage, along with more gloves. I was always losing one," Gavin said.

"Sully, grab the box of bags and gloves while you get the equipment," Xavier said.

"Will do," Sully said and headed back inside. "Gonna try to open up the garage from the inside. There's a way to do it without power."

"Go ahead," Gavin said.

"Time to clean up," Xavier said. "Samuel, Chandler, Jude, you three up to helping?"

"Of course," Samuel said.

Chandler looked around and worried his hands together. "Once I have the gloves. You never know what is on all this stuff."

"Sure," Jude said. He gave up when Dawson dropped to the grass and rolled back and forth. "Crazy dog."

"Let him be. He's fine," Xavier said with a chuckle. He stooped over to give the dog a good belly rub. When he heard a knock on the garage door, he went over and called out to Sully. Through that kind of communication, they managed to lift the door and send it back on the rails.

With gloves passed out and bags ready, the group went around to begin cleaning the aftermath from a hurricane's side-swipe.

Pausing only for water breaks and a simple sandwich lunch, they cleared out Gavin's yard. With a collection of neighbors, they spread out to help the rest of the neighborhood. Most of the street had gotten away with only missing shingles, two damaged patio screen covers and some other light damage. Other than the power issue, things were looking up.

Another hour later, Malcolm and Reece returned from their field trip.

"Roads throughout the area are blocked by fallen trees, a few telephone poles and lots of wires. We had to circle around and find different routes multiple times. Took longer than we thought to go a few blocks. Crazy stuff," Reece said after accepting a fresh bottle of water.

"What happened?" Sully asked.

"You have a smashed lanai. That southern red cedar snapped and toppled it," Reece said.

"Shit."

"Sorry, man. Other than that, you're good." Reece glanced at Jude. "You and Doc have some torn lanai screens and loose shingles. Saw some bare spots on the roof."

"That's not too bad, considering what could have happened," Jude said.

"There's deep puddling left over from the storm surges, so I don't know about water damage," Reece said.

"Happy to report that his greenhouse is still standing underneath all the wood he wrapped around it," Malcolm added.

"Hey. After all the work we did to put it up, it better still be standing," Dakota said.

Everyone chuckled.

"What about the beach?" Chandler asked.

"The beach is a mess by our homes. That's all we could get to. Some erosion. Lots of debris. We have sand piled up around the lanais that will have to be transferred back. Don't know what it's like with the southern-facing beach. I'm sure that's a bit worse," Malcolm said.

"There's no major physical damage to homes and businesses, which is a minor miracle. A couple of trees are on roofs and garages, but it doesn't look like they went through," Reece said. "There's no way even your big truck can make it through the roads, Sully. Don't think we can reach the Charm until the roads are cleared."

"Damn. Was hoping at least you might get through, Sully," Dakota said.

"Same here. Guess that's a no-go," Sully said.

"I can contact the sheriff and see if one of the deputies can check it during a loop," Xavier said.

"That would be wonderful if you could, Gray," Samuel said.

"Need to check in anyway," Xavier said and headed inside to get on the radio.

* * * *

Throughout the next three days, the power remained out to most of the counties.

As promised, Xavier contacted the station to request a check on the Charm. He mentioned to Gavin that they didn't need him. They had enough coverage, and the EMTs couldn't move the ambulances through the streets. After another check-in, he headed outside to where the others continued to clean.

"Hey, Samuel, Dakota," Xavier said.

They looked over at him.

"Any news?" Dakota asked.

"Everything remains standing. All three buildings. There's no visual damage other than landscaping and the beach. That includes your home. Sully did one helluva solid renovation and building of the new reception space. They heard the emergency generator running next to the restaurant," Xavier reported with a smile.

"Thank heaven for that," Samuel said.

"Ahh, great, the generator is mainly for the cold storage spaces," Dakota said. "Tell Sheriff Robin that we appreciate everything."

"Will do."

Reece groaned. "Sonofa —"

"What the hell?" Malcolm asked while everyone stared at Reece.

"Looks like my company will have majority of clean-up around the entire town. Shit. Not what I wanted, but damn, we're going to be busy as hell," Reece said.

"It's a lot of money...for you and the crews," Malcolm said.

"Yeah. But damn. We're going to have to pace ourselves. Call in the tree trimming companies I know to help out—not to mention all the insurance bullshit," Reece said and shook his head.

"Could you start with the tree on my truck? I took pictures of the damage, but the insurance company requested pictures without the tree. I don't expect it to go much further, other than a total write-off," Xavier said.

"Sure. Lemme get my tools," Reece said and headed toward his truck.

"I'll give you a hand. We might as well get through what we can on the street," Sully said.

Like before, everyone else pitched in to continue gathering the scattered debris, downed branches and other messes.

Within a couple of hours, Reece and Sully had managed to unearth Xavier's truck. Reece also took pictures of the entire area to help prove that the homeowners were at fault. When the homeowners came out, luckily not drunk, Reece glared at them.

"What did I tell you about this tree the last time you contacted my company? I told you the tree was dead and would fall—either on its own or with the next tropical system. Now you're at fault not only for the tree but the damage it caused to my friend's truck," Reece snapped. He handed his chainsaw to Xavier and stormed over to have another session with the idiotic couple who hadn't bothered to join in the clean-up.

Sully and Xavier snickered while they continued to toss the pieces onto the neighbor's yard and away from Gavin's lawn.

"Holy shit," Gavin said while he helped.

"Yeah. Whenever you ignore the basics of landscaping and tree care, especially after contacting his company, Reece takes it personally when people don't follow through. He calls it pure neglect," Sully said.

"In other words, don't get on Reece's bad side. He's a freaking certified arborist and knows his shit. Follow through with whatever recommendations he makes regarding your yard," Dakota said after he wandered over.

"Crazy," Gavin said and looked at Xavier. "Hey, what did the sheriff or chief say about you?"

"Stay here and help with whatever I can. If they need me, they know how to reach me. While I can't drive, it's a short walk to the station."

Finishing with the idiots, Reece handed Xavier a piece of paper with their insurance information. "Pass that on to your people."

"Thanks for this," Xavier said and pocketed the paper.

"No problem. Idiots, I swear." Grumbling, Reece snatched back his chainsaw and helped Sully finished cutting down the tree. Then they moved on to the next downed tree after talking to the homeowner.

"We're going to make lunch for everyone. There's enough deli meat and bread for everyone who is working," Dakota said. "Mal!"

"On my way."

The pair headed inside. Within an hour, they returned with boxes filled with stacks of wrapped sandwiches, bags of chips and two jugs of fresh iced tea. Seeing what they held, Gavin raced into the garage and carried a small folding table and set it down for them.

"Come and get food," Dakota hollered. "For anyone who helped out with the clean-up, this is for you." He added the last bit after glaring at Gavin's horrible neighbors.

"The kids are there," Xavier said. He picked up four sandwiches and chips. Gavin picked up the bottles of water. They carried everything over to the house. "Hey, Danny, are you around?"

"Gray!" Danny pushed past his parents and raced over. "Wowee, that was a wild storm."

"It was crazy. This is my boyfriend, Gavin. He lives next door. We have a generator going so we can share some food. Would you guys like some sandwiches, chips and water?"

"Wowee. Yeah," Danny said.

"Danny, don't take food from strangers," his mother said.

"Gray is an EMT and helped us before the storm, Mom. The girls, Jesse and me are hungry. We got nothing here. I'm taking it," Danny said. He turned back to Xavier and Gavin.

"What do you mean you have nothing there?" Xavier asked.

"They got beer and bottles but nothing to eat — at least stuff we don't need to cook. Jesse and I grabbed the last bread, peanut butter and jelly, along with crackers, and hid it in our bathroom with our stuff. It's all we got, along with water. That all works still."

"Is it always like that at home? Where your mom and dad get alcohol and no food?"

Danny nodded. "Since they lost jobs due to that virus thing."

"They haven't gone back to work?"

Danny shook his head.

"Can I call a friend who can stop by and check on you guys? She can help make things better."

"You talking about CPS?"

"How do you know what that means?"

"My aunt threatened it to my mom. She was gonna call CPS, who would take us away from Mom and Dad," Danny said. "I wish she did call. Cassie and I don't wanna stay here anymore. She cries from an empty belly, and Dad hits her. Me, too."

"Oh my God," Gavin said while he set down the bottles. He pulled the thin boy in for a gentle hug.

Xavier pulled out his phone and asked for the aunt's phone number. Then he stood and walked away. When the aunt answered, he explained who he was and the nature of the call. Finishing it, he returned to them. "Okay, Danny, I spoke with your aunt. She knows what is happening and is going to start things in motion. She asks that you hang in there with Cassie and that she loves you. This time, she's not going to let things drop. It seems your mom wasn't telling her the truth. If you need to reach me, I'll give you my number. Gavin, do you have paper and pen?"

"Let me get some from the house," Gavin said and raced off. He returned in minutes with a pen and Post-it pad. "Here is my number, though you can knock on my door if I'm home. This is Gray's number. The last one is for the sheriff's office. He's a good friend. Gray will let him know what is happening, along with his contact at the CPS. Okay?"

Danny took the paper and studied the numbers. He glanced over his shoulder and shoved the paper into his pocket. "I'll keep it hidden. Thank you." His brown eyes were earnest and teary. Then he rubbed his wrist against them.

"If you need more to eat, come next door and we'll give it to you," Gavin said. "If they...pass out or something, come on over with the other kids and watch some TV with us."

"Okay. Thanks."

"Take this food for now. This isn't for the adults," Xavier said and carefully placed the sandwiches and chips in the boy's arms.

"Jesse!" Danny hollered.

Another small boy pushed past the adults, now all four of them in the doorway, and ran to his friend. "Yeah?"

"Take the bottles. It's food for us and the girls. No one else."

"Yay! Not peanut butter and jelly," Jesse said and took the bottles from Gavin. "Thank you!"

"You're welcome," Gavin said.

The boys ran back, ignored the adults and went inside.

"Holy shit," Gavin said.

"I know. Let's get back to the others. We're not going to let this go. I'll keep in touch with the aunt. Good thing I met them when I did," Xavier said and led Gavin away.

The adults went back inside and slammed the door shut.

"What was that all about?" Dakota asked when they returned.

Xavier explained what had happened between them and Danny.

"Holy shit," Dakota said.

"That's what I said. Why do some parents do that?" Gavin shook his head.

"Don't know, but this time these kids have someone looking out for them. Someone else knows what is happening and isn't going to let it go."

Gavin squeezed Xavier's hand and went back to work.

* * * *

With news that the bridge damage was minor and fixed, there was hope that the power trucks could come through sooner than predicted.

In awe of his first hurricane, Gavin continued to follow everyone else throughout the clean-up process. They went beyond their neighborhood, especially Sully and Reece with their tools. Throughout their time outside, Gavin was amazed at nature's fury.

What's even more important?

It was how this small town came together. Neighbors helped each other. Everyone supported and shared when they could.

Throughout the pandemic, he'd noticed pieces of this sharing and friendliness. This was now on a big-time expansive endeavor.

"I can't believe how mostly everyone comes together to help each other. It's a sight to watch." Gavin mentioned this to Xavier when they returned for food and water.

"It's one of my favorite things about living in Shore Breeze. I don't know if it's unique to our town, but it's special," Xavier said while he enjoyed his barbecue baked personal pizza that Dakota and Mal had created for each person.

"Isn't it weird what chefs think is important to pack for foodstuff, not like most other folks? Especially if you let them know you have a generator," Gavin said with a chuckle. "I wouldn't have thought to grab blocks of mozzarella, basil, tomatoes and other pizza fixings. But they did."

"That's why they're chefs and we're mere mortals and helpless wannabe cooks," Xavier said.

Laughing, Gavin leaned against Xavier. He stretched out his legs on one of the picnic blankets he'd spread across the front lawn. While the sun was out and bright, there was a light breeze to cool them off.

"Better not be laughing at my puffy pizza," Dakota said.

"Nope. Enjoying the hell out of it. It's the last thing I expected to eat during a power outage," Gavin said.

"A barbecue is a different style of oven. Just need to know how to get the most from it," Dakota said from his blanket.

"So yummy, Mr. Dakota," Danny said from the blanket he shared with his sister and friends.

"Need another one? I can start things up again. Got plenty."

"We're good. Gotta get back. They're angry we left for pizza," Danny said while he crammed the last bites into his mouth.

"Did you talk to your aunt?" Xavier asked.

"She'll be here next week, no matter what happens. Cassie and I are gonna pack up some stuff and hide it. We wanna leave," Danny said.

"Good. Don't lose our numbers."

"I won't. Bye," Danny said and took Cassie's hand. He led his little group back to the house.

"Poor kids," Gavin said.

"There's a bit of a bright spot for them. Just gotta hope," Xavier said.

Hoping it was true, Gavin helped Samuel and Mal clean up the remnants of the lunch.

"Oh my God! Is that what I think it is! Look!" Chandler called out. He jumped and raced to the edge of the lawn.

Jude and Dawson followed him. "Holy crap! It is! Power trucks! Two of them!"

With those words spreading across the neighborhood, everyone raced to the street. They stared at the sight. Then everyone cheered and danced around. Two electric company trucks parked by the downed tree and line.

"Let's get the saws and help them," Sully said to Reece.

"Hell, yeah!" Reece said.

They raced to the truck, pulled out the saws and gloves then rushed down the street. Everyone else gathered their gloves and gear and followed.

Explaining to the crews who they were, Reece and Sully helped cut down the massive broken trees with their chainsaws after the crew made sure there was no power. Samuel and Malcolm used one of the elongated pruning shears on other branches. The rest of them dragged the branches away.

The truck lifted the bucket and a lineman figured out how to fix the problem.

"Could you help with the rest of the streets?" the other driver asked.

"We cleared everything that wasn't snagged on the lines. We know not to touch them unless cleared by one of you," Reece said.

"That's why our crews made progress. Thanks for the help," the driver said.

"Figured you guys could use some food and cold water," Dakota said. He handed over bags of multiple sandwiches, a bag of chips and bottles of water. "This should be enough for all of you."

"Appreciate it. We'll get to work and connect everyone back to the grid."

"We'll do all we can to keep you guys going. We're lucky to have a generator, but most folks don't," Gavin said. "Appreciate all the work."

* * * *

By the end of the week, power was restored to multiple blocks. The television reports were encouraging.

The same news repeated after couples returned from walks around the neighborhoods. Power lit up everything. Streets were cleared of most obstacles. There were piles of debris at the end of yards, but that was to be expected.

By Friday evening, Gavin teasingly kicked everyone to scoot them out.

"Dakota, Samuel, you are cleared to go home. Power is restored. There was a down maple tree that had to be removed before they could go down the lane," Xavier said after his latest call with the sheriff's office.

"Hallelujah," Dakota called out. "Let's go home, babe."

"Good thing everything is packed," Samuel said. He went to Gavin and pulled him into a long hug. "Thank you for opening your home to everyone. It was fun."

"I loved having everyone here. It was fun. Crazy times," Gavin said and hugged him back.

"Keep working from home. I'll let you know when to return. Okay?"

"Can do. We pushed back the events."

Samuel then pulled Xavier into a tight hug. "You're one of us now, Xavier. One of the Charm men."

Surprised by the hug and the words, Xavier hugged Samuel back then accepted a quick embrace from Dakota, who echoed Samuel's words. He smiled and stood next to Gavin.

Dakota tugged Gavin in for a hug. "I'll send money to you for the food. Don't say anything. Samuel insisted," he whispered to Gavin.

"Okay. Okay." Gavin knew there was no arguing with them.

After squeezing again, Dakota released him.

Gavin and Xavier helped them carry the last suitcases to the SUV and load them into the back. Then they waved bye to the last of their friends.

Gavin closed the door and leaned against it. "Holy crap."

Xavier dropped into an armchair. "Want me to leave, too? I'm in no hurry. Don't care much about the apartment. It's on the second floor, so shouldn't have damage to it."

"No, I don't want you to go anywhere. I do want you to consider the idea of moving in with me."

"What?"

"Move in with me," Gavin said while he dropped in the chair next to Xavier's spot. He grabbed Xavier's hand. "Think about it. We're good together. If we can survive a hurricane with a house filled with friends, we can get through anything...together."

Xavier smiled. "I'll think about it."

"Until then, stay here. I'm closer to the station than your apartment is. You can drive my Soul to college."

"I might need to do that."

"Good. Now…" Gavin looked around the house. "Ugh. Need to…"

"Get this all back in order before my OCD goes crazy?"

"Exactly."

Laughing together, they got back to cleaning the house.

Chapter Twenty-Seven

"Julia, I know you're worried about everything being repaired in time for the wedding. I feel the same way. Shore Breeze got side-swiped by the hurricane. There was some surge and wind damage. The electricity came back on this week. Everyone is assessing the damage. All this takes time." Gavin bit back a groan at the crazed bride, but he did his best to hold back his frustration. This wasn't the first bride or groom going crazy since the hurricane had swept through.

It had taken the last two days to get through his client calls, only pausing to be one of the witnesses when the aunt had arrived next door with her lawyer, a CPS agent and a pair of deputies to serve papers, review the house and collect Danny and Cassie. Gavin and Xavier knew the little ones would be safe with their aunt in Tallahassee.

"Right now, everything is on track for your November wedding. Yes, Julia, there is plenty of time." He paced again while he listened to the bride's rants and raves about Mother Nature, the wedding, the cost and back to rants. "No. No. I see no need to cancel anything. I'll learn more within the next couple of weeks. Yes, I'll keep you updated. Of course. Promise. Calm down, please, and enjoy your dress fitting appointment. I wish I could be there, but I'm needed here. Of course, you'll be a beautiful bride." He paced again. "Take care. Bye." Gavin hit the button. "Oh my God. Please let this be over. I hate hurricanes."

There was a knock on the door.

"Oh, no, please don't be another crazed wedding couple."

Another knock.

"Be right there." Gavin left this phone on the coffee table, picked up his cup and took a few gulps of coffee. Then he headed to the alarm to pause it, then the door and pulled in a deep breath. He unlocked and pulled on the handle. "Hello. How can—" His eyes widened. He swallowed past a hard swollen knot in his throat. "What—?"

"Don't scream. Don't run."

"Maurice—"

"Step back inside, Gavin. I don't want to do this outside." Maurice waved the black gun to force Gavin to move.

Gavin stepped back a few paces. He trembled and shook the entire time. He wrinkled his nose at the horrible stench wafting from the unkempt Maurice. "You don't look so well."

"Don't even think of touching that alarm. I cut the wires." Maurice closed and locked the door. "A lot has happened since the expo."

"Why don't you tell me about it? You d-d-don't need the gun." Gavin stopped and swallowed after the tremble. "I'm not going to do anything but listen." He held up his hands and backed away a few more steps. He wanted to reach for his phone but didn't want to set off Maurice…or the gun.

"Let's see. Things didn't work at the expo. Patricia and Hillary whined and complained to Carole Anne all about me, all about you and back to me." Maurice paced and turned to faced him. He waved the gun at Gavin and moved closer. "Always back to you, even when you're not around. It's always about you. You find a way to aggravate my nerves and frustrations. Gavin the wonderful. Gavin the great coordinator. Sweet Gavin. Kind Gavin. Precious *fucking* Gavin."

"I haven't done anything to you. I left Atlanta and a profitable career. I got the hell out of your way," Gavin said.

"And fucked things up in the process, like you always do!" Maurice waved the gun at Gavin's face. His spittle splashed on Gavin's cheek and chest. He stepped away and dragged fingers through his greasy hair. Then he faced Gavin again. "Carole Anne was even more of a hard-ass since you left. No one from high society wanted anything to do with her company when they found out you were gone. She got on our cases to bring in new events. Always on our cases. It got even worse after the expo. Whine. Whine. Nag. Nag. 'No, Maurice,' no to this. No to that. No to everything. Whine. Complain. Pathetic. So pathetic." He shrugged while he paced away and returned. A nasty smile curled his lips. "Until I shut her up. That was most pleasant. Shut her mouth good."

"Should I ask how?"

Maurice waved the gun. "Carole Anne. Patricia. Hillary."

"Oh my God." Gavin felt the blood drain from his face. "All of them. You killed all of them. Why?"

"Nag. Nag. Whine. Whine. Then Carole Anne tried to fire me. That fucking bitch thought she could fire me. That topped the shit list. They pissed me off, so I shut them up. Permanently. Possibly all over the news by now, not that I give a shit. They deserved a shot to the head...each. Felt damn good."

Gavin's eyes widened.

"I realized how it all came back to you. Always back to you. The precious, perfect Gavin." Maurice stalked closer, held up the gun and pointed it at Gavin. "Everything that went wrong with my life happened after I got together with you. Every. Fucking. Thing." He moved his finger to release the safety.

"I left—"

"Didn't change a fucking thing in my life. I told you so many times, Gavin. No one leaves me. *No one.*"

"Maurice, you don't want—"

"If I can't have you, no one will." Maurice cocked the gun.

The clicking sound definite. It rang through the silent house. It even beat the A/C turning on and blowing chilling air.

Gavin's skin pebbled with gooseflesh. It was more than the chilling air conditioner. The sight of the cold black steel barrel pointing at him froze him down to his heart.

Xavier! I'm so sorry. I wish we had more time.

"No! Maurice, *no!*"

Maurice shot the gun four times.

Gavin screamed when the bullets sliced into his body. Heat tore through his shoulder, chest and abdomen. Collapsing under the pain, Gavin fell to the ground. Pain overwhelmed him. Spots wavered in his eyes. He cried out, but stifled by the blood.

"No one else will have you. No one can stop me."

There was one more shot.

Gavin braced for the final shot to end his life.

Instead, Maurice dropped to the ground across from him with a black hole in his temple. Blood pooled and covered the ground. His eyes were empty of life.

Xavier.

Help.

Xavier.

Help.

He needed Xavier.

Gavin groaned while he raised a hand and patted the coffee table.

The coffee mug knocked over. Papers went flying.

Gavin found his phone and pulled it down. The phone slipped out of his bloody hand and spun away. It took a second try to get the phone closer.

Instead of dialing 9-1-1, he hit the option button for Xavier.

"Gavin, hon, how are you? Everything —"

"Maury here. Shot... Bad... Need...help..."

"Gavin? Baby?"

"Shot... Bad... Help me."

"Stay with me. I'm on my way. Stay awake."

"Can't. Hurts. Bad..."

"Stay with me, Gavin."

"Love... Sorry..."

The phone dropped from his hand.

Gavin slid back into the darkness with Xavier's beloved voice in his ear.

Chapter Twenty-Eight

"Gavin? Gavin? Talk to me. Gavin!"

The call went quiet.

"No. Chief! Someone shot Gavin Hartfield in his home. He's hurt bad." Xavier burst into the fire chief's office. "I need everyone. The sheriff, paramedics and, shit...all of you. He's on the phone. Weak. We need to alert the ER. I gotta get to him."

Chief Fromme hit the alarm. "Get on the bus with Ryder and Aiden. You do *not* take care of him. You're too close," Chief Fromme said while he rose and grabbed his jacket.

"I know. I know." Xavier raced out to get to the ambulance.

"What's happening?" Aiden asked.

"Gavin was shot. Multiple times. By an ex. I don't know if the ex is still there. Gavin managed to call me. Had trouble speaking. We need to get to him *fast*." Xavier gave them Gavin's address. "Chief will alert the sheriff and get deputies out there."

Ryder climbed into the driver's seat, closed the door and hit the sirens while he drove out.

The fire truck raced after them.

Sirens from the deputies added to the chaos.

"Come on, Gavin. Stay strong. Stay strong," Xavier whispered. He flipped the phone between his hands and pocketed it.

Deputy cars raced past them and screeched to a stop in front of Gavin's home.

When the ambulance stopped, Xavier jumped out and bolted to the house. "Gavin!"

"No, you need to wait here until we clear the house," another deputy said while he grabbed Xavier's arm.

"My boyfriend is in there. This is his home. He's been shot."

"I know. There may be an active shooter."

One deputy appeared in the doorway. "House cleared. One dead. One alive. Send in the paramedics."

Ryder and Aiden hastened with their gear.

Xavier moved to follow.

"Don't contaminate my crime scene, Grayson."

Xavier spun to find Sheriff Robin Burke standing next to him. "It's Gavin. I must get to him. I promised him."

"Not inside. Let Ryder and Aiden get him stable and bring him out," Robin said. "Tell me what you know."

"But—"

"Xavier," Robin said, using his true name, "focus on me. Take in a breath."

With everything circling inside him, Xavier knew Robin brought a good point. He couldn't help Gavin in this state. He pulled in a deep breath and calmed himself.

"Good. That's the way," Robin said and placed a hand on Xavier's shoulder. "Tell me what you know, Gray. I need the background to figure out what happened."

Even though he wanted to get inside and be with Gavin, Xavier knew Robin needed to know everything. He went through the basics of what Gavin had said happened back in Atlanta before he'd moved to Breeze and the continued harassing phone calls. Then he added in his own interactions with Maury at the expo.

"Would you suspect him of doing something physical?"

"I wouldn't put it past the man. I mentioned to Gavin that he should speak with someone at your department, but I don't know if he got around to doing it," Xavier said. "After meeting that bastard, I should have pushed for more, but—"

"This isn't your fault, nor is it Gavin's. The blame rests on the perpetrator of the crime. Now I need to do my job and make sure this is investigated," Robin said. "My detectives are good at their job. Let them work the scene."

"One dead. One alive. That's the crime," Xavier said. "What if—?"

"Gavin's alive," Ryder hollered from the doorway and stopped Xavier's questioning. "We need the stretcher. *Now!*"

Xavier and Robin ran to the ambulance and pulled out the gurney. They pushed it up the driveway and walkway to the door.

Ryder, Aiden and two deputies carried the backboard outside. Gavin was strapped down, his shirt opened with multiple leads and bandages spread over his chest and abdomen. An oxygen mask covered his face. Aiden also held two IV bags high.

"Oh God, oh God, Gavin," Xavier said. "What happened to him?"

"Shot close range four times — once in the shoulder, two in the chest and one in the lower abdomen. Pulse and BP are low. Breath sounds are compromised on the left side. We need to get him to the clinic. He needs a chest tube and surgery," Ryder said.

They secured the board to the gurney, and everyone pushed it to the ambulance. Ryder and Aiden lifted and secured it inside. Aiden raced to the driver's side while Xavier and Ryder climbed into the back.

"Get him to the hospital. I'm sending you with an escort. I'll figure out what the hell happened here," Robin said and closed the doors. He banged to let Aiden know to take off.

Aiden hit the gas with full sirens, along with the deputy in front of them.

"Gavin. I'm here. We're taking you to the clinic," Xavier said while he sat in the jump-seat.

Gavin somehow managed to open his eyes. He looked at Xavier and closed his eyes again.

"How are his vitals?" Xavier asked Ryder.

"Falling. It isn't a long trip. The shorter the better. Can't do much for him right now other than to support him with oxygen and fluids. You know that." Ryder turned up the oxygen and increased the pressure. He did the same with both IVs to replace the blood volume loss.

"As an EMT, yeah, I know. Emotionally?" Xavier shook his head. "Doesn't matter. We'll get him there. He'll pull through. He's strong. Keeps in shape. This isn't going to take him from me, not at the hands of that bastard."

"I hope not."

"We're here," Aiden called when he pulled to a stop and opened the back doors. "Doc Elliott and nurses are waiting. They'll take care of him. You know Doc Elliott will do everything within his power to save him, Xavier."

"I know. I know. It's Gavin. Everything is different."

"Great," Ryder said while he unhooked everything for the transfer to the ER.

Xavier got up to make the process faster and assist Ryder. Then he unlocked the wheels.

When they transferred the gurney to the ground, Doc Elliott was right there to check the situation. "What happened?" He pulled on his stethoscope and listened to Gavin's chest.

"His ex shot him. If the bastard weren't dead, I would kill him myself," Xavier said.

"Not the update I wanted," Doc Elliott said while they pushed the gurney into the ER. "Ryder? Stats?"

Ryder gave the rundown on the vitals and steps he'd taken on scene and in the ER. "Breath sounds were compromised on the left side by the gunshot. Vitals dropped. Hard to keep him stable. Opened his eyes once at Xavier's voice but no other response."

"Thanks. Xavier, stay out here. Please let me do my job. Call Samuel and Dakota. They need to know what is happening. They're his family. They need to know. Can you do that for Gavin and me?" Doc Elliott asked.

"Yeah. Yeah, it will give me something to do," Xavier said.

With a nod, Doc Elliott whisked the curtains closed and called out his orders. He told someone to notify the surgeon and get the blood bank ready.

"Come on, Gavin. Stay strong," Xavier said while he moved away from the priority area. He tugged out his phone and dialed the Charm.

"Southern Charm, this is Elise. How may I direct your call? Would you like to make a reservation?"

"Elise, this is Gray. Could you patch me through to Samuel?"

"Hello, Gray, of course. Give me a moment."

Xavier waited through the transfer beeps. He let out a long breath. This wouldn't be a pleasant call.

"Morning, Gray, what's up?" Samuel asked.

"Can you get Dakota and Chandler and put me on speaker?"

"Umm. Okay. Is something—"

"Please, Samuel."

"Okay. Hang on…"

Xavier heard Samuel set the phone down and holler for Dakota and Chandler. He only wanted to go through this once. Then he hoped the sheriff would take over.

"Okay, Gray, you're on speaker. What's happening?" Samuel said.

"Gavin's hurt. It's bad…really bad," Xavier said in an unsteady voice. He paused to control himself. "I'm here with him in the clinic. Doc Elliott is working on him right now. He'll be heading to surgery."

"What? What the hell happened?" Samuel asked.

"We need to get down there," Chandler added.

"Hold on. Gray. Is there more?" Dakota asked.

"Do any of you know about Gavin's ex and the other reason why he left Atlanta?"

"Gavin told me a little bit after I overheard a threatening call and saw a bunch of scary emails. That was within the first few months of him being here," Samuel said. "Was it him?"

"Yes, it was Maurice. I don't know all the details. Sheriff Robin is at the crime scene with his detectives."

"Crime scene?"

"Maury shot Gavin."

"Shot? Oh my God," Samuel said.

"What about the bastard? Is he in custody?" Dakota asked.

"Dead. Coward shot himself. Gavin is hanging on, but I..." Xavier swallowed past the lump in his throat. "His vitals are weak. They think his lung collapsed. There were four bullets, close range. Somehow they missed his heart and brain."

"Gavin is strong and in good health. He'll get through this, Gray," Dakota said. "We're going to close up what we can here and get over to the clinic. We'll rally the family."

"Will you stay there with him?" Samuel asked.

"As long as he needs me, I'm not going anywhere. My chief was with me at the scene and knows where I am."

"You two got tight," Dakota said.

"Yeah, I'm falling for him, Dakota. Hard."

"Good for you. Hang in there. We'll be there as soon as we can."

"I'm inside the ER, but they'll be moving him up to surgery—" Xavier turned his head when he heard movement and commotion. "Now. They're wheeling him out now."

"We'll meet you upstairs by the surgical waiting room."

"Gotta go." Xavier ran over to the gurney.

Gavin appeared pale underneath all the wires and connections. There was a chest tube in his left side.

"What's happening?" Xavier looked over at Doc Elliott. Though he wanted to touch and kiss Gavin, he kept his hands to himself.

"Taking him to surgery," Doc Elliott said. "Need to get the bullets out and repair the damage. It's going to be a long one, but someone will come out and update you. Did you call Samuel and Dakota?"

"They're on their way." Xavier stopped at the elevator and watched Doc Elliott and the nurses push the gurney inside. He wasn't allowed with them.

"Good. Not sure how this one will turn out. He's strong, but there's a lot of damage. Just want to warn you—"

"No, he'll come out," Xavier interrupted. "I know him. There's too much for him to do. He's planning Samuel and Dakota's wedding. Nothing will stop him from doing that."

The door closed between them.

"Please, don't take him away from me." Not accustomed to being on this side of things, Xavier returned through the ER and back to the customer side.

"Hey, Gray, there you are. Figured I run this over, considering you're staying here," Ryder said when he appeared. He held out Xavier's backpack. "I clocked you out of the system per the chief's orders."

"Thanks. Appreciate it." Xavier slung one strap over his shoulder.

"What's the news on Gavin?"

"A lot of damage. Collapsed lung is the biggest one. They took him up to scans, tests and surgery. Doc said he couldn't tell the outcome on this one."

"He's strong and healthy. That's something in his favor."

"I know. Gavin has a lot going for him, but you can't predict anything."

"We'll cover everything at base. Norman is on his way to cover your spot. Take care of Gavin," Ryder said.

"Things are still new."

"Doesn't matter. You belong by his side, and don't worry about work. Other than Gavin, it has been quiet."

"Is the sheriff still working the scene?"

"Yeah. I think they'll be there a while," Ryder said. "The forensics teacher guy is on site. The whole situation is crazy. The dead guy's blood stunk of booze."

"Add a gun to a volatile situation and death almost always follows or is involved."

"Lucky for us, guns aren't a huge issue in Breeze...unlike those big cities." Ryder waved away the conversation. "Go on up where you belong. I gotta get back to base."

"Thanks for bringing my bag to me. Tell everyone thanks for their speedy response."

"That's our job." With a wave, Ryder walked away.

Xavier searched for the elevator bank and headed in that direction. He smacked the Up button and waited for the elevator to respond. Soon, he was inside for the quiet trip to the surgical floor.

"Hello, Gray. Didn't expect to see you up here," a nurse said.

"Hi there. My boyfriend, Gavin Hartfield, was brought here by Doc Elliott," Xavier said when he stood next to the desk.

"Oh, dear, that's a rough situation. He's in Operating Room Three with Doctors Snyder and Ward. Doc Elliott also scrubbed in to assist. Go on and have a seat. I'll get an update when it's available."

"I'm expecting some friends from Charm and around Breeze. They're all close to Gavin."

"No problem. Help yourself to the coffee and snacks. Gavin's in the best hands."

"Thanks." Xavier went to the waiting room and dropped his bag on a chair. He poured himself a cup of coffee from the pot, checked it with a sip and added some cream to lighten it. While he didn't want it, he needed something to occupy his hands. Then he returned to his chair to begin the long wait.

* * * *

Barely acknowledging the arrival of the Charm guys, Xavier kept his seat and cooling coffee cup. Then he maintained his watch between the ticking clock that never seemed to move and the closed doors that led to the operating rooms. Though he did recognize in some fashion through the emptiness in his belly and the ache from sitting for so long, that hours had passed since the frantic morning call.

"Damn clock. *Move*. Give me something," Xavier muttered. He tried to sip the coffee and grimaced. When he set the cup aside, Malcolm moved over to exchange it with a fresh one.

"This is fresh brewed by one of us from the Charm's stash. Better stuff," Malcolm said.

"Don't really need more caffeine rushing through me."

"Good to keep something in your hands," Malcolm said and crouched in front of Xavier's chair to get in eye contact. "How are you holding up?"

"Don't know. Can't lose him. Not like this." Xavier shook his head. "Not like this."

"No one thought it would get that far with his ex. Samuel filled me in on what happened. No one knows what can push a person," Malcolm said.

"You didn't see him in Atlanta. He was constantly around Gavin—needling him, harassing him, not leaving him alone, making sure Gavin could always see him. He didn't give a shit about the expo or his job. His focus was on Gavin—laser-type focus. That twisted version."

"Holy shit..."

Xavier nodded. "I didn't tell Gavin, but it scared the shit out of me, especially if I was away and came back and found that bastard stalking and threatening him. I tried to always be next to Gavin, but there were times I couldn't be—not if Gavin wanted me to get a snack, refresh our drinks or a bathroom trip. The expo was huge and spread out."

"You did everything you could to keep him safe."

"I knew there was something darker in that man. I've seen it, especially the aftereffects of what happened." Xavier shoved his fingers through his hair. "I should have reported it or something. But...there was no physical evidence or proof. It was just behavior and threats. Nothing physical or tangible."

"You can't blame yourself for what happened."

"I left Gavin alone. I should have made sure he followed me out of the door and got to the Charm."

"Why didn't he leave?"

"He wanted to stay home, finish cleaning up after the hurricane and make some calls. It was easier to do his work there and leave you guys alone to clean up without him getting in the way. That's how he put it." Xavier shook his head. "As if he could ever be in the way."

"Gavin's always like that. He still feels on the outside, though none of us think the same."

Samuel wandered over and sat next to Xavier. "You did everything possible to save Gavin. He called and you answered. Your quick thinking and position helped to save him." He reached out and squeezed Xavier's shoulder.

Before Xavier could respond, the doors pushed open.

Doc Elliott walked out, dressed in operating scrubs with dark spots on them and his hands free from gloves. He removed his mask and surgical cap. While studying the room, he smiled at everyone.

It was at the smile that Xavier let out a long breath. Setting the cup aside, he rose to his feet but didn't move forward.

"He's okay," Samuel said.

"Yes. Gavin made it through the surgery. We repaired all the damage. He's in recovery and will be moved to an ICU room for care. There's still a long road ahead of him. We have to worry about the usual things like infection, clots and other potential complications," Doc Elliott said.

"Can we see him?" Xavier asked.

"Not yet. We need him to finish waking up from the anesthesia, manage his pain and settle him into an ICU room. Everyone can stay here. I'll send a nurse to speak with you when we move him. Even then, only two visitors for a few minutes can see him. He needs his rest. Once he's out of ICU, he can have more visitors for longer periods of time."

"Can we stay here?" Samuel said.

"I'll leave it up to you. I'll let him know everyone was here. Again, it takes time." Doc Elliott shifted his attention until he focused on Xavier. "Right now, Gavin is going to be okay. He survived the surgery."

"Now he needs to rest and let his body heal," Xavier said.

"That's going to be a problem," Dakota said. "Gavin doesn't know how to relax and do nothing."

"Unlike leaving him mobile with an ACE bandage and crutches, Gavin isn't getting up anytime soon. He's hooked to multiple IVs, ports and other tubes in bad places. Plus, he's quite drugged," Doc Elliott said with a grin. "I'm not letting him up anytime soon."

There were some soft chuckles.

"Hang in there, everyone. I'll see you again when I know more," Doc Elliott said and walked back toward the doors.

"Thanks, Doc!" Xavier said.

Doc Elliott waved and hit the pad to walk through.

In relief and exhaustion, Xavier dropped back into the seat. He lowered his face in his hands and let the tears come.

Gavin is safe. Gavin is alive. Gavin isn't going anywhere.

"Hello, everyone. Is there an update on Gavin?"

Looking up, Xavier watched Sheriff Robin enter the waiting area.

"Yeah, you just missed Doc Elliott. Gavin came through surgery like a trooper. He's in Recovery and will go to ICU next," Dakota said. "Can you tell us what you found?"

"Investigation is still ongoing, but I can share some of the details. I have a question for Gray," Robin said.

"Umm. Yeah. Sure." Xavier rose and walked over to Robin. He rubbed his hands together and shoved them into his pockets.

"Can you provide an ID for me?" Robin pulled out his phone, pressed something and held the screen toward his body. "It's not a pretty picture."

"You know I've seen worse."

With a nod, Robin turned the phone toward Xavier. "Can you tell me who this man is? There wasn't ID on the body."

"Body?" Dakota said.

Robin held up his other hand to stop Dakota.

Xavier lowered his gaze to study the phone. "That's the man from the Atlanta Expo. The one called Maurice Hirschinger, known as Maury. He's an event coordinator for an Atlanta company called Mosaic Events. A 'Carole Anne' owns it, but I don't know her full name. Gavin worked for Mosaic before he came here."

"She's not a nice lady, either," Samuel spoke up. "I called to verify Gavin's employment and spoke with her. She tried to make it sound like Gavin was a horrible person who couldn't plan anything. Luckily, Gavin had jotted down clients, and they all glowed and revered him," he added.

Robin nodded while he listened. He jotted the name and details on a pad. Then he contacted the station. He connected with the evening precinct commander. "Hey, Clive. Got the name. Maurice Hirschinger. Check for all known vehicles. Registered in Atlanta. Worked for Mosaic Events, owned by a woman called Carole

Anne. Yeah, ID verified by Gray. Saw him in Atlanta with Gavin. Yeah, I'll wait," Robin said.

Xavier waited for Robin to finish the call.

"What? Wait. Repeat that—" Robin said and paused. His eyes narrowed. "Are you sure? Verified?" He shook his head. "Unbelievable. Okay, have Detective Lancaster get in touch with the Atlanta detective. Make sure he knows to offer up the gun for forensics, along with anything else we find. No. No. I'll tell Gray and the others here. Right. Good." Hanging up the phone, he slid it back in his pocket.

"What? What happened?"

"Atlanta found three bodies, all female, at Mosaic Events. All shot with a gun. The perpetrator is caught on CCTV, and the Atlanta PD is investigating to identify the possible suspect. I'll have my detective get in touch with them and relay the details of our crime," Robin said.

"You think Maury went on a spree, shot them and ended here to find Gavin," Xavier said.

"That's what it looks like to me, but I don't have all the details. Ballistics will tell us for sure. There were no bullets left in the magazine. We found no extra magazines, until we find his vehicle." Robin studied him. "Atlanta might need to speak with you and Gavin, when he's able to answer questions. My detective will definitely need to speak with Gavin."

"Not until he's stable in the ICU. Questions can wait until then. Gavin's been through hell," Dakota said while he moved closer.

"You know I'm not that harsh or cruel, Dakota. I'm not forcing anything, especially on Gavin," Robin said. "It will have to happen sometime, though. I'll speak with Doc Elliott and have him contact my detective when it's a good time for Gavin. I swear it."

"When can we go to the house and clean it? There's no way we're letting Gavin go home to that nightmare," Reece asked while he stepped forward.

"Soon as the forensics finish and we captured everything, I have a specialized biohazard cleaning team that will clean the entire area. They have the correct chemicals and tools. After they're done, I'll contact..." Robin looked at the gathered group.

"Samuel and me," Dakota said.

"I'll contact you, and you guys can take over. A couple of tables will need to be replaced. The sofa will be cleaned, but—"

"Gavin shouldn't have to look at it and be reminded," Xavier finished.

"Cost isn't a problem," Samuel said.

"I'll leave it in your capable hands after the biohazard team finishes," Robin said.

"Then contact me if the Atlanta people or your detectives need me," Xavier said.

"Will do. Thanks for the assistance. You helped us connect a lot of pieces," Robin said.

"Wish I had it before all this happened—"

"Stop," Robin said and held up a hand. "Remember... None of this is your fault or Gavin's. It's all on Hirschinger—his decision, his motive, his crime. Be grateful Gavin survived, unlike those ladies. Remember...Gavin survived. Hirschinger is dead and can't hurt him again. Got it?"

"Yeah. Yes. I got it." Xavier rubbed his hands together and nodded.

"That's all you need to concern yourself with right now. My detectives and I can oversee the rest. You know we have one of the top forensic guys. No one can top our Keegan."

"Best man to have on your side," Sully said. "He can figure out the clues to any crime-scene puzzle."

"Exactly. Keegan will get our answers, along with the Atlanta team. Until then, keep watch over our friend. He needs you more," Robin said. "I'll be in touch." Then he walked away.

"That's what I plan on doing, no matter what happens," Xavier muttered, pulled away from Dakota's touch and returned to his chair to maintain his surveillance.

Chapter Twenty-Nine

While bullet wounds were dangerous and destructive, somehow Gavin's wounds weren't. Though Maury had shot to kill him, the sheriff suggested that the man had been so drunk that he couldn't control the gun or the recoil, which had altered the paths of the bullets. Either way, with Doc Elliott and the clinic's help, Gavin was able to leave within two weeks.

Driving Gavin's Soul since he didn't have an insurance resolution on his truck, Xavier drove him home where the Charm guys had created a surprise.

"Just tell me what is happening. There's not a lot of time, and I'm not in the mood for a party. Not yet," Gavin said. He continued to tire easily and lose energy, but Doc Elliott had said that was normal. His body was healing and would use the extra energy to focus on that part. Until then, he would have to endure it.

"After the special team cleaned and removed what they couldn't, Samuel, Reece and Jude went into organizing and redecorating mode. They redid your entire front room from the door to the kitchen. The security company fixed the alarm system. The sheriff returned your laptop and phone to Samuel after forensics gathered what was needed to help solidify the case."

"What case? He's dead."

"It's needed to close the files—with the sheriff, Atlanta and the courts in both places."

"Whatever. The bastard is dead," Gavin said while he looked out of the window.

"It'll take longer to heal the mental and emotional wounds. Doc Elliott gave you the names—"

"Of therapists to talk to," Gavin interrupted. "Yes. I'm thinking about it. There's more to what happened than being shot. I don't know if I'm ready to talk to anyone."

"One of the therapists will be there when you are ready. Please, find a way to reach out to them." After turning into the driveway, Xavier parked and placed his hand on Gavin's thigh. "Reach out to me."

Gavin trailed his fingers over Xavier's hand. "You moved in like I asked. Right?"

"Gav—"

"Right? You admitted your finances were a wreck with the loss of your truck and the increase in rent. Staying with me would save you so much, and we can be together during the little free time we get. I want you to live with me, Xavier."

"I know." Xavier smiled when Gavin lifted his gaze. "I ended my lease and moved in."

"Your furniture and big stuff?"

"In a storage unit, for now. Forget about that. Let's get you inside and settled. It's almost time for your next round of meds and a snack."

"Oh, great, an EMT and nurse-in-training for a caregiver. Just what I need."

"Exactly what you need to keep you recovering and not overdoing it. You did the same for me, now I get to return the love and support," Xavier said while he pulled the keys and got out. He opened the door for Gavin.

Holding an arm against his chest and belly where he'd taken the brunt of the damage, Gavin allowed Xavier to assist him. He would admit that he needed the extra help in a lot of things.

Xavier pulled the two bags from the back seat and locked everything up. Then he wrapped an arm around Gavin to support him. "Lean against me," he said.

"Why didn't you pull into the garage?"

"Samuel wanted you to walk in the front door and get a different memory to replace that last one," Xavier admitted.

"Really?"

"He loves you, like everyone does. He's trying to do what he can to help you. Let him."

"I already did. He wouldn't let me pay for the hospital, made sure I had my own room and all the best treatment. He and his family did that for me."

"Give him a little bit more," Xavier said. He put his hand on the door, and it opened to his touch.

"Welcome home!"

The cheerful cries hit Gavin when he entered the doorway. He winced and leaned against Xavier.

"Samuel, not so loud," Xavier said.

"Oh, shit, sorry, sorry," Samuel said while he moved forward. He motioned to tell others to turn on the lights. Then he held out his hands. "Welcome home, Gavin."

Blinking and restoring his balance, Gavin stepped deeper into his home. The anticipation of fear, pain and so much hatred gnawed at his mind, sped up his heart and put cement in his lower legs so that he couldn't move.

"He isn't here. You *are* safe. Your home *is* safe and secured. Cleansed. I swear," Xavier whispered. He clutched Gavin's shoulders.

The soft words and warmth loosened Gavin's fear.

"Look at your home. See what your friends created," Xavier said.

Opening eyes that he hadn't realized he'd closed, Gavin looked around. Instead of the simple lines of basic furniture, Samuel and the others had given him an edgy industrial media stand that held his flat screen and various electronics. They'd paired it with multiple shuttered bookcases to showcase his favorite books and chosen gifts he'd received from clients over the years. Light streamed through the front and side windows that were framed in simple floor-length curtains. The extended Chesterfield leather sofa lent a masculine grounding without distraction while the sack-cloth pillows would offer comfort after a long day. The matching industrial coffee table provided additional storage options. One of Gavin's treasured paintings hung on the wall over the sofa. A couple of wooden side tables with new lamps set by the light gray linen guest chairs anchored the seating arrangement. A patterned antique rug centered the room and gave a bit of warmth against the wooden floors that gleamed with a cleansing and polish. Thanks to Jude, there were multiple vases of fresh eucalyptus branches, grasses and a couple with brilliant flowers.

"This is…" Gavin couldn't finish the words.

"We weren't sure about the placement of the accessories. We grouped many together from our memories during the hurricane party, but feel free to change everything around. Obviously, it's your home," Samuel said.

"We wanted to make things a little easier for you to come home to," Jude added.

"But with a different look to not remind you of the original," Reece said. "Plus, Samuel said we could spend his money. Always a bonus."

Gavin smiled, then chuckled. The laugh was soft and broken, not well used. But it was there.

"Do you like it?" Samuel asked.

Gavin nodded. "It's wonderful. I love all of it—better than the simple furniture I purchased after leaving Atlanta."

"I remember you mentioned during the hurricane party wanting to change things around and go with something more industrial but edgy and with a touch of leather," Jude said while he stepped forward. "When Samuel mentioned getting you something new, I figured, why not give this a chance?"

Gavin touched Jude's shoulder. "Thank you…for everything."

Jude moved in for a gentle hug, mindful of Gavin's healing.

Gavin returned the hug. When Jude released him, he embraced Samuel. Then he hugged Reece. "Thank you to all of you for making this better."

"Xavier helped, too," Jude said. "Since he's living here, we figured he should have some input." He nudged the slightly taller man with his elbow.

"Didn't do much," Xavier said.

Still, Gavin stepped into Xavier's warm, familiar embrace. He would always feel safe there. "Thank you," he whispered.

"Anytime. I'm not going anywhere."

"Come sit. Dakota and Mal made a bunch of light meals to enjoy while you recuperate," Samuel said.

Gavin turned his head against Xavier's chest to look at Samuel. "Still planning your wedding."

"I hope so. Wouldn't trust it to anyone else," Samuel said and added a smile. Then he held up a finger to stop Gavin. "You can do it from here. All the trades know to come to you. I'll swing in for the visits."

"I can make that work—until the week of the wedding and I'm feeling better."

"And you get the release from Doc Elliott."

"Yes. And that, too. What about the reception meal?"

"Leave the reception meal and massive BBQ to Dakota. He knows how to plan that with his fellow chefs. This is the one thing he wants to do. The rest he conceded all decisions to you and me."

"That's a big deal."

"I warned him, but he said go for it."

Xavier nudged them forward until he got Gavin to the sofa. He assisted Gavin down to a relaxing position, though Gavin snagged a pillow to hold it against his side.

"Get a cup of water and something for him to snack on, Samuel. He needs his medications and a nap," Xavier said.

"Will do," Samuel said.

Xavier set the bags on the nearby chair. Then he dug through the backpack and pulled out the different bottles of medication and a piece of paper. He checked the paper, which was a schedule, and opened two of the bottles and poured out the pills.

"Ugh," Gavin said.

"Pain creeps up on you when you least expect it. This isn't the strongest pain medication, but it'll get you through the worst of it. Then we can switch you down to an OTC med, if you need or want it," Xavier said.

"Here you go." Samuel returned with a glass and small plate and fork. "A bit of easy pasta salad, light and filling."

"Eat the salad first. These pills need a cushion of food. We should have stopped and gotten yogurt. It would help with the antibiotics," Xavier said.

Samuel handed Gavin the plate and fork.

"Thanks," Gavin said and ate the simple meal.

"We can pick some up and bring it back. Anything else?" Samuel asked.

Xavier located a pad and pen. He jotted down a few items and handed it over.

"Any flavor but coconut, banana and vanilla. Prefer the berries," Gavin said.

Samuel chuckled. "Berry-flavored yogurt it is. I'll kick everyone out. Your laptops are in your home office. Your phone is charging on your nightstand. I dropped off our wedding binder. I answered calls from your clients and explained the situation. Everyone is understanding and not upset."

"Oh, jeez, I completely forgot about them. We didn't have anything on the calendar for the next couple of weeks, other than your wedding. We don't get busy again until Thanksgiving and through New Year's."

"Then there's plenty of time to rest and heal up," Samuel said.

"Ugh. Don't wanna stay still," Gavin said.

"Too bad. Orders from the doc." Samuel shifted his gaze to Xavier. "That's your job, Xavier. It's a tough one."

"Tell me about it," Xavier said with a grin. "I know what I'm facing with him."

Chuckling, Samuel shoved the paper into his pocket. He called out to the others that they were heading out.

Everyone followed Samuel out of the door. They scattered to their different homes and jobs.

Xavier locked the door after them and kicked off his boots. He left them by the door. Then he returned to remove Gavin's sneakers and added them to the row of shoes. "I know you don't like having shoes on when there's no visitors."

"Thanks." Gavin wiggled his sock-covered toes.

Then Xavier sat near Gavin. "Take the pills."

"I know."

"Then you can either stretch out on the sofa and try it out for a nap or use the bed."

"Bed. *Our* bed."

Xavier smiled and kissed Gavin's knuckles. "Our bed then. Finish your meal and meds." He gathered the bags and carried them upstairs.

Gavin watched him move around and hoped Xavier felt at home, too. He glanced around at the new furniture. Then he noticed some pieces that must belong to Xavier mixed in with his accessories. It felt perfect.

* * * *

Within two weeks, Gavin had steadily made progress in his recovery. At the same time, he continued to expand his basic plans for Samuel and Dakota's wedding.

After another conversation with the couple and with everyone settled on the plans and invitations — both paper and e-invites — were sent out. The couple chose a classic sunset wedding on the Charm's beach. It would be only for family and close friends. Gavin and Jude had the freedom to create and decorate the ceremonial space. Dakota's brother, Cal, would provide the music for the ceremony and part of the reception, along with a DJ.

With the grand opening of the new reception space scheduled for the middle of October, they wouldn't have access to it. Instead, they would open all the doors to the Delights' floor space and the expanded patio. There would even be picnic blankets spread out across the lawn and beach. Along with the ceremony guests, the couple wanted to open the reception to everyone in Shore Breeze. They knew that without the townsfolk, the B&B and restaurant wouldn't have survived all the challenges they'd faced, including the pandemic. This would be a time to celebrate.

"Thank you so much. I'm going to sketch out some ideas, and I'll send them to you for a finalized version. Then after approval, I would like the flyers spread throughout all the stores, restaurants and bars — and perhaps a single mail-out. That will depend on the pricing, though. Right. Okay. Thank you again," Gavin said and ended the call to a local printer. Then he looked around his office. "Where did I put that pad and those pencils?"

It took a few minutes, but Gavin unearthed a drawing pad and a container of colored and drawing pencils.

Holding everything, along with his phone, he went back downstairs. Turning on the TV for some background noise, Gavin curled in the corner of the Chesterfield sofa with a drawing pad. Setting the container and phone down within easy reach, he opened the pad to a fresh page. He sketched out multiple ideas for the flyers that would be posted throughout town to alert everyone to the event.

"How long have you been sitting there?" Xavier asked when he walked in the front door. Dressed in his EMT uniform, he carried both his backpack and duffel bag.

"An hour or so. Trying to work on this flyer. I found a local printer who can finalize my sketch, print and help distribute everything." Gavin looked up and smiled. He snagged the remote and turned down the volume. "How was your shift?"

"A normal one like all the others—some crazy emergency stuff, some regular patients who needed a bit of extra support or a ride to the hospital." Xavier pulled off his boots and set them in place. Picking up his bags, he dropped them near the coffee table. Then he moved closer, leaned down and captured Gavin's mouth for a long kiss. The shift had been forty-eight-hours long, one of the first extended ones since Gavin had been hurt. "Hey there," he whispered when he pulled back a touch. Then he kissed him again.

Gavin returned the kiss. He raised his hand to wrap his fingers around the back of Xavier's neck. Then he moved his hand to brush his thumb along Xavier's bristled jawline. "Hey there, sexy man. Missed you."

"Missed you, too," Xavier said while he sat on the edge of the sofa, next to Gavin's hips. He rested his hand on Gavin's lower belly, his thumb brushing against the helm. "Tell me you didn't work the entire time."

"Umm."

"Gav."

"I need to get this wedding planned and organized. It's the most important event for the Charm. This is for her owners. If I screw this up—"

"Gavin, when have you ever screwed up an event?"

Gavin fell silent.

"See? This is what I mean." Xavier moved his hand from Gavin's belly to stroke his thumb along the smooth chin. "You need to take a break, Gav. Stop, take a breath and calm down. You're still healing. Doc Elliott said you're making good progress, but you're not at full power."

"I'm not pushing myself. I promise. Everything is being done either by phone, email or through the Internet. Next week I can go out to the stores with Samuel."

"Says who?"

"Doc Elliott. I called him earlier. If Samuel remains with me and I stay within town, take breaks and eat, I can do my job." Gavin captured Xavier's hand. "I'm okay, Xavier. I survived all of it. Yes, I know I need to talk to someone, and I will."

"When?"

"After the wedding," Gavin said.

"Gavin—"

"Please, Xavier. I want to concentrate on that, because planning a wedding lifts my spirits and emotions. It fills me up and gives me the energy I need to make everything bright, beautiful and perfect. If I tap into my emotions and break it out, it'll change everything and I'm afraid what will happen to the event." Gavin lifted Xavier's hand and kissed his knuckles. "I promise that I will make that call once the wedding is over and before the holiday events begin."

"Promise?"

"I swear to you," Gavin said.

Twisting their hands, Xavier placed a kiss on Gavin's knuckles. "You know I'll stand by you, no matter what happens. If you break, I'll be there to help put you back together. If you need a shoulder or support, you know I'm here."

"That's why I know I can get through the planning and wedding. Because I have you, I'm not alone. I know and believe that," Gavin said.

"Damn right."

Gavin chuckled. "Go take a shower. Get into comfy clothes. Do you need to sleep? What about studying?"

"I can hold off for a little bit. It wasn't that busy, so we could grab some sleep. I also did some homework. I can still take my class on the computer, but I'll need to go back to school next Tuesday."

"You can use my car."

"I think I can work around the money for a down-payment on a used truck. Sully is taking me to a place he knows, and we did some research."

"Are you sure?"

"I can do it. You were right. Moving in with you is saving me a lot of money. Though, that wasn't the main reason why I agreed."

"I know. There's something between us, and we work and live well together. Even with crazy schedules, we mesh well."

"*So* well. But the benefit is I can afford a down-payment and monthly payments on a used truck. Plus, I finally got the payment from the insurance company."

"I wish I could go with you."

"That's okay. We'll go for a drive when I get back. I'll take you out to dinner."

"That Irish restaurant in Pensacola?"

"We can do that."

"Yay."

"Now, what do you need after my shower and change into comfy clothes?"

Gavin chuckled. "I need your help with this design. I can't settle on a single option or if it's good enough. This is going everywhere."

"I'll help you decide."

"Then we'll figure out what to do for dinner."

"Sounds like a plan."

"We can catch up on *Lucifer*. There are new episodes to enjoy. Then" —Gavin drew a finger down Xavier's jawline and neck— "you can take me to bed."

Xavier smiled. "Definitely agree to that plan."

"Then get, and go to it."

Laughing, Xavier captured Gavin's mouth for another series of kisses. Then he pushed away and ran upstairs to begin their evening together.

Chapter Thirty

The time for the wedding finally arrived — the one day no one had been sure would happen for Samuel and Dakota.

Gavin knew it would work out, especially after sitting them down for that deep heart-to-heart talk.

The first families to arrive were Dakota's five siblings. The two older sisters, Carolina and Montana, brought their husbands and six children. Instead of staying at the Charm, they'd chosen rooms at one of the hotels in Pensacola Beach so the kids could enjoy the pool, beach and play areas.

When Samuel wondered if they could add the kids to the wedding, Gavin had scrambled to figure out what could happen. The three girls could drop flower petals while the boys could escort them — until one little boy insisted he wanted to drop petals, too.

With that situated, Gavin, Samuel, the moms and the kids all went to Pensacola for an emergency shopping spree to find adorable dresses for the girls and shirts and pants for the boys. Gavin even found matching ties for the boys to match the adults. The moms found shoes for all the kids. Then Gavin called Jude with an additional order of four baskets with petals of all the different flowers he was using for the kids to drop.

At the same time, the rest of Dakota's siblings arrived. Del and Cal were singles. The last to arrive was Georgia, the youngest sister, and her fiancé, who was stationed overseas and able to get leave. Del and Cal shared a room at the Charm while Georgia reserved a room at the same hotel as her sisters.

The siblings were gregarious, cheerful, numerous and all gorgeous like their oldest brother. Gavin adored all of them, especially the children. He happily accepted Carolina and Montana's assistance with wedding preparations.

Though not expected after their talk, Dakota's parents didn't make an appearance. Things remained strained between the siblings and their parents. Gavin understood parental issues, because he wasn't close to his parents after he'd come out.

On the other side, Samuel's family remained prim, proper and a little stuffy when they'd arrived. Samuel and Chandler double-checked everything in the three rooms and changed out a couple of items. Gavin didn't know if this was Samuel's parents first time seeing what he'd accomplished. He couldn't believe how different Samuel contrasted with them, but Chandler mentioned it was due to his time living in Shore Breeze. Plus, the love of Dakota added to the mix.

When the crisp October day started, Gavin couldn't be any happier for the couple. He moved around, taking care of all the details.

"You should sit and relax," Xavier said while he followed Gavin. He wouldn't let Gavin do anything physical besides walking and rearranging something light.

"I feel fine. I promise. I assigned Carolina and Montana to each groom. They're in charge of that room and herding the four groomsmen. They'll help with their attire and boutonnières. Georgia and Samuel's sister-in-law, Abigail, are riding herd on the kids to get them dressed and in position. I have Victor, Dorian, Cal and Del escorting guests to the wedding area and finding their seats." Gavin brushed a kiss against Xavier's cheek. "Everything is perfect. I promise."

With those words, Gavin continued to move from the beach to the porches, the restaurant and the kitchen to review everything. After the nuptials, workers would spread lots of blankets for reception guests to sit and enjoy their barbecue dinner.

"Oh, man, that barbecue smells better with each passing hour," Xavier said after a long sniff of the deliciousness spreading out. "Are you sure we can't have a sample?"

"Nope. These chefs won't allow it. I can't bug Mal, because he's one of the groomsmen and isn't cooking. We'll have to suffer. There's Katie..." Gavin said and helped open the doors when Katie's van pulled into the drive. He motioned for Xavier to hold the other door.

Katie, who was beautifully dressed for the ceremony, and her assistant wheeled out a cart from the back of the van. On a careful count, they placed the boxed-up cake and multiple boxes of cupcakes on the lower tiers. They wheeled the cart up the ramp and through the doors.

"Hello, Gavin, Gray, it's a beautiful day. I'm a little late because I wanted to set this up before the wedding," Katie said.

"Go right into the restaurant, Katie. There's a table against the far wall with everything you need," Gavin said and waved down the elegant hostess, who was also dressed in her wedding finery. "Cecile, can you show her where to go?"

"Of course," Cecile said in her liquid New Orleans accent.

Gavin checked his tablet. "That's the last thing to arrive."

"Hey, Gavin," Victor said while he walked over with Dorian.

"How's everything outside?"

"Good. All the guests have arrived and are waiting. Del is staying there in case anyone has problems or needs a bathroom fix. The officiant is here. Cal is tuning up his guitar, along with the violinists. I sent the DJ to set up his table on the mid-level patio, but he'll keep out of sight during the wedding. The videographer and photographer are also here. The photographer is getting early shots of both grooms in their rooms and will get shots of the guests and set up in the restaurant. When the cake is ready, he'll take those pictures, too," Victor said.

Gavin checked everything off his tablet then looked at his watch and out of the windows. "The sun is starting to drop. Time to get this wedding started. Go back and alert everyone. I'll send the ladies out to you and Del to help them find their seats. Thank you, Dorian, for helping out."

"It was my pleasure. Everyone has waited for this day to come," Dorian said and headed outside with Victor.

"Time to get our grooms."

* * * *

As the sun sank, Gavin sent each groom to walk down the aisle to Cal's beautiful music with the violinists. Together, the grooms stood under the flower-covered arch where the officiant waited. In the background was the beautiful rolling waves of the ocean.

Dakota stood tall in his lightweight taupe suit with a rust tweed vest and tie. His groomsmen, Sully and Reece, were in the same colors.

Next to him was Samuel in a matching suit with a caramel tweed vest and tie that brought out his caramel-brown eyes. His groomsmen, Chandler and Malcolm, were in the same colors. Malcolm had subdued his hair color with soft caramel highlights against his natural reddish-brunet color.

The little girls wore sand-colored dresses with caramel and rust accents. The boys wore either a caramel- or a rust-colored shirt with taupe pants. Gavin had finished their looks with the taupe bow ties. All the kids sat in chairs and remained well behaved under their mothers' supervision.

Watching from the back, Gavin leaned against Xavier, who remained by his side.

After the officiant welcomed everyone to the ceremony, she continued into the wedding. Cal sang another song that Samuel and Dakota had requested. Then the grooms moved together and held hands.

Their vows were personally written.

As they were spoken, the vows brought tears to everyone's eyes.

Gavin reached for Xavier's hand and entwined their fingers. He exchanged glances with his lover and chosen partner.

Love you, Xavier mouthed to him.

Love you more, Gavin mouthed back.

Xavier lifted their joined hands and kissed the back of Gavin's hand.

When they returned their attention to the ceremony, the grooms exchanged engraved wedding rings and promises under the guidance of the officiant.

"Ladies and gentlemen, may I be the first to introduce you to Mr. and Mr. Ashford-Mitchell. You may kiss your husband," the officiant said.

"Happy to do so," Dakota said. He tugged Samuel close and dipped him for a celebratory kiss to everyone's laughter and cheers.

"Go, Dakota," Gavin called out while clapping his hands.

Reece and Sully let out multiple whistles.

Cal and the violinists played a celebratory song while the newly minted husbands walked together down the aisle to the cheers and applause of their families and friends.

Then it was time for the party.

Food. Crowds. Music.

All the sights and sounds of an ever-expanding crowd grew as the reception seemed to continue deep into the night.

When the DJ turned on his table after the feast and filled the entire area with music, everyone got to their feet to dance the night away—from the little kids bouncing around to older couples, both heterosexual and LGBTQ+, swaying and showing off their moves honed by years of experience. Singles mingled and connected.

Abandoning his duties for a bit, Gavin let Xavier drag him into the middle of the dance floor with the rest of the Charm couples. Xavier spun him around into an embrace.

Tossing his head back with laughter, Gavin followed Xavier into multiple dances. Their bodies moving together in near-perfect harmony.

Dancing, laughter and frivolity happened late into the early morning hours. It was a party no one wanted to end—even the newlyweds.

For a wedding and event planner, it was the best possible outcome.

"Perhaps next time will be our moment to shine," Xavier murmured in Gavin's ear during a slow dance.

Gavin glanced into those beautiful eyes and smiled. Oh, yes, he would enjoy that.

Want to see more like this?
Here's a taster for you to enjoy!

Bad Boyfriends, Inc.:
Awfully Ambrose
Lisa Henry & Sarah Honey

Excerpt

The voice was loud and obnoxious, at odds with the restaurant's muted soundtrack of clinking cutlery, soft jazz and murmured conversation.

"Really appreciate you paying for dinner, Tom. I'm between opportunities right now but I'll be damned if I'm gonna take just any job and be a corporate drone. Better to take a free meal when I can get one, right?"

It was followed by a braying laugh that made Liam wince and want to drag his nails down a blackboard, because that would have been preferable to listening to this honking, snorting nightmare.

Liam prayed he wouldn't have to wait on whoever the loud idiot was, but judging by the smirk on his co-worker Judy's face, he had a sudden sinking certainty that the table was his. Sure enough, when he glanced over to check, there was Braying Man in the middle of his section—elbows on the table, wearing a backwards baseball cap and a flannel shirt, picking at his teeth.

The idiot caught Liam's eye and snapped his fingers. "Hey, man, can we get a bread basket or something? And booze. Lots of booze. Her old man's paying, so make it the good stuff." He winked, then gave Liam honest-to-God finger guns.

The guy was an utter dickhead, Liam decided. Still, part of the job was keeping his opinions to himself, so Liam made his way over to the table, face carefully impassive. His mask slipped for a split second when he recognized the girl who was gazing at Dickhead with something like worship. It was Kelly, who he shared a Marketing Communications class with at the University of Sydney, and the last time Liam had talked to her, she'd been dating someone completely different—a nice, if slightly scruffy, guitarist in a pub band. He wondered what had happened to him.

The other couple at the table had to be Kelly's parents. They were looking at the guy with a slightly confused expression on their faces, like he was one of those hairless cats, and they couldn't decide if they were fascinated or horrified by his existence.

Liam had to admit, Dickhead was objectively attractive when he was keeping his mouth shut. He could have been a model, with his well-muscled physique, dark hair and carefully sculpted stubble. He had a strong, straight nose, killer jawline, and even white teeth. He was just Liam's type—or would have been, if Liam dated.

Liam cleared his throat and did his best to pretend he didn't know anyone at the table as he said, "Welcome to Bayside. Would you like to order some drinks?"

Dickhead rolled his eyes. "Wow. I guess you weren't listening, huh? I mean, I *literally* just asked you to bring us good booze."

Liam kept his face pleasantly neutral—he'd had plenty of practice, working as a waiter in a high-end Sydney restaurant—and clarified, "What, specifically, would you like to drink, sir?" He made sure to address Kelly's father, since he was obviously the one footing the bill.

The man smiled gratefully and started to say, "I'd like a gin and tonic, and my wife will have—"

Arsehole interrupted. "Just give me a bottle of that Don Paragraph stuff"—as someone from a family of winemakers, Liam died a tiny death at the mangled pronunciation—"and the quicker the better, yeah?"

"I'll check if we have any *Dom Perignon* in stock, sir. How many glasses with that?" Liam asked through clenched teeth. God, he hoped they weren't celebrating Kelly's engagement to this douchebag.

Dude wrinkled his nose. "Just one. It's for me." He turned to Kelly and winked. "Gotta watch for extra calories in drinks if you wanna stay in shape, am I right, sweet pea?"

Liam waited for Kelly to rip the guy's balls off—he hoped literally, but he'd settle for metaphorically—because he knew she had a hell of a temper when she was wronged. He'd been on the receiving end of it during one disastrous group assignment. But Kelly just smiled like a Stepford Wife and murmured, "Yes, Ambrose."

Liam was pretty sure the shock on her father's face was mirrored on his own, but he schooled his features and nodded. Ambrose tilted a menu at Kelly's father. "This seafood platter's meant to be for two, but you're cool with me ordering it, right, Tom?"

Kelly's father cleared his throat. "Kelly's allergic to seafood."

"That's cool, I wasn't planning on sharing anyway," the dickhead—*Ambrose*—said with an easy grin that lit up his entire face and really, it wasn't fair that someone who was such a colossal arsehole could be so attractive.

But of course, that was how the world worked, right? Beautiful people got away with murder.

Liam turned back to the older man. "And the rest of your drinks order, sir?" he asked, taking petty satisfaction at the way Ambrose snorted and muttered under his breath.

"A gin and tonic for myself, and a glass of Connelly Cellars' Perfect Pinot," Tom said, and Liam suppressed the urge to preen, just like he did every time someone ordered one of his family's wines.

"Make mine a tonic water," Kelly said.

Liam blinked. *Wow, what happened to the girl who always claimed she'd never drink water because fish fucked in it?*

Something weird was going on, and whatever it was, Liam didn't like it. He especially didn't like that it was happening here at Bayside. People didn't come into Bayside wearing backwards caps and being dicks. Bayside had standards—standards that Liam was beginning to worry he might have to attempt to enforce. It had water views! You could see the Sydney Harbour Bridge from the wide dining room windows! It was both fancy and trendy, and it *always* made the list of the top ten places to eat in Sydney. Diners weren't supposed to wear flannel to Bayside, and Liam panicked quietly that he didn't know if the dress code was actually enforceable or not. Liam had only been working here for eight months, but it had never come up before. People usually treated Bayside like it was a special occasion, not three a.m. at the counter of Macca's.

"Good choice, babe. You know you're a sloppy drunk," Ambrose said, leaning in and patting Kelly's face. Then he hauled himself out of his chair, scratched his belly and farted. "I gotta go take a dump. I always shit when I'm out. Make someone else deal with that, am I right?" And with that Ambrose sauntered towards the bathrooms, leaving Kelly's parents staring after him open-mouthed.

Liam couldn't help himself. "Kelly —"

"Hi, Liam, I guess you've met my new boyfriend now!" Kelly cut in, following that with a tinkling laugh that was pitched a little high with nerves. "He's an entrepreneur."

Liam opened his mouth to ask what happened to Greg the bassist, but Kelly shot him a glare that said she would hunt him down and personally set his dick on fire if he said another word. Liam knew that look, so he shut his mouth, went to fetch drinks and said a prayer that he wouldn't have to be the one to clean the toilets at the end of the night. Frankly, he wouldn't have been surprised to learn that Ambrose had just decided to take a shit on the floor and stolen all the paper.

When Ambrose wandered back out again at last, he didn't walk straight back to his own table. Instead, he approached another table where a group of shiny and fashionable young women who were probably Instagram influencers or something were eating.

"Hi, ladies," he said. He put both hands on their table and leaned forward. "My name's Ambrose."

"Is he —?" Kelly's mother's mouth dropped open. "Oh my God."

"Ambrose is very sociable," Kelly said. "People love him."

A ticking vein in her father's temple called her a liar.

Liam saw the way that Tom started to strangle his linen napkin, and hurried over to the influencers' table. "Excuse me, sir," he said to Ambrose. "Can you please return to your own table?"

Ambrose gave him finger guns, and sauntered back over to join Kelly and her parents.

What the everlasting *fuck*? And Liam obviously wasn't the only one thinking it. Kelly's mum looked close to tears, and her dad looked half a heartbeat away from either a stroke or a homicide. In the event he actually did murder Ambrose, Liam decided to tell the police it was justified. Hell, at this point he'd probably give the guy an alibi. And the murder weapon. And a bucket of bleach to clean up the murder scene.

Kelly, though, just beamed at Ambrose like she was under some sort of spell. "I missed you, boo." She blew him a kiss.

Ambrose shrugged. "Have we ordered yet? I'm starving. Service here is soooo slow," he said loudly, stretching his arms over his head and attracting stares from the other tables. "Probably can't get decent staff."

Liam seethed and wondered if he and Tom could come to some sort of agreement regarding mutual alibis and body disposal. The walk-in freezer out the back would be a good place to store a corpse while they figured out their next step.

Liam woodenly went through the specials, which nobody ever ordered anyway, then took their menus back and excused himself. He'd only made it a few steps away from the table when the obnoxious click of someone's fingers pulled him back again.

"Garçon!"

Ambrose. Of-fucking-course.

"Hey, change Kelly's order to a garden salad," Ambrose said. He grinned at Kelly. "We don't want you getting too chunky, right, babe?"

That vein in Tom's temple looked about ready to pop. "Kelly can eat what she bloody well likes," he hissed in an undertone.

"A salad sounds great, actually," Kelly said. "Ambrose knows what's best. Babe, tell them about your business ideas."

Ambrose straightened up, his eyes gleaming. "Have you guys heard of multi-level marketing?"

This time it was Liam's jaw that dropped. Kelly was a *business major*.

"So," Ambrose said to Kelly's stone-faced parents, "what you do is, you have a product, and you recruit people to sell it for you. They're called a downline. Like, some people say that it's predatory and cult-like, but I've been in a cult, and ha! You won't fool me like that twice! Well, three times. Did you bring your chequebook, Tom? I mean, I can take cash if you want to get on board too, I guess. Like, what do you think? Five grand?"

Liam stared at Kelly for a moment, wondering who the fuck she even was, then escaped to the kitchen to put in their orders before he finally snapped. He managed to resist the urge to tell the chef to spit on the seafood, but it was a close-run thing.

About the Author

Ever the quiet one growing up, Nicole Dennis often slid away from reality and curled up with a book to slip into the worlds of her favorite authors. Over the years, she's created a personal library full of novels filled with dragons, fairies, vampires, shapeshifters of all kinds and romance. Always she returned to romance. Still, there were these characters in her head, worlds wanting to be built on paper, and stories wanting to be told and she began writing them down whether during or after class. She continues to this day. Only recently has it begun to become fruitful, spreading out to let others read and enter her worlds, meet her characters, and see what she sees. No matter what she writes, her stories of romance with their twists of paranormal, fantasy and erotica will always have their Happily Ever Afters.

She currently works in a quiet office in Central Florida, where she also makes her home, and enjoys the down time to slip into her characters and worlds to escape reality from time to time. At home, she becomes human slave to a semi-demonic tortie calico.

Nicole loves to hear from readers. You can find her contact information, website details and author profile page at https://www.pride-publishing.com

PUBLISHING

Sign up for our newsletter and find out about all our
romance book releases, eBook sales and promotions,
sneak peeks and FREE romance books!